MONSTERS AREN'T BORN

Wildefae

THE LAST HEIR OF ELSEWHERE

USA TODAY AND INTERNATIONAL BESTSELLING AUTHOR

KATE KING

This book is a work of fiction. All characters, names, places, and incidents, either are the product of the author's imagination or are used fictitiously. Any resemblance to real persons, living or dead, events, or locales, is purely coincidental.

The Last Heir of Elsewhere © 2024 by Kate King

All rights reserved.

No part of this book may be reproduced in any form or by any electronic or mechanical means, including information storage and retrieval systems, without written permission from the author, except for the use of brief quotations in a book review. For more information, please email hello@katekingauthor.com.

First Cover edition April, 2024

Cover design and typography: Flowers and Forensics

Alt Cover design and typography: Story Wrappers

Copy Editing: One Love Editing

Formatting and Edge Design (Printed edges edition): Painted Wings Publishing Services

Unique Character Art: @damianintheden, Rin Mitchell

Published by Wicked Good Romance

For anyone who has ever lost a sibling

M.A.C. September 19th, 1999 - October 22nd, 2023

AUTHORS NOTE

In book two, I experimented with adding a summary of the previous book. It was my first time trying something like that, and the results were primarily positive, so I've included it again.

The first couple of chapters of this book give a recap of the last book, but if you need a more extensive refresher, I have put **a detailed encyclopedia** at the back of the book, which includes a **summary of book two**, a **glossary of important locations** and **terms**, and **a character list with descriptions.** That is also where I have moved the **pronunciation guide** and the **family tree.**

I hope this is helpful for readers who (like me) like to look up the Wikipedia articles on every series they read. There is some background information sprinkled in there that hasn't yet made it into the books, but no major spoilers (beyond book one and two, which are well and truly spoiled).

That said, I want to make clear that **you do not have to read any of this.** This isn't homework, and your reading experience will not suffer if you don't read my musings. I am not dropping any easter eggs; it's just to help you out, and you can absolutely skip it. Do as you wish!

For those reading on Kindle, you can find it in the table of contents under THE WORLD OF WILDE FAE. In physical books, it begins after the final chapter.

Enjoy!

Kate M. King

CONTENT WARNING

PROLOGUE: BAEL

THE WAYWOODS, HUNTING DAY, ONE YEAR AGO

"The dead are loud today."

Scion let out a long-suffering sigh, and dug his heels into the sides of his horse. "I have never known you to make a single statement without some insipid follow up, Bael. What are you getting at?"

"I was merely commenting." I grinned. "I think they know it's hunting day."

He snorted with derision. "What a wretched existence. To be foolish enough to die in the hunts and then to haunt the grounds where one died. I'd rather face true death."

I chuckled darkly. "If you say so."

Scion offered me another contemptuous glance. He still rode his war horse, even in the quiet woods on the outskirts of the palace grounds, and it was a testament to how well he'd trained the beast that it didn't break stride or react to his constant movement.

My cousin and I looked nothing alike. Where he was dark-haired, silver-eyed and pale, I was golden in all ways. Even his expression was opposite mine: set in a perpetual scowl. Scion had only been back in the capital for a matter of weeks and clearly the confines of court life were grating on his temper.

Selfishly, I didn't care.

Miserable or not, I was thrilled to have my companion back. I'd been painfully bored this last decade. There was hardly anyone to talk to except Gwydion, who was duller than dishwater, and Aine, who was away from home almost as often as Scion. Still, it was plain to see that Scion was miserable.

Of course, that was hardly a novelty in our family.

To be an Everlast was synonymous with misery, and had been for the better part of seven thousand years.

"This is pointless," Scion groused as we crossed over a small stream and into a denser patch of trees. "There wouldn't be anyone foolish enough to enter the woods today."

I hummed in agreement. King Penvalle had sent us out today to make sure that the hunting ground was secure. It was a pointless task that anyone could have done—we had thousands of servants and any number of them could have ridden through the woods, yet he'd demanded that we go personally. It wasn't clear to me if it was a power play or if he was simply mad. Perhaps a bit of both.

My gaze caught on the path ahead, where the sun shone through the trees. A translucent spirit flew past, chased by an errant Underfae. I raised an eyebrow. It was as I'd told Scion: the dead were loud today.

They always were on hunting days.

Perhaps because the first hunt of the season was always held in the capital. It was impossible to count how many souls had been lost here over the last seven thousand years. These woods were full of the imprints of those who had lost their lives—or rather given their lives—to the Wilde Hunts.

Interrupting my thoughts, Scion craned his neck back to me again, this time turning nearly fully around in his saddle. "Are you planning to attend the hunt?"

I tensed. What he really meant was: "are you still going to tow the family line and stay well away from the woods this evening." He could have asked straight out, but for some reason he did not. While it was rude in the Fae court to be so direct, we never followed such laws amongst ourselves.

I shrugged. "I thought I would attend the party at the very least."

"Hmmm," Scion said.

"What?"

He paused, and it was only the tiny stiffening of his shoulders that told me he was struggling to come up with a reply. "You know I would prefer you came with me, but it might be too dangerous for you."

I rolled my eyes. "If you're concerned about my getting caught up in the violence, don't be. You haven't been here for the past years, so you haven't seen how bad the court has become. If I were to be overtaken by bloodlust it surely would've happened already."

Scion's hands clenched around his reins, his knuckles turning white. "If I didn't know better, I'd call you a fucking liar. Grandmother wouldn't allow that."

I laughed. "She always had a blind spot for her sons, you know that more than most."

Scion fell into an uncomfortable silence. His father had been our grandmother's oldest son, the one who, if not for his untimely death, would wear the crown now instead of our Uncle Penvalle.

I would've liked to say Belvedere would have been the better choice for king, but then I really would be a fucking liar. Penvalle was bad—half-mad, violent, and power hungry—but Scion's father had been worse...whether my cousin acknowledged that or not. Not that I should judge anyone for having a monster for a father. The heinous actions of my own father—my real one—would easily outweigh anyone else's crimes two times over.

I opened my mouth to say something about it, but lost my train of thought as leaves rustled up ahead and a breathy moan reached my ears. I turned my head toward the sound like a wolf scenting prey. "Did you hear that?"

"What?" Scion asked sharply.

I glanced briefly at him, then dug my heels into the sides of my horse's flank. "I'll be right back."

"You can't be fucking serious," Scion shouted after me. "You might not care about wasting your own time, but do not waste mine."

I laughed. "Go back, then. No one is holding you captive, Sci, least of all me."

The snap of twigs and panting breaths grew louder as I urged my horse forward. My ears pricked up.

"Put me down!" a soft female voice whispered.

"What's wrong?" a man replied.

"Shhh."

"Bael!" Scion said again, his impatience evident. "What the fuck are you doing?"

He might not have time for anything other than exactly what was expected of him, but he would get to leave again as soon as the hunts were over. I would be stuck here for another hundred years, miserable and completely alone. I'd been bored for so long it was the small things that broke up the monotony. Who was here breaking the rules? Who might I get to punish?

"Patience," I said. "I want to check on something."

I swung down from my horse and strode forward at double the speed any human could have walked, my hair blowing back from my face. My gaze skimmed over the trees, searching for whomever was speaking too loudly, doing such a terrible job at trying to be quiet. Even if we'd been human we would have heard them. As Fae, they had no chance of hiding from us.

My eyes landed on the couple in the trees. I glanced at the male and immediately forgot his face—one guard looked much the same as every other to me at this point. My eyes traveled to the girl and my lip twitched.

She was pretty for a human. Pretty generally, I supposed. Her wild red hair was falling loose from some vain attempt at taming it, and there was a flush across her pale, freckled cheeks.

Not enough of a flush, in my opinion.

It was plain to see what she'd been doing with the guard, whose unremarkable face was becoming uglier by the second. Unbidden, the image of shoving her up against that tree myself flitted through my mind. Tearing that hideous dress off her and putting a real flush on her pretty face.

Fuck. What was I thinking?

I had no qualms about human lovers—preferred them, in fact. They were easier to talk to than high Fae, oddly more honest and forthcoming. A good quality in a sexual partner. Still, I didn't know anything about this woman. I'd never noticed her before, and there was no reason to be standing here now, as if bewitched.

I shook my head slightly, as the sound of Scion's boots hitting the earth sounded behind me. "As I said, I don't see why you have to waste our time chasing after…what? Shadows?"

He was being intentionally obtuse, now. I glanced back at him sharply to show my displeasure. I opened my mouth to retort, but before I could the girl moved out of the corner of my eye. I turned back abruptly, and froze, watching her. Beside me, Scion seemed to be doing the same. None of us moved, as if frozen in an odd sort of standoff.

She was staring right at me. Or rather, she was staring at the clearing where she probably heard the hooves of our horses or felt some disturbance in the wind. She couldn't actually see me, as Scion's illusion kept us invisible from the eyes of mortals. Except, as I watched, she reached slowly for the hand of her guard, as if taking comfort in his presence.

That was…unusual to say the least.

Some humans had a sort of natural awareness of magic. Usually those who were either changelings—humans taken from across the veil as children and raised to serve the courts—or those who had some far distant Fae ancestor. This woman looked too young to be a changeling. We had stopped taking changelings before I was born, and the redhead couldn't be more than nineteen? Twenty? Perhaps she had a great-grandfather who was Fae, and that was all there was to it.

"Fuck this," Scion said sharply. "I thought you saw something interesting. If I've seen one guard fucking some Slúagh whore in these woods, I've seen them all."

I laughed. He was right, of course. There was nothing remarkable about the woman aside from her pretty face. She couldn't see us, it was merely an odd coincidence. I began to turn away.

"What are you staring at?" The guard asked the woman, his voice cutting sharply through my internal dialogue.

"Be quiet—" she breathed, softer than the sound of her own rapid heartbeat.

I froze again, the sound of her voice rooting me to the spot.

"Why?" her guard scoffed. He reached for her arm, pulling her around to look at him. "What the hell are you doing, Lon?"

She stared frantically between him and us, swallowing hard. I watched a bevy of emotions cross her face: Confusion, terror, realization, and then her skin went so pale that whatever color had been in her cheeks looked as if it might never return. "I—"

Realization flooded me and I cackled a harsh laugh. She *could* see us, and her lover thought she was insane.

He was missing the beauty in the situation. Insane, she might be, but I found her fascinating.

I leaned over to my cousin, keeping my eyes fixed on the girl. If she could see us, she could likely hear us too. "I think you're losing your touch. The pretty Slúagh girl can see us."

Even as I spoke, I wondered if I'd inadvertently lied. Perhaps she was not Slúagh—human—after all. Maybe she was something else.

"No," Scion disagreed sharply.

He moved so fast I barely had time to wonder if the humans would be able to see his movement. He took a step toward them, raising a hand to cast an enchantment. Something rose in my chest unbidden—a strange desire to step between my cousin and the girl, whose name I didn't even know. But before I could act on the absurd impulse, Scion stopped.

She gasped a full second too late and squeezed her eyes shut even as Scion had already stopped. There was the answer to one question, then.

She was at least partly human. Her reactions were too slow, her movements too weak.

She was far too breakable.

"Did you mean to stop?" I asked Scion thoughtfully.

Scion stared at her, clearly horrified, then gave a tiny shake of his head, which I knew would be all the confirmation I'd get. He'd intended to kill her, but could not. I knew of only one reason why the Fae would be physically unable to harm someone… "Fascinating."

Scion made an angry sound in the back of his throat, and spun on his heel to leave. "Let's go."

I didn't move, keeping my gaze fixed on my new puzzle. My new obsession. The air shifted, like something in the fabric of the world had been set in motion, and as the breeze hit my face the scent of honey and magic drifted toward me.

If that was how she smelled, I had to know what she'd taste like.

"Bael!" Scion barked a harsh command.

He felt the pull too, then. He must, or he wouldn't be so eager to run in the opposite direction.

It didn't matter. Whatever it was, would come regardless, and I felt sure I would see this girl again.

"I'm coming," I replied, my mouth turning up in a wide grin. "I've seen all I needed to see."

PART ONE
Blood and Fealty

1
LONNIE

THE CUTTHROAT DISTRICT, INBETWIXT, ONE WEEK SINCE THE RISE OF THE REBELLION

"Focus, little monster." Bael's breath grazed my neck sending tingles over my entire body. "Try to imagine nothingness. Like, darkness that stretches on forever."

I gritted my teeth. "Should I imagine nothing or darkness?"

He paused, and there was humor in his voice when he replied: "Whichever."

I squeezed my eyes shut tight, but all I could think about was the warmth at my back and the shivers dancing over my skin. Clearly, Bael was oblivious to the fact that his presence alone was enough to shatter my focus.

Although, I supposed it was better to be distracted than terrified. At least I'd grown beyond that point in the last week…mostly.

Bael and I stood in a dark, musty store room, lit by a single lantern and dirty window overlooking the city street. It had been a week since our escape from the fallen obsidian castle, and five days since we found refuge with the Thieves' Guild in Inbetwixt. Downstairs, the guild was bustling with conversations and footsteps—something I never would have noticed had I not spent the last hour trying to think of *nothing*.

Shadow walking—or the ability to magically propel oneself between one place and another—was not something that came naturally to me. Truly, magic in general didn't come naturally to me. Nevertheless, I'd spent the better part of the last week trying to learn to control whatever untrained abilities lay dormant inside me.

The results had been...mixed.

I'd been taught all my life not to use magic or something horrible would happen. In the last weeks, I'd leaned that my fears were not baseless. Whenever I'd tried to call fire to my hand, I seemed to call other things as well, and deadly monsters would flock to my side like moths to...well, *a flame*.

Perhaps that was why I struggled to practice.

I'd managed to stop trembling with terror every time I thought about my power, but thus-far hadn't had any luck conjuring anything more than red-faced frustration. I certainly hadn't mastered the ability to disappear and reappear at will, and I was starting to wonder if I ever would again.

"Go stand over there." I pointed aimlessly across the room, even as I took a large step forward, putting some much-needed distance between us. "It's a bit difficult to think of nothing with you breathing in my ear."

The prince chuckled. "A likely excuse."

"Excuse or not, I can't do this with you hovering over me."

With an over-dramatic sigh, Bael stepped out from behind me and sauntered across the room to lean against the wall by the window. To my dismay, my eyes followed him without my permission and my heart fluttered.

It was no wonder I was struggling to focus.

There had always been something slightly unnerving and dangerous about Bael, but his joking demeanor and too-pretty face camouflaged his darker nature. In the palace, the prince invariably appeared as if he had just stumbled out of a wild party or overslept by several hours. His red-gold curls were always too long, and he hardly ever wore shirts underneath his brightly colored waistcoats revealing both his well-defined muscles and intricate swirling tattoos.

Now, his hair was cropped short, having been burned in the fire, and the dimly lit room glinted with the reflection of his black, obsidian-plated armor. He carried no sword or knives in his belt, practically screaming that he could kill just as easily without them. It was as if, without the layers of silk and smiles, it was evident that there was nothing golden about this prince—and there never had been.

As if he could read my thoughts, the corners of Bael's lips twitched upward, revealing a mischievous gleam in his yellow irises. "You're still thinking."

"How can you tell?"

"Just your expression. If you let yourself get too distracted you'll end up traveling somewhere you didn't intend. We can only hope it's just downstairs and not halfway across the city."

I made a frustrated noise in the back of my throat and opened one eye. "I doubt there's much danger of that. I'd have to actually move first."

He grinned, but only waved a hand for me to hurry up. "Get on with it. I have other things I want to do with you before the meeting."

If he'd intended to motivate me, his mention of the meeting had the opposite effect. I glanced out the window, where the sun seemed far brighter than it had been when we began practicing. "How long have we been doing this? Should we not be downstairs already?"

We were due down in the thieves' den an hour before noon, to meet with the rest of the displaced royal family and Cross's crew. There had been many meetings since we'd been here, most regarding the ongoing rebel conflict, but none that I wanted to attend so much as this one.

I'd decided days ago that I would not be going to Nevermore for the next event of the Wilde Hunts, or even to Overcast with the rest of the Everlasts. No, I wanted desperately to travel across the country to the far northern province of Aftermath where I'd been born and had once lived with my mother and sister before relocating to the capital. Now, for the first time, we'd be meeting about when I might be able to leave on my journey and, equally important, who would be accompanying me.

Bael didn't bother to look out the window as he answered. "I'm not worried about time, little monster. Stop stalling, or I'll find another way to motivate you to try again."

An anticipatory tingle traveled down my spine, but I ignored it. Instead, I shook my hands out, and rolled my neck, before standing straight. "Fine. One more time."

I squeezed my eyes shut and tried desperately to think of nothing. Darkness. Anything but the thousands of other thoughts that threatened to overtake me.

Frustrated, I tried to recreate the sensation of plunging sideways into an endless void, but even without looking at the too-gorgeous male in front of me, it was nearly impossible to clear my mind. How could I, with everything going on in the country? With all the mysteries still left to solve, and battles still looming?

I groaned. "I give up. Perhaps I simply can't shadow walk again."

"You'll manage it, eventually," Bael said, pushing off the wall to stand in front of me.

I hung my head, defeated. "Your confidence in me is likely displaced. I'm starting to think I used up what little abilities I had back in the capital. There's simply nothing left."

The prince moved forward another step. He was so tall I had to crane my neck back as he placed his hands on my waist, turning me toward him, before bending to drag his tongue over the column of my neck. "No," he said against my skin. "You still taste of magic, little monster. It's still inside you, you simply haven't found the right motivation to use it."

I let out a slightly incredulous laugh, even as my pulse throbbed to life beneath his lips. "What are you doing? I thought you were trying not to distract me?"

He skated his lips over my collarbone. "And I thought you said you were giving up, so I can be as distracting as I want."

My pulse pounded between my legs, and the laughter fled from me as I tilted my head back, giving him better access. My voice was breathy, my protest half-hearted. "But did you hear me? I'm sure we've been practicing too long already. We're likely late to the meeting as it is."

"I do not think they can start without us," he countered as he dragged his tongue over the scarred shell of my ear. "Do you have any fucking idea how hard it is to look at you for hours and know I can't be *distracting*? I've been planning how I would fuck you against that wall since the moment we walked into the room."

My breath caught, and I felt my cheeks heat, and the blush seemed to cover my entire body. *Shit.*

Even a month ago, I never would have believed that I'd willingly stand in the arms of, not just a fairy, but a Fae prince. But, of all the absurd changes in my life lately, somehow Bael's presence felt the most natural. I supposed that was due to our mating bond.

It had only been just under a week since I'd first acknowledged our bond, but every day it became harder to ignore the instinct to complete the mating. That seemed crazy, as it hadn't been long ago that I would have denied it was possible for a human to be the mate of a fairy. Fuck, only weeks ago I wouldn't have known exactly what a mate *was*, but now Bael seemed to fit in a place in my life I hadn't realized I was missing anything. We didn't know all of each other's secrets yet, and in many ways were still getting to know one another, but somehow it *felt* right.

I reached up and threaded my fingers into his short curls. Pulling his face to mine, I captured his mouth with a kiss. His hands on my waist guided me backwards until I felt the heel of my boot hit something solid. I leaned into the resistance and realized it was a sturdy wooden barrel, likely full of some stolen thousand-year-old wine.

I pulled back, my lips hovering just a hair away from Bael's. I could feel his heart beating against my chest, matching the rhythm of my own. "Should we go back to our room?"

The prince's eyes flashed, hungry with anticipation. "Fuck no."

His fingertips traced the curves of my body, his touch sending shivers down my spine. He raised me effortlessly onto the wooden barrel and my breath caught, my knees falling open of their own accord. Bael moved to stand between my parted legs, his hand trailing down to grasp my hip over my skirt.

He kissed his way down my neck, nipping and licking at my skin until he reached the top of my blouse.

"Do not rip it," I gasped. "I don't have time to keep mending them."

He smiled, showing every one of his too-sharp teeth. "You are talking far too much."

He wrapped both hands around my calves before sinking to his knees on the floor before me. His hot breath sent shivers up my spine, and a moan escaped my lips as he pushed my skirt up, and pressed a kiss to the inside of my thigh.

I tipped my head back. "Fuck."

"Only say that when you mean it, little monster."

I was tempted to tell him I meant it *now* and bypass any preamble, but forgot the words when he forced my knees wider apart and moved his lips to the other thigh, hands sliding upwards, to discover his path was unimpeded. "Do you mean to tell me, that you've been wearing nothing beneath this skirt the entire time we've been in here."

My cheeks flushed, and I glanced away, realizing now what that probably looked like. "Well, you keep tearing my clothing, and—"

I broke off, gasping, as he leaned forward to press a kiss right over my clit. It sent tingles racing through my body, making every inch of me stand at attention for him as he slowly licked and stroked, causing me to arch into him greedily.

He reached up and palmed my breast, pinching my nipple through my blouse, and the spark of pain embedded itself in the base of my spine. Pleasure built, hot and consuming, and I whimpered. My hips rose of their own accord, and Bael pushed my thighs wider, as if to feast on me—to taste me completely.

I gripped his hair, whimpering as he sucked my throbbing clit into his mouth, his sharp teeth scraping just slightly. Then, without warning, he pushed his long fingers all the way inside me and I braced my palms on the edge of the barrel as my back bowed and I screamed, all my muscles clenching and shaking all at once.

"Fuck me." I breathed. "I need to feel you."

There was no hint of hesitation.

Too fast for human eyes, Bael rose to his feet. He undid his belt and let it fall to the floor with a metallic thump, which I forgot the moment his hands landed back on my thighs.

He looked down at me, eyes flashing. His fingers curled, digging into my thighs, hard enough to bruise, and lined himself up with my entrance before slamming into me. I gasped, my body reacting instinctively to the fullness and clenching around him.

His thrusts were slow at first, but they grew faster and harder as we both lost ourselves in the rhythm of our bodies moving together. I let out a moan, feeling him stretch me wider, filling me more completely. Our hips locked together, and I bit my lip hard enough to taste blood, quickly wiping it away before he could notice. Sex and blood—that was how a full mating bond formed, and we couldn't do that. At least, not yet.

Bael's hips snapped forward, driving himself deeper into me, making my walls clench tighter around him in response. His hands gripped my hips firmly as he took control, pulling me back toward him before slamming into me again. Each time he entered me was like a jolt of electricity coursing through my core; shooting sparks straight to my clit with each powerful thrust.

A knock sounded on the door, and I whipped my head toward the sound.

"Ignore it," Bael growled.

His thumb found my clit, and he rubbed up and down, then rhythmic circles, as he thrust into me, our ragged breathing falling in sync. I whimpered, pleasure building in me again, as I rolled my hips against him.

The knock sounded again, harder this time.

"It's probably Iola," I gasped. "The meeting..."

Bael growled. "She'll wait."

"But..." I couldn't finish my thought, much less my sentence, when he kept stroking his fingers over and over me in time with each thrust.

I gasped, unsure what I intended to say. The sensation was too much, my body was too tired, and I couldn't go any higher without crashing.

Bael placed another kiss on my throat, sucking lightly on the skin. An unexpectedly strong tremor shot through me, curling my toes, and settling deep in my core. "Oh gods."

He made a satisfied male noise in the back of his throat. "One day, I'll mark you here, too, and then we'll see whose bite makes you moan louder."

"Hmm?" I jerked, realizing what Bael was talking about—where he was kissing me. A spark of self-loathing crept through my happy haze of lust, and I reached up to push his head away from the all too obvious bite scar on my throat that seemed unwilling to heal.

"Wait," I breathed.

His eyes flashed with wicked intensity, and before I could protest, he grazed his teeth deliberately over the scar.

Every muscle in my body clenched, and I let out a sharp breath as the sensation pitched me over the cliff I'd been climbing since the first brush of his lips. My knees shook, my entire body clenching, and I bit down hard on my own lip to stifle my scream as I shattered around him. Seemingly spurred on by my reaction, Bael's movements stuttered then stilled as he followed me over the edge.

I stared up at the ceiling, panting, as I came down from the adrenaline high that was better than any fairy wine. The mark on my neck throbbed, and I closed my eyes, an odd combination of satisfaction and guilt washing over me.

It shouldn't matter—not really, when Bael and I fit so well together and I was nearly as happy as I could ever remember being.

Except, he was not the one who'd left that mark on my neck, and no matter what I did, my conflicting feelings seemed likely to be as permanent as the scar.

2

LONNIE

THE CUTTHROAT DISTRICT, INBETWIXT

It took several minutes for the stars to stop bursting behind my eyelids, and for both of us to collect ourselves.

Now dressed and looking far less rumpled than I likely did, Bael took a step toward the door. "I told you they would wait, little monster."

I put a hand out to halt him. "No, let me go. Iola is afraid of you."

Bael frowned, and one of his bright yellow eyes rolled into the back of his head, showing me the white. I'd seen him do this before, and knew he was simply checking to make sure it really was Iola on the other side of the door. After a fraction of a second, the prince blinked, and grinned at me. "Alright, you go."

I checked once more that my clothing was back in place, then crossed the small room and swung open the door, smiling sheepishly. "I'm sorry to make you wait. We were—"

"Please, save me the explanation," Scion said, without inflection. "The entire house could hear you, I don't need a reenactment."

Words failed me.

Instead of Iola, it was Prince Scion who stood on the other side of the door, close enough that if I wanted, I could have reached out and touched him.

I looked up to meet his gaze and immediately regretted it.

It had been days since Prince Scion and I had so much as made eye contact, now, our eyes met and a pounding ache radiated through me, settling in my chest, and beneath the bite on my throat. *Damn.*

Scion had always been almost too-perfect looking. More overtly dangerous than Bael, he seemed at home in armor, and gave the impression that he doled out pain with his pleasure. Since the battle, his flawless features had been marred by a slash that ran the length of his face, from his temple down his cheek to his chin, narrowly missing his silver eye. It had been done with a Source-forged blade during the battle, and therefore would not heal immediately like any other wound, but I'd thought that perhaps Gwydion would be able to fix it for him. Apparently not since the cut was still red and raw, and oozed slightly whenever Scion moved or spoke.

My lips parted, words stalling on the tip of my tongue. Then, silently, Scion quickly averted his gaze, leaving me feeling hollow.

I could have kicked myself. *Every. Damn. Time.* And yet, I couldn't simply learn to look away first. Or better yet, never to look at him at all.

It had been like this all week, since that morning in the fishing village when he'd kissed me as if he could not stop himself. I knew the feeling, because that was exactly how I felt every time we grew close.

"Sorry," I stammered to my shoes, finally remembering how to speak. "I thought you were Iola. See, Aine keeps making her run errands or do chores, like she's still a servant, so I thought she'd sent Iola to tell us we were late for the meeting again. Because, well…"

"Stop speaking." Scion put up a hand. "I do not care."

He shouldered past me into the room, knocking a bit too hard against my arm for it to have been an accident. My brow furrowed, my irritation at his dismissal overtaking my embarrassment. "You can't just barge in here."

Scion ignored me, instead focusing on Bael. "Have you lost your mind? What the fuck are you doing?"

Bael looked entirely too unfazed. He ran a hand through his ruffled hair, and smiled impishly at his cousin. "I would have thought that was obvious."

"Let us pretend it is not," Scion said, every word sounding like it pained him. "Since I would not have imagined you to be this stupid."

"Oh?" Bael quipped, still sounding far too calm. "And I wouldn't have imagined you to be so transparently jealous, but here we are."

Scion spluttered, seeming too angry for words. My stomach turned over uncomfortably, and I closed my eyes. I could hardly stand to listen to this.

Only last week, Scion had seemed different—less abrasive, and helpful at times. For the briefest moment, I'd even thought he might have feelings for me. Unfortunately, it seemed like that version of Scion had been the false one, and the cruel, mocking prince had returned with full force.

"Take a breath, Sci." Bael said. "I was merely trying to teach Lonnie to shadow walk."

"That's an inventive teaching method you've devised." Scion threw the pair of us a scathing look. "You're going to kill us all. Is it worth it?"

My heartbeat pounded too hard against my ribs, and a fresh wave of guilt crashed over me.

Scion was right. We were playing with fire, Bael and I, and if something went wrong then it wouldn't be merely we who got burned. The entire Everlast family, Scion included, were at risk of paying the price for our mistakes.

The Everlast family was cursed, so that they could never experience true happiness. The moment any one of them did, anyone who shared their blood would die. This meant that while Bael had known for some time that we were true mates, and I'd finally been sure of it when I couldn't bear the thought of losing him during the battle, we couldn't complete our bond. There was too great a risk that he might experience real joy for the first time, and doom his entire family in the process. It was a miserable curse, in more ways than one.

I glanced up at Bael, and gestured vaguely toward Scion. "Perhaps he's right."

"No," Bael snapped, finally seeming annoyed. "He's not. No one is dying today."

"You're so sure that you're willing to bet your life on it?" Scion sneered, "How's your control today? Do we need to start looking for another cage?"

"Alright, that's enough," I said. "Maybe we should just—"

"You want to talk about control?" Bael took a step forward, reaching for me. Whatever I'd meant to say flew from my mind, as he gripped my hair and pulled my head to the side, just hard enough to expose my neck to the room. "What about your control?" he demanded of Scion. "I didn't mark her, *you* did that."

A ringing silence filled the room, and I shifted to extricate myself from Bael's grip. When I stood straight again, it was to find Scion looking resolutely away from me.

"She's not my mate," Scion ground out after a long, tense moment. "It's different."

"Like hell it is." Bael let out an exasperated sigh. "Part of me would welcome death, if only to spend eternity reminding your immortal soul what a fucking idiot you were."

I stiffened. If they argued—truly argued—I didn't know what I would do. For that matter, I didn't know if we would all survive the carnage. "Stop!" I said, unsure which of them I was speaking to—perhaps both. Bael let go of me, and I turned to Scion. "Is this really why you came all the way up here?"

Begrudgingly, and perhaps looking a bit embarrassed, Scion shook his head. "No."

I sighed. "Then what are you doing here?"

The prince took a deep breath through his nose and seemed to struggle to control his anger, before replying calmly. "You are late. Extremely so, in fact."

Bael rolled his eyes. "I told you, I was teaching her—"

Scion's silver eyes flashed, a bit of his rage leaking out. "Teach her to appear downstairs then, *quickly*, because we're all growing fucking old waiting for—"

Scion broke off, coughing, and it took me a beat to realize why. The Fae could not lie—ever. To do so would result in extreme pain, like flames searing one's throat. Because of this, they made games out of being misleading, while speaking only technical truths, and took great enjoyment out of tricking others into believing a misdirection. But Scion had just lied casually, as if by accident. Looking furious with himself, and still clearing his throat, the prince disappeared.

Baffled, I turned to Bael, "What just happened?"

To my surprise, he grinned in satisfaction at the spot where his cousin had stood a split second before. "Nothing gives me greater satisfaction than when he gets so angry he lies by mistake. It's hyperbole to the point of insanity."

I shook my head, trying not to smile. "You would enjoy that, because you're already insane."

"Trust me, little monster." Bael wrapped his arms around me, and pressed his face into my hair, breathing in, as if not ready to let me go just yet. "You don't know Scion like I do. I would actually call this outburst progress."

"You can't be serious," I almost laughed. "Progress toward what? The two of you turning this house to toothpicks?"

He shook his head. "You'll see. Anger is good. All he's doing is the same thing he's been doing for months."

"Which is what? Trying to murder me? Cursing the day I was born?"

"Proving how much he thinks about you."

My heartbeat sped up, my chest squeezing uncomfortably. Even if that were true, I couldn't see why Bael would be so happy about it. Fae as a whole were non-monogamous, but it still seemed like a stretch to expect the cousins to share me equally…if that was even something I wanted. I was not yet sure it was.

With Bael, I never questioned how he felt about me, but with Scion I was in a constant state of confusion. We could hardly stand each other at the best of times, but I'd been unable to keep myself from falling into his bed the night before the castle burned.

Had there been no rebellion, no battle, I was not sure what I'd expected to happen. It had seemed as if our relationship—if there was one—had begun to move beyond barbed banter and threats, yet, Scion never again brought up any of what happened in Inbetwixt or the kiss in the village. He'd hardly spoken a word to me in the last week, and now every time we looked at each other, the mark he'd left on my neck throbbed and my chest felt as if it might burst with...something.

Shaking my head to clear it, I squirmed to escape Bael's hold. "If you mean that your cousin spends a truly alarming amount of time plotting my demise, then yes, I'd agree."

Bael shook his head. "You're both infuriating. I've never met two people better at lying to themselves."

My shoulders slumped. "Regardless, he's right. We should go, this meeting is important."

"Whatever you say." Bael drew one arm from around my waist, and reached up, brushing a fingertip against the bite on my neck, and chuckled when I shivered. "I'm happy with how things are, you know, I'm just waiting for the two of you to join me."

I yanked out of his grasp and spun to look him in the eyes, barely registering anything he'd said beyond the word "Happy." "You're not perfectly happy, though, right?" I demanded. "Not true happiness?"

Bael's gaze widened, taking in my stricken expression, before his face softened. That word alone gave all the more credence to Scion's concerns, and if Bael was truly happy...then this could not continue.

He reached out and pushed a rebellious curl behind my ear, then leaned in to kiss my forehead. "No, little monster. I could never be truly happy until you are."

I relaxed. He didn't have to worry then, because I might not be cursed, but as long as they were, and as long as the dark cloud of mystery continued to hang over my very existence, I was in no danger of happiness.

Despite Scion's suggestion, I still couldn't shadow walk, so Bael and I took the normal, human way down to the secret underground den.

Cross's home was almost as grand as the obsidian palace had been before it was reduced to ashes. Despite its picturesque interior, however, it was nothing more than a facade for the headquarters of the guild.

Or, it used to be.

When Scion and I stayed here, we'd been the only inhabitants of the townhouse—aside from Cross himself. The other three dozen or so guild members slept in the barracks below ground. Now, the house was being used for the overflow of Everlast loyalists and soldiers who did not want to swear fealty to Ambrose Dullahan and his rebel army.

We passed one such group on the landing. Five or six soldiers in black obsidian armor, who all pressed themselves flat against the wall as Bael and I passed. Bael made no sign to indicate he saw them at all, simply walking on by as if they were not there.

I nodded awkwardly at the nearest man, and turned sideways to pass by. "Sorry."

The soldier paled beneath his helmet, and his voice shook with fear as he answered. "My fault, my lady."

I frowned, and opened my mouth to question the odd reaction, but Bael gripped my arm, steering me away with a purposeful stride. When we'd turned a corner into another hall, this one slightly less ornately decorated than the first, with lower lighting and no ornate carpeting along the wooden floors, I looked up at him. "Why stop me from speaking to them? We're no longer in the palace, it shouldn't matter if my manners are up to your standard."

The prince rolled his eyes. "It's not that, little monster. Don't always assume you're being insulted."

I bit my lip, not wanting to acknowledge that he had a fair point—I did tend to assume I was being insulted, especially when it came to anything any of the Everlasts did. "Well? Why stop me, then?"

"The soldiers are afraid of you," he replied easily. "We need all the support we can get, especially from those trained to use a weapon. I'd rather you not scare them away."

I glanced down, considering this as we approached the door to the tunnels. He was right, of course. In the last months, I'd had to grow used to being treated as something other than a servant, but even with a crown on my head I'd never had any real power—never been shown true respect. Now, I was having to get used to a different kind of reaction: fear. Wariness.

One week ago, Ambrose Dullahan, leader of the rebel army and former crown prince of the Everlast family, seized the capital with his army and took the obsidian crown. In the midst of chaos, he offered me a proposition that led me to unleash my long-concealed magic. The prince turned rebel leader had offered me information about my long-lost family in exchange for my loyalty. According to him, my mother—whom I'd assumed dead for some years now—may still be alive. As Ambrose was a seer, and the Fae could not lie, I had every reason to believe him. But, before I could give him an answer, I watched helplessly as the castle crumbled and—to my knowledge—Bael and Scion were swallowed by the raging flames and collapsing walls. Without meaning to, or fully understanding how I'd done it, I'd channeled all of my pent-up grief and anger into one explosive burst of energy, summoning forth twisted creatures from the depths of my anger—the afflicted.

Now, in the wake of the battle, I was filled with constant conflicting emotions. Not only had I revealed my hidden magic to others, but also to myself.

Throughout my entire life, I'd known in the back of my mind that there was something different about me. Knowing that my mother warned me never to go digging for answers, or worse, to try to use the powers. I'd firmly believed—or perhaps convinced myself—that I was human, and there was nothing more to it.

Now, however, I wasn't entirely sure.

Even if I hadn't managed to conjure fire or shadow walk in the past week, I could no longer pretend it was impossible. I could no longer ignore Bael's comments and explanations of Fae culture, or insist he was a fool to suspect that I might be more than human. Still, that didn't bring me any closer to knowing the truth of who I was.

Each time someone mentioned my abilities or observed me with inquisitive eyes, my chest tightened and my palms began to sweat. Even Bael pushing me to hone my magic only fueled the anxiety threatening to choke me.

Still, as much as I wanted to deny it, using magic during the fight felt exhilarating. A part of me craved the power, while another part was terrified by it.

Not wishing to think any deeper on the issue, I turned my attention back to Bael. "At least I don't ignore everyone as you do," I mumbled. "Are you not concerned that the few soldiers who have remained loyal will be offended and leave?"

He actually laughed at that. "I pray you never lose your naiveté, because then I'd know we truly ruined you."

"Meaning?"

"Meaning that if we do not want our guards to fear you, my presence will do you no favors."

I considered that as we made our way through the tunnels and emerged into the thieves' den. I supposed, Bael was right, especially now that he'd given up his courtly attire and false smiles. He'd had an entire lifetime of being feared by all those around him—except perhaps his immediate family—and knew that it could be as much a hindrance to leadership as it was a requirement for royalty.

Of course, I didn't desire to rule anyone.

And thanks to Ambrose Dullahan, I no longer did. In name, or otherwise.

3
LONNIE

THE CUTTHROAT DISTRICT, INBETWIXT

The thieves' den was a large, rectangular room with a bar on one side and a training ring on the other. The ceiling was adorned with shiny copper panels, while the walls were constructed of stone and illuminated by small wisp lamps every few feet. On the left side of the bar, a heap of crates and barrels leaned against the wall. On the right, a handful of small tables and chairs were arranged. When Scion and I had visited, the tables had rarely been occupied, but in the last week they were often used for strategy sessions. That seemed to hold true today.

Every seat around the tables was occupied, and there were more people leaning against the walls or sitting on the floor. Many faces turned toward me, and unlike the last time I'd been here, there were few smiles in the crowd. Most expressions were anxious, some outright fearful. I sighed. Being the object of so many stares, and terrified ones at that, was entirely too exhausting.

I pushed through the crowd, and finally spotted a genuinely friendly face. Making my way over, I leaned against the edge of the table where Iola sat. "Morning."

Iola looked slightly better than during the battle, having had a few meals and a bath. But she was still recovering from being accidentally poisoned over a month ago. Her tea-stained hair was braided and her borrowed clothing was clean, but she remained pale, sickly, and bedraggled. Every time I saw her the guilt that had taken root within me over these last several days seemed to grow, like it was a living thing within me.

"Oh, hi," Iola said, flustered. Her cheeks turned slightly pink. "Hello."

I raised a bemused eyebrow. "Are you alright?"

"Of course. I'm glad you finally came—down here that is." Her cheeks flamed scarlet. "Oh, gods. Here, do you want my chair?"

I stared at her, nonplussed. "No, you sit. What is wrong with you this morning?"

Behind me, Bael laughed, and leaned forward to whisper in my ear. "Scion doesn't knock, little monster. I think you were right—your friend was sent to get us, and probably gave up, so they sent...reinforcements."

Now, my face was growing hot as well, and I stared down at my shoes as I mumbled. "Well, your sister should stop ordering Iola around. It wasn't her job to fetch us in the first place. This whole thing was entirely avoidable."

"I don't disagree."

"Where is Aine, anyway?" I asked, glancing around.

Before Bael could respond, he was cut off by a jovial shout across the room. "Good of ya to finally join us, lass!"

A boisterous voice echoed through the room and I looked up. Through the crowd, I could make out Cross's bright red hair, and Scion's dark head beside him, bent low over something spread out over the bar. To my mingled relief and disappointment, the prince didn't look up at me, but Cross met my gaze over the heads of the many thieves.

The leader of the guild was clad in a suit of molded armor, resembling Scion's obsidian gear but with a lighter weight and a leather-like texture. It was a stark contrast from his usual casual attire, giving off the impression that he expected to be ambushed at any moment.

"Apologies for my lateness," I called back. "I see my penance is there are no chairs left."

The thief master grinned. "Not to worry, we've almost finished planning."

I tilted my head to the side. "Planning?"

"We'll be moving you out tomorrow night."

My heart skipped a beat, and a real smile spread across my face. That was the first truly good news I'd heard in days.

We'd been searching for a way to leave the city safely, both because I wanted to travel to Aftermath, and because most of the Everlasts were eager to join the rest of the family in Overcast. Unfortunately, news of the capital attack had spread quickly, and now other cities were beginning to show where their allegiance lay. When we'd arrived, the streets of Inbetwixt had still been safe to walk on, but now, only five days later, we would have to leave under cover of darkness, or risk a run in with the rebellion.

"What if he's waiting for her at the gates?" Bael asked loudly.

There was no question in my mind—or anyone else's, as far as I could tell—whom he meant by "He."

"Our spies in the capital report that the afflicted are keeping the entire rebel army busy for the time being," Cross replied. "Even if Dullahan does realize we're moving tomorrow, I doubt he'd be able to make it here."

"Is there any way to be sure the Dullahan won't see us?" asked one of the thieves sitting too far into the crowd for me to make out their face. "We all know he's a seer, but every seer I've ever met had limitations."

"That's a good question," Cross commented. "Sci, do you know how much your brother can actually see?"

All eyes turned to Scion, and he visibly stiffened. I could practically see him struggling to resist the urge to deny that Ambrose was his brother, but apparently, he was unwilling to scald his own throat twice in an hour.

"He's not fucking omniscient, if that's what you're asking," Scion ground out. "He doesn't know *everything* we do."

"But what's his range?" Cross asked. "Is he limited by distance? A certain amount of time into the future, or certain people…" He trailed off, looking hopefully at Scion to pick up the thread of the conversation.

Scion set his jaw, looking furious as he mulled over his answer. Anyone would assume he just hated his brother, but I would've bet everything I owned that the real problem was Scion didn't want to spread information about the Everlast family's abilities to such a large audience. Ambrose Dullahan might be a traitor, a murderer, and an exile of the royal court, but he was still an Everlast, and what hurt one, hurt them all.

"Ambrose is much the same as our grandmother was," Scion said finally. "He's not limited by distance, but is more aware of those he is close to. He cannot see anything of his own future, however, so he always travels with a companion."

"Anything else?" Cross asked.

Scion's frown deepened to the point that if his face could've wrinkled, the expression would be permanently etched there. "I'm not certain," he admitted. "At the height of her power,

Queen Celia was plagued by such constant visions she was effectively blind to the world around her."

I raised my eyebrows, and was far from the only one in the room to look surprised. I hadn't known that about the former queen, though, it did make sense. In all the years I'd worked in the palace, I'd only seen Queen Celia one time. She rarely left her room, and was almost more of a myth than a living person. If she saw so much of the future that she'd lost track of the present, that explained much. It might also explain some of Ambrose Dullahan's behavior, except…

"He didn't seem unaware of his surroundings when I spoke with him," I piped up. "And I certainly would have noticed if he were blind."

Bael leaned over to me, speaking low. Though as the room was made up of mostly Fae, it hardly mattered. "Ambrose is only two hundred odd years old, little monster. Grandmother Celia was over one thousand when her visions reached that height. He's likely not there yet."

I pressed my mouth into a thin line. Bael had probably meant his comment to be helpful, but as with so much else he shared with me, it only sent my mind reeling. Never before had it occurred to me that magic might grow with age. Most of the Fae I knew personally were relatively young by their standards. How powerful would they be in one hundred years?

I supposed it didn't matter. I was mortal, and wouldn't be here to see it.

"Alright," Cross spoke over the now whispering room, and raised a hand to call everyone's attention back to him. "I've always thought it was near pointless to try to outrun a seer, and given this information, it's best to just assume the Dullahan knows everything, which makes it all the more important that we have a strong plan in place if we're to get everyone out alive."

"If you've already determined that the rebels are busy ridding the capital of the Afflicted," I said, trying to ignore the guilt that rose higher in my throat. "And we all agree that there's no way to evade Ambrose Dullahan, can we return to the plan at hand?"

"You seem entirely too flippant about your own life," Scion snapped, addressing me directly for the first time.

"He doesn't want to kill me," I said, my voice rising above the crowd again. "I mean, if that's what you're worried about...he didn't seem that way when we spoke."

"He doesn't want to kill you, *yet*," Bael muttered. "But if we wait too long to leave, I'm sure he'll make a more direct threat."

I nodded. That, I agreed with, but we weren't talking about what might happen in several weeks, only how to leave the city.

I'd had a lot of time to mull over why Ambrose Dullahan might want me to join him, and there were only two options as far as I could tell.

One, that he wanted to use my magic. However, as I'd barely been able to do that so far, and according to Cross, I'd created nothing but problems for the rebel army in the form of afflicted monsters, that seemed unlikely. The second option, and the one that I tended to think far more plausible, was that he *did* want to kill me—just not yet. Bael agreed.

While I'd all but completely rejected the Wilde Hunts, and had openly refused to travel to Nevermore for the third trial and had lost the obsidian crown, I was technically still the queen. If Ambrose believed in the validity of the hunting season, as the rest of his family seemed to, we suspected he wanted to kill me on the correct night to ensure that there was no challenge to his leadership. If so, there was just under two weeks until I'd meet the rebel king again, and I did not want to be in Inbetwixt if that happened. Nowhere would be perfectly safe, especially when trying to evade a seer, but I'd prefer that Cross and his thieves not have to die just to protect me from another attack.

"How will we be leaving?" I asked loudly, practically begging Cross to step in and redirect the conversation.

To my relief, he took the hint. Cross spoke as if addressing me alone, but the room listened with rapt attention. "Our tunnels extend all over the city, and we can escort you to the edge of the wall."

"And then what?"

"And then we can ride to the nearest town." Bael muttered under his breath. "We can always shadow walk if need be, but horses would be preferable."

"We can get you horses," Cross said.

I shot him a grateful look. "Fine. So you'll be bringing me and Bael and..." I trailed off. This was a bit of a sore subject, and the ensuing pause emphasized my discomfort.

"I would like to come," Iola said. "But..."

She trailed off, and my eyes shot to her. Truthfully, I was not sure if she would be able to handle a journey across the country with her health as poor as it was, but if she wished to come then I couldn't leave her. I'd agreed, during the battle, that we would stay together. In a way, I felt responsible for her, at least until she learned to stand on her own.

"You do not have to if you don't wish to," I said quickly.

She looked uncomfortable. "It's only, I don't know where else I would go."

I met Cross's eyes over the crowd, a question in my gaze. "I'm sure there's room for more refugees here."

"Yes, of course," the thief master answered.

I smiled, as did Iola. At least here, she had a good chance of recovering fully, whereas on the road to Aftermath...in truth, I was not sure she'd last a week.

"Anyone else?" I asked.

"Not us," Gwydion's voice said from somewhere behind me, interrupting my thoughts. "We'll be taking Elfwyn to Overcast."

I stood up straighter and craned my neck to see him, having not realized he was in the room. Bael's brother stepped forward, the crowd shuffling to make room for him. Taller and more muscular than Bael or Scion, who were both large in their own right, Gwydion was the largest fairy I'd ever seen. He had the build of a fighter, rather than the healer he claimed to be.

"I suppose that's you and Thalia, then?" I asked, lightly.

Gwydion nodded, and gave me an apologetic smile. "I'm sure you can understand, Aftermath is no place for a child."

I snorted. I'd been raised in Aftermath, but it wasn't worth pointing out. They all knew, they simply didn't care, and I didn't want to travel with Gwydion, anyway. I'd been suspicious of him since realizing that he'd not fully healed Iola. Now, looking at Scion's face, and the multitude of injuries on everyone else, I was more concerned than ever.

I searched for Thalia in the crowd. "Are you content with returning to your parents' home?"

She gave me a sad smile. "It's the best option."

That was not really a "yes" but I took it to mean that she'd made up her mind as well. I nodded, and turned away from them.

"Fine. I assume Aine will go with them as well."

"We'll smuggle them out, much the same way we are doing with you, tomorrow evening," Cross offered. "It's easier to do it in two groups."

I nodded, having not really expected their help. Most of the Everlast family—everyone who'd managed to escape with us, that was—seemed to believe I'd lost my mind wanting to go to Aftermath. Their firm belief that Aftermath was nothing but a desolate, dangerous, wasteland, won out over anything else.

Bael reached up and squeezed my thigh. "We'll be better off in a small group, anyway, little monster."

I smiled at him, and leaned back against the table, somehow exhausted from nothing more than this conversation. There was a long silence, and it took me a beat to realize that one person had yet to voice his intentions.

My gaze met Scion's silver eyes across the room, as if he'd already been watching me. I expected him to look down as he had done every time we'd mistakenly caught each other's eye in the last few days, but he didn't.

I forgot to breathe as my heartbeat sped up, my pulse pounding in my throat. My lips parted, and I leaned forward slightly, unsure if I intended to move, or had simply lost the ability to hold myself up. I watched his hand twitch, clenching at his side, and then he tore his gaze away from me, staring at the floor.

"Are you alright, little monster?" Bael asked, bemused.

I sucked in a breath, like I'd been underwater, and shook my head to clear it. "I'm…tired."

A technical truth, if not the full truth. I was *tired*, but more so, I was reeling from the realization that I never once thought Scion wouldn't accompany us to Aftermath. It never even crossed my mind that we'd have to leave him…and why? Why would I assume such a thing when he'd made no mention of it, never shown any indication of wanting to come? Worse, why did I care?

Why did I feel like I was about to lose something vitally, crucially, important?

4
SCION

THE CUTTHROAT DISTRICT, INBETWIXT

"Alright, mate?"

I looked up at the sound of Cross's voice and blanched. The room was nearly empty. The meeting must have ended some time ago, and I hadn't bothered to notice.

I shook my head, struggling to think of a truthful answer that would appease him. "I'm...tired."

That was true enough. I'd hardly ever slept worse than I had this week, for a number of reasons, not least of which was the constant noise of the thieves' den.

Cross seemed to read some of this in my expression, because his grin widened behind his copper beard. "The barracks not what you expected?"

I gave a stiff jerk of my head, that could have meant anything, being neither a nod nor a shake. I didn't have the energy to come up with a satisfactory misdirection, nor did I want to openly insult my only friend outside my own bloodline by telling him that, if not for our long friendship, I would have slaughtered every single one of his children for just one hour of peaceful sleep.

"You could always sleep up in the house. No one is forcing you into this exile, Sci."

"No." I grunted. I'd heard enough this morning to confirm my decision not to set foot anywhere near the townhouse bedrooms. I'd rather take my chances fending off Cross's many daughters.

I pushed my chair back from the table, and the sound of wood scraping against stone sent a new throbbing through the back of my skull.

"Did you want something?" I asked, realizing Cross still hadn't moved from where he stood beside my chair.

"Not especially, just curious to know your plans."

I raised a sore eyebrow and pressed my lips together in a flat line. It was clear he really wanted to ask if I was planning to go with Lonnie, or if I'd be traveling to Overcast with the rest of my family. If only I knew the answer to that myself, I'd gladly tell him.

Unfortunately, whenever I considered Aftermath, my mind was stuck on the same scenes, replaying them over and over. The thick, black smoke clouding the air and suffocating me. The unrelenting flames devoured everything in their path, reducing buildings to rubble. The desperate cries of villagers, a mix of Fae and humans, as they fled for their lives.

I had absolutely no desire to set foot in that hell ever again, but still, I was considering it, and I wished desperately that I could convince myself there was any reason other than the obvious; where that infuriating, stubborn, beautiful woman went, I felt compelled to follow...even if it was the worst decision I could ever possibly make.

"Just say what you came to say, Cross, or I'm going to go try to sleep."

"I just thought I'd let you know we'll be leaving tonight instead," he replied.

"Why the change?"

"Siobhan's idea." He jabbed a thumb behind him, indicating one of his crew I knew he was especially fond of. "It's good, yeah? Always best to leave a false trail when dealing with your brother, so he might see the meeting, but get the details wrong."

I grunted in lackluster acknowledgement. His efforts were undoubtedly good, but ultimately pointless. The truth was that if Ambrose had seen Lonnie leaving the city and wanted to go after her, no amount of planning could stop him. It was impossible to out maneuver a seer as talented as my brother. I'd learned that lesson time and time again, but the destruction of our home had finally made it stick.

When I met my brother in battle, it would be no surprise, but a test of pure strength, and I took some satisfaction in the knowledge that he'd know I was about to kill him.

It was barely mid-day, and I already knew that no amount of exhaustion could force me to sleep at this hour. Still, anything was preferable to lingering out in the den. I'd found Lonnie's constant presence impossible to ignore when we inhabited the same enormous fortress. Now, I would have traded anything for my most pressing problem to be the woman haunting my tower.

I stepped into the barracks and was reminded of telling Lonnie that I'd die before letting her sleep here. The sentiment hadn't been nearly strong enough.

The room was nearly as long as the den itself, with two-dozen beds placed end to end along each wall. At a glance, nearly every bed was occupied. Some people were sleeping, others talking, while still more engaged in far livelier activities until the sounds of heavy breathing, snoring, whispers, and sex filled my ears.

I strode toward the nearest bed, and kicked it. "Move."

The occupant, a young-looking Demi-Fae male, rolled over and blinked sleepy eyes up at me. "What's wrong? Is father calling?"

I glowered. I would never get used to anyone calling Cross "father." Not when I'd known him since he was barely older than the idiot in this bed. "Get up."

Seeming to realize whom he was speaking to, the boy rubbed his eyes and blanched. "But…I was working all night."

"What gives you the impression that I am a sympathetic sort? Get the fuck out."

He scrambled to his feet, leaving the bed unoccupied. I sat on the edge to unlace my boots and sighed before lying flat on my back. I stared at the cobwebbed ceiling and ground my teeth, listening to the raised voices from the next bed over.

There was nowhere to hide in the thieves' den. Nowhere to go for a moment's solitude, where my entire cursed family could not find me, or sixty-odd thieves were sleeping or fighting or fucking at any given moment. Nowhere to go where *she* wasn't.

The end of my mattress dipped, and I glanced up, startled. My eyes widened slightly. A curvy, lavender haired female dressed in the same training leathers as the rest of Cross's crew sat at the foot of the mattress. I raised an eyebrow, saying nothing.

"Hi," the thief said. "I'm Maeve."

I stared at her, unaffected. This was becoming a daily occurrence, as if those I'd already rejected had spoken to friends, and now they'd made a game over it. Normally, I'd enjoy the attention, but not now. Now, I wanted nothing more than to be left alone.

My continued silence seemed to rattle the thief, because she shook herself before continuing again. "You're in my bed."

Thinking of the male I'd just displaced, I raised an eyebrow. "Is that so?"

"Yes." She giggled. "But, I don't mind sharing."

The corner of my lip tipped up in a sneer. Even if I'd been in the mood to fuck anyone, the woman's lies would have made me turn her away.

I couldn't stand any more lying humans.

 "Even if these beds were assigned, which I know they're not, I'd still tell you to go sleep on the floor. I don't want company."

Her smile vanished, and she leaned back, affronted. Frankly, I thought she got off rather easily. If I'd had the energy to truly scare her, perhaps I would not have to deal with any more of these propositions. Only, somehow, I was beginning to feel guilty over breaking humans just for the sake of it.

I rolled over again, attempting to ignore the sounds of the barracks. With every passing second, I regretted my refusal to sleep in the main house. But then, the memory of this morning would creep into my subconscious—of storming into the same upstairs hall that I'd comfortably walked only last week, and hearing her familiar breathy moans. I knew the sound instantly, and that alone was alarming. How many cries of pleasure had I heard over the years? Too many to count, yet for some reason I could have picked hers out of an entire chorus of voices. Horrifying to say the least.

Footsteps sounded beside the bed, and I ground my teeth without opening my eyes. "I thought I made it clear I'm not going to fuck you."

"Well, I suppose I'll have to find some way to quell my disappointment."

I opened my eyes abruptly at the sound of the unexpected voice. Lonnie stood at the end of my bed, arms crossed, jaw set. She looked like she was trying very hard to seem aloof, but her hands shook and I could hear her erratic heartbeat thrumming too fast to be normal.

I sat up too fast and my head spun. "I thought you were someone else."

"Obviously," she said, almost bitterly, keeping her huge brown eyes fixed on the bed. "I'm well aware of how repulsive you find your attraction to me, my lord."

I cocked my head. Lonnie was dressed unlike anything I'd ever seen her wear, in clothing no doubt borrowed from Siobhan. Her trousers and bodice were leather, with a low-cut white blouse and a black beaded belt. Her long curls were left loose and untamed, falling in a halo around her shoulders. I blinked slowly at her. "You don't know fucking anything."

"Don't I? You can't lie, so you must've meant it when you said you wanted me, but you won't do anything about it. What am I meant to assume?"

If not for the persistent noise of the room, and the throbbing pain in my face, I might have thought I'd fallen asleep after-all. This felt like a dream. Or a test. She could not truly have come to find me just to ask if I wanted her, there had to be something else she wanted. "What are you doing here?"

She took a step forward, still not looking me in the eye. "You didn't say anything during the meeting."

My brow furrowed. "That's not true."

She swallowed heavily, and I was distracted for a second watching her throat work. If I didn't know better, I'd say she was in pain. "I meant, you didn't say anything about if you intended to travel with us."

"There's nothing in Aftermath except ruins and afflicted and the source knows what other fucking creatures. Going there is suicide."

The corner of her mouth tipped up unexpectedly. "Bael said much the same thing."

Good. At least he hadn't completely lost his mind. "Then why go?"

"I've explained this. If my mother is alive, she is most likely in the north. In any case, I was born there. You are correct that there are dangers in the north, but that's not all there is."

I shook my head. "And you seem to forget that I spent a decade in Aftermath. I know perfectly well what hell awaits us there, and I have no desire to return."

She pressed her lips flat together. "So, you are not coming with us?"

I sat up straighter, so we were nearly eye-level. "Are you asking me to?"

"Would it matter if I did?" she asked, answering my question with a question in a way that would make any of the Fae proud.

For a long moment, I forgot the sound of the room. I could hear nothing but my own heartbeat, and her breathing. I licked my lips. "Perhaps."

"*Perhaps*." She sneered. "*Perhaps* you could be doing anything. Just say what you mean, Scion."

The sound of my name from her lips seemed to resonate through me like a siren song, but I pressed my own lips together, saying nothing, because I could not—could never.

Perhaps if she said she wanted me, I wouldn't be able to deny her.

Perhaps I'd thrown myself head-long into the plans for taking back the capital, filling every waking hour with work, because I was determined to keep the vow I'd made to Bael in the crumbling tower; resolute in my conviction to avoid Lonnie until he asked otherwise, and never to betray our friendship again over this damned woman.

Perhaps I'd never had a reason to envy my cousin anything, but now I feared I'd grow to hate him because he was the one whom she'd deemed worthy of forgiveness; the one sharing her bed every night and making her late to breakfast.

Perhaps...

"Will you go to Overcast with the rest of your family?" she asked when I remained silent too long.

"No," I replied, realizing this for the first time myself. Until I'd spoken I had not been certain that I had no intention of going into hiding along with the others, but now that seemed as if it should've been obvious all along.

"What, then?" she asked. "Or were you planning to make me keep guessing?"

"I wasn't planning on anything. You're the one who sought me out, rebel."

She shook her head. "I wouldn't have to if you weren't avoiding me."

My lip curled. "Did you ever stop to think about why that might be? What if I don't want to see you?"

She shook her head, brow furrowed in anger, and stepped back toward the door. "Right, never mind. I don't know what possessed me to come down here."

My jaw clenched as I turned my head away, unable to mask the anger boiling within me. Her leather boots thudded against the floor, a constant reminder of her presence and my frustration. But just as she reached the door, I heard her steps falter. My chest tightened, and I bit my tongue to keep from blurting out something I'd surely regret.

She hesitated before speaking, carefully choosing her words. "I know better than to ask a favor, so I won't ask you to come with us... but I do wish you would offer."

My head snapped up, caught off guard by her request, and my thoughts scattered when our eyes finally met.

Even though I expected it by now, the searing pain that shot through my body still caught me off guard. It was like wasting away from starvation, every fiber of my being screaming for relief. Like a thousand knives were being driven into me at once, each one piercing deeper, twisting in my gut. The intensity of it left me breathless, my muscles tensed and trembling with the effort of enduring it. How could something as innocent as a glance produce such an excruciating physical response?

I'd made an entire career from pain. I'd defined my immortal existence by it, and learned its intricacies so well that I knew the exact point at which a mind would splinter, unable to handle another moment of agony.

With every glance, she shattered me.

5
LONNIE

THE CUTTHROAT DISTRICT, INBETWIXT

*I*n my dreams, I was eleven once more.

The sun hung low in the sky over the meadow, nearly obscured by the smokey clouds around the mountains of the Source on the horizon, and the sound of humming insects was almost louder than the wind rustling the nearby trees of the Waywoods. My eyelids drooped with exhaustion, as I shifted onto all fours, and inched forward, imagining I was a sleek mountain lion on the hunt.

Everyone knew to fear the monstrous mountain lions in the valley of Aftermath almost as much as we feared the Fae soldiers. It was rumored in our village that they stalked the same target for days on end, sometimes weeks before they finally made their strike. I didn't think I would have to wait that long — not as long as the real lions would — but I had my doubts. After all, my sister, Rosey, was terrible at this game.

My sister was awful at nearly every game I invented. She didn't enjoy playing pretend, or anything that might involve running, and she always forgot to creep through the grass, trying to muffle her footsteps so I wouldn't hear her.

Sure enough, my heart leapt at the sound of footsteps on the nearby path. They grew closer, grass crunching. With a rush of excitement, I *leapt from my grassy hiding place to tag my twin. "Got you, I—oomph."*

I slammed into something hard and unexpected, and bounced off. Light danced behind my eyes and my breath left me in a whoosh as my spine slammed into the cold ground, still hard this early in the spring. I gasped as my lungs spasmed, struggling for air.

An unfamiliar, too-pleasant voice pierced through the quiet air. "Who is this?"

My eyes snapped open, and I gazed up at the overcast sky, only to see the silhouette of two, tall strangers towering over me. My blood ran cold.

Fairies.

My eyes snapped open and my heartbeat raced as I jolted upright. Disoriented, I rubbed my bleary eyes and dragged my tongue over my lips, clearing the fuzz of sleep from my mouth.

A sharp sting of pain pulsed through my hip, reminding me that I had dozed off on the unforgiving wooden floor of the bedroom. My half-packed satchel lay strewn haphazardly beside me, its contents spilling out onto the floor in a chaotic mess of clothing, food, and weapons. It didn't look much different from when I had started.

After the disastrous conversation with Scion, I'd intended to spend the rest of the afternoon packing to leave. I had no idea what possessed me to seek out the prince, or more embarrassing still, to ask him to come with us—as if he'd care what I wanted. He hadn't even replied to my question, and finally I'd fled from the room, humiliating rejection hanging over me.

I couldn't face the shame of explaining to Bael what was bothering me, and vowed not to leave our room again until we left the city tomorrow evening. Therefore, I'd never been happier than when I was told we'd be leaving tonight, rather than tomorrow evening.

When evening came, Siobhan met Bael and I in the hallway outside the bedroom to escort us down to the tunnels that would take us out of the city.

"Ready?" she asked, when I opened the door.

I held up my small satchel. "There wasn't much to pack."

Tall and thin, but with corded muscles like a dancer, Siobhan didn't look deadly, but I'd long since learned that looks could be deceiving. Her long, midnight-black hair was braided tight against her head, and she wore a hood with her dark thieves armor, that made it difficult to discern her expression as we set off down the hall.

"Will you be traveling with us?" I asked.

"Yes." Her tone made it sound as if she were smiling beneath her hood. "Me, Arson and Cross will be coming along, at least as far as the wall."

"Do we really need such a large group?" Bael asked.

"Don't worry, my lord," she said with humor in her tone. "We won't draw too much attention to your girl."

Though Cross had said the network of tunnels extended all over the city, I had no real notion of how accurate that statement was without seeing it for myself. Siobhan brought us through the house to the same entrance tunnel we usually used to enter the dens. However, once we entered, she turned left, and pulled on a small chain hanging from the ceiling. After a long pause, a passage slid open along the wall.

I stared in amazement "I never would have noticed that."

"Precisely." Siobhan said, clicking her tongue. "Come on, we've got a tight schedule tonight."

"Where does this lead?" I asked, as we hurried along a stone passage nearly identical to the one we'd just left.

"This passage connects to the wine cellar below the bar next door," she explained. "But that's only where we're meeting the others. We have a ways to go yet before you're clear of the gates. Keep up."

I snapped my mouth shut, resolving to try to hold in my questions—however difficult that might be.

As it turned out, we need not have hurried. An hour later, we still stood in a huddle in the crowded wine cellar, waiting for the rest of our party to arrive. The chill of the wine cellar seeped into my cloak, freezing me from the inside out. Had I been thinking about it, I might have worried that I'd be colder the moment we stepped outside, but there was no room in my mind for such thoughts. Not tonight.

My hands were clammy with anxiety, my pulse erratic as I glanced around. Bael's shadow loomed over the rows of dusty bottles, his yellow eyes glinting in the darkness, like a cat peering out of some winding alley. Cross stood with arms folded, a scowl etched into his usually smiling face, and beside him Siobhan and Arson perched on barrels, like sentinels waiting to strike.

I sucked in a breath, managing to keep my voice even despite my trembling hands. "Let's go."

Bael cleared his throat, and glanced toward the door. "We could wait another moment."

He was the one who'd insisted on waiting for Scion, and though I felt sure that after our conversation earlier that he was not coming, I had to admit Bael's certainty lit a tiny spark of hope in my chest.

Now, after an hour, that spark had been well and truly doused.

"Is waiting any longer going to matter?" I asked, bitterness lacing my tone.

He opened his mouth to reply, but stopped as the sound of distant footsteps down the hall made everyone tense. My heartbeat sped up in excitement, and I turned toward the door.

Aine stepped into the room, dressed as if she intended to travel in a long, woolen coat and heavy leather boots. Tan, with a slim figure and honey-brown curls tied back in a long braid, her expression was set in a tight, determined, line.

My momentary excitement fled, leaving me emptier than I'd been before. My eyes flicked to Bael, hoping for some understanding or reassurance, but he stood just as stunned and wide-eyed as I did.

"What are you doing here?" I asked.

"Are you not leaving tonight?" Aine replied primly.

"Yes," I said slowly, "and you are leaving tomorrow."

She took another step forward, letting the light from the hall flood into the small room. "My mistake. I was under the impression that there was an open invitation to travel to Aftermath."

"Why would you want to travel with us?" Bael demanded.

"I wouldn't," Aine said bitterly, "but the alternative is worse. Anyway, you know I'd be useful."

Bael cocked his head to the side, assessing. "I know you *could* be useful. Whether you will is an entirely different matter."

Her face flushed with anger, and her voice grew sharp as she retorted, "I will be. I have no desire to be hidden away any longer."

Bael paused, assessing his sister before shrugging. "Fine."

"Wait." I reached out and grabbed his arm, trying to convey my misgivings with my eyes alone.

As far as I'd seen, Aine had never once done anything one might consider useful. She'd been at the palace when it was attacked, and as far as I'd heard, had done nothing to stop it. More concerning still, Aine had not acclimated well to losing her comfortable palace lifestyle. She had suddenly taken on many traits I might have associated with her mother, Raewyn: sulking, ordering everyone around, and making snide remarks at every possible opportunity. Even pompous Gwydion was handling the upheaval better than his sister.

I longed to unleash a diatribe of complaints, but instead, I only said: "I thought you were unwilling to use magic?"

"And we thought you didn't have any magic," she snapped. "Things change."

Bael looked like he might already be regretting his decision. "She'll use her abilities…correct?"

"Correct," Aine ground out.

"Then there's no problem," Bael said.

I was not so sure about that. "But—"

"Leave it, little monster. If Aine is willing to come, we'd be foolish not to let her."

I snapped my lips shut. Neither of them seemed inclined to share precisely how Aine might be useful, which might have swayed me. Still, I supposed I would have to trust that Bael knew what he was doing—at least for the time being.

"Right," Siobhan said briskly. "Shall we go, then? Or are we waiting on any other royal relatives?"

Bael and I looked at each other, and foolishly, the last tiny shred of hope lit once more within me "Is it worth waiting any longer?"

He sighed, giving me an almost pleading look, before rolling his eyes into the back of his head. After a moment, his face twisted into a grimace. "No, you're right. We should go."

I nodded, saying nothing, and stepped forward to take his hand. He squeezed my fingers, and even though I appreciated his comfort, I felt somehow lopsided, and my chest ached in a way it had no right to for someone who clearly never thought twice about me.

6
LONNIE

THE SEWERS, INBETWIXT

Even knowing we'd be walking through the sewers, somehow I had not thought the smell would be quite so potent.

I tried to think of anything else as we trudged along, the stench of decay clawing at my senses, but the sewers were a suffocating maze; a foul miasma that threatened to overwhelm me. The scurrying of rats echoed off the walls, their tiny claws skittering in the darkness. Fortunately—or unfortunately, as it were—I had much to dwell on that was equally foul.

Glancing at Bael, I found him already looking at me. "What are you thinking about, little monster?"

Nothing good.

I kept my voice low, though, with the echoing tunnels and the closeness of our group, it hardly mattered. "Did you not want to go to Overcast? Even the slightest bit?"

He scoffed. "I take it you've never been to Overcast."

Cross laughed a few paces ahead of us. "Dreadful place, lass."

"I thought that was your northern outpost," I said, more of a statement than a question.

"It is. But simply in terms of the land itself, there are many reasons to avoid a visit." Bael gave an affected shudder. "It's built almost on top of the Wanderlust, and it's downwind from Aftermath. Trust me, little monster. We'd be happier in the center of the Source itself."

I laughed, though I did not feel all that humorous. "I take it you've never been to the Source, itself?"

He rolled his eyes, seeming to assume I'd been joking. I hadn't been.

We walked for nearly twenty minutes, the dark tunnels stretching endlessly like tangled yarn. A rat ran across my feet and I stifled a scream, if only to avoid breathing in any more of the putrid air.

Finally, when I was not sure I could take another minute of the stench, it seemed that the stone beneath our feet began to slant upwards. I nearly skipped with excitement. "Are we nearly there?"

"Almost," Cross replied.

"Where does this tunnel end?"

"It goes around the entire city, of course, but we're going to be stopping off near the eastern gate."

I pressed my lips together, and only nodded. I was not overly familiar with the geography of Inbetwixt, but it was easy enough to understand where each gate must lead by the name alone. Aftermath was in the North-west of the country, on the opposite side of the walled city from the eastern gate. That gate would lead to the shipping docks, and was the furthest from any road that might take us toward our destination. Still, complaining would do little good now.

To my immense relief, we finally came to a halt at the base of a simple, metal ladder, which ascended into a hatch in the ceiling.

Cross stopped in front of it, flanked by Siobhan and Arson, and I stood behind him, with Bael and Aine hanging back slightly. Again, as in the wine cellar, I could see what Bael had meant about the too large group. Hopefully Cross knew what he was doing, and there would be no problem with being overly conspicuous as we left the city.

"You'll need to stay below ground for a moment while I check the area," Siobhan said. "The gate isn't far from here, so as long as no one is waiting around for you it shouldn't be difficult to leave."

I swallowed and nodded, feeling a bit like her statement was a bad omen—almost inviting trouble the moment we moved above ground.

Siobhan received a leg up from Arson, and began to ascend the ladder. "I'll shout when it's safe."

Reaching the top of the ladder, she opened a hatch and there was a small whoosh of a fresh breeze, a sliver of night sky, before she disappeared and we were plunged back into semi-darkness.

"I'm going with her," Arson said roughly, speaking for the first time all evening.

Cross nodded, and he too climbed out of sight. The passage immediately felt roomier, though I still wished for nothing more than to escape into the open air.

Bael squeezed my hand and I gave him a weak smile, unable to muster anything in the way of words. I should be ecstatic to be finally beginning our journey, but I couldn't help but focus on what I was leaving behind.

The hatch opened once more, and Siobhan stuck her head back through the hole. "Safe."

"Go," Cross said roughly. "Quickly."

I swept my long, dark wool cloak out of the way, and stepped onto the first wrung of the metal ladder. It wasn't very high to climb, but the scum on the bottoms of my boots made me move carefully, afraid I might slip as I ascended. Siobhan reached a gloved hand out, and I took it, allowing her to help me the rest of the way out into the clear night air.

The air smelled of salt and the sea, and even the faint odor of fish was a welcome change after so long below ground. Sucking in a breath, I practically laughed with relief as I looked around, taking everything in. We'd arrived behind what looked to be some sort of boat house, if the barrels and nets covering the ground were anything to go by. Behind Siobhan, I could see a sliver of a long dock, water lapping at its edge, and the masts of several tall ships.

I stepped out of the way of the ladder to allow Bael to climb out, and squinted into the darkness near the harbor. "I thought we were coming out near the wall."

Siobhan didn't respond to me directly, but shook her head as she shot a meaningful look at Cross. She addressed him the moment he pulled himself out of the hole in the ground. "The gate is down, like we expected, but there are only two guards."

Cross frowned, then turned to me, finally addressing my question. "The wall is over there." He pointed to somewhere beyond my eye-line. "It surrounds the entire city, and the eastern gate is at the harbor. Usually, this gate remains open to the road, even at night, because traders come in at all hours, but the gate is down."

"Why?" I asked, thinking I already knew the answer.

"Because we're in the city," Aine's drawl answered.

I turned to see her climbing up the last rungs of the ladder. Arson stood beside the hole, his hand outstretched as if to help her, but she didn't so much as glance at him.

"No one knows for sure that we're here," I argued.

Aine brushed dust from her knees and straightened. "Do try to be serious. Of course word has spread by now, and as I thought you knew, the lord and lady of this city are no supporters of ours."

"They won't be a problem much longer," Cross said with a shadow of darkness behind his usual smile.

Aine raised an eyebrow, looking interested. "Only time will tell if that's an improvement or not."

"Try not to make new enemies." Bael eyed his sister warily. "We can hardly afford any more."

"Right," Cross straightened. "Let's carry on then. There are two guards on the outside of the gate, but there shouldn't be any trouble as long as…" he trailed off, glancing at Bael.

"Just point them out," Bael said, without inflection.

I frowned, but said nothing. In the past, I might have argued over the necessity of Bael killing two random guards, but since the castle had fallen I'd had to get far more comfortable with the use of force.

Cross led, with Bael directly behind him, as we crept single file through the harbor. The wooden planks beneath my boots creaked softly as I paced back and forth, my thoughts drifting to the dangers lurking in the darkness around us. Every shadow seemed to hold a hidden threat, every rustle of the night breeze sending a shiver down my spine.

The wall came into sight, the huge wooden gate looming, casting long shadows over the already dark harbor.

Suddenly, a distant crashing noise echoed through the quiet night, followed by the sound of voices raised in alarm. We exchanged worried glances as the commotion drew nearer. Shadows flitted along the alleyways leading to the docks, and the unmistakable clatter of armored boots on cobblestones filled the air.

Cross's gaze hardened, his eyes scanning our surroundings for any sign of danger before he positioned himself protectively in front of us, and drew his sword. "Rebels."

7
LONNIE

THE DEADEYE DISTRICT, INBETWIXT

T ime felt as if it stopped on the dark, windswept dock, and I froze. Then, all at once, movement erupted around me.

A shout cut through the night, piercing and terrible, sending fear pounding through my veins. "For the Dullahan!"

Cold dread washed over me, the sound of those words bringing back too many memories and sending me running. Sound was everywhere, roaring in my ears, and my feet were moving before my mind had fully caught up with the far too familiar sight of black, hooded cloaks.

Across the dock, Cross gritted his teeth as he swung his sword, the metal glinting in the pale moonlight. Behind him, Siobhan shot one arrow after another into the oncoming crowd, but for each enemy she sent toppling into the harbor, it seemed two more would appear out of the darkness.

I ran a few paces, only to come skidding to a shocked halt. I stared in disbelief at the space between two buildings. Where a moment before there had been no one, there now stood one of the many black cloaked figures, his face completely obscured by a hood.

With slow, sluggish clarity I realized he had appeared out of thin air, which could only mean one thing: he'd shadow walked into existence.

Thus far, the rebel soldiers we'd come across had primarily been human, but apparently not anymore. Either Ambrose Dullahan had been recruiting among the most powerful High Fae, or he'd kept back the best of his soldiers until the castle was won.

Both possibilities had terrifying implications.

In one swift motion, a strong hand yanked my cloak and made me stumble backwards. I let out a piercing shriek, and reacting on pure instinct, I kicked out, my foot connecting with the male's knee. The rebel tripped, and I scrambled back, stumbling to regain my footing.

His hood fell back and our eyes connected.

As I'd thought, it was a fairy that looked back at me. All Fae were lovely, but as compared to the Everlasts, this male was almost plain looking, with hard, dark eyes and pale blonde hair pulled back in a knot at the nape of his neck. Source-forged scars crossed his face, and they pulled tight as he grinned at me. I didn't recognize him, but upon seeing me, his eyes lit up with excitement.

"There you are," he said in a low rasping tone. "The mortal queen, right? You're the one we've been looking for."

My blood ran cold. I knew, of course, that Ambrose Dullahan was searching for me, but I'd been lured into a false sense of security by the word of Cross's spies. Seemingly, the Dullahan would not wait the several weeks we'd expected to come searching for me. Perhaps then, he wouldn't bat an eye at killing me here and now.

I took a step backward, my hands curling into fists at my sides. "Don't touch me," I hissed.

The rebel laughed. "Or what?"

Anger sparked at the back of my mind, and I focused on the sneering, arrogant face of the Fae. My hands shook, and the telltale heat of magic crawled up my skin for the first time since the battle at the castle. Distantly, I realized that perhaps I needed to be in danger for it to work. That perhaps practicing within the thieves' den truly had not been enough motivation, and only now would I know what I was really capable of.

But then, I looked around at the dozens of people filling the harbor, and the flames just below my skin seemed to flicker and die.

I couldn't do this. Not now…perhaps not ever.

Nearly every time I'd used my magic, either consciously or unconsciously, afflicted creatures seemed to spring from nowhere, like moths drawn to the flame. The afflicted were not sentient creatures, they were the echoes of former Fae, warped by Wilde magic. They could not be controlled, and calling them to this harbor would only put all our lives in greater jeopardy.

Real fear washed over me, such as I hadn't felt in sometime. Not the fear of losing something precious to me, or of battle, but of knowing without a doubt that I was too weak to fight back. If I could not call forth any of the magic I hated as much as I relied on, for fear of destroying my friends, then the Fae would kill me. Just like I'd always expected them to.

I took a slow step back, knowing it would not matter where I ran, the rebel would follow.

Out of nowhere, a silhouette emerged from the darkness behind him. Bael, towering and muscular as compared to the other male, materialized out of nothing. His intense yellow gaze was furious, predatory, like that of a lion stalking its next kill.

Feeling the shift behind him, the rebel turned his attention from me to Bael, his eyes widening in fear. With a swift and fluid motion, Bael reached out and gripped the male's neck.

The rebel let out an inhuman scream, which was cut short as Bael twisted his head sharply, snapping the bones with a sickening crack.

I watched the body go limp in the prince's hold, but he didn't stop there. He glanced up at me, meeting my eyes, and kept twisting.

My heartbeat sped up, my skin heating as I watched. I recalled Scion once telling me that Bael had ripped out twice as many hearts as he had, and it was my hypocrisy that didn't allow me to see that. I saw it now, as he tore the scarred Fae's head from his neck, holding it from a rope of unkempt hair, its vacant eyes staring blankly into the night sky.

I saw, but I didn't care.

Tossing the head to the side with a wet thump, Bael advanced on me. I didn't flinch away as he grabbed me with his blood-stained hands, and forced my face up to focus on him. "Did he touch you, little monster?"

My mind worked to follow what he was saying, when all I could see was his heated gaze. A deeper flush covered my entire body, and a hum of awareness traveled through me. Truly, I could have kicked myself. It was neither the time nor place to be thinking of how those bloodstained hands might feel tracing over my skin.

After a long beat, in which the fight around us seemed to fade away, I shook my head.

The prince smiled, showing every one of his too-sharp teeth. "Good. If he had then that would have been far too quick a death."

Before I could formulate an answer, he'd taken a tighter hold of my waist. Without asking my permission, he dragged me forward, the shadowed darkness swallowing us.

We only spun for a fraction of a second before reappearing. The same scent of sea air and sounds of shouting, metal on metal, told me that we'd only moved to the other side of the dock. Bael quickly dropped me, and my feet hit the ground too hard, my feet wobbling slightly before I could steady myself.

"Run. I'll catch up with you."

"What?" I demanded.

"They're here for you." His tone was almost exasperated. "Not to kill, most likely, but to capture. You need to go."

"Not without the others," I said stubbornly.

He muttered a string of words I couldn't understand, most of it being in the old language, though I gathered from the tone it was likely curses.

"They'll be fine," Bael insisted, switching back to the common tongue.

"But Cross and Siobhan—"

"Aren't who they're looking for." He looked up, as if appealing to the gods. "I can't heal you if you get hurt, so please, I need you to act against your nature and *run*."

I bit the inside of my lip, but nodded. Bael's yellow gaze locked onto mine, a silent promise passing between us before he dashed off toward the chaos.

I stood there for a moment, before turning and fleeing into the darkness, the clash of steel still ringing in my ears.

The land outside the gates of Inbetwixt was wild.

As I sprinted through the dense forest, the branches whipped against my face and it felt like the darkness was closing in around me.

The sounds of the battle slowly diminished, and my mind was flooded with memories of my first night in the Waywoods. A wave of dread cooled my skin, my mind conjuring images of an unknown entity lurking in the shadows.

A branch snapped behind me and I whipped around.

My heart pounded. That had been a footstep, I was sure of it.

I stood still, straining my ears for any sound, but the only thing I could hear was the faint rustling of leaves in the wind. Letting out my breath, I turned back around and continued.

Without warning, agony seared through my shoulder.

I closed my eyes, and for a moment the pain almost stopped, my breath catching, as if I momentarily lost consciousness between breaths. I let out a scream of agony a beat too late, everything seeming to occur just slightly delayed.

Finally, I looked down, and nearly gagged. A crossbow bolt, as thick as my middle and pointer fingers held together, jutted out of the side of my chest. From the angle, I guessed it would be sticking out my back as well, somewhere just above my right shoulder blade.

Behind me, leaves crunched. Footsteps pounded, no longer bothering to creep along in the darkness. My eyes darted back and forth like a frightened rabbit, but the forest was too dense to see who might be following me. Worse, I couldn't run like this, and whatever rebel had followed me had to know that.

My heartbeat quickened, the throbbing ache in my chest radiating outward, burning, like a hot poker against my skin. I closed my eyes, willing myself to disappear, when an idea struck. I could, *literally* disappear.

It was a terrible idea, if only because it was nearly impossible.

I hadn't even been able to shadow walk out of the store room into the hallway, and most Fae could not shadow walk while injured. That was how Aine, Thalia and Gwydion had been stranded in the burning tower, and even Bael said he'd rarely managed to disappear while in pain.

The sound of pounding footsteps echoed closer and panic set in, making my decision for me. I had to at least try to escape, because the alternative would be infinitely worse.

The pain was almost unbearable, but I closed my eyes and took a deep breath, feeling my body tremble with the effort to hold back the tears. I could feel the magic pulsing within me, like a strong current running through my veins. I could hear it, like the crackle of electricity before a storm.

I tried to focus, to concentrate on the image of the place that I needed to go, but my mind was jumbled. I couldn't think of anything clearly, except the pounding *ache*.

Without meaning to, I let my eyes flutter open once more, just in time to see a stranger sprinting toward me out of the dark. I caught a glimpse of his hard face, and the tattoos covering his scalp, before the edges of my vision blurred and I felt myself sliding to the side. Distantly, I thought I heard a raven cry, and the wind seemed to beat at my face, as if with a rush of wings, then my unfocused gaze went dark.

I just barely had time to wonder if I'd managed to shadow walk, or instead, fainted on the forest floor.

8
SCION

THE CUTTHROAT DISTRICT, INBETWIXT

Gwydion danced across the stone floor of the thieves training ring, grinning as he waved his sword in large figure eights. "Come on," he taunted. "Are you giving up so easily?"

I fixed him with a stony look, and deliberately lowered my own sword arm. "I've changed my mind. This is fucking pointless."

My cousin threw back his head, laughing merrily. "You only say that because you're losing."

I pressed my lips together. He was right, of course, but I wouldn't give him the satisfaction of agreeing.

After the day I'd had, I had felt the extreme desire to fight someone.

This morning's argument with Bael, combined with the meeting, and finally, Lonnie's appearance in the barracks had been the straw that finally broke my resolve to avoid everyone, less I explode on an unsuspecting bystander. At this point, I would welcome the confrontation, if only to let out some energy.

I'd sought out Gwydion for exactly that reason. We were not particularly close friends, which meant he'd likely not inquire about my mood. Better still, as my cousin did not possess any combative magical talent, he was by far the best sword fighter in the family.

If Gwydion and I were sparring with any other weapon in the world—magic, intellect, or even fists—I would have destroyed him easily, but sword play was my weak point and the evidence of that was painted all across my face. It seemed as good a way as any to vent my frustrations and practice my least favorite method of fighting at the same time. Except, as he kept beating me, it was having the opposite effect, and I was more on edge than ever.

"I've changed my mind," I told him. "I don't care for you to help with this."

"Suit yourself," Gwydion said jovially, stabbing his sword through the air at an invisible opponent. "I only hope for your sake that you never have to fight Ambrose without magic."

I stiffened. "What does he have to do with this?"

Gwydion gave me a suspicious sideways glance. "Isn't that what you're planning to do? Go after him, that is."

I pressed my lips firmly together. Again, he was right.

Not agreeing to go to Aftermath had been almost physically painful, and I still was not sure if I'd done the right thing in leaving Bael and Lonnie alone to go on their adventure. Knowing Lonnie wanted me to go made it all the worse, but it still didn't change anything. Joining them would inevitably ruin not only me, but my relationship with my cousin, and I couldn't bring myself to ignore that, no matter how much I wanted to.

Not accompanying them, however, left me with few options. I didn't want to go into hiding in Overcast, nor could I stand to stay here among so many people. My only purpose in life—to rule—had been pulled out from under me, and now I could think of nothing else to do but hunt down my brother.

I nodded stiffly. "Is it that obvious?"

He laughed. "Yes. I would advise you to wait until our army has had time to rebuild, but I know you won't."

"I don't need an army to face Ambrose," I said stubbornly. "You forget, this last decade I practically *was* the army."

"And you forget that I grew up with Ambrose, and know him well—perhaps better than you do. He's an excellent physical fighter, and he knows he can't beat you with magic."

"So?" I snapped. "Unfortunately for him, there's no chance we'd ever stand off without magic."

Gwydion shrugged. "Perhaps, but you weren't held at the top of the tower as the rest of us were. Those rebels did something to prevent anyone from fighting back with magic."

I furrowed my brow. I vaguely remembered having trouble with magic when I finally fought my way to the top of the tower, but with everything else happening, I hadn't thought to question why or consider that it might happen again.

"How do you know for certain it was something the rebels did?" I asked. "Maybe Aine was simply living up to all our expectations, refusing to use her powers even to save her own life. In fact, why are you not harassing her about this instead of me?"

"Because she's gone," he said, his eyes widening slightly.

"What?" I stood before I realized what I was doing. "Gone where?"

The corner of his lip tipped up. "Did you not know? Aine went with Bael and your…whatever you're calling her now."

I schooled my expression back to neutral. "That's surprising."

The thought hit me like a punch to the gut: they were really gone. Lonnie and Bael had left, and I couldn't shake the feeling of regret for not going with them.

Without thinking, I immediately searched the back of my mind, as if looking for a thought half remembered. A dream where one knew they were dreaming. Quill was circling high above the city as I'd requested, but dove to land on a nearby roof when he felt my summons. Return home.

If I couldn't be there physically, I could at least keep an eye on them through Quill.

In a fit of frustration, I let the sword slip from my grasp and clatter to the ground. "I'm done," I declared, exasperated.

"Fine," Gwydion said, as I stomped my way across the room. "But don't say I didn't warn you."

My face twisted in disgust as I turned to confront him. But before I could even let out a shout, a sharp and sudden pain pierced through my chest. It was like a hot poker stabbing me from the inside, causing me to gasp and double over in agony. The nausea rose in my throat with each wave of pain.

"Sci?" Gwydion's voice was faint, as if coming from a far distance. "What's the matter?"

A sharp gasp escaped my lips as my chest constricted with a sudden knowing. A primal, all-consuming desperation took hold of me.

Lonnie was hurt, and there was nothing in the world that would keep me from finding her. Not even myself.

9
LONNIE

THE WAYWOODS

I fainted.

Or, at the very least, I collapsed forward into the mud. My consciousness swam, and I experienced the strange sensation of hearing my own scream, without feeling my mouth move—like my mind was picking out the most relevant moments and discarding the rest as my vision went white from agony. The arrow in my chest hit the ground first, and dug deeper into my flesh, propelled by the weight of my own limp body.

I lay on the cold, hard ground, my chest heaving with each gasping breath. My heart pounded in my ears and tears rolled down my face into the mud, where I could not bring myself to lift my head, even to watch for my attacker. I strained my ears to pick up any sound other than my own ragged breathing, but all I heard was the eerie stillness of the empty forest.

The silence pressed in on me, and I waited, growing more confused with each passing second. Where was the tattooed attacker? The footsteps that had been pursuing me seemed to have vanished into thin air. Had they given up? Lost track of me in the trees?

I blinked my eyes open with difficulty, glancing around from where I lay with my cheek in the mud. My heart skipped a beat. The trees were...different, less dense, and the dim sky peeked through the overhead canopy enough that I could see more than a few feet in front of me. In the distance, I could make out the outline of what looked to be a house.

I sucked in a startled breath—that house certainly had not been there before.

Apparently, I *had* shadow walked...and *then* fainted.

That was more than good enough for me.

Excitement rose in my chest for a moment, only to come crashing down at the realization that I had no idea where I was. Taking another look around at my surroundings, I saw little more than trees. I could have screamed with frustration as well as pain. I knew too well that losing one's way in the Waywoods was almost as sure of a death sentence as the arrow piercing my chest. I might have gone one hundred yards, or twenty miles, there was no way to know. Traveling by magic would do me no good if I still died before Bael could find me again.

My thoughts raced like a madman, conjuring up endless scenarios of gruesome deaths - Blood loss. Delirium. Starvation. Infection. I needed to get off the ground, and get my wound out of the mud.

With a guttural cry of agony, I heaved my body up off the ground. My muscles strained and trembled under the weight as I stood, wincing with each movement.

I sucked in another rattling breath, and although it was painful, I was distantly grateful at the realization that my breathing was not overly labored. The bolt probably had not punctured a lung. *Probably*? Still, I couldn't raise my right arm to feel the damage, but I could tell from how the jacket caught as it fell away that the arrow was indeed sticking out of my back. Thankfully, it seemed to have gone through at the point where my arm met my torso. If I'd been standing even a few inches in any direction, I would have died instantly. The shaft of the arrow had been embedded even deeper by me fainting, and I couldn't remove it as it was the only thing currently preventing me from bleeding out. But nor could I leave it sticking out of my flesh, a foot in either direction—not if I wanted to search for Bael and the others.

Pondering this, I staggered a few steps toward the house in the distance, thinking vaguely that perhaps there was a village nearby, or at least someone who could tell me where I was. I made it only a few steps, before exhaustion winded me and I slumped back against the nearest tree, and closed my eyes.

It was a mistake.

The moment my eyes closed again, it was all I could do to keep from slipping away into oblivion.

"Can't sleep. Can't s-sleep," I chanted dully, as I forced my eyes to stay open.

To sleep while gravely injured was to never wake again, but my entire body ached, and my eyelids felt as if they were weighted down with lead and there was little to focus on.

Then, for the second time, I thought I heard a distinct caw of a raven in the distance. As I pried my eyes open, a colossal black bird swooped down and landed gracefully on a patch of moss-covered forest floor nearby. Despite its size, the bird made little noise as it touched the ground.

"Q-quill?" my voice quivered.

The bird hopped forward, standing on the ground slightly to my left. He was so enormous, even for a raven, that I found myself staring into his too-large golden eyes as he cocked his head at me, as if to say: *There you are.*

In all the months I'd known Prince Scion, I had hardly seen him without his raven companion, except during our stay in Inbetwixt when he was trying to blend in and go unnoticed. Other than that, Quill was always by his side, yet I saw no prince. Was I seeing things? Had the blood-loss affected my mind to the point of hallucination? Furthermore, did I want to see Scion?

I'd asked him to come with us and he'd rejected me, making it perfectly clear that whatever I'd thought was between us was in my mind alone. In fact, for all I knew, he'd decided to go back to being my enemy, and Quill's presence here was an omen rather than a sign of rescue.

If I'd had the energy I would have laughed as I put out a tentative hand. "What are you doing here?"

Quill replied with an agitated caw. *Looking for you, fool.*

"I doubt that. Your master abandoned us." I mumbled, struggling to keep the bird in sight. "You tell him that I said he can go fuck himself."

My vision blurred and darkness crept in at the edges. Were those to be my last words then? A curse spoken to a bird.

I opened my mouth, thinking I should perhaps say something else. Something more meaningful, when I felt strong arms encircle me, drawing me in close, and a voice I recognized all too well whispered in my ear. "Fuck you too, Rebel."

10

LONNIE

THE WAYWOODS

"What are you doing here?" I asked.

"Saving your life, apparently," Prince Scion said darkly, as if the very idea angered him.

Without waiting for my reply, Prince Scion bit down on his wrist with the same intensity I had seen Bael do many times before. He held the bleeding wound to my mouth.

A mix of emotions flooded through me - a sense of relief mingled with disgust. Still, I didn't resist as the taste of blood, salty and metallic, filled my mouth. Perhaps I should have.

One of the things that Bael had mentioned, though never satisfactorily explained to me, was that by sharing blood he had tied me to him. In essence, he had made me more likely to think of him, to want him. If I was honest with myself, everything Bael had described about the connection—the changing feelings, the obsessive thoughts, the wanting to be close...I already felt that way about Prince Scion, but what if this made it worse?

I pushed the worries away as I swallowed, gulping down the life-saving liquid. Scion made a strangled sound in the back of his throat, somewhere between a groan and a sigh, and within seconds, I started to feel the effects of the blood take hold. The pain in my chest ebb slightly, and my eyes flew wide—suddenly alert—but that was where the healing stopped. The wound in my chest spasmed, and I glanced down and was almost startled to see the arrow still protruding from my chest.

I pulled my mouth back, blood coating my lips. "How did you find me?"

Prince Scion grimaced. He was wearing his full obsidian armor, and his black hair was windswept off his face, like perhaps he'd sprinted all the way here. "That's not important right now. How the fuck did this happen? Who did this to you?"

"That's not important, either. Why isn't it healing?"

Scion shook his head. "I won't know until you show me. We need to get you somewhere where I can take a look at that wound."

Somewhat reluctantly, I dropped his wrist, and wiped at my mouth with the back of my hand. "Fine."

I pushed to my feet—or, at least, tried to. I staggered, and Scion threw out both arms to catch me, before lifting my entire body into the air. Carrying me as if my weight made no difference to him, he strode toward the same house in the distance I'd been trying to reach earlier.

With every step, the house grew clearer. Finally, I beheld not a house, but a dilapidated old barn, that I was sure had not been used in longer than I'd been alive. Disappointment surged. We likely would not find any village here, but I supposed, at least I was no longer alone.

"We need to go to a healer," I said stiffly.

"No healer will be able to fix this."

Dread washed over me, because I knew he was right. Even now, I was starting to feel light headed again. "If even your blood did not heal me, and I cannot see a healer…I'll die."

"No you won't," he growled, shouldering open the rotting barn door and stepping inside. "I won't allow it."

Strangely, a shred of hope rose in my chest. "If I were to trust anyone to make demands of death itself, it would be you, my lord."

"Not demands, rebel," he said thickly. "Prayers."

The barn turned out to be hardly better than the forest in terms of shelter. It was large, and mostly empty, with rough and rotting beams, and cobwebs hanging from every corner and rafter. Some rusted tools, a few empty stalls, and piles of filthy hay made up the entirety of the interior, and although I could not see outside from any angle, the sound of the rushing wind made me glad it was not raining, as I doubted the roof would have held up.

The moment we stepped inside, Scion lowered me to the floor, looking slightly apologetic when I hissed in pain.

"Take off your shirt," he demanded.

I shrank back. "No."

He rolled his eyes. "This isn't some ruse to get your clothing off, rebel, I need to see the wound."

I felt my cheeks heat, and my mind flooded with the memory of looking down at his perfect, unscarred face as he said, "Take off your nightgown. I want to see you." We both knew he hadn't needed any ruse or trickery to get me naked only last week.

Praying he didn't somehow know what I was thinking, my hands trembled as I reached up to try to undo the buttons at my throat, but found it was too painful to lift my arm. Tears blurred my vision, and a strangled cry escaped my lips. "I can't."

Scion lurched forward, as if pulled by invisible strings, and grabbed for my hand with trembling fingers. "I'll do it."

I nodded, closing my eyes so I didn't have to look at him as he gripped the fabric of my tunic in both hands and tore it cleanly down the center as if it were tissue paper. The two even halves hung uselessly off my shoulders, and I shivered as the cold air hit the bare skin of my stomach and chest.

Scion's expression was unreadable, as he leaned closer so he could inspect the wound. His breath skated over my bare skin and gooseflesh rose on my chest and arms, my nipples turning to hard peaks. I saw his eyes flick to them for the briefest second before he stepped back. "I need to pull the arrow out."

"No!" I hissed, shrinking back from him. "The arrow itself is the only thing preventing me from bleeding to death."

"I know," he snapped. "But it is also the thing preventing my blood from healing you. I need to take it out, so the wound will close."

I shook my head vigorously. "Absolutely not. Do you even understand how quickly I will die once it's removed?"

He scowled. "You do not need to explain mortality to me, I've killed enough men to know far better than you how much blood you can lose before there's no returning from it, and I daresay you're past that point already."

"So, what, you're hoping to speed things along?"

He laughed without humor. "How many times must I save your life before you stop accusing me of trying to kill you?"

"I don't know," I replied, my blood heating. "Perhaps I wouldn't think that if you didn't blow so hot and cold. Do you hate me today, or is your other personality making an appearance? What are you even planning to do, if not simply let me bleed out?"

Scion's silver eyes darkened, and slid to mine, then he smiled as he reached up and began unbuckling the breastplate of his obsidian armor, until it finally fell with a ground-shaking clang against the barn floor. Then, he did the same with his arm guards. "Press your back against the wall and brace yourself. The arrow will hurt when I pull it out, quite as much as it did going in."

"Are you just going to ignore my question?" I seethed.

His tongue swept over his bottom lip and my eyes widened as he began to shift out of the heavy looking chain mail undershirt that covered everywhere on his body that was not protected by stone. "I'm not ignoring you, rebel, I'm simply unwilling to waste any more time arguing with you when I could simply show you how I intend to help."

Scion straightened and stood shirtless in front of me, every inch of his muscled chest gleaming with sweat. My breath caught, and I swallowed, not entirely from nerves this time as he sauntered toward me. He put his hands on my shoulders, steering me to stand against the wall as he'd directed, then bent low over me, bracing one hand behind my head.

My heart pounded too fast, my breath catching. "Wait no! What are you going to do?"

His magnetic eyes darted over me, and then narrowed, like he was making up his mind. "It's not what I'm going to do, rebel. It's you."

"Excuse me?"

Then, he tilted his head to the side, baring his neck to me, and raised an eyebrow. "I'm going to pull that arrow out, and you're going to take my blood to heal yourself."

I blinked at him, finally shocked into silence. He could not be serious, could he? "I...I can't do that."

"How else did you think you were going to survive this? You need far more than a taste from my wrist."

"No. I'm not even sure my teeth will break your skin."

He looked almost like he was suppressing a smile when he said: "Bite hard."

I could think of nothing to say, because he was right. There was no other option, but that didn't make me feel better about the idea. I might have thought this was one of those strange cultural differences between humans and Fae, simply impossible for me to understand, except that I knew it wasn't. Bael had been perfectly clear that even to fairies, sharing blood was taboo, and Scion had never struck me as one to dabble in the gray areas of society. "You seem far too calm about this."

He looked down at me, and as so often with Scion, I couldn't read the expression behind his eyes. His arrogant, perfect features always hid whatever he was really thinking from me. "Not calm, rebel. Focused."

Scion braced his hand on the wall above me. He hovered his other hand over the arrow shaft, but didn't yet touch it. We were so close, I could see every silver spec in his eyes. "Are you ready?"

"No," I blurted out.

Seeming not to care about my answer, Scion gripped the back of my head and pressed my face into the curve of his shoulder. It was the only warning I got before a sharp, burning agony tore through me. My eyes watered involuntarily as the extreme pressure on my chest suddenly released, and I screamed into Scion's neck.

I'd never hated him as much as when my head swam, and I could feel hot, viscous blood pouring over both of us, soaking our bare skin and the tattered shreds of my tunic top. Distantly, I heard something clatter against the floor, which could only be the broken arrow, but my head was spinning, and I couldn't think of anything except the pain.

"Now, rebel," he said in a strangled half-whisper.

Giving in, I closed my eyes and drew a deep breath. Then, trying not to think about what I was doing, I sank my teeth into his pulse point.

The metallic taste of his blood flooded my mouth again, thick and warm, but this time it felt so much more potent. He groaned, and it sounded somewhere between pain and pleasure, and I sucked harder against the wound.

With each pull of blood, I forgot to be revolted or embarrassed, until at some point I realized I was enjoying it. He tasted like salt and iron and something else, something undefinable that sent electricity skating over my skin. Finally, I understood what it must mean to taste of magic.

The pain lessened, and I swallowed desperately, my throat burning with the intense craving for more. The beat of his pulse under my teeth was like a drum, driving me to drink until there was nothing left but crimson stains on my lips.

Scion reached up and wound his hand into my hair, but instead of pulling my head back as I'd expected he pressed my mouth more firmly against his throat.

His skin radiated a comforting musky scent, reminiscent of the forest, and felt surprisingly smooth against my face as I brushed against it with my lips and nose, grazing his collarbone. Without thinking about it, I ran my tongue up the side of his neck to the tip of his pointed ear.

Scion shuddered, and as the last sharp sting of pain faded away, a different kind of warmth spread through my body. I pulled back to look at him. Our gazes met, and this time there was no pain inside me, just a throbbing, aching need.

I ran my tongue over my bottom lip, cleaning off the blood that still lingered there. His eyes snapped down to my mouth and his pupils dilated until only a hint of silver remained around a circle of burning black.

"Rebel..." he breathed, neither a statement nor a question.

Meeting his intense gaze, I could see the hunger there. The magnetic energy between us crackled as our lips collided once again. Everything with Scion was always more intense than I expected. More consuming, more demanding. He craved my complete surrender with every touch.

A mix of anger and overwhelming lust surged through me, wanting to punish his mouth for the pain he caused me while also craving his touch intensely. Feeling almost drunk, I leaned forward and pressed my bloodstained lips to his

A strangled groan came from the back of his throat, and it was as if the tension shattered.

His lips opened against mine, his tongue sweeping in to savagely claim my mouth. I could taste the anger on his lips, the hunger and need, and the magic that buzzed in the blood that still coated both our mouths. Our hands tore at what was left of our ruined and bloodstained clothing, and all rational thought fled.

I felt my feet leave the floor as Scion picked me up and slammed my back against the wall. I gasped, expecting it to hurt, but there was no pain left in my shoulder. His hard length pressed into my core, and I wrapped my legs around his waist. Shadows sprung out of nowhere, and wrapped themselves around my body, holding me against the wall and leaving Scion's hands free to roam down my sides, over the curves of my breasts.

A low growl escaped from him as he reached down and slid his fingers between my thighs, dragging them through my folds before he thrust two fingers inside me. "Fuck, you're so wet."

A shock of arousal hit me, fogging my mind. "Gods…"

He drove his fingers in and out, holding me painfully close to the edge. I wriggled in an attempt to urge him to move faster. Just when I was about to scream, Scion pulled his fingers away and brought them to his lips. "I thought I'd imagined how fucking sweet your cunt is. You taste like magic, rebel."

I burned at those words, the heat around us seeming to actually rise as he brought his mouth to one nipple, and then the other, sucking hard enough that I could feel it all the way down in my core.

A soft hiss escaped my lips as he bit down on the top of my breast with just enough force to cause a mix of pleasure and pain. The shadows wound tighter around my arms, my waist, and pulled taught around my throat. I arched my back, pressing closer. He nipped at the pebbled flesh, not taking care to be gentle, and each pull from his mouth and graze of his teeth sent sparks of pleasure straight to my clit.

He moved his mouth up the column of my neck back to my lips. He bit down on my bottom lip, sucking it into his mouth as I reached between us, and traced my fingers along his chiseled chest, savoring every ridge of muscle beneath my touch. I reached the belt of his trousers, and I shoved them down. My hand wrapped around his shaft and I moved my fingers up and down, slow and teasing.

He hissed, and pulled his head back to look me in the eye. "Do you want this?"

The answer came immediately to my lips. "Yes."

Scion licked his lips, and his gaze widened, burning with some combination of lust, and something else impossible to name. Like he was almost hoping I would be the one to put a stop to whatever this was, and give him a reason to close himself off again.

"I won't be gentle," he warned.

"Don't be," I leaned in, and ran my tongue over the still visible bite mark on his neck. "Fuck me like you hate me."

11
SCION
THE WAYWOODS

I felt the moment my self-control splintered. It shattered like glass all around me, and I couldn't remember why I had been denying myself in the first place.

I wasn't thinking about mating bonds, or politics, or responsibility as I ducked my head and wrapped my lips around her perfect breast. I swirled my tongue against her nipple, sucking, and nipping, and she moaned, her head tipping back.

I had no thoughts except for her, and how sweet she tasted, and how much I wanted to both own and be owned by her when I gripped the backs of her thighs and drove my hips forward, taking every inch of her with my cock.

Lonnie made a strangled sound, neither a moan nor a scream, and stared directly at me, her huge brown eyes locked on mine.

My breath caught. Thoughts came flooding back, and I waited for half a second, pulsing inside her, wondering if something should happen. If I should feel different, or be filled with some sense of *knowing*. Or even if I should drop dead on the spot.

Nothing happened.

I drew a long, sharp breath as realization flooded me in waves, crashing over me all at once. Except, it was not the realization of any bond, but rather, of my own fucking feelings. Of everything I'd been blind to.

I had her wrapped around my cock with a brand on her shoulder and my blood on her tongue and in her veins, yet I was still breathing. That could only mean one thing: Lonnie was not my mate. She was not fated for me.

Until now, I hadn't realized that part of me thought she was.

I had thought that was why I could never manage to kill her, why she had bothered me to the point of obsession from our very first meeting, why I had felt willing to sacrifice my entire family to be with her.

There was no intervention of the gods, no magic drawing me in, which could only mean that I loved her. I was in love with her, and I had no excuse for it.

"Please," she begged, writhing her hips against me, asking me to move inside her.

In a matter of seconds, my elation transformed into rage, almost as if someone had flicked a switch. I was angry at myself for falling into this trap, and at the gods for cursing me, and at Lonnie for being the cause of all my misery.

I shook slightly from the effort of not moving, and I wrapped my fingers around her hair, yanking her head to the side to bare her neck. My teeth sank into the soft skin of her throat.

I gripped her chin, not letting her turn away from me as I held her there, trapped between my chest and the wall, with ropes of shadows binding her arms.

"Please…" she said again.

I couldn't bear to look at her like this. Couldn't see that it was only the bloodlust and adrenaline causing her expression and nothing else. I couldn't let her see anything in my face that would reveal the depth of my obsession.

I let her feet fall to the floor and spun her around until her cheek pressed into the rough wooden wall of the barn. She raised her hands above her head, laying her palms flat, and arched her back, seeking contact.

I pressed my body against hers, and slid sharply into her in a single stroke. She gasped and her back arched as I entered her deeply. A soft moan escaped her lips.

Shadows swirled, covering every part of her skin I couldn't reach with my fingers, skating over her nipples and lower to graze the skin of her lower belly.

The faint scent of smoke seemed to fill the room, hot and suffocating, but I ignored it. Bringing my hand down hard against her ass, I smiled when she cried out and her scream was cut short by the rising shadows covering every part of her I couldn't reach.

A sharp crack echoed behind me, the sound of splintering wood breaking through the heavy rhythm of my thrusts. But I didn't bother to turn my head as I reached around, my fingers finding her clit, and rubbed up and down in punishing strokes. She shook, every muscle quaking.

I smacked her ass again, harder this time, and she screamed into the wall, all her muscles tightening around me.

"Fuck," I hissed.

I dug my fingers into her hips and my vision went white. I let my head fall forward into her tangled hair, and didn't let up as I came, filling her completely.

We stood, panting, for a full minute before I became truly aware of the scent of smoke filling the room. I slid out of her and turned around, before my eyes widened in shock.

Thick smoke billowed into the room, blinding and choking me. Through the haze, I could hear the ominous creaking of collapsing wood above us. Suddenly, a massive beam snapped and split, sending sharp splinters raining down.

The barn was burning—and I wasn't sure which one of us had caused it.

12
BAEL

THE DEADEYE DISTRICT, INBETWIXT

A tremendous roar rattled across the harbor, and my heart raced as I charged back through the eastern gate of Inbetwixt.

The battle raged on, just as furious as how I'd left it. To my left, cloaked figures streamed in and out of the dark alleys between the fisherman's shacks, and on the right the docks were coated with blood and limp bodies. The smell of blood permeated the air, causing my hair to stand on end and my nostrils to tingle with curiosity.

I swung an arm out and grabbed the nearest cloaked figure, not even bothering to glance at if they were male or female before I tore into their throat. Blood covered my hands, and I rolled my neck, feeling the surge of adrenaline that only violence could bring.

Dropping the body with a wet smack, I looked around until I saw my sister on the other side of the docks. Aine stayed on the outskirts of the battle, but that didn't mean she wasn't contributing.

My eyes widened as I watched several rebel soldiers walk toward her in a neat line, before drawing their swords and plunging them into their own stomachs. A smile spread across my face. She'd kept her word to use her magic.

"Feeling a bit rusty?" I shouted to my sister.

Aine scowled at me between the fighters. "Hardly."

"I'm not so sure." I strode toward her, stepping over one of the soldiers she'd hypnotized into ending their own lives. "That was quick. It was almost a kind death."

Aine's scowl deepened—she looked slightly guilty. "Not all of us are sadists, Baelfry."

My eyes widened. She was correct, of course. Not everyone in our family took pleasure from violence—only the majority of us.

My sister, however, was not a member of the majority. Aine had a similar ability to our late uncle, but while Penvalle had reveled in controlling others, she despised it. It had been at least a decade since I'd seen her use a shred of magic.

I skidded to a halt in front of Aine and grinned widely at her. "You kept your word."

"Is that a question?" she snapped. "What are you doing here? I thought you escaped with your pet."

It was my turn to scowl. "Don't call her that."

Aine sighed heavily. "Whatever. I really don't know what you all see in that human."

I set my jaw, my amusement from a moment before leaving me as quickly as it had come. "She's not human."

"Is that what you took out of what I said?" She sneered. "What she is barely matters. I'd say the same if she were the most powerful Fae in Elsewhere. I don't understand how she's managed to captivate all of you."

I didn't bother to ask whom she meant by "all of us." Aine was quite as close to Scion as I was, and since they'd both been avoiding me in the thieves den, she'd probably spent more time in his company in the last few days then I had in weeks. If after seeing how miserable he'd been, she didn't understand why we'd be interested in Lonnie, there was no way to explain it to her.

"Why would you return alone, then?" Aine asked when I did not reply. "I'd like to think it was to help me, but I know you…"

I grinned, not feeling the least bit guilty. Helping had been the last thing on my mind.

After making sure Lonnie was out of harm's way, I couldn't resist the urge to return and finish the battle. All the members of my family who possessed an offensive magical skill were trained as warriors. Everyone, that was, except for me.

For me, violence came naturally.

I'd never allowed me to be on the front lines of the war like Scion, or fuck, even like Ambrose, and I couldn't deny that perhaps there had been a good reason for that. I loved the fighting, and couldn't turn away from it. It felt like a compulsion, an irresistible addiction that pulled me back in.

That wasn't the only reason I'd returned, though. The information I needed from the rebellion was crucial and one of these pricks was going to have to give it to me, whether they liked it or not.

"I need to find whoever is leading this group," I muttered, knowing that if any Fae were listening they'd be able to hear us even over the sounds of fighting.

Aine cocked her head to the side. "Ambrose, you mean?"

I laughed hollowly. "If only I were so lucky, but no. I doubt he's here."

She nodded in agreement. "No, likely not. This fight screams of disorganization."

I grimaced. She was entirely correct, and that was what worried me. If the rebels goal was to capture Lonnie, then this was a poor attempt at doing so.

Shaking my head, I pushed that thought to the back of my mind. "Will you help?"

Aine sighed with resignation. "Fine."

I waited for more, expecting her to suggest that I'd owe her something in return, but she didn't. I smiled in gratitude as Aine scanned the remaining rebels, finally settling on the small, thin-faced male. She motioned lazily for him to follow and he trotted after us with a glazed look in his eyes, then stood with his back against the wall of a dilapidated fishing hut. His knees trembled as we stepped in front of him.

I didn't bother with any greeting or explanation—not when this male had no choice but to answer me. "Where's Ambrose?"

The man said nothing. His eyes were wide and unblinking, darting back and forth as he trembled uncontrollably. He was terrified.

Aine hovered over my shoulder. "I can't make him tell you what he doesn't know. You need to be more specific."

I shook my head, and glared at the male. "Where was the last place you saw him, then?"

Again, he said nothing, and I growled with frustration before pulling my arm back and slamming my fist into his jaw.

"I don't know what you mean," the man screamed, pressing a hand against his face.

"Wait, that's not what they call him," Aine hissed. "He doesn't know who you're talking about."

Oh, shit. It had slipped my mind that not all of the rebels were aware of Ambrose's real name or who he truly was. This person in front of me was a human, probably too young to remember when the crown prince abandoned his duties and started the rebellion.

I held my hand back, ready to strike. "Where's the Dullahan, then?"

"Not here," the man screeched before I could hit him again.

"Where did you last see him?"

The man shook his head. "I don't know, I can't remember. No one has seen him lately. He hasn't been traveling with the army."

I glanced at Aine, who shrugged. If that was true, it was even more concerning.

I stepped back from the rebel man, and growled with frustration. I had to locate Ambrose before anyone else, but I couldn't reveal my reasons in front of my sister. I couldn't disclose my desperate need for the crown he had stolen, or how long I had been trying to retrieve it, only to have my attempts foiled time and time again.

As far as I knew, Ambrose had been in our dungeon, right under my nose for the last several months. Then, for reasons I couldn't begin to understand, Scion had freed him, only for the castle to be attacked less than a week later.

My rebel cousin had been present for that fight, at least long enough to speak to Lonnie, but where he'd disappeared to after that was anyone's guess. I'd figured he'd be in what was left of the castle, enjoying the spoils of his victory, but perhaps not?

Without any warning, a sharp, searing pain pierced through my chest, causing me to stagger backwards in shock. Panic set in as I instinctively looked down, half-expecting to see a knife lodged in my chest. But there was nothing, and an overwhelming sense of dread washed over me.

"What is it?" Aine asked.

"It's not me..." I gasped. "It's her."

I wasn't sure how I knew, or where she was, but Lonnie was hurt. Hurt badly enough for me to feel it, even without a completed bond. Anger consumed me, drowning out the throbbing ache in my chest.

I shook my head, as my eyes rolled backwards. I couldn't see anywhere in the world, only places I'd been before or was familiar with, so if Lonnie had run beyond that point...

"Go," Aine said briskly.

I snapped my eyes back to her, my adrenaline rising. "Are you coming?"

She furrowed her brow and scanned the bustling harbor, her eyes landing on the intense struggle between the thieves and the rebellion. It was clear that Cross and his crew were gaining the upper hand, but they hadn't won yet. "No, I'll stay and help."

I hesitated, unsure of whether I could rely on Aine's aid. She was known to be fiercely protective of those she cared about, but I wasn't sure if the thieves' guild fell into that category. Still, I had no other options than to put my faith in her.

I gave a small nod, acknowledging our silent understanding, and disappeared into the inky blackness of the night.

I took a staggering step out of the darkness and into the forest clearing where I'd left Lonnie earlier. A faint yet alluring fragrance of wildflowers and honey filled my senses, mingling with the sharp metallic scent of blood.

A growl bubbled in my throat. She was gone.

My heart pounding in my chest, I pushed through the thick tangles of branches and leaves, desperate to find her. I needed to see her, to know she was safe.

Something moved out of the corner of my eye and I whipped around just as a sudden shadow engulfed me. Before I could react, an enormous raven swooped down from the sky and landed on my head, its sharp claws digging into my scalp. My heart raced as I cursed loudly and frantically batted at the bird with both hands, trying to chase it away.

"You!" I hissed. "Fucking miserable bird."

Scion's raven perched on a nearby tree branch, cawing mockingly as I tried to catch my breath. He tilted his head and glared at me with malice.

Straightening, I glared back. "Were you watching, then? Where the fuck is she?"

The raven made a tittering sound, suspiciously close to laughter and my blood boiled. I might feel foolish speaking to a bird, except that Quill was no ordinary animal. It followed Scion everywhere, and attacked virtually everyone that wasn't him. Worse, I would swear it talked sometimes, but only when I was just out of earshot.

"If she dies because you wouldn't help, I swear I'll eat you."

Fuck, I might eat him regardless. The monster in my head wanted desperately to snatch the creature out of the air, but right now I needed him.

The raven cawed, as if he could understand me, and leapt into the air, his dark wings beating furiously as he flew just a few feet above the ground. He looked back at me with an urgent expression before darting off again.

With a muttered curse, I sprinted after him.

I ran along behind the bird for what felt like an hour, but was probably mere minutes. I was only vaguely aware of how far we'd traveled. Miles, I could only assume. It didn't matter, I would have run all the way to Aftermath to find her.

The only thing keeping me from panicking, was that wherever this accursed vulture went, Scion was sure to follow close behind. I didn't know how it worked between this creature and my cousin, if he could see directly through the birds eyes or if it was more of a general knowing, but I hoped somehow he'd reached Lonnie before anyone else did.

It was strange—only a few short weeks ago, I'd have been terrified that it was Scion himself who'd hurt her. Now, I suspected my cousin would tear his own heart out sooner than hers.

With gritted teeth, I urged the raven to pick up speed. It dipped and weaved in front of me, taunting me with its agile movements. My heart pounded as I tried to keep my eyes locked on its erratic flight pattern. It seemed to revel in my frustration, swooping close before darting away again, clearly enjoying this game of cat and mouse.

Finally, we reached a clearing, and I skidded to a halt as the bird landed on a branch overhead.

The scent of smoke wafted toward me, and I spun around in a daze and froze when I saw the bright orange flames dancing in the distance. The heat was intense, even from this far away, and the crackling of the fire echoed through the woods. Fear seized me, making the hair on the back of my neck stand on end as I approached the raging inferno.

I spotted two figures in the distance and relief washed over me.

Lonnie stood in front of the old wooden barn, swaying slightly on her feet, as if with anxiety. Her once neatly braided hair was now a tangled mess and her clothes were ripped and stained with blood. Beside her, Scion stared up at the flames.

My tense shoulders relaxed as I let out a long sigh, but my mind was still racing with confusion. The metallic smell of blood filled the air and I couldn't help but notice the crimson stains on their clothes. What had transpired? Whose blood were they drenched in?

"We need to go," Lonnie was saying, her voice high with nervousness.

"Why?" Scion asked.

"In case the afflicted arrive."

He cocked his head at her. "...are you saying you know for certain that they will?"

Lonnie didn't answer him. Instead, as if she sensed my presence, her head whipped around and her eyes widened in recognition. Her lips spread into a beaming grin.

She moved toward me with a determined look on her face, her hair flying behind her like a wild banner. As she reached me, she wrapped her arms around me in a tight hug, dispelling any lingering fears that she was injured. She leaned back slightly and pressed her lips against mine. I could taste a mixture of blood and longing on her mouth, and smell the lingering sex on her skin. My eyebrows flew up. What the fuck was going on here?

"How did you find us?" she gasped.

"I'll always find you, little monster."

Her cheeks flushed and she looked down. "Is everyone alright?"

"Are *you* alright?" I countered, not wanting to scare her with the knowledge that the battle still raged on at the harbor. "What happened?"

She flushed, and looked down. "I'm fine. I'm—"

"Alive," Scion finished for her, darkly.

I slowly looked up and saw Scion lingering in the shadows behind her. He was shirtless, his skin smeared with fresh blood. Our eyes met, and we shared a silent understanding.

If he'd accepted his bond with her and was still breathing, then perhaps everything would be fine. I'd never been so happy to think I'd been wrong in my life.

I couldn't stifle a grin, as a wave of true happiness washed over me, entirely unexpected. Then, just as quickly, my head throbbed with blinding pain, and I resisted the urge to fall at the wave of nausea that washed over me.

"Are you alright?" Lonnie asked. "You look sick."

I swallowed the bile in my throat, and struggled to catch my breath. Looking up at her, I shook my head, and forced a smile. "I'm fine, little monster." I lied, barely aware of the searing pain in my throat over the throbbing in my skull. "I'm just happy you're safe."

13
LONNIE
THE WAYWOODS

Over the next several hours, no one so much as spoke of what had just happened in the barn. In fact, Bael, Scion and I barely spoke at all, as we shadow walked across the woodland, searching for a town in which to rest.

It felt to me like the day we'd spent disappearing and reappearing all over Elsewhere, searching for a place to hide following the attack on the obsidian castle. On that day, however, we'd visited only towns which we could walk directly into, as someone within our party had been there before. Now, we were in a part of the Waywoods that neither of the princes, and certainly not I, was familiar with, and searching for a town turned out to be harder than finding a single grain of rice on a sandy river bank.

"Where are we?" I asked as we tumbled out of the dark and into yet another section of unidentifiable woodland. The gnarled trees surrounding us looked much the same as every other tree, and the underbrush picked at my ankles like every other thorn and vine, making it impossible to know where we'd landed.

Scion turned to me, and pushed his rumpled hair out of narrowed eyes. "Surely you have learned enough not to keep asking such vague questions. You know we can't answer you."

I scowled at him. "*And surely* you have learned to be more flexible with your interpretation. You know what I meant."

Bael made an exasperated noise in the back of his throat. "I suppose that answers all my questions."

I glanced sideways at him, and asked: "What questions?" at the same moment as Scion said: "The fuck is that supposed to mean?"

Bael shook his head. "Just that your stubbornness defies all intervention...both of you."

Scion made a hiss of anger, but I thought there might be slightly less bite behind the sound than usual. As if he were putting on an act, rather than being truly annoyed with me.

Or, perhaps that was merely what I wanted to hear.

We hadn't spoken a single word about what had happened in the barn, but awareness of it pulsed between the three of us, like a firework poised and ready to go off at any moment. I knew we would have to broach the subject soon, but until then, it was as if nothing had changed.

Or rather, nothing except the fact that Scion now seemed determined to stay with us...at least as far as the next town.

In the meantime, I had other, equally pressing things to worry about.

I glanced over at Bael, and narrowed my eyes, as I had every time we'd shadow walked to a new section of forest over the last hour. I could swear he seemed pale, as if he might be injured, but I couldn't see anything wrong with him.

"Are you sure you're alright?" I asked, losing count of how many times I'd asked already.

"I'm merely sick of wandering around, little monster," he replied.

I had to admit he had a point. The forest was so large, and everything looked so similar, it was impossible to shadow walk in the correct direction since we didn't know where we were going. Looking for a village had therefore become a chore, and I was growing exhausted. I'd assumed that it wouldn't take us more than an hour or so to find a town.

I was wrong.

The sun rose, and started to dim again in the time we searched. The surrounding forest didn't look all that different from the area near the palace. Or, for that matter, the woods surrounding the quarry that I'd walked through during the second hunt. I looked this way and that, trying to take in landmarks, but there was nothing but trees and mile after mile of winding pathways through the underbrush.

The longer time wore on, I was barely able to hide my growling stomach. I gathered that Bael and Scion were doing no better, though they did a better job hiding their displeasure than I did.

I did notice that the Underfae, which usually followed me when I ventured off the pathway or too far into the Wildes, steered mostly clear of us, only peeking out from between the branches to nod at me as we passed. Bael and Scion, who could of course see them as well as I could, made no comment. I supposed they were as used to the creatures as they were to birds and squirrels, so the little figures warranted no mention. Still, as I'd never been able to comment on being able to see them before, I had to bite my tongue to keep from crying out every time we came across one.

Finally, when the chittering sounds of the forest were beginning to sound more sinister than cheerful, and I was nearly ready to ask one of them to carry me, we finally spotted chimney smoke in the distance.

Excitement rising in me, I wanted to sprint toward it. Instead, however, I threw out an arm, and caught Bael across the chest. "Wai—ouch."

At my yell, Scion jerked, as if my voice had startled him, and Bael gave me a sideways glance as I rubbed my arm where I'd hit him. His chest was like stone, and I might as well have punched a boulder.

"What is it, little monster?"

"Wait," I repeated, reproachfully, shaking out my hand. "We have no idea if this village is sympathetic to the rebellion. We can't just walk in there without a plan."

Scion made a disgruntled noise in the back of his throat. "I don't care what your plan is as long as it involves finding an inn. I haven't had a good night's sleep in a fucking week."

I wholeheartedly agreed, but I didn't believe we could enter the village without drawing attention. I turned my gaze at Scion, and the glance alone confirmed my fears.

Scion had retrieved his armor from the wreckage of the barn, and it looked no worse for wear, as if the flames and crumbling beams had made no mark upon it. Quill sat proudly on his shoulder, above the Everlast family crest, banishing any shred of doubt about Scion's identity.

On my other side, Bael suffered from the same problem, though it had little to do with his clothing. Even if I'd never seen him before, I would have instantly been suspicious of anyone as sickeningly handsome. Worse still, his eyes and razor-sharp teeth stood out, even if the village was made up entirely of Fae.

Both of them were far too recognizable, but I could not say the same of myself. My human face and ears were enough to blend in almost anywhere, and more, I now wore Bael's long, dark traveling cloak over the shreds of my torn and bloody tunic. My own jacket and cloak were little more than ash, and I supposed I should merely be grateful to still have trousers.

That thought sent color to my cheeks, and I shook my head to clear it before addressing Scion. "I should go alone, while you wait here. Both of you are far too recognizable."

"It doesn't matter who sees us, little monster," Bael said. "We're not letting you enter that village alone."

Scion growled in agreement, and I pushed my hair out of my face in exasperation. Fucking overprotective, unreasonable Fae males.

"You know I'm right, though," I argued. "Even before we'd ever spoken, I recognized you both immediately."

"In the forest?" Bael clarified.

"Yes, when I wasn't supposed to see you, and—" I broke off, coming to a sudden realization. "Wait, could you not simply do that again?"

I looked to Bael for help, but he only shrugged. "Ask the illusionist." He jerked his head at Scion. "He has all the useful powers, I can't do anything unless you want to murder the entire village in one go…"

"I could do that as well," Scion said, sounding almost bitter.

"Yes, but with as much flavor as me?" A wide grin stretched Bael's face, and his yellow eyes flashed with mirth. He raised a hand, and a tree in front of us disintegrated. "I think not."

"So, will you do it?" I asked Scion, before they could meander off on some tangent that would take the better part of an hour.

"I suppose," Scion said slowly, his brow furrowing with annoyance. "But I'm still not sure I see the point. I doubt there's anyone in a woodland settlement we need to worry over."

"Try not to light us on fire by mistake," Bael said, grinning.

Scion grimaced, as he raised a hand to cast the illusion. "Shut the fuck up."

THE SCENT OF BAKING BREAD AND ROAST MEAT MET ME AS I STOOD at the edge of the village. I sucked in a deep breath, my empty stomach roiling. That smell had to be coming from an inn, and it was all I could do not to run toward the center of town.

The village was small and run down, hardly different from the many that we'd visited in the days between escaping the castle and staying in the thieves' den. There was only one long Main Street, with gray-washed wooden houses on either side, and the occasional fenced in yard where a dog, or a skinny cow was tied to a post.

I walked down the center of the street, the hood of Bael's cloak pulled low to hide my hair and face, as well as my torn and bloody clothing. I'd appear alone to anyone who bothered to look outside their grimy windows, but in truth, I had two tall guards standing on either side of me.

Bael grinned, seeming to enjoy himself, while Scion stalked behind me, his expression like he was attending a funeral march. I could swear, if I didn't know they were related, and more importantly, friends, I never would have been able to guess. There was nothing about them that was in any way similar.

Nothing, I supposed, except me.

I came to a halt in front of a house that could only be the local inn. It was taller than the others around it, with a few strong horses in a paddock out front, as if they were waiting for their riders inside the bar.

"Please do not draw attention to yourselves," I reminded my invisible companions, holding the door open wide enough that the princes could slip in behind me, I stepped into the inn.

Neither prince answered, which I assumed meant they refused to make any promises.

Later, I would reflect that I should have made them swear an oath.

14
LONNIE

THE INN, THE VILLAGE OF FORLORN

Having seen one tavern in Elsewhere, I would bet I'd seen them all.

Like the inns in the capital, the inside was dark and smelled of tobacco and that delicious bread I'd smelled along the road. The long bar took up most of the room, with mismatched tables and chairs covering the remainder of the floor space. In the back corner, a staircase led to what I hoped were rooms for rent.

I made a beeline for the bar, and caught the eye of the thin, green-eyed man pouring ale. I let out a sigh of relief. He was human, perhaps ten years older than my own age of twenty-one, and carried no weapons that I could see. As far as barkeeps went, this male seemed harmless.

"Evening," the man said gruffly, not looking at me.

"Hello," I replied, trying to sound friendly.

The man looked up sharply at the sound of my voice. His eyes lingered on my body, then panned up to my face with interest.

He smiled with a slightly lecherous gleam in his gaze. "Looking to stay the night?"

"Yes, actually. Do you have any rooms available?"

The man's grin widened. "Even if I didn't, I'd kick someone out for you, beautiful."

Bael took a lurching step toward the bar, and I stepped as hard as I could on his foot. "Thank you. How much?"

I silently prayed that he was not greedy, as I only had a few coins in my pocket. The money I'd intended to bring with us was left in my bag, long lost back at the harbor, and as a rule neither Bael nor Scion carried much money on their person. I supposed, they'd never had to before, when the whole of the country belonged to them.

The barkeep grinned. "Three bronze pieces, and one more for dinner if you're hungry."

"I'm starving," I replied, letting out an honest sigh of gratitude as I passed him the coins.

He nodded to one of the bar stools. "Sit there. I'll bring you something."

I paused, my heartbeat quickening. There was no chance I could sit so close if I wanted the princes to stay hidden. I glanced around, and spotted a shadowed table on the far side of the room. "I'll sit over there if you don't mind."

The barman winked. "Don't feel like talking?"

This time it was Scion who moved so fast, I was nervous the displaced air would be visible. He moved around behind the bartender, grabbed a glass off a shelf, and smashed it on the floor.

I jumped, at the sound, and glared at the prince's unapologetic smirk behind the bartender's back. "You're welcome," he mouthed.

I shook my head, as the man whipped around, seeing nothing except the broken glass on the floor. "Fuck, did you see that?"

I grimaced. "Must've fallen."

I gritted my teeth as I made my way to the table, and sat down gingerly in a wooden chair with my back to the bar, letting the princes slide onto the bench across from me facing the room. As long as I kept my back to the room and my voice low, no one would realize I was speaking.

"Was that necessary?" I muttered under my breath.

Bael and Scion glanced at each other, a silent understanding passing between them.

"Very necessary, little monster," Bael said, speaking for both of them.

"Stop that," I said, acidly.

"Stop what?" Bael asked.

"You're always leaving me out of conversations, as if you need to take care of me at every turn."

Scion made a derisive noise low in his throat. "We do."

Bael rubbed the back of his neck, looking only slightly more apologetic. "You do find a truly baffling number of ways to injure yourself, little monster."

I scoffed, but could not answer as at that moment, the barkeep appeared behind me carrying a plate of food. He placed it on the table and grinned. "Let me know if you'd like company."

"Er, right. Thank you." I pursed my lips as he walked away.

"See?" Scion muttered. "If you were truly alone, then that man—"

"Would what?" I interrupted. "Flirt with me? You're ridiculous."

Scion's gaze burned, and he shot another dirty look at the bartender, but said nothing. Perhaps we'd ventured slightly too close to the topic of what might be between us. Or, perhaps he simply didn't care to keep arguing. I'd never truly know.

Bael put a hand flat on the table, and leaned forward. "Eat, little monster, while it's still hot."

I picked up my fork, and used the edge to saw at my chicken. "I'm sorry I couldn't get something for you two. It would have looked strange to order three plates."

Bael waved me off. "We're fine."

I looked guiltily at the chicken and vegetables on my plate. "Aren't you hungry?"

"Of course," Scion replied. "But the difference is we can't starve to death."

"We have more important things to discuss, anyway," Bael added. "Clearly, we were wrong. Ambrose isn't going to wait until closer to the third hunt to come after you."

I took a bite of chicken and chewed slowly, thinking. "Maybe he doesn't want to be king."

"Impossible," Scion spat. "He led a fucking raid on the kingdom and took the crown, and more importantly, you don't know him."

"Do you?" I asked, my curiosity taking over. "Do you really know him either? Hasn't it been decades since you two spent any time together?"

Scion clenched his jaw. "Yes, but believe me, I know my own brother. Ambrose wants to be king. He was literally born for it."

I raised an eyebrow. "Fine, then what is he trying to do?"

"I don't know, little monster," Bael said. "But I think we should assume he'll keep trying whatever it is. Perhaps we should reconsider if Aftermath is the safest option, right now."

I shook my head vigorously, forgetting entirely to be inconspicuous. "No. I refuse to join the hunts again, if that's what you're thinking. Or go to Overcast."

"But if you're constantly under attack—"

"Then I would be under attack anywhere," I said fiercely. "Rather than hiding, the two of you might try teaching me to defend myself."

"We can if you like," Bael said with a sideways grin. "But as I recall, we've tried that before."

I let out an exasperated sigh. "At least tell me all the ways I could kill a fairy."

Bael laughed, and I had to kick him under the table to remind him to keep his voice down. "Sorry, little monster," he chuckled. "I just never thought you of all people would have to ask that."

I felt a flush creep up my cheeks. He was right, of course. I was only sitting here now because I'd killed the most powerful Fae in Elsewhere with my bare hands, long before I ever consciously attempted to use any magic. I'd seen dozens of Fae die since, and killed a handful myself…but that had been mostly luck.

"I know about weapons from the source," I said, somewhat defensively. "But there must be other ways that I don't know about."

"Why does it matter?" Scion asked, almost suspiciously.

I rolled my eyes. "Because despite my best efforts, you're right. I am injured constantly, and perhaps the next time someone decides to shoot me with a crossbow, or lock me in a dungeon, or take on another face to creep into my room, the two of you won't be there."

They fell silent, and shared another of their infuriating silent glances. No one was laughing anymore, presumably because I was right. I needed to know every possible way to defend myself, as I'd inevitably use them all.

"First is as you just said," Scion said finally. "Weapons forged in the source. Iron, steel, silver, it doesn't matter as long as it came from the source forge."

I glanced at the thin, pinkish line that still crossed the prince's face. Only hours ago, it had been an open wound, but evidently I was not the only one to benefit from the effects of blood healing. Scion looked almost back to normal, though the pale scar remained, and I suspected it would always be there from now on. Still, the prince seemed nearly as uncomfortable as I'd ever seen him, and I remembered suddenly that he'd executed many people for the queen while in the military. Perhaps this was bringing up bad memories.

"Why don't wounds from Source-forged weapons heal completely?" I asked quickly, hoping to give him something else to focus on.

"Because that's the source of our magic," Scion said, as if that was all the explanation needed.

I frowned. "Alright, what else?"

"Wilde magic in general," Bael said. "Like the smoke at Aftermath that turned the Fae into the afflicted, or the afflicted themselves." I opened my mouth again, but he answered my question before I could ask. "That's for the same reason as the Source-forged weapons, and also why we say that the elderly have returned to the Source, if they choose to move on to the next life."

I held up the fingers on my right hand, and put two down, as if I was counting down a list. "What else? Or are those the only ways?"

"Not the only ways, no," Scion said heavily. "We can't starve, freeze, suffocate, drown or bleed to death, but dismemberment or burning will eventually kill nearly anything. Beheading, also. There are not many creatures that can live without their heads."

"There are also curses," Bael said. "That's probably what will get us in the end."

From his tone, Bael meant the comment in jest, but I didn't find it all that amusing. Nor, it seemed, did Scion, as all humor wiped off his face.

I quickly searched for something to say. "So, why don't you take precautions? Ban source forged weapons or destroy the forge or…something, I don't know."

To my surprise, they both laughed, and I looked around quickly to make sure no one had heard.

"Because, little monster," Bael said. "If we destroyed the source we'd all die. Anyway, getting run through by a Source-forged sword is a fairly uncommon way to go."

"What's the most common, then?"

"Magic drain," Scion answered darkly, his eyes shadowing over again "Which is precisely what it sounds like. Magic, like any other skill, is finite. Like an athletic ability, even the most gifted magical practitioner will eventually hit their limit and grow exhausted. If any magical being exhausts themselves to the point of full depletion, they'll die."

I bit my lip. Was that something I needed to worry about? How did one know how much magic they had?

Like he read my mind, Bael reached out and put a hand over mine. "You'll be fine, little monster. We wouldn't let that happen to you."

I shook my head. I wasn't entirely sure how he believed he might prevent it from happening, especially if draining was common, but that wasn't the point right now.

The point was, that for immortals, there certainly were a lot of ways to die, and for once in my life, I was worried about someone other than myself or my family.

If the rebellion continued coming after me, and if Ambrose Dullahan confronted Bael and Scion, I feared it could be the death of all three of them. I couldn't let anyone sacrifice their life for me.

"Hope this is alright for you." The barman stopped in front of a shabby wooden door at the end of the hall. "Since you're on your own I put you farther away from the other guests."

I bared my teeth in something between a smile and a grimace. "Thank you…I'm sure it will be fine."

The moment I'd finished eating, my exhaustion finally caught up with me. Against my better judgment, I allowed the talkative barman to lead me up to my room, with the princes trailing invisible behind us like stalking shadows.

Now, I stood in front of the door to my chamber, waiting for the barman to step aside. Instead, he remained rooted to the spot, seeming entirely unaware that I wanted nothing more than to be rid of him.

Pushing lank hair from his eyes, the man shifted on his feet. "So, where did you come from?"

"The city," I replied vaguely, not clarifying which one. "I'm quite tired though, so if you could just…"

"Will you be staying long? If you're spending more than one night, I could—"

"I'm leaving early in the morning," I cut him off. "Now, excuse me."

Not caring much how rude I seemed, I elbowed my way past him to open the door of the room. I held it open wider than necessary, allowing the princes to slip in behind me.

"Goodnight." The barman grinned suggestively. "Just shout if you need *anything*."

Behind me, Scion made an angry sound in the back of his throat. I coughed to cover the sound, and slammed the door shut in the man's face without so much as returning his "goodnight." Bolting the door behind me, I slumped against the wall in exhausted relief.

"Want me to kill him, little monster?" Bael asked, striding over to the bed.

I glared at him. "I truly hope you are joking. You can't murder every person who annoys you."

His lips curled into a mischievous grin, and he gave me a playful wink. "I could, but I won't as long as he stays downstairs where he belongs."

I shook my head, and gestured down at my dirt stained and bloody clothing. I'd yet to find a mirror, but I was sure my face looked no better. "How anyone could be interested in me when I look like this is the great mystery of the age."

"You really don't see yourself clearly, rebel." Scion said flatly.

I turned to look at him, where he still stood rigid by the door, but he'd averted his gaze to the floor.

Not knowing what to say to that, I instead surveyed the cramped bedroom. It was just as dilapidated as the rest of the inn and the dirty walls and creaky floorboards gave it a sense of neglect and abandonment. There was no tub, or even a basin for washing, but I had spotted a bathing room several doors down as we made our way down the hall. The real problem, then, was the small single bed pushed against the wall.

Bael sat down on the end of the bed to unlace his boots, and even sitting he looked too large to fit. I swallowed uncomfortably. Of course, it would have been impossible to ask for multiple beds, but now I wished I'd thought of a way. Would all three of us fit in such a small space? And if not, how would I choose who to leave out?

As if reading my mind, Scion cleared his throat. "It will be fine, rebel."

My cheeks flushed with embarrassment and the room suddenly felt warmer. Suffocating.

So far, no one had commented on the hum of sexual tension hanging over all of us, and it didn't seem as if the princes were likely to fight. But, if they were jealous over a bartender, how would it be if they got angry with each other? Or worse, with me? The world may never recover if these two truly fought, and I didn't want to be the cause of that kind of destruction.

"I-I need to take a bath," I stammered, hurrying toward the door.

"No," Scion said fiercely, stepping sideways to block the door.

I stopped in my tracks, surprised by his sudden aggressiveness, and looked up at him sharply. "I must. I feel disgusting."

"Deal with it. Over my dead fucking body are you going anywhere alone."

"That's ridiculous. I'm only going down the hall."

Scion crossed his arms. "No."

With a frustrated sigh, I turned back to Bael for help. His expression turned sour, and he avoided making eye contact with me. "He's not wrong, little monster. That innkeeper seemed a little too curious about you, and we don't know who else might be staying here."

"He's harmless, and I haven't seen another living soul since we arrived."

Bael fixed me with a hard stare. "I'm not willing to take that chance.

"Then one of you will have to come with me because I refuse to go to sleep covered in this." I gestured at the blood and ash coating my skin.

They looked at each other, sharing one of their silent conversations, and finally seemed to come to an agreement.

"We'll all go," Bael announced, standing up.

I looked down, stalking angrily toward the door. It seemed I was to be allowed no reprieve from either of them, and I couldn't decide if I preferred this new protectiveness, or when both had been out to kill me. At the moment, I might rather have the latter.

15
LONNIE

THE INN, THE VILLAGE OF FORLORN

The air felt heavy and charged with unspoken tension as we entered the dim, grimy bathing room.

The room was small and cramped, less than half the size of the too-small bedroom. The wallpaper was peeling in places, and only decorated by a cracked mirror hanging above a dingy sink. The large circular bathtub in the center of the room was rusted beyond all belief, but I didn't care. It could have been a worm-infested hole in the floor, and I still would've seriously considered using it to wash the grime from my skin.

To my immense relief, the water ran clear and hot when I turned on the rusted faucet. I stepped back, waiting for the tub to fill, then flushed when I felt the eyes of both princes on me.

It seemed foolish to request they turn around while I undressed, but equally embarrassing to simply strip my clothes off while they watched. A blush immediately heated my cheeks at the unbidden thought of having them both watching me, perhaps joining me in the water at the same time…

"Everything alright?" Bael asked, a hint of humor in his tone.

I nodded, but couldn't answer as my mouth had gone impossibly dry. I forced a deep breath and clenched my jaw to keep from trembling as I turned away. My hands shook as I hastily stripped off my grime-covered clothes.

I avoided meeting anyone's gaze, but could sense the weight of their stares on my back. My breathing turned uneven and my heart raced with a mix of nervousness and excitement as I swiftly slid into the bathtub.

The tense atmosphere and lack of conversation made it clear that they were silently communicating once again, then slow footsteps echoed through the room. Bael walked around to stand in front of me beside the tub. He looked down pointedly, possessive hunger in his gaze. I resisted the urge to cover myself, and was reminded strongly of the first time he'd stood beside my bathtub, and how pointedly different this felt—still torturous, but now in an entirely different way.

Bracing his hands on the sides of the tub, he leaned down until our faces were level and mere inches apart. His yellow eyes locked onto mine, and he raised one hand to run his thumb across my bottom lip. "What are you thinking about, little monster?"

My eyes widened with mortification, as I recalled that they could likely smell even the barest hint of my arousal. I shook my head, wishing I could simply say "nothing" and instead finding no words to describe my thoughts. "Nothing important."

"Liar."

I opened my mouth to protest, but he pressed his thumb between my lips and instead I let out a deep moan. I swirled my tongue around it, sucking the salt from his skin. He groaned in response.

Our mouths were so close, I could almost taste his lips without even moving. A current pulsed through every inch of my skin as he grasped my chin in his strong hand, and leaned further over the water to drag his tongue over my bottom lip.

I opened to the kiss, hungry and desperate, and wound my fingers into his curls. His lips moved against mine with an intensity that sent shivers down my spine, igniting a heat within me that only grew with each passing moment.

"Are you going to join me?" I asked, my mouth dry.

His eyes rolled upwards to gaze at the ceiling, as if he was desperately searching for the willpower to resist. He shook his head. "I don't think that's a good idea, little monster."

"Why?" I asked, knowing I sounded needy. Desperate.

His expression was slightly pained, and he pulled back from me. "I'm already far too happy with you," he confessed. "And if you keep looking at me like that, I don't care if it destroys me, I won't be able to resist the urge to claim you as mine."

My eyes went wide, even as I heard the creak of the door. I whipped my head around, to see Scion halfway out into the hall. *Fuck.*

I hadn't meant to ignore him, in fact, even now it was impossible to decide whom I would prefer more.

"Wait," I called sharply. I looked between them, helpless, my heart pounding as if I were on the brink of leaping from a cliff.

"No," Scion's shoulders sagged and his head hung low, his usually confident posture now hunched and defeated. "I'm not your mate. I shouldn't be here."

Bael scoffed in disbelief. His expression had changed from one of arousal to annoyance in an instant, his brows furrowing and his lips thinning into a tight line. "And what's made you so sure of that?"

"How can you ask me that?" Scion's eyes widened, as if it were already obvious. "Look at her."

"I am," Bael snapped back. "It's a bit late to claim modesty, don't you think? I can smell you all over each other. I can see the marks on both your necks—"

"—and yet you and I are still breathing," Scion cut him off. "So whatever you're thinking, you're wrong."

My breath caught and my mouth fell open. A shred of doubt crept into my mind, as I realized for the first time that Scion and I had done exactly what Bael was warning against…hadn't we? Hadn't we marked each other, shared blood, and yet nothing seemed any different. Yet, even as I thought that, my pulse seemed to throb beneath the mark on my throat. My entire body tingled with a sudden awareness that seemed to embed itself in my chest.

"What does he mean?" I asked Bael. "What are you thinking?"

He shifted his gaze back to mine, but his expression was unreadable. "What I've been trying to tell both of you for weeks. It's not only you and I who are meant to be together, it's you two. The way you've always been mine, little monster, you've really been ours."

My eyes widened and words failed me. Was that right? Was it even possible to have more than one mate?

Yes, I thought, answering my own question. It had to be, because I'd heard stories about it. Queen Aisling, for one, had three mates. But then, she was a Fae queen, and I was…just me.

"You're delusional," Scion snapped at Bael, his voice breaking through my haze of wonderment. "If that were true, then you and I wouldn't be here to discuss it, would we? There's no fated bond here, and no excuses." He laughed humorlessly. "I don't understand why you haven't tried to kill me yet."

"I think you're too fucking neurotic to be happy," Bael hissed at his cousin. "I'd always assumed I was the more fucked up of the two of us, but at least I can recognize my own damn emotions."

Scion straightened, his face morphing back into its usual mask of arrogant rage. "Careful."

"No, I won't." Bael snapped. "You won't do shit no matter what I say. You can't hurt me because it would hurt *her*, and you can't do that, can you?"

Scion spluttered, words seeming to fail him.

"I'm almost jealous," Bael continued, "that you seem to have found a way to circumvent a generations-long curse, but I could never hope to be so inherently miserable that I could claim my own mate and not know it."

"That can't be right," Scion replied, his voice rising in frustration.

"No?" Bael laughed without humor. "I've been watching how you two look at each other for weeks and all I want is for you to get over yourselves and admit what's fucking obvious to everyone around you."

"And what's that?" Scion demanded.

"You're in love with her," Bael practically shouted. "It's so fucking obvious, Sci. Everyone can see it. Everyone knows except you, and *you*," he looked at me, and I reeled back, not having expected to be addressed directly in what seemed to be a fight between them alone.

"I don't—"

"You don't know?" Bael interrupted, sounded almost mocking. "Then explain how I can't even think about anyone else looking at you without being ready to murder them, but you're naked right now, practically begging to be fucked, and the only thing bothering me is how we're all going to fit in that tub."

I blinked in complete and utter shock. His frustration had clearly been simmering for some time, and he'd reached a boiling point without my ever noticing there was a problem. This had gone way too far.

I looked over at Scion, and tried to keep my voice as calm as possible. "Shut the door."

"Gladly," Scion hissed, taking a step further into the hall.

"No." I stopped him with the command in my tone. "Shut the door and come over here."

Bael reached down and ran a hand through my hair, petting me as if to silently apologize for raising his voice. I leaned into his hand.

Scion watched from the doorway, one hand gripping the frame, his body halfway in and halfway out of the room. His eyes were downcast and his face contorted, like whatever was going on in his head had completely broken him. "Rebel..." he breathed, his tone turning almost pleading. "I can't."

"Why?" I replied mercilessly.

Bael twisted his fingers more firmly through my hair. "Because somewhere deep down he knows one day the bond will break through even his damaged fucking psyche, and he'll end up killing us both just to be with you."

Gods, that shouldn't have sounded so hot. He was talking about their death, but all I could focus on was the way my pulse throbbed between my legs at the idea of owning anyone so completely.

"That's not why," Scion said doggedly, even as he stepped back inside and shut the door behind him. He fixed his too-intense gaze on me, and his silver eyes flashed with rage. "Do I have to fuck you again to prove there's no bond here?"

My chest screamed as I struggled to take in a breath. My thighs clenched, as I grew wetter at just the idea of that. I knew he wanted me to reject him—to turn away in disgust—just as he'd tried to force me to be the one to say no in the barn.

Just like he'd been trying to push me away since the very beginning.

I forced myself to keep my tone even, my face neutral. "Yes, my lord."

I turned away, waiting for what he would do.

Bael looked down at me with something like approval, as behind me, I heard the now familiar clanging of metal and the dull thud of discarded armor hitting the ground. My heart raced as the distinct click of Scion's heels echoed through the room. I held my breath as each step brought him closer.

My pulse throbbed harder between my legs, and I twisted to see Scion step up beside the tub, his intense gaze locking with mine. He was entirely naked, and already half-hard. I licked my lips, and his gaze darkened, following the path of my tongue with his eyes. "Slide forward, Rebel."

I raised a skeptical eyebrow at him, but he was already lifting one foot and sliding his leg into the warm water. I scrambled to make room for him, splashing in my haste.

Settling behind me, he sank deeper into the bath, his arms flung out to the sides, and he let out a deep sigh as he tilted his head back against the cool porcelain. My mouth went dry, even as wetness pooled between my legs.

Smirking, Scion pulled me backwards until I relaxed against his chest. I could feel the warmth of his body even hotter than the bathwater. He hummed contentedly and his breath tickled my neck, making me shiver.

I could hardly believe that Scion was going along with this. He must truly believe that we were not meant to be bound together. I couldn't wrap my mind around that idea, and wasn't sure what I wanted to be true.

If he was also my mate, then this was incredibly dangerous and if not, then what was I thinking?

Doubts and questions tangled together in my mind, and I craned my neck to meet Scion's gaze. I opened my mouth to ask what he was thinking, when the words died when the warm press of his lips made every muscle in my body loose and malleable. I couldn't help but whimper at the sensation, craving more.

I bit down on his lip hard enough to draw blood, and Scion let out a feral sound from deep within his throat. Our kiss became more aggressive as he fought for control. He dug his fingers into my thighs, spreading them wider beneath the water and causing a delicious pain that only added to the heat pooling between my legs. He ran delicate fingers over my core, and I moaned into his mouth as I felt him grow harder against my ass.

Next to the bathtub, Bael let out a low growl as he watched Scion's fingers dance over my clit. My attention shifted to him, and he quickly removed his shirt with one fluid movement.

My eyes went wide, and I couldn't help but stare at the white, vine-like tattoos that traced his toned chest, and disappeared into the waistband of his trousers. I'd seen every inch of him before, traced my tongue over those hard muscles, yet the sight still had me pressing my thighs together.

He smirked down at me and ran his hand through his tousled red-blonde hair before taking another step closer. Bael leaned forward again, bracing holding himself over the water by the edges of the tub. His lips closed around my breast, and a jolt of pleasure shot through me. I gasped and arched my back, desperate for more.

His hand slid down to the front of his trousers and gripped his own hard cock through the fabric, as he flicked his tongue over my nipple. My eyes fixed on the movement, and I struggled to form coherent words while Scion's fingers expertly teased and stroked my sensitive clit. My exhaustion seemed to evaporate, and I completely forgot everything except my pounding pulse. I needed one of them inside me, now.

"Are you sure you won't join us?" I asked Bael, my mouth dry.

He smiled wickedly, but shook his head. "No, little monster…I don't need any help to realize the hold you have on me."

I made a pleading sound in my throat, and Scion seemed to understand. He lifted me with ease and switched our positions so that I straddled his lap. I gripped the edge of the bath and my breath hitched as I moved to settle onto his hard length beneath me. Except, he gripped my hips holding me off him, and looked me in the eye.

This felt vastly different from the first time. In the barn, it was hot and frenzied, whereas now my heart squeezed, and his gaze lit me on fire, saying everything without a single word.

Keeping his gaze locked with mine, his hands firmly grasped my hips, guiding me down and impaling me on his cock. A sharp gasp escaped my lips as I felt the exhilarating fullness inside me.

Rising up on my knees, I began to ride him, feeling every inch deep within me.

He buried his face in my neck, as if he too felt the need to hide from the intense emotions that were passing between us. His breath tickled my skin, and I fought to hold on to myself as the awareness in my chest seemed to heighten.

Blindly, I reached a hand behind me, feeling for Bael, wanting both of them touching me.

Bael's footsteps echoed as he circled the large, claw-footed tub and leaned over Scion's shoulder to kiss me gently on the lips. "You look so pretty like this."

I moaned into his mouth and reached out to palm him through his pants. Following my lead, Bael pulled away and took his cock out, to run the tip of himself over my lips. I opened, taking him down my throat. He closed his eyes as if in pain as I flicked my tongue, tasting all of him.

I sucked hard, making Bael moan as Scion gripped my hips harder. I could feel his fingers dig into the soft flesh of my ass. He guided my body up and down with force, grinding my clit against him with every stroke and causing me to bounce and the water to splash out onto the floor.

My entire being quivered in anticipation, my breaths quickening as an intense wave of pleasure began to rise in my lower belly.

Bael threaded his hands through my hair, pulling hard until I looked up at him, my lips still wrapped around his cock.

"Give me your hands," he said, his voice strangled.

I raised an eyebrow in silent question, and licked the tip of my tongue over his throbbing tip.

"Let me hold your hands," he said more urgently. "Unless you want to burn this inn to the ground."

My shocked jolt had me pulling back, wanting to ask any number of questions, but he gripped my hair and held my head in place.

I reached up and held out my hands for Bael to hold onto, as Scion guided me to go faster. Electric tingles coursed through my limbs and I arched my back, meeting every thrust with a soft moan. It was as if his touch was setting off an explosion inside me, and I couldn't tell whether it was madness or pure ecstasy coursing through my veins.

My breathing turned uneven, and Bael squeezed my hands so hard it was painful, as a final wave of pleasure crashed over me. I screamed silently, my vision going white as my legs shook uncontrollably.

Spurred on by my release, both men spilled inside me. I swallowed hard, and then finally slumped forward against Scion's chest.

Bael reached out to pet the top of my head. I felt the soft brush of his fingers through my hair, and a tingling sensation spread down my scalp. "You're perfect, little monster."

I felt Scion suck in a deep breath and hold it. I didn't dare to even try to look at him, afraid of what might happen if we saw too much in each other's eyes. Instead, I closed my eyes and listened to the frantic sound of all our hearts beating out of sync with each other.

An intense feeling of contentment washed over me, and in that moment, two things became incredibly clear:

First, that I would never be able to choose between them because both were wholly and completely mine; my mates. My *everything*.

And second, I had to leave them.

16
LONNIE

THE INN, VILLAGE OF FORLORN

A dim light seeped in through the dirt-caked window of the small room, casting a faint glow on the dusty floor. I lay on my side, squashed between Bael and Scion on the creaky, narrow bed, our limbs tangled together. Bael spooned me from behind with his arm securely curled around my waist, while Scion faced me with his arm draped over my hip, our mouths so close I could feel his warm breath on my skin. I breathed deeply, trying to give the impression I was asleep, even as I counted every second that passed.

I was counting down the time remaining until I had to leave them.

Though the scene earlier was meant to bring some awareness to Scion, it had done far more for me. Everything came into sharp clarity—the curse, my role in it, my feelings. I had to escape tonight or I never would.

It was ironic, really.

I'd spent so much time worrying that they were going to kill me, and now I was leaving to avoid the reverse. If I stayed, one way or another, they'd die, and I couldn't let that happen. Still, my heart ached every time I thought of leaving. *Just a few more minutes.*

Bael stirred behind me, his warm breath tickling the back of my neck as he murmured soft words in his sleep. My heart swelled and I struggled to catch my breath as tears pricked at the corners of my eyes. My time had run out.

Ever so slowly, I unraveled myself from their arms and slipped out of bed. Padding on tiptoes across the cold wooden floor, I barely breathed, afraid the slightest sound would wake them.

I'd left my muddy boots by the door, but didn't dare stop to put them on. Picking them up in one hand, and grabbing for Bael's abandoned cloak with the other, I slowly eased the door open.

It made no sound, but still, I paused and held my breath. Stepping into the dimly lit hallway, my ears strained for a creak of the bed or an angry curse from Scion. No such sound came, and I let out a shaky sigh of relief before continuing down the hall, careful to avoid any loose floorboards.

I didn't have any firm plan as I stumbled down the rickety stairs, two at a time, and burst into the dimly lit tavern. I supposed I should have spent the hours lying awake in bed deciding where to go—what I was going to do next—but no such thoughts had broken through the fog swirling my mind. I was so focused on leaving, I hadn't worked out what I would do next. I hadn't even had time to be afraid yet, to worry what might be waiting for me alone in the forest.

I supposed it didn't matter.

I'd never had much of a plan for my life—my future—before the princes came into it. Why should that change now that I was leaving them?

. . .

The street outside the inn was desolate, not a single soul in sight as I paused to sit on the front stoop and lace up my boots. The air smelled of rain and damp earth, and I sucked in a heavy breath before standing and wrapping Bael's cloak around my shoulders.

Suddenly, the world stretched wide before me.

I looked right, then left down the dark street, as if an idea might spring out of nowhere and present itself to me. Unsurprisingly, nothing happened. I supposed the only thing to do was to keep heading north.

The moment that Ambrose Dullahan suggested my mother might be alive back in the midst of the battle at the castle, I'd known that the first place I should look for her was in the valley where I'd grown up. Not only had Scion once mentioned that my mother had been sent to Aftermath as a prisoner, but mother had grown up there. She was more familiar with that province than anywhere else in Elsewhere, and I felt certain that if she could not return to be with my sister and I, that's where she would've gone.

My heart panged at the thought—as so often happened when I thought of my mother or my childhood, I wished Rosey was still here with me. Wished we were making this journey together, and wondered what she would've said about all that had come to pass in her absence.

Without warning, the first drops of rain touched my face, and I pushed them aside along with the sudden tears that burned at the backs of my eyes. *Stop,* I told myself firmly. *There's no time to wallow—not if I want to escape before anyone realizes I'm gone.*

Making a quick decision, I swallowed my emotions and crept around the back of the inn. The rain kicked up as I stepped carefully through the mud, and in the distance a clap of thunder rattled through the wood. I groaned. Of all the times to be out of doors alone, the beginning of a storm was far from ideal. Although, with any luck, it would drive the creatures of the Waywoods into their homes, keeping them off my path.

One could always hope for small miracles.

I let out a sigh of relief as I reached the backside of the inn. Perhaps there were miracles to be had tonight, as I found myself looking at the wall of a rundown stable. I darted quickly inside, eager to avoid the rain.

The barn was dark, and it took a moment for my eyes to adjust as the door swung shut behind me. The air in the barn was thick with the smell of wet hay and manure, mixed in with the musty aroma of old wood. There was an old mule in one of the first stalls, who couldn't be bothered to even look up at me as I walked by. I cast it half a glance before moving on, making my way further down the rows.

If there was a horse worth stealing here in this miserable swamp town, I'd take it as a good omen.

As soon as the thought flitted through my mind, I spotted a strong chestnut mare on the far end of the right-hand row. The horse looked up at me with intelligent interest, and excitement flooded me.

"Hello there," I breathed in hushed tones. "Who do you belong to?"

The horse stomped her hoof, as if in answer, and I grinned. It didn't matter who she belonged to, she was mine now.

I practically skipped forward, only to stop short as a loud clang echoed behind me.

I froze, and glanced over my shoulder. I glared at the mule, and scanned the other dark shadowed stalls. Nothing jumped out at me, or even breathed aside from the sleeping mule. I let out a breath—it must have been nothing.

In any case, I kept forgetting that I did not have to be quite so vigilant anymore. I could protect myself now…at least, I hoped I could.

Taking a calming breath, I turned back toward the mare, and gasped. My eyes widened, and I took a staggering step back. Ambrose Dullahan leaned against a stall in a space I was positive had been empty only seconds before. His arms were crossed, his posture casual, as if he'd been waiting here for me for some time. Which, I supposed, he could've been.

"You…" I gasped, unable to form the words for anything else.

"Me," the prince replied, flashing me a cocky grin. "Were you expecting someone else?"

I stuttered, words failing me entirely.

Ambrose looked every part the rebel king, in mahogany stained leather armor with a sword strapped to his back and another on his hip. His obsidian gaze seemed to swallow the light around him and his silver hair was wild, shaved short on one side and pulled into a tight braid on the other. He had dark, swirling tattoos climbing up his neck and wore several hoop earrings and what looked to be a small bone stabbed through one of his pointed ears.

He exuded a rougher, more rugged aura than his brother, Scion, so while their features were similar, no one would confuse the two. If Scion could be described as 'intense,' and Bael as 'dangerous,' then Ambrose was 'aggressive.'

Like a bucket of ice-cold water poured over my head, fear fell over me. "What are you doing here?"

The rebel leader grinned wider, as if he'd been hoping I would ask that. "You can leave the horse," he said, nodding to the mare. "You won't need her where we're going."

"Excuse m—"

I didn't get a chance to finish my sentence as a sharp pain cracked against the back of my skull, and everything went white.

PART TWO
Flame and Sea

17

AMBROSE

THE INN STABLES, VILLAGE OF FORLORN

"Was that really necessary?" my friend Riven asked, stepping forward out of a shadowed alcove.

I looked up at him, then down at the redheaded woman on the floor. "Absolutely."

Riven was a large man—nearly as tall as I—with a hard, square face and hair cut so short it was possible to see the tattoos that crossed his skull. He'd been my primary companion for some years now, and was used to taking on unusual requests without question. He'd conducted my meetings at the brothel in Inbetwixt, and most recently, had shot Lonnie in the forest. This, however, was apparently beyond even *his* ability not to question.

"If you're sure," he grumbled, sheathing his long sword in his belt.

A moment before, he'd cracked the hilt of that sword against the back of Lonnie's head from behind, just as I'd instructed. Part of me was disappointed at how easy it'd been to subdue her. I'd wanted to see more of the magic she was only just beginning to use with conscious effort.

No matter—I'd see it all soon enough.

"Trust me," I grumbled, as I bent to pick up Lonnie's limp body off the floor. "This one will require careful handling."

"How do you know?" Riven asked. "I thought you couldn't see her."

I glanced down at her unconscious face, and I shook my head resignedly. "I don't need magic when it comes to her."

While I couldn't see everything going on in the world at any given moment, some people were easier to keep track of than others. Since the first time I'd met her as a child all those years ago, I'd never been able to see Lonnie and therefore she'd become the ruler by which I measured my own abilities. She was the stone with which I sharpened my talent, the dragon standing between me and the ultimate prize of total omniscience.

I'd spent the better part of ten years trying to see any glimpse of her future, but to no avail. As a result, I'd watched her grow up through others' eyes, and learned her temperament so well that I'd have been able to predict her movements even without magic. Though we'd hardly spoken, I felt as if I knew her. She was outside my power, and therefore my weakness in every possible way.

A part of me felt slightly guilty for the pain the blow to the head would no doubt cause her, but it had been necessary. Even without prophecy, I knew her well enough to guess that left awake to argue she'd talk endlessly, wasting precious hours that we didn't have.

I knew, because she'd been difficult even as a child and I knew, because she was just like her mother, and in the decade that I'd known her, Rhiannon had never once accepted anything without a fight.

In the end, Lonnie would have agreed to come with me anyway. This was merely expediting the inevitable. Every pain I caused her was for the greater good.

I only hoped she would see it that way.

We walked through the shadows, and reappeared in the Inbetwixt harbor.

At this early hour, most of the world was still asleep, but not the sailors and merchants coming in and out of port. The early morning skyline was a sea of towering masts and billowing sails, bobbing gently in the rhythmic sway of the waves. The salty tang of the ocean mixed with the fresh scent of rain. Seagulls cried out overhead, their calls echoing off the docks and mingling with the distant shouts of sailors. Everything looked as it normally did. In fact, without the remnants of dried blood still splattered across the docks, you would never have guessed that a fight had occurred here just two nights ago.

I strode down the deck toward my ship, Lonnie unconscious and still cradled in my arms.

Because of her unpredictable detour, we were running late. Originally, I'd planned to find Lonnie the night of the fight on the docks and begin our journey together two days sooner, but she'd managed to dodge my men quite skillfully. Of course, she didn't do it alone. I shook my head, sighing. My younger brother was still finding ways to irritate me, despite the fact that we'd hardly spoken in thirty years.

Perhaps because he himself didn't know what he was planning to do before he did it, Scion's future was almost as difficult to predict as my own. It wasn't until Bael had rejoined the group that I'd been able to find all three of them. Unlike Lonnie or Scion, my cousin was always resolute in his decisions, making him an excellent subject for my particular brand of magic.

I knew, for instance, that Bael would soon wake at the inn in Forlorn, and find Lonnie gone. I knew that while Scion would take hours to calm down enough to focus, Bael would immediately begin searching for his mate, using the talent he'd inherited from his Unseelie father.

Unless our ship left within the hour, both he and Scion would arrive to rescue their mate. If we were already at sea, however, it would take them days—perhaps weeks—before they saw her again. I was hoping for the latter.

At the very end of the dock, my ship bobbed slightly in the choppy water of the harbor, its sails billowing in the wind like great white wings. Riven led the way up the ramp to the main deck, and I followed, walking carefully with Lonnie in my arms. As we stepped onto the deck, the crew all turned from whatever they were doing to stare, but no one questioned me about the unconscious woman.

They'd learned a long time ago not to ask questions.

Before I could take a single step toward my cabin, a thin woman with close cropped black hair ran up to me. "We're nearly ready to sail, sir."

"Good," I said shortly. "Thank you, Lin."

Lin danced between her feet, and made every effort not to look at Lonnie. Like the rest of the crew she knew not to ask questions, but as the captain in all but name, she was allowed more leeway than most.

"Should we move out, then?" she asked. "The wind is picking up, so we might not even need magic to move the ship out of the harbor."

I gazed up at the crow's nest, where two crew members with a knack for manipulating the weather were already perched. It was fortunate they could conserve their energy, considering the rough seas that awaited us along the coast and beyond. If the rain in the village of Forlorn was anything to go by, storms were inevitable.

I smiled slightly. I enjoyed sea travel because for some reason the weather was one thing I'd never been able to predict. Sea travel, which was almost entirely dependent on weather, felt unpredictable in an otherwise painfully boring world. There were no surprises in life when I already knew what was going to happen at any moment...perhaps that was why I was so fascinated by the woman in my arms.

"Yes, finish raising the sails," I said briskly. "I want to be far away from the shoreline that it's a distant memory by the time dawn truly breaks."

"Yes, sir." Lin gave a little tilt of her head, somewhere between a bow and a nod of agreement, and scurried away.

"Wait!" I called after Lin, an idea occurring to me a moment too late.

She was halfway across the enormous ship already, but skidded to a halt, slipping slightly on the wet deck. "Yes sir?"

"Have someone bring a vial of Gancanagh to my room."

Lin raised a shocked eyebrow, and glanced at Lonnie as if she couldn't stop herself. "An entire vial, sir?"

I rolled my eyes at her concern. I wouldn't be using the drug for what she obviously thought, but I didn't want to bother explaining myself. The less people knew why we'd been shipping Gancanagh's dust all over Elsewhere, the better.

. . .

My cabin on the ship was a cozy yet cramped space, resembling a hybrid between a bedroom and an office. The walls were lined with maps and charts, their corners curling from years of use. A neatly made bed took up one end of the room, while a sturdy desk sat at the other, cluttered with papers and navigational tools.

"I could get the dust for you," Riven said, the moment the door snapped behind us. "I'm not sure we should be letting the entire crew know what we're using it for. Not everyone here is one of ours, some are just merchant sailors."

The corner of my lip tipped up as I strode across the small room to lay Lonnie down on my bed, before turning back to Riven. "I thought much the same thing, but they won't guess why I need it. They'll think it's for her."

Riven pressed his lips together in a disapproving line. "I don't know why you feel the need to let everyone think you're a monster."

I smiled ruefully. "I am a monster. Just not the type the world thinks I am."

18
BAEL

THE INN, VILLAGE OF FORLORN

I barely noticed or cared as the sound of breaking glass rattled through the room.

Scion tore through the tavern of the dilapidated old inn, smashing tables and chairs, flipping over shelves and breaking windows. Destruction chased him, leaving a mess of splintered wood and shattered glass in his wake. I'd seen Scion break dozens of things over the years, and today was no different.

Well, it was no different except for the fact that I almost felt like joining him.

"Stop," I heard myself say. "This isn't helping anything."

My cousin fixed me with furious silver eyes. "Maybe I'm not trying to fix anything."

That much was obvious, and it was hard to demand he stop when I had little idea what to do myself.

Only yesterday, I'd been the closest to happy I could ever remember being. Lonnie had stopped fighting me at every turn, and even Scion seemed to be calming down, his legendary rage quelled by her presence. We were alive, and all together, and then…*nothing*.

I'd awoken this morning to Scion's angry yell, and rolled over to find the space beside me in bed entirely empty. Lonnie's honey and magic scent was long gone, and for once in my life I had no fucking idea what to do.

Part of me wanted to be angry, to lash out at her for causing such chaos, but I could have turned this entire building to dust, and it wouldn't have fixed anything. It wouldn't explain what happened. It wouldn't tell me how she could leave without a single word.

Another splintering crash rattled the very floor we stood on, and I looked up. The dining room of the inn was in splinters, and Scion stood in the very center of all the wreckage. His shoulders shook as he breathed hard, spinning around and scanning the floor, no doubt looking for something else to destroy.

I ran a hand through my hair, annoyed. "Perhaps you could put all that energy into searching."

He ignored me, and instead took a jerking aggressive step forward, shadows rising around him to tear the very rafters from over our heads. Instinctively, I leaned back, wincing as a heavy wooden beam smashed on the floor some two feet from where I was sitting.

It wasn't that I was afraid of my cousin—far from it. He'd been the only real friend I'd had growing up, and I knew it was only because of him that I wasn't shipped back to my father at birth.

A bastard, half-Unseelie prince would never have been allowed in the high court of Elsewhere, except that Ambrose had just left a mere few years before, and there was concern that Scion, the new heir, wouldn't have any peers to socialize with. Like an overgrown house cat, I'd been practically gifted to my cousin as a companion—it was a role I never resented, but it did set the parameters for our relationship practically in stone. I never commented on his tantrums in a way that he could take seriously, and I never challenged him—that was, until recently.

"I'm telling you, she left on her own," I said for perhaps the third time this hour. "Destroying everything will not help."

"Don't say that as if it's a fact," he barked back, smashing another chair against the already condemned bar.

"Isn't it?" I laughed bitterly. "Have you met Lonnie? Whatever the simplest thing to do is, she will inevitably do the opposite."

Scion glared at me. "She could just as easily have been taken."

I groaned. We couldn't keep arguing about this. "Whether Lonnie was taken or not, it barely matters. Either way, we have no idea where to begin looking for her."

Knowing that nothing would have changed since last I checked, I rolled my eyes into the back of my head, searching.

Visions of the forest path crossed through my consciousness, but it was like searching for a single tree within the woods. All I could see was the same stretches of woods over and over, like a reoccurring nightmare meant to drive me out of my mind. It was made all the more difficult because I could only search in areas I'd either been or knew well, where the spirits whose eyes I borrowed felt familiar.

"Anything?" Scion asked.

I blinked, and returned my gaze to the room in front of me. "No. You try."

He rounded on me. "And how the fuck do you suggest I do that? You're the one who can—" he broke off, waving his hand beside his right eye. "Do whatever it is that you do."

"Check in with your stupid bird," I sighed. "Didn't he find Lonnie before?"

I held my breath, a tiny shred of hope lighting inside me, as he fell silent, his eyes sliding out of focus. I had no fucking idea how he talked to that demonic creature, or if indeed he was speaking at all, or perhaps seeing through its eyes as I did with the departed. It didn't matter, however, if the bird found her I'd never threaten to kill it again.

"Nothing," Scion said roughly, returning his gaze to me. "He's circling the Wanderlust marshes, now."

I raised an eyebrow. "Why?"

He gritted his teeth. "Because she's nowhere in the forest, and the marshes are only a few hundred miles away. I couldn't think of anything else."

I groaned. A few hundred miles would be impossible for her to travel by foot, and as far as I could tell, Lonnie could so far only use her magic when she was in imminent danger. But, if she'd finally managed to shadow walk without first being under attack...it was possible, I supposed. Improbable that she'd manage to get so far, but I wasn't going to shoot down any ideas at this point. "What we really need is a seer."

"*You're* supposed to be a damn seer," my cousin snapped back.

"Barely," I replied darkly. "But if you think my taking a nap will help I'd be happy to try it."

He said nothing. We both knew my minor prophetic talent was far below the caliber we'd need for something like this.

"We could contact my mother," I said halfheartedly, already knowing it was a terrible suggestion.

Scion snorted a derisive laugh. "That would be the height of desperation."

"I *am* fucking desperate, aren't you?"

He didn't answer, and with little else to do, I lowered to the floor and sat with my back against one of the few remaining walls. My eyes rolled again, and I moved my search further—back to Inbetwixt, to the harbor, the city, even the quarry where the second hunt was held.

As I searched—not expecting to find anything—I tried to think of where we might find a seer.

The ability to see into the future was a common trait among those with magical abilities. It was so widespread that nearly anyone with magic might get a vision or two in their lifetime. Those small flashes, however, were almost nothing compared to a talented seer.

Because of Grandmother Celia—and I supposed, whatever ancestor she'd inherited her talents from—prophecy was even more common in our bloodline than most.

My mother was a dream oracle, but her talents lay in large scale phenomena. Wars, important deaths, major weather events. She was excellent at predicting earth tremors, but terrible at noticing anything that stood directly in front of her. Conversely, I'd been known to have the occasional prophetic dream as well, but only about mundane things, and nothing as strong or as clear as we would need at present.

I wasn't looking for just any dream oracle or someone with a light prophetic gift; I needed the best. Someone who could see every possible path, every decision, long before they occurred.

We needed Grandmother Celia.

Or—the irony nearly choked me—we needed Ambrose.

I blinked, the room coming back into focus, and looked sideways at my cousin. The war had made him bitter and he hated his brother far more than I did. I couldn't imagine that he'd simply put that aside, now. Though he'd spoken to Ambrose before in regard to Lonnie, perhaps he'd do it again now if it meant finding her.

"Listen…" I began slowly, unsure how to broach the subject without getting a chair thrown at my head. "What if—"

"You seem far too calm considering your mate is missing," Scion blurted out, interrupting me as if he hadn't heard a word I'd been saying.

Distracted from what I'd meant to ask, I narrowed my gaze on him.

He was wrong. I wasn't calm at all, far from it in fact. I'd simply shut down, unable to think beyond anything but the present moment. If I let myself get as angry as Scion had the luxury of being, if I let the monster in the back of my mind out to play, I'd lose control.

Losing control for me wasn't as manageable as it was for the rest of my family. If my magic leaked as Scion's shadows did, I could destroy an entire village. If I removed the wall I constantly kept around my mind, I'd shift into my other form by mistake, and then we'd have an entirely different problem. I needed to maintain the appearance of calm…for now.

"Don't say that as if she's only mine," I hissed. "Look at the state of this fucking room, this is not the behavior of someone who doesn't care."

He glared at me. "I'm only pointing out, you seemed far more concerned during the second hunt."

"Of course," I snapped. "Then, I knew she was in danger. There was a gigantic fucking snake…" I trailed off, realization dawning. Ambrose was not the only seer in the area.

"A snake?" Scion asked. "I never heard about a fucking snake."

I ignored him, my eyes rolling again as I flicked through various angles of the quarry. This time, I wasn't looking for Lonnie. My target now was much, much larger.

Finally, I spotted a disturbance in the water, enormous ripples covering the surface as if something large and serpentine were moving just out of sight. With an excited shout, I jumped to my feet. "I've got it."

"Where is she?" Scion demanded, the mingled panic and relief evident in his tone.

"Not Lonnie," I said, grinning as I returned my eyes to his. "But I know how we're going to find her."

19
LONNIE

ABOARD THE FORESIGHT

*I*n my dream, I stared up in abject terror at the two Fae males.

Though I'd never encountered the Fae this close, there was no mistaking either of the men for human. One had long, chestnut colored hair, tied back in a braid at the base of his neck, and wore a black cloak that shifted with every movement, revealing a glint of a sword at his belt. The planes of his face were sharp, almost feline, and his sharp golden-yellow eyes held only cruelty as he watched me. The other male, looked somehow younger than the first. He was certainly cleaner, and his clothing was made of fine, evenly dyed fabric. His hair was silver— not the gray or white of age that I'd seen occasionally on those humans that were lucky enough to grow to old age, but silver, like mother's knives.

A cold terror washed over me and I stumbled backwards, the gravel beneath my feet scraping and clattering.

The Fae were evil, twisted creatures who'd stolen my mother away from her real home in the night, never to see her own family again. I'd heard countless stories of the terrible court of Nightshade, that once stood on this land before the Gods had seen fit to punish the Fae for their wickedness. Mother made sure that from the moment we could speak, Rosey and I learned that our only weapon was to lie, and to hope never to be noticed. She said that the best thing a fairy could be was dead, and if we were ever taken by them that we should either kill them or hope to die trying. Still, I'd never had cause to take her warnings seriously. Not until today.

My heart raced as a large hand lunged toward me, aiming for the neckline of my dress. I could feel the fabric tighten as the chestnut-haired male dragged me to my feet. "What are you doing in the grass, girl?"

I opened my mouth wide and let out a high-pitched scream, using every ounce of air in my lungs. In a moment of panic, I swung my leg up and aimed a hard kick at the male's legs.

Chuckling, the male turned to his companion. "Vicious little thing, isn't it? Do you think it speaks the common language?"

"Leave her, Commander," the silver-haired male said flatly. "We hardly have time for this."

The commander yanked harder on my collar, shaking me so my feet dangled a few inches above the ground. "It's been many years since I encountered a human, but I daresay this one looks familiar."

"Familiar, sir?"

"Do you not see the resemblance? I think we've come across that Slúagh bitch's child."

The silver haired male stepped forward slightly, and I met his black eyes. He seemed to be trying to look through me, as if he could see something that was not there. Then, his brow furrowed and he shook his head. "Perhaps. But, if so, then that's even more reason to leave the child alone."

The commander ignored him. He leaned close to my face and spoke slowly and loudly, as if unsure if I understood him. "Slúagh, where is your mother?"

I tried to kick him again, and this time he dropped me. I landed hard on the ground, and gasped for air, my chest heaving as I let out another blood-curdling scream. The shadow of the male's hand loomed over me for a split second, poised to strike me across the face.

"Don't," the silver-haired male said sharply, grabbing his commander's arm and holding him back.

The commander swiveled his neck around, to look at his companion. His tone was sneering. "Am I offending you, Prince Ambrose? Do your delicate Seelie sensibilities extend to letting your heart bleed for humans?"

The other male's expression didn't change, and he looked bored as he made a derisive noise in the back of his throat. "Hardly, but if you murder Rhiannon's child before we've even seen her, it certainly won't win her over to your side. Is the greater good worth sacrificing over one human?"

"Fine," the commander growled after a pregnant pause. He bent down to my eye level. "Human, take me to your mother. Or I won't see any further reason to keep you alive."

I AWOKE TO A DULL THROBBING IN MY SKULL, AND THE FEELING OF the ground swaying beneath me.

My mind still chased the memory of my dream, which slipped further away with every passing second. Eyes closed, I tried to force myself to fall back into the story…to remember what happened next…but the face of the silver-haired fairy was lost.

The bed made a distinctive lurch, as if the floor really was moving, and my eyes snapped open. *What in the name of Aisling?*

Alarmed, I sat up with a start and looked around.

Wherever I was, the room was dark except for the faint glow of a wisp lamp. Bookshelves lined the room, and maps were tacked to every available open space on the wood paneled walls. I reached up and felt a lump on the back of my head, causing me to wince even as I sighed with frustration.

It had never once happened in the first twenty years of my life that I awoke with truly no notion of where I was or how I'd arrived there. In the past year, however, it happened so often that I was starting to become accustomed to confusion. *What a disheartening thought.*

The clink of metal on metal caught my attention, and I turned abruptly, making my head pound even more.

Ambrose Dullahan sat beside a foggy port window, his feet up on the wooden surface of a small table. I gaped at him, remembering the last thing I'd seen before something obviously struck me into unconsciousness. His smirking face blinked in the back of my memory, and anger rose in my chest.

"Where am I?" I demanded, my voice coming out raspy with disuse.

Dullahan looked up, eyes widening as if surprised to find me awake. He had changed his clothing since accosting me in the barn, and now wore a thin, off-white shirt with a tie undone at his throat. His sleeves were rolled up, and I could see more of the swirling black tattoos that adorned the right side of his throat covering the flesh of both arms. He held a sword nearly as long as I was tall across his lap, and those muscular, tattooed arms were busy polishing the blade with a cloth. On the table in front of him sat two bottles, one a dusty, amber-colored whisky, and the other a clear glass bottle with no label, filled with a moon-bright liquid.

"How's your head?" he asked casually.

I bit back an angry growl. "Painful, as you no doubt already know."

"My apologies for that, love. Would you like something to drink?"

In truth, I would've liked to take him up on the whisky, if only for my nerves, but out of pride I ignored the offer. "No, I'd like to know where I am, since obviously you've taken it upon yourself to kidnap me."

"Would you say this is kidnapping?" he asked thoughtfully. "I would view it more as speeding up the inevitable."

"Pardon?" I hissed. "What is that supposed to mean?"

"Only that you would have eventually decided to join me on your own, I've simply made that decision easier for you."

I scoffed. "All you fucking royals are so damned entitled. You think you can make decisions for everyone just because you were born lucky."

"Whatever you say, love." He looked back down at his sword and continued polishing, as if he hadn't a care in the world. "But I thought you'd softened to royals as of late."

I felt heat creep up my cheeks. What did he mean by that? Was he such a talented seer that he'd had a front row seat to everything I'd done in the last weeks, or was he simply making an observation based on the distress I'd shown when the castle crumbled with Bael and Scion still inside? I looked down, hiding my burning face. "Even if I have, it doesn't make it any less true that you all think you can drag me around without any concern for my opinion."

"Fair enough," he said flatly. "It did seem easier to beg for forgiveness than ask for your permission. My apologies once again."

I blinked at him, more confused now than ever.

Only last night I'd sat with Bael and Scion discussing the likelihood that the male in front of me would kill me, but clearly I wasn't dead...yet. Stranger still, neither Bael nor Scion had apologized to me upon our first meeting, or indeed, admitted they might have any faults until we'd grown to know each other well. When judged against his peers, Ambrose Dullahan was almost... nice. Or, as nice as anyone who'd struck me in the back of the head could be.

Deciding to press my luck for more information, I sat up straighter and leaned toward him, "I want to know where we are."

"On my ship." His response was delivered with an almost chilling calmness, as he reached up to a map pinned on the wall behind him. Pressing his pointer finger into the space between the island of Nevermore, and the coast of Inbetwixt, he shrugged. "Somewhere in this vicinity."

Cold dread washed over me. "That's impossible—" I blurted out, only to break off, a hacking cough bursting from my mouth as pain shot up my throat.

Any other time, the fact that lying had once again caused me pain would be of far larger concern. Now, however, it barely registered in the face of far worse things. The third hunt would have taken place in Nevermore, had the kingdom not fallen beforehand. Perhaps the original theory Bael and I had devised while in Inbetwixt was correct after all, and I was being ferried to the winter island only to be murdered in the hunts.

Looking entirely unbothered by my coughing fit, Ambrose plucked the unlabeled, white bottle from the table, he held it out to me. "Drink this, it will help."

I swallowed again, but didn't take the bottle. As the burning subsided, I narrowed my eyes. "That's not water."

He glanced down at the translucent white liquid shimmering in the bottle. "I never said it was, but it's not poison either if that's what you're concerned about."

I scowled. The fact that it might be poison had not even yet occurred to me.

If he wanted to kill me here and now, rather than waiting for some opportune moment in the future, he undoubtedly would have already. Still, I should have been more vigilant, just as I should have paid better attention in the stables. I'd heard a second sound on the other side of the barn before his presence in front of me had erased it from my mind. Now, I realized there must have been an accomplice waiting to strike.

The too-late realization didn't make the blow to my head or my pride hurt any less, nor did it change the fact that we were in the middle of the ocean.

"What are you planning to do to me?" I asked.

"I wasn't planning to do anything to you, per se. *With you*, might be better phrasing."

"What are you planning to do with me then," I asked, trying not to roll my eyes. This situation was far too serious for such pointless word games.

He tried to shove the bottle into my hand again. "Drink this and I'll tell you."

I cast a suspicious glance at the bottle. I wasn't about to take any food or drink from a male who'd knocked me unconscious, only to force me onto a ship. "No."

He looked apologetic. "For all our sake, love, I really must insist."

"Why do you care? What is it?"

I wasn't really expecting him to answer, but to my surprise he immediately replied. "It's diluted Gancanagh's dust, mixed with sea water and clary sage, and I care because—"

My eyes widened. *Shit.*

He didn't get a chance to finish the sentence, as I was already leaping off the bed and rushing for the door. Nice? I couldn't believe I'd thought so for even a moment. The rebel leader was the complete opposite of nice, if this was what he was trying to give me. "Stay the fuck away from me."

I'd learned of the existence of Gancanagh's dust back in the brothel in Inbetwixt. It was a fairy drug, that caused insatiable lust, lack of inhibition, and with too much use would eventually lead to madness. Scion and I had fallen under its effects, leading to the bite mark now permanent on my throat. At the time, we'd been trying to discover where Ambrose Dullahan and his army were, and learned instead that they were transporting the dust in and out of Elsewhere and the neighboring country of Underneath, by way of Inbetwixt harbor.

We'd never learned what they were doing with the drugs, but now, I supposed, I knew where at least some of the horrible substance had ended up.

My fingertips gripped the metal handle of the door, and I pulled, only to jerk back when I found it locked.

Behind me, I heard Dullahan rise from his seat and move toward me. "Wait, you don't understand."

I turned and pressed my back against the door. I shrank away, and threw a hand up to block him. I still didn't know exactly how to summon magic at will, and feared what would happen when I used it, however right now I would be more than happy to summon afflicted to my side if it meant avoiding the rebel king. "Don't touch me. I know what that does."

"You don't know anything," Ambrose spat. "You're proving why this is necessary without even realizing it."

As he moved closer, I felt the telltale heat of magic rising to my fingertips. "Oh?" I let out a slightly hysterical laugh. "And how is that?"

"You have no idea how to control yourself, and I'm not about to let you figure it out on a wooden ship in the middle of the ocean."

"There is no world where you can force that down my throat."

He let out a humorless laugh. "I don't typically force women to do anything. Yes, this is Gancanagh's dust, but it's significantly diluted. In this state it's used to prevent magic. Put your damn hands down and I'll explain how it works."

I scoffed, trying to seem unbothered, but in truth I was nearly trembling. As if sparked by my fear, a flame lit in my shaking hand. I looked at it for half a second, shimmering with blue and orange, before Dullahan's own hand shot out and he grabbed my arm.

He forced my hand to close before dragging me forward away from the door. He barely seemed to feel it as I kicked out, landing a blow against his abdomen. Winding his fingers into my hair, he pulled my head back, and dragged me around until my back pressed against his chest. The white bottle dangled in his hand, next to my face.

"Drink," he said harshly, his breath hot against my ear.

"Make me," I spat. "Is this your idea of not doing anything to me?"

"Fine." He let out a growl of frustration, then flipped our positions. With one hand on my throat, he held me against the wall. Unstoppering the bottle with his teeth, he spat the cork onto the floor and pressed the mouth of the bottle against my lips. "Don't be so fucking stubborn. It won't hurt you, just make it so you can't burn the damn ship down."

I longed to throw a retort back, but I refused to open my mouth. I choked, and clawed at his hand as he pressed the bottle harder against my lips. I kept my teeth pressed firmly together, and refused to relent even as he squeezed my neck. I narrowed my eyes at him in defiance, silently telling him he'd have to knock me unconscious before I stopped fighting him.

His black eyes bore into me, looking more conflicted than angry. "I hate hurting you, Elowyn, but I will. Don't make the mistake of thinking you mean more to me than the greater good."

I gave him a questioning look. Why would I think that? Why would I think I meant anything to him at all, much less more than whatever he believed his mission to be?

With an apologetic look, his fingers tightened and finally, I gasped for breath. Not wasting a second, he shoved the little bottle into my open mouth and tipped the entire contents down my throat.

The potion tasted bitter, like wine gone bad. I coughed, and tried to spit it out, but couldn't entirely manage not to swallow. Roughly half the liquid trickled down my throat, and I waited in abject terror for the effects of the dust to take over, for my vision to blur, and that uncontrollable lust to cloud my mind.

Nothing happened.

Looking satisfied, Dullahan let me go and stomped back across the room toward his chair. "See? I told you, love, it won't hurt you."

I struggled for breath, gasping, as I massaged my throat. "I'm just waiting to feel whatever horrible effect you intended."

"Wait forever if you must, but you won't feel anything. In its original state, Gancanagh's dust removes all inhibitions. We've blended it with other herbs, to instead rob Fae of their magic before battles. Otherwise, it would be pointless to train human soldiers."

I narrowed my eyes. "I suppose I should simply be grateful to still have my clothes on."

He cast an almost offended look at me. "I wouldn't harm you, Elowyn...at least, not in such a lasting way."

"You didn't seem to have any problem hurting others while you destroyed the palace, or on the docks the other night."

He raised his eyebrows. "Others, certainly, but not you."

I didn't know what to make of that, much less what to say, and so fell silent, leaning against the door while I struggled to gain control over my frantically beating heart.

I had to admit—albeit begrudgingly—that he was correct. I didn't feel any different, but if his explanation was true, then he'd not only prevented me from defending myself, but also from leaving through the shadows.

The reality of the situation, and how far we were from the shore suddenly hit me with renewed force, and for the first time real fear outweighed my anger. "Even if you have stopped me from using magic, it doesn't matter. I've killed Fae before without magic, I'm sure I can do it again."

He laughed. "I don't doubt that, but you won't."

"Are you truly so arrogant that you don't think I could ever hurt you?"

"Not at all," he replied. "I'm sure you will kill me eventually, but not today, and not for a very long time."

I stared at him, nonplussed. He spoke in even more infuriating riddles than any Fae I'd ever met. "I won't hurt you." "I'm sure you'll kill me…" What was I supposed to make of that?

As I remained silent, questions flitting through my mind, Ambrose rose and took a step toward the door. I furrowed my brow. "Where are you going?"

He cast a look back at me. "To dinner. I've spent the better part of a day watching you, and now that you're awake and subdued, I'm going to go eat."

"First tell me where we're going," I demanded. "You dragged me onto this ship for a reason, no doubt, and I deserve to know what for?"

His lip curled. "Oh you do, do you? I don't see any reason why I should tell you anything."

"I…" I trailed off, and snapped my lips shut, unable to think of any argument to the contrary. I supposed if his goal was to murder me in Nevermore, then he really wouldn't have much reason to give me prior warning.

In the silence that followed, my stomach growled loudly.

Dullahan grinned even wider. "Would you care to join me for dinner?"

"No," I replied automatically.

It had been some weeks since I'd felt truly disadvantaged around the Fae, but all those feelings of helplessness and inferiority were swiftly returning in Ambrose Dullahan's presence. He'd robbed me of my only defense, and now I was as much at his mercy as I had been of the other Everlasts in the dungeon, or during the hunts.

The truth was that it had been mostly Bael who kept me alive in those first days, and Scion in recent weeks. Without the use of magic, I had little defenses, and was just as helpless as I'd been before.

"How's this, Elowyn," Ambrose said, hovering by the door. "You must join me for meals, and so long as you're sitting at the dinner table I will tell you anything you like." His grin took on a wicked gleam. "You will not eat while on this ship unless it's with me, and for every question I answer, you must answer one of mine in return."

My eyes narrowed. That was not going to happen. "How could you possibly have questions for me, when you know everything about everyone in the world?"

He pressed his hands into his pockets and moved around me to reach the door. "I suppose you'll have to come to dinner and ask."

"No," I said stubbornly.

He shrugged, and reached for the handle of the door again. "Fine. Come and find me when you change your mind. I expect hunger will overtake your spitefulness eventually."

I fumed. *Fucking rebels. Fucking...fairies.*

No matter how much my opinion on certain Fae had changed lately, I was always rudely reminded that on a whole, most were spiteful, wicked creatures who took pleasure in tormenting me. Ambrose Dullahan was no different from the nightmares I'd had all my life.

"Wait," I said suddenly, as the object of my derision moved to close the door behind him.

Dullahan looked back, his expression curious, rather than angry. "Have you changed your mind so soon?" he asked in an almost pleasant tone. No doubt he was putting on an act, luring me into a false sense of security. I would not fall for it.

"So, if I refuse to eat with you, am I to be a prisoner here?"

He cocked his head. "We are all prisoners here. We're in the middle of the ocean, Elowyn."

"But do you intend to keep me in this room forever, or am I allowed to see the sun at some point?"

He seemed to think about it, then shrugged. "I suppose there's no reason you shouldn't be allowed to go where you wish aboard the ship, but be careful. Don't do anything foolish."

"Like what?" I asked, in spite of myself.

"Like trying to escape. You would not make it very far, as even I could not swim to shore from here without falling prey to one of the creatures that lurk beneath the waves."

"Fine." I smiled, picturing him being eaten whole by some slimy serpentine creature. I supposed there was always hope he'd fall overboard. Fall, or get pushed…whichever.

He took another step toward the door, holding it open this time as he hovered on the threshold. "Oh, and don't think you can sneak down to the galley and I won't know about it. You will not eat unless it is with me, and should you try, I'll know." He tapped his temple. "I know nearly everything that goes on this ship."

My smile fell from my lips.

That had indeed been what I'd planned to do; find my own food, then perhaps steal a life boat and make my escape. "If I didn't know you were an Everlast, I would now. All of you love to offer bargains, and throw me around as if it's your source-given right to do so. You're exactly like your family."

He glanced over his shoulder at me as he unlocked the door, and his black eyes flashed with sudden anger. "Wrong, love. I'm nothing like them. I'm worse."

20
LONNIE

ABOARD THE FORESIGHT

Several hours passed, and I laid flat on my back on the creaky, single-person bed, my eyes squeezed shut. I remembered Scion's explanation that his brother was not omniscient, but I wasn't willing to risk it. If the Dullahan really could see everything within the ship, all he would see of me was that I was sleeping. He wouldn't know that I was waiting for the sun to set outside the small port window, or that I was silently planning my escape.

There was no possible way I would willingly remain on this ship, bound for Aisling knew where, without any means of protection. Neither though, did I think I could fight my way out. I assumed that the ship's crew was made up of the same rebels who had stormed the obsidian castle, and attacked our party in the harbor. Whatever else one might say about them, it was clear they were well trained and fiercely loyal to their leader. It seemed unlikely therefore that I'd be able to hold my own against any of them, or find a friend on the ship to help me.

I was well and truly on my own, but that only made me more determined to escape.

As the sun slowly descended below the horizon, the once busy sounds of the crew working on deck began to fade. I supposed they would all have to eat eventually, and perhaps there was less to do on a ship like this during the evening. Not that I had any idea what sort of ship we were on, but I imagined it must be large to carry an entire army to Nevermore, or wherever else we might be going.

Finally, when the sky outside the window was nearing total darkness, I rose from the bed.

Creeping toward the door as if my mere footsteps would send the rebels running, I held my breath and tried the latch. To my shock, it opened readily, and a huge gust of salty winter air flew in to greet me. It rustled the maps on the wall, and the tattered ruins of my clothing—still destroyed from the last few days' events.

Something between frustration and embarrassment washed over me. Had I truly never bothered to try the door until now? I'd assumed it was locked, but apparently the Dullahan had kept his first promise too: I was allowed to roam the ship, I was simply not allowed to leave.

I peered outside and took one cautious step onto the deck, then gasped. The sky was wider than I'd ever seen, every tiny star somehow brighter and more lovely than I'd ever noticed before. The rush of waves moving past the ship was almost soothing, and though the air was cold, it didn't hurt my skin as I moved further out of the cabin.

The ship was massive, its deck stretching the length of several royal dining halls, and it stood completely and utterly empty. I'd thought I might need to sneak past a guard, or avoid the evening crew, but I was entirely alone in the middle of the star-filled darkness.

For a long moment, I simply stood, marveling at the beauty of the silent ship, then I shook my head. What was I doing? One only knew how long I would have before someone else came out to work, or because of the sounds of my feet. There was no better time than now to search for a way to escape.

I didn't allow myself to worry about Ambrose Dullahan or his visions as I made my way around the edge of the ship. Either he would see me, and come running, or he wouldn't. There wasn't a single thing I could do about it either way, but I could do my very best to leave this cursed ship in the meantime.

The ship was long, with a deck reachable by stairs on either side. The cabin I'd been sleeping in must have been Ambrose's personal cabin, as it was the only one accessible from the main deck. On the opposite side of the ship, below the huge wooden steering wheel, was another door that I presumed led to the lower levels.

As I passed the wheel of the ship, I had a moment of alarm, realizing there was no one up there steering. Then, I noticed that while the waves crashed against the sides of the boat, we didn't appear to be moving much at all. I supposed the wind was not strong enough to carry on, and Ambrose had allowed the crew a brief rest, as we drifted softly on the waves.

That, or this was some elaborate ruse, meant to give me hope of escape only to snatch it back again when the crew emerged from wherever they were hiding.

In truth, both options seemed equally plausible.

Quickening my steps in case I had less time than I thought, I continued my inspection of the ship. I'd never been aboard one before, but I thought there must be some smaller boats somewhere, to escape in the case of a crash, or perhaps to row to shore when anchored.

Finally, tied to the edge of the ship with two long, thick ropes, I found what I was looking for. A rowboat, no larger than the bed I'd woken up in, hung ready to be lowered to the water below. It didn't look large enough to carry more than one person, but that didn't matter. I didn't need a large vessel, only one that would not capsize.

Leaning my head over the edge of the ship, I took a quick survey of the water below and the distance to reach it. Immediately, it became clear that there was another problem beyond any monsters in the water. We must be very close to Nevermore, as large chunks of ice floated along the waves, bumping against the hull of the ship.

In a ship this size, the ice hardly mattered, but in the small rowboat…Well, I supposed I would just have to be careful to avoid it. Despite Ambrose's warnings about the creatures that lurked beneath the oceans, I would much rather face them than the creatures aboard this ship.

Clambering up onto the side of the ship, I put one leg over the edge, and eased myself down onto the small rowboat.

Immediately, my heart flew into my throat as the boat sank several feet downwards before jerking to a halt. I froze, and my breath heaved, as I sat perfectly still for a moment, processing the realization that I had not just fallen fifty feet into freezing water.

I swallowed a fearful gulp, and looked up at the two creaking ropes that held the boat, and me inside it, suspended in the air. There was a pulley on one rope, clearly intended to lower one's self down slowly, although after that fall I was not sure how much I trusted its strength.

Still, I had little other choice. Now, hanging midway between the deck and the water, I couldn't pull myself back up onto the ship even if I wanted to. There was nowhere to go but down.

Gripping the rope in both hands, I took a deep breath and began to lower myself down into the waiting water.

There were no further problems as I slowly descended, and after a minute of straining my arms, I felt the bottom of the boat touch down. The water seemed more ominous from here, and the waves larger. I shivered when the salty spray hit my face, lapped against the edges of the boat, and sprayed over the sides to pool by my feet.

Looking out into the silent night, I suddenly became aware of the vastness of the ocean, and the empty skyline ahead. Had this been a fool's errand, and now I would find myself sinking to the bottom of the ocean, just as Ambrose had warned? Perhaps, but if so, it was better than a death in the hunts in Nevermore, or whatever else the rebels intended for me.

Resolute, I reached for the oars on the bottom of the boat, and used one to push off from the side of the large ship.

I ROWED FOR SEVERAL MINUTES, AND BARELY FELT LIKE I'D MOVED an inch.

Already my arms were aching, and my belly growling with hunger. I wouldn't be able to keep this up for more than a night —perhaps two.

Judging from the cold, I supposed we were closer to the winter Island of Nevermore than even I'd thought, and therefore decided to row in the direction the ship had been traveling in hopes that I would reach the island faster than the mainland of Elsewhere.

That decision, however, presented its own challenges.

The ice was harder to avoid than I'd anticipated, and all too often I had to stop to go around some tiny, snowy iceberg, so that after what I thought was a full hour of rowing, I could still see the rebel ship in the distance.

I pulled my oars back into the boat, and flopped on my back to rest. The wet, wooden floor of the boat was hardly comfortable, but I didn't care, my exhaustion taking over.

I would just rest for a minute…maybe two.

As soon as my eyelids fluttered shut, a loud thud echoed from the side of my small boat. My heart raced as I sat up and scanned the dark water. *Shit!*

Suddenly, another force slammed into the side of my vessel, causing it to rock violently. Panic rising in my chest, I braced myself against the sides, unsure of what was trying to tip me overboard.

Despite whatever reassurances I had given myself regarding Ambrose's warnings, the last thing I wanted was to be devoured by a sea creature.

I grabbed for my oar, and held it aloft as if it were a battle ax. Holding my breath, I waited for whatever had knocked into me to surface again. A long silence stretched, and I began to feel foolish. Maybe I'd imagined it. Maybe it had been nothing more than ice, and I was overreacting.

A towering wall of water suddenly rose, and crashed down on me, soaking my clothes and skin. Then as I cleared the water from my eyes, a colossal tentacle burst from the ocean's depths and reached toward me with fierce determination.

In my panic, I completely forgot about trying to avoid detection from the distant ship and let out a blood-curdling scream. I closed my eyes, waiting for the huge sea beast to wrap its slimy arm around me and pull me beneath the waves.

A heavy weight landed in the middle of my boat and I flinched, unwilling to look at what might have climbed within, except...

"There you are, love."

A large, distinctly human feeling hand wrapped around my upper arm, and then, the familiar feeling of being pulled through the shadows overtook all my other senses.

Suddenly, we were landing back on the deck of the ship. As soon as my feet hit the wood, Ambrose released his grip and I stumbled forward, crashing to my hands and knees. Salt water sloshed around in my mouth and nose, making it hard to breathe. I coughed and sputtered, struggling to catch my breath. My whole body shook uncontrollably, teeth clattering together from the cold.

I felt his presence looming behind me, and pushed up to sitting before turning to look.

Like me, Ambrose was drenched and his shirt clung to his chiseled muscles. However, unlike my shivering from the cold, he shook with fury. His body was rigid and his expression was a steely mask of anger. "What the fuck were you thinking?"

"That I would rather drown than be a prisoner," I sniped back.

"Stupid Slúagh," he hissed. "You were not a prisoner, but after this, all you've done is force me to make you one."

I reeled back, more surprised by the use of the slur than anything else. "Is that how you talk to your human rebels, Dullahan? Or, should I call you Prince Ambrose?"

His eyes widened, and he seemed a bit surprised himself, as if only now realizing what he'd said. Then, he stiffened, and his face returned to its flat, emotionless look. "Get up."

"No," I said instinctively.

He reached for my arm and dragged me to my feet. "If you don't get warm you'll die anyway, and then I'll have wasted my time for nothing."

He was right. My teeth chattered and I could hardly feel my arms and legs, let alone my fingers, which made it hard to protest as he half dragged, half carried me across the deck to his cabin. As we walked, I saw that most of the crew had emerged from below deck and were watching us with expressions varying from curiosity, to anger, to smug satisfaction. I refused to meet anyone's eyes, and let my wet hair fall down into my face.

Ambrose reached his cabin and kicked the door open, before stepping inside and slamming it shut behind us. A cold, uncomfortable silence fell over the room.

He released his grip on me and marched toward a trunk at the end of the bed, which I had barely noticed until now. He forcefully lifted the lid and grabbed a shirt and what appeared to be trousers before tossing them in my direction. The fabric hit me in the face with a gentle slap, but I managed to catch them before they fell to the floor.

"Put those on," Ambrose demanded, before pulling out another shirt and trousers, presumably for himself.

My numb, red fingers shook as I held up the shirt to inspect it. It was massive, clearly meant for him, and would probably be the size of a tent on me. Still, I preferred it to the wet, torn clothing I currently wore. "Fine." My voice quivered and my teeth clacked together. "Get out so I can change."

He looked up at me with a mean smirk. "Absolutely not. I'm not going anywhere if you're just going to try to run away again."

I pressed my lips together and tried to stop shaking. I was not, in fact, planning to run away again. Even if I hadn't destroyed the only boat, I now realized I would likely be better off waiting until we arrived wherever we were going and trying to slip away there, then launching myself back into the unforgiving ocean. I didn't bother to explain that, however. He never would've believed me.

Instead, I stood a bit straighter, trying to regain some of my dignity. "You can't stay with me at every moment. Even you have to sleep."

"Yes," he said, reclining backwards on the bed. "And I'll do so right here where I'll hear you if you try to leave."

I blanched. "Where do you expect me to sleep?" I asked, already sure I knew the answer.

He looked sideways at me, before casting his gaze onto the edge of the small bed. "Here is fine, or the floor. Your choice."

I gritted my teeth. "You cannot be serious."

He didn't look at me, but his lips tipped up in a smile. "You'll soon realize, love, that I am always serious. I have no time for games."

21
SCION
THE QUARRY, INBETWIXT

"This is a miserable place to hold the hunts," Bael said, clambering over a group of jagged rocks, and stepping gingerly onto the mud on the opposite side. "There are more spirits here than even in the woods by the palace."

Glancing back at him, I rolled my eyes. "You never cared what the hunting grounds looked like before."

"There are a lot of things I never cared about until recently."

I paused, refusing to indulge the conversation he was clearly trying to trap me into having. "True enough."

It was nearing nightfall when we left the inn and arrived in the forest near the quarry to hunt for one of the old ones.

The obsidian quarry in Inbetwixt had been exhausted and abandoned for over a hundred years, leaving behind a massive crater that gradually filled with rainwater to become a seemingly bottomless lake. The lake was home to many monsters, including the enormous serpent that guarded the surrounding woods.

I hadn't met the snake myself, but from Bael's description, I agreed that it was one of the old ones—the ancient creatures that had protected this land long before the Fae ever arrived. We might be the dominant race in Elsewhere, but we were far from the oldest, or even the most powerful. There were things in the depths of the Waywoods, the high mountains of Nevermore, and the swampland of the Wanderlust that even I feared.

"What do you plan to do when we find it," Bael asked, his tone unnaturally cheerful.

"Ask our questions, then kill it before it kills us first."

"I'm not sure it's possible to kill one of the old ones."

I didn't look back at him, this time keeping my gaze on the steep, muddy ground so as not to slip. "Anything can be killed with enough effort."

I fell silent again as we trudged closer and closer to the murky, algae-covered edge of the lake, my boots sinking slightly into the muck with each step. My mind raced with half-formed ideas on how to lure the monster out of hiding and toward us.

"Forget killing it," I commented. "How do you suggest we find it?"

Even without looking, I could tell Bael was grinning from his tone. "We could use your bird as bait. It would be like killing two birds with one snake."

I kicked a stray rock at him. "Fuck off, be serious."

"I was," he replied. "I'd be perfectly happy to be rid of that cursed creature. But in truth, I expect it won't matter. We will not have to do the finding."

"What do you mean?"

He nodded toward the water through the trees. "From the looks of that, *it* will find *us*."

Frowning, I followed his gaze, squinting at the amorphous shapes floating over the surface ahead. We were still some fifty paces away from the edge of the water, and for a long moment, I couldn't tell what I was looking at. Then, as realization dawned, I turned away swallowing the bile rising in my throat.

Rotting bodies, bloated and practically unrecognizable, floated over the surface of the water. I could only assume they'd been here since the second hunt, which meant well over a fortnight. Anything that disposed of its prey like that was a creature I had no desire to ever meet.

For her, though, I would face any number of murderous creatures.

Waking up this morning to find Lonnie gone had caused a torrent of mixed emotions. I was livid, and more importantly, terrified of what might have happened to her. But also, somewhere in the back of my mind, I was relieved.

Guilt ate at me for feeling that way, but I'd spent every waking moment of the night before dreading the inevitable conversation of the morning. She'd expect some kind of explanation and I couldn't give that to her.

I knew Bael believed Lonnie to be my mate as well—he'd done everything to make that clear but scrawl the words across my forehead—but still, I couldn't agree with him. I didn't feel it.

He was right about one thing though: mate or not, I loved her.

I loved her enough that I hadn't been able to stay away when somehow I felt the pain of her flesh being pierced by the arrow. I loved her enough that I'd been unable to let her die, even when it meant deepening the connection that was already driving me insane. And I loved her enough that if she asked me directly, I wouldn't be able to lie.

So I could never let her ask.

That was too cruel, even for me, to insert myself in the middle of a mating bond I had no right to destroy.

Last night was a one-time mistake, and now, losing her felt like the gods swift punishment. I'd never realized what it truly meant to be cursed with misery. Now, I wondered how I'd ever managed to live this long with the despair constantly finding ways to torment me.

I would help Bael find Lonnie, and then I'd leave. I'd let them go off on their adventure alone, just as I'd tried to do back in Inbetwixt, and I'd find a way to defy the prophecy my brother had made, and never let her become my wife.

My thoughts came crashing to a halt as behind me, an ominous rattling sounded and I whipped around. Bael, several paces back, had also turned to look. Without my realizing it, or even thinking of where we were going, we'd reached the edge of the dark, churning water.

Bael swiveled back around, and we made meaningful eye contact before moving as one closer to the water itself.

I held my breath and waited for a long heartbeat, then another. Nothing moved in the forest or beneath the surface of the lake, and I relaxed slightly. Opening my mouth to suggest we keep moving, my words were lost as a menacing voice hummed through the trees, seeming to come from everywhere and nowhere at the same time. "Is thisss my reward?"

I spun in a circle, searching for the voice, then halted. My stomach turned over, horror flooding me as a massive blue-black serpent emerged from the water, its scales gleaming in the setting sun.

My blood ran cold. How the fuck had Lonnie escaped this thing? And worse, why the fuck had I insisted she enter the second hunt alone?

I didn't have long to dwell.

The snake's sharp gaze locked onto me as its forked tongue flicked out of its mouth, tasting the air between us like it was salivating at the thought of devouring both of us in one gulp. Its scales glittered as it coiled and uncoiled, its eyes fixed on me.

My heart pounded against my chest as I stood frozen, unable to move as if in a trance. My fingers tingled as I thrust my hand forward, instinctively, aiming to halt it with my magic.

"No!" Bael's voice rose in a desperate yell, and he forcefully pulled my arm back. "Stop! We need it alive."

The shadows that I held in my hand dissipated quickly, and I scowled at my cousin. We also needed *us* alive, but I couldn't deny he had a point. We'd come all this way, and despite my best efforts I couldn't think of another way to find Lonnie.

I lowered my hand slowly, keeping a shred of magic tingling on my fingertips, just to be safe. Perhaps this had been a foolish plan—a deadly mistake.

"Have you brought me royal blood?" The creature's enormous head lowered until it was level with mine, swaying back and forth, mesmerizing me with its movements. "Are you here to repay my kindnessss?"

"What kindness?" I asked, half-entranced by its swaying head.

"What kindnessss," the snake repeated, its voice rising as if in excitement…or anger. "What kindnessss, asks the king, as if I have not been waiting far too long for my prize. As if I am not ssstarving. Ravenousss."

Bael and I glanced at each other, and I could tell instantly we were of the same mind. This had been a fucking terrible idea, and likely a deadly mistake. If both of us left this lake unscathed, it would be a damned gift from the Source.

Hiding his hands behind his back, no doubt to maintain some element of surprise should he decide to use his magic, Bael stepped forward toward the snake. He smiled pleasantly, and offered it a courtly bow. "Forgive us, old one, allow me to introduce myself, I'm—"

"I know who you are, ssshadow prince." It thrashed its long tail, and the water splashed some twenty feet into the air, the floating bodies churning on the newly formed waves. "I know all that goes on in these woodsss."

I swallowed thickly, before offering a bow of my own. The back of my neck prickled, and I stood quickly, not liking the feeling of taking my eyes off that enormous swaying head even for a moment. "That is why we've come to you, old one," I said quickly. "To seek your assistance."

"Assssssistance," it hissed, drawing the word out so it echoed all around the quarry. "Why should I offer anything, when the lassst favor I granted has not been repaid?"

Again, Bael and I shared a look. It was entirely too focused on whatever bargain it had recently made to be of any use. Perhaps, then, we should leave and find another way?

I widened my eyes at Bael, trying to convey with a look that we should retreat while we both still breathed. Evidently, he misunderstood my meaning.

"What was your bargain?" Bael asked the snake. "And with whom?"

The serpent hissed in rhythm, almost as if it were laughing. Its twisted mouth curled into a sinister smile. "The queen...Ssshe promisssed me her life in exchange for another. Her mortal blood, for that of a born royal. Ssso, I ask you again, are you here to repay her debt?"

Shock rocked me. "The queen" could only mean Lonnie. This, then, was her bargain. This was how she'd escaped during the hunt—by offering another in her place.

I couldn't help but wonder who Lonnie had planned to offer up as a sacrifice to the snake in order to save her own skin. And deep down, I knew it was me.

I almost couldn't blame her.

That thought rattled around the back of my mind, and I warred with myself. On the one hand, I wanted nothing more than to fix this for her. Give her no other reasons to hate me, and ensure she would never doubt my love for her again. On the other hand, perhaps it was fate that I'd heard this. Perhaps it would be all the easier to walk away from her now, knowing that not so very long ago she'd meant to offer me a gruesome death.

Perhaps it wouldn't matter either way, because the snake had every likelihood of ending my life before I ever saw Lonnie again.

"Answer me," the snake demanded. "I am famissshed, ssstarved, Unsatisssfied."

"We didn't know of the bargain," Bael said. "But if we could negotiate the terms, perhaps we can all come away with a boon."

The snake assessed him, and was silent for a long moment, evidently thinking. "What do you ssseek?"

"The queen who bargained with you…do you know her whereabouts at this very moment?"

The snake cocked its head, looking almost surprised before it replied just as slowly. "Yessss."

Bael straightened, as if steeling himself. "Tell us, and you can take my blood as payment."

The snake's tongue shot out again, whiplike. "The bastard born blood of a lesser prince is hardly a prize."

"What say you to the blood of two kingdoms?" Bael asked confidently.

I gaped at him. We never spoke of Bael's parentage, even among ourselves. It was as if to admit it aloud, to acknowledge the unseelie, would be to put power behind it. Of course, for some years now it had been harder and harder to deny who his father was, but suspicions were nothing to confirmations.

"Shut up," I murmured. "No good can come from this."

Indeed, Bael didn't have a chance to answer before my prediction came true. The snake made an angry hissing sound, and thrashed its long tail once again. "I do know of your parentage, Prince Baelfry, but I do not recognize the court of the unseelie, as I was born before their country was ever formed. Your blood, therefore, is only half royal, and would only sssatisfy me if I were to have all of it."

That settled it. *Fuck this.*

We'd find another way. Shit, I'd track down my source-forsaken brother if we needed a seer this badly. There was no world in which we'd learn anything useful from this horrible creature.

"Let's go," I said, wanting to leave no room for Bael to misunderstand me once more. "We can find her another way."

The snake bent its enormous head even lower, swaying in front of me so I found my eyes flicking back and forth, trying to hold its gaze. "Go then," it said. "You might find your wife without my help, King of Elsewhere, but it is unlikely that you will do so."

My mind went blank, every thought fleeing, as if time around me had come to a screeching halt. Bael whipped around to stare at me, his expression as astonished as my own had to be. I felt my mouth fall open, and heard my own voice as if it came from someone else. "She's not my wife."

The snake opened its huge mouth wide, showing rows of razor teeth. I flinched, and it let out another hissing laugh. "You marked her, did you not? Allowed her to claim you in return, and shared blood as well as flesh. Queen Elowyn is your wife in the eyes of this land, and you her king consort."

My heart raced as I looked at the snake, my mind struggling to comprehend the words it spoke. The fact that it had just uttered her true name—something I'd wanted to know for well over a year—hardly mattered in the face of this new information. Even the fact that the old one had named me king barely registered, my mind too full of the echoing words: *my wife, my wife, my wife.*

"Take my blood instead, then, in exchange for her whereabouts," I blurted out.

Flicking its tongue out to taste the air around me, the snake paused, seeming to savor the moment. "A generous offer, King of Elsewhere," it said, "But perhapsss not a wise one."

"Wait," Bael said, seeming as eager to save my life as I'd been to save his. "What if—"

I cut him off, speaking only to the snake. "Take the offer, for there will not be another."

"Indeed, I accept your offer."

I stood perfectly still as the serpent slithered forward, its long, slim body coiled tightly around my torso, and it was nearly impossible not to move or fight it as it let out a sharp hiss.

"Tell us first," I said. "So I will be awake to hear the answer."

The snake moved faster, winding around and around as if it meant to squeeze the breath from me before using its long teeth. "The queen is still alive, and journeys by boat to the land of Underneath."

"Why?" I asked, my breath catching in my throat even as I fixed my gaze on Bael, begging him not to misunderstand what I could not say out loud.

Pain and illusion would not kill instantly, but Bael's magic could. He was better suited to killing in the short term than I was, and seconds could mean the difference between life and death if the snake decided against a mere taste of blood and intended to eat me whole.

Seeming to understand, my cousin nodded behind the serpent's huge head, and I gritted my teeth, hoping his aim had improved since the last time I'd seen him use his magic on something of this size.

"Why," I gasped, again, as massive jaws opened over me.

"To sssee the heir," it hissed, as its jaws closed around me. "The lassst true heir of Elsewhere."

22

BAEL

THE WAYWOODS, INBETWIXT

My heart pounded too fast as I kept my gaze fixed on the serpent.

The moment Scion had offered his blood to the snake and not struggled as it began to wind around him, I'd known what he was planning. I so rarely got to use the strongest of my magical abilities, because instant death wasn't all that useful except on a battlefield, and I'd never been allowed to set foot on one.

From an early age, I'd been capable of destroying multiple lives with one wave of the hand. The problem was, and always had been, that I enjoyed doing it.

It didn't seem to matter to my family that I was far from the only one with that particular character flaw. They didn't acknowledge or care that both my uncles had been far more blood thirsty than I ever was, or that Scion crippled anyone who mildly annoyed him. They didn't want to think that perhaps I'd inherited a love of violence from their side of the family, and it had nothing to do with my father. No, the family line had always been that I was broken, dangerous, and too Unseelie to be trusted.

The family had worried for years that my control would waver, and I'd destroy far more than their intended target. I didn't have to summon power as others did. No, my issue was keeping it under control, and not letting it leak out. Destruction always lingered just below my skin and I myself wasn't entirely sure how precise my aim was. There was no time like a life-or-death situation to find out.

As the snake lowered its jaws over Scion's head, I raised a hand, and in a blink the creature was gone. Surrounded by a mound of ash and crumbling scales, Scion sat on the ground, his face completely drained of color.

My hands were trembling, and I could feel the magic coursing through my body as I approached to offer him a hand up. "Are you alright?"

Breathing heavily, my cousin looked up at me. He scrutinized my trembling palm with apprehension, before hesitantly grasping it and allowing me to help him up.

"I'm fucking fine...obviously," he said roughly. "More importantly, are you alright?"

I wanted to laugh, but I was too exhausted to even manage a chuckle. He had just been moments away from being devoured in front of me, yet he seemed more worried about the energy it took for me to kill the creature attacking him.

What did that say about my family's faith in my control? Nothing I wasn't already well aware of, I supposed.

"I'll be fine," I told Scion. "I just need to rest for a bit."

A bit, or several days—but I didn't want to alarm him.

"Are you close to draining?" Scion asked.

I shook my head, because I wasn't sure I could deny it out loud. Even if I was close to using too much magic, I wasn't sure I could die from drain, as others could. I'd shift before reaching that point…though, that was almost as dangerous.

"What about Lonnie?" Scion demanded.

I pressed a hand to my throbbing temple. "What about her?"

"Did you use her power as well?"

I shook my head. "Our bond isn't sealed, and I haven't shared power with her in weeks."

"But, the last time you used that power—"

"I know," I cut him off, thinking darkly of the afflicted attack in Inbetwixt where I'd nearly drained not only myself, but Lonnie as well. "But I'm telling you she's fine."

Mates could share power back and forth, giving bonded groups a nearly unlimited supply of magical life force. *Nearly unlimited*, being the operative phrase. It was a useful side effect of mating that each partner would become more powerful, however the danger was that once one mate drained, they'd start feeding off the power of the other. It was possible, therefore, for one mate to kill the other by mistake.

I'd nearly drained Lonnie on the day after the second hunt while escaping from the afflicted, and sent her into a coma for several days. Now, though, that was unlikely to reoccur. At least, not unless I could mimic Scion, and find some way around the curse that prevented us from sealing our bond.

I glanced at my cousin, who looked relieved now, that at least Lonnie was not in danger. That his wife was not in danger.

We would have to talk about that eventually—that, and everything else the snake had said, but first all I wanted was to sleep.

Scion and I stared unseeing at each other over a small fire, the only sounds that of the forest, the crackling flames, and our heavy breathing.

Sleep had so far evaded me. Nevertheless, several hours of silence had done almost as well at replenishing my energy. The same could not be said for Scion.

I looked up at him across the fire. His color had returned, but that was about the only normal thing about him. His expression was dark, almost defeated rather than his usual mask of anger. I itched to ask what he was thinking, but wasn't sure I wanted to know.

"So, she's in Underneath," I said to break the tension.

"Not yet," he corrected dully. "On her way there."

"Whom do you suppose is traveling with her?"

He made a strangled sound, somewhere between a laugh and a scoff. "Who the fuck do you think is?"

There was no need for me to respond; we both understood the situation perfectly: It was clear that Lonnie had joined the rebels. The only question remained if she had done so willingly or if Ambrose had forced her.

"At least they're not going to Nevermore," I said without enthusiasm. "Our theory is wrong, then. He isn't trying to kill her during a hunt."

Scion's face twisted into a bitter scowl. "I have no doubt that he still intends to kill her, just not in Nevermore."

I didn't disagree with him. All I wanted was to chase after her immediately, but I felt stuck in place with no clue where to begin. Worse, going to Underneath wasn't an option for me. My only consolation was that it would take days to reach Underneath by boat, so she was hopefully not in any immediate danger. More importantly, if she were hurt, I'd know.

"Who the hell is the last heir of Elsewhere?" I asked, remembering the last thing the snake had said.

Scion shrugged. "I don't know…could it be your father?"

I shook my head, even as I said: "Perhaps? But I don't think I've ever heard Gancanagh called that before."

Scion flinched when I mentioned my father's name, like he was afraid the monster himself would appear in the forest with us. I rolled my eyes. King Gancanagh was powerful, but not that powerful. Otherwise, I was sure we'd have met by now.

"Whoever the heir is, it doesn't matter," Scion said. "That sounds like something Ambrose would care about. All I care about is finding Lonnie before he does something to her."

I nodded, pleased he was at least admitting out loud that he was worried for our mate, regardless of what he chose to view their relationship as. "It would be fastest for you to travel to the Hedge, and try to head them off, rather than searching for a ship we have no good way of finding."

Scion looked up at me sharply, his eyes narrowing. "What do you mean, 'fastest for me to travel to the Hedge.'"

"What, do you not agree? It wouldn't take you more than a day to reach the Hedge, and then you could wait for the ship to arrive." I cocked my head, thinking. "I suppose it might be difficult to cross the border, but I have no doubt you—"

"Shut up for a moment," Scion snapped. "Why do you keep saying 'you?'"

I scowled darkly. "Do not try to tell me you're going to fuck off again and not go after her. I'm getting really tired of playing this game with you, Sci. Don't call her your mate, fine, but now you can't deny that she's at least your damn wife."

He visibly flinched at the word "wife" but didn't correct me. "Only technically, and I'm sorry—"

"I wish you would stop apologizing. It's quite disconcerting, you know," I smiled, trying and failing to make a joke. "I don't think I've heard you apologize once in the last thirty years, and now it's all you can do."

"I don't understand why this doesn't bother you," he said sharply. "If you would just react, then—"

"Then what? You could confirm to yourself what a bad person you are?"

"Perhaps!" he said a bit too loudly. Overhead, a flock of birds startled and took off into the air. "If it were me in your position..."

I ran a hand through my hair, so exasperated it was hard to form a coherent sentence. "You *are* in my position, you stubborn fucking bastard. I don't have any more right to her than you do."

His mouth became a thin line. "I'm not going to debate this with you. Just tell me why you're talking as if you're not going to come with me to Underneath?"

I raised a surprised eyebrow. "You cannot be serious, Sci, you know why I can't go."

To my surprise, Scion waved me off as if there were no issues. "It's another week until the full moon. I'm sure you can handle yourself, you just killed an old one."

I gaped at him.

It wasn't even that I disagreed entirely, it was that Scion had never once been so blasé about anything. "To be perfectly clear, you're saying that even though I wasn't allowed to join the army in case I got a taste for it; when I spent a week every month caged in the castle, and when I was hardly allowed to leave the grounds for the first twenty years of my life, *now* you want me to step into Underneath."

He didn't even have the decency to look embarrassed. "Yes. Don't you want to?"

I bit back a growl. Did I want to make sure my mate was safe? Of course, but I was all too aware that my presence might be more dangerous to her than anything else in that cursed city. If I hadn't been completely sure that Scion would destroy anything in his path to find Lonnie, it would've been different, but as it was, I'd only make things worse for both of them. "What happens if someone recognizes me?"

He cocked his head, looking at my face as if he'd never seen it before. He closed one eye, and frowned. "You look more Seelie than Unseelie...and who knows, perhaps there are a lot of yellow eyes in Underneath."

I snorted a genuine laugh. "You've become quite adept at lying to yourself in these last weeks."

He scowled, looking far more like himself. "It's not that."

"Then what is it?"

He glanced away. "I just know from experience that you won't be able to stay away for long, anyway. I'd rather stay together."

I closed my mouth, merely nodding. It was the closest he'd ever come to admitting that we might share the same feelings when it came to our little monster, and that he too was compelled to follow her into the underworld.

I only wished that sentiment wasn't so literal.

"Fine. We'll both go." I let out a short burst of laughter. "With the both of us, your brother and my father, it will be like a fucking family reunion."

23
LONNIE
ABOARD THE FORESIGHT

In my dream, I pushed the door open, the Fae males walking close behind me. My mother stood at the long wooden counter in the corner of the small kitchen, chopping roots with a long knife. Immediately, I felt safer.

"Mother," I began, but didn't get a chance to finish.

"Rhiannon," the frightening man interrupted me. "I'm glad to see you're well."

My mother dropped her knife at the sound of his deep voice and turned with a gasp.

Her face was pale and heart-shaped like mine, her hair a shade brighter red and tied back in a long braid. She barely looked at the second Fae, who stood near the door, all her attention focused on the frightening man. "What are you doing here?"

"Did we not agree to meet?" he said pleasantly.

"Yes, but—" she looked at me, her eyes darting anxiously toward the door. "Lonnie, where's your sister?"

"Outside," I said quickly.

"Why don't you join her."

The frightening man laughed. "It seems the children aren't safe outside if they are running into strangers at every turn."

My mother bristled. "They're fine. You are the problem here."

"Is that any way to greet an old friend?"

Mother snatched her knife off the ground. She brandished it at the commander. "I'll greet you with this unless you tell me what you're doing here. We were not supposed to meet for months."

"Plans change," he said, honey dripping from his voice. "I need you to do something for me."

Again, mother glanced at me, as if only just realizing I was still there. "Lonnie!" she snapped. "Go outside."

"But—" I cast around for some excuse that would keep me in the room. My curiosity burned like fire within me. "I thought I heard a mountain lion earlier."

To my surprise, the commander threw back his head and laughed. "Why doesn't Ambrose here watch the children while we talk. In case there are any more lions lurking around."

The second Fae male looked up suddenly. "Commander, you're not fucking serious. You didn't bring me here to play wet-nurse to human infants."

I wrinkled my nose. I was hardly an infant—I would be eleven next year.

"I brought you here to do whatever I asked of you," the commander barked. "Go."

My mother wrung her hands in her skirt, but nodded for me to follow.

Over the next several days, Ambrose Dullahan held true to his word.

Every morning, he'd remind me that if I wanted to eat I could join him in the dining room, then he'd leave, shutting me in the room all day. Every night, he'd return, and I would stubbornly sleep on the floor like a dog, so as to avoid touching him.

This went on for two straight days, and at first, the gnawing ache in my belly was manageable.

I'd been hungry in my past life as a servant, and even starving while in the dungeons. I was no stranger to finding ways to distract myself from the shooting pains in my stomach. Happily, the cabin was filled with books, and I distracted myself from the bleak situation learning history and geography that I'd never before had the time or opportunity to know.

Finally, however, I couldn't take the hunger anymore, and on the morning of the third day since my attempted escape, I gave in.

Rising from the bed, which I occupied during the day so as to rest my aching joints, I dragged myself across the small room and tried the door. It was not locked, and I found myself staring out at the wide-open sky, and the bustling deck of the ship.

Stepping out onto the deck, I shivered slightly at the cold winter air that blew in huge gusts, picking up the ends of my hair and the hem of my borrowed shirt. I turned my head this way and that, trying to take in everything at once.

Men and women barked orders at each other, while others hoisted sails and scrubbed the wooden planks clean. The sound of creaking ropes and splashing waves created a symphony of maritime activity. Far in the distance, I could just barely make out Dullahan standing on the captain's platform at the wheel, his long white hair almost shining in the bright sun.

I scanned the faces of the crew members as I walked nervously down the center of the ship. Not a single person paid me any mind, but still I couldn't help but notice that almost all of his crew were humans.

That only fueled my dislike of the rebellion. A fairy war fought by human soldiers gave an uncomfortably real meaning to the word "Slúagh." The literal translation of the Fae slur for humans was "Sword fodder," and that had never felt so real as it did in this moment.

Grinding my teeth, I reached the other side of the ship and stopped at a set of stairs leading up to the captain's deck. I glanced around again, half expecting someone to stop me, or at least ask where I was going. No one did, and with a final anxious glance at the crew I began to climb.

There were three people on the captain's deck—or rather, two Fae males, and a woman who looked to be half-Fae.

My mouth fell open as I looked over the group. Ambrose Dullahan stood at the wheel, steering the ship, while the tiny black-haired woman spoke to him in rapid, too-quiet words I couldn't make out. They were not what shocked me, however. The other male—tall, with close cropped hair and tattoos covering his scalp—glanced at me as I approached. I met his green eyes, and instantly recognized him. "You!" I exclaimed. "You shot me, you fucking bastard."

I took a quick, jerking step toward the male. I was absolutely certain it had been him whom I'd seen in the Waywoods, just before I shadow walked. Not only that, but while back in Inbetwixt, Scion and I had sought a male of this exact description in the brothel owned by one of the city's many guilds. We'd never found him, but I'd suspected it was he who had scribbled my mother's name on Phillipa Blacktongue's client book, as some sort of cruel taunt on behalf of his rebel commander.

Before I could demand an explanation, Ambrose Dullahan raised his voice to a volume I could actually hear over the rushing wind. "Riven, Lin, leave us."

I gaped after my attacker as he followed the small woman down the stairs and out of sight. Every bone in my body wanted to chase after him. To attack, to do…something. Only, it was now more clear than ever that my true enemy still stood before me.

The rebel leader hadn't even looked at me as I approached him, though he would certainly have been able to see my entire walk from end to end of the ship. Now, he kept his eyes firmly on the horizon, entirely focused on steering the ship.

"Dullahan," I said, bitterly. "You ordered your man to shoot me."

It wasn't a question, but Dullahan answered as if it were. "Yes." He cast me a sideways glance. "And 'Ambrose' is fine."

"Don't like your nickname?" I asked with a harsh laugh. "What does it mean anyway?"

"I'll tell you over dinner, assuming you share something about yourself first, Elowyn."

I wrinkled my nose. "Here's something," I snapped. "No one has called me Elowyn since I was a child."

He looked contemplative. "Right, sorry love. Old habits…"

I reeled back, surprised by his casual tone. This male had ordered someone to kill me in the forest, knocked me out and dragged me onto his ship, no doubt bound for my death, but he'd also saved my life from the sea monster, and talked as if we were…not friends, perhaps, but at least as if we knew each other.

My mind spun with questions, and I forgot for a moment what I was doing here in the first place, but Dullahan reminded me. "Are you willing to eat yet?"

I ground my teeth, and as if on cue my stomach rumbled loudly. "Yes."

"Good." He looked at me for the first time, his face impassive, as if he were staring through me. "I'll have something appropriate for you to wear brought to the cabin."

I frowned. In truth, my stomach was almost weeping with hunger, and I didn't want to spend another second waiting, now that I'd given in. Dressing up for him was the last thing I wanted to do, especially if it prolonged my meal. "I don't remember that being part of the agreement."

Ambrose cast me a condescending look. "If you'd prefer to keep wearing my clothes, be my guest, but you should know you're becoming quite the source of gossip among the crew."

I snapped my mouth shut, my cheeks heating. I longed to point out that there would be nothing to gossip about if he'd just let me sleep in another room, but didn't feel like wasting my breath on pointless arguments. "Fine. I'll wear whatever you want, just bring it quickly."

He grinned. "I'm glad you see it my way."

I'D BARELY CROSSED THE DECK OF THE SHIP AGAIN, ARRIVING IN THE cabin where I'd been sleeping, before there was a knock at the door. I rushed to open it, and came face to face with a young, chestnut-haired man. He was covered in freckles from the top of his forehead down to his hands, which shook slightly as he held out a tangled ball of burgundy silk.

"For me?" I asked, glancing down at the fabric.

The man nodded, and shoved the bundle at me. Holding it up, I realized it was a gown that looked at once too formal and too delicate to wear on a ship such as this.

"Wait!" I called, as the man had already turned to leave. "Do you have anything else? Trousers perhaps?"

The man looked over his shoulder at me, and finally spoke in a clipped, rasping tone. "This is what the captain sent, miss."

I took that to mean that even if he could've found other clothing, he wouldn't. I groaned. "You can tell your captain that he is only confirming my opinion of him."

The man paused. "Which is what, miss?"

"That he's a controlling fucking bastard."

"Yes, miss."

Slamming the door, I made my way across the room and laid the dress out across the bed. Something heavy fell from between the folds of fabric, and I jumped in shock, as whatever it was landed beside my foot and rolled across the floor and under the desk.

My heartbeat increasing inexplicably, I got down on my hands and knees and poked my head under the heavy wooden desk. I blinked in surprise, and stretched my hand out to reach the black, glittering object. Pulling it out, I straightened and held my breath as I stared down at the dangerous looking obsidian crown. *What the fuck?*

The crown sparkled without anything to reflect off of, and I glimpsed my own distorted reflection in its smooth, black face. It seemed to pulse with a strange sort of energy, like it was alive and not a chunk of carved stone.

I shivered, and tossed the crown unceremoniously on the bed. I didn't care about the crown in the same way Bael and Scion did, but I didn't want to wear it either. Something about it sent cold shivers up my spine, and turned my stomach.

Ignoring the crown, I instead looked down at the dress it had come wrapped in. The gown reminded me simultaneously of all the intricately decorated clothing Scion bought me in Inbetwixt, and of the iron and purple gown Iola had made for me back at the palace on the occasion that I'd attended the ball with the prince's raven.

At that thought, I looked over at the window, half expecting Quill to be hovering outside, as if summoned by my thoughts. Nothing but the sky and the ocean stretched before me and I sighed heavily.

I'd done my best not to think of Bael or Scion in the last days, and for the most part, I managed.

That was one reason I despised Ambrose Dullahan's similarities to his brother and cousin. They too, liked to drag me around, and seemed to enjoy buying me clothing I never would have otherwise worn. I hadn't lied when I said Dullahan reminded me of his family, but they had better qualities which outweighed the rest.

Ambrose Dullahan might have some of the same mannerisms and proclivities, but only those which I disliked. Everything he'd done was closer to the cruel, smirking princes who had once tormented me. He was nothing like the males I'd left in the inn, who looked at me as if they couldn't turn away, and who'd saved my life more times than I could count.

I hated to allow myself to think of them, as it left a gaping wound where my chest should be. A large part of me felt guilty for leaving, and another part hoped they'd soon arrive to rescue me.

It was a selfish thought, and one I refused to voice, less I somehow wish it into existence.

I'd left to keep them safe, and I supposed one benefit to this mess was putting even more distance between us than I ever could've managed on my own.

Someone had brought a bathing tub into my room while I'd been gone, and I took a quick bath, trying not to dwell on thoughts of the last time I'd stepped into a tub. Once finished, I reluctantly unwrapped the new dress and laid it out on the bed.

Fortunately, it was not a complicated pattern, and I didn't require any help to do up the lacing in the front. Unfortunately, however, the size was slightly too small and I looked down in dismay at how the fabric clung to my body like a second skin, and pushed my breasts up below my chin.

It could be worse, I supposed. I could still be covered in blood.

The sailor—or perhaps he was a servant, I wasn't sure—returned in due course, and knocked three times on my door. I hurried to let him in, already dreaming of whatever food might await me.

The freckled sailor looked up at me, his eyes lingering on my head. "You're not ready, miss?" He phrased it like a question. "Should I come back?"

"No, I'm quite ready," I said quickly, trying to usher him out the door. "Let's go."

He shook his head vigorously. "The crown, miss. I was told 'specially to make sure you didn't forget it."

I gnashed my teeth. *To argue, or to eat?*

"Fine," I said viciously, and dashed back across the room to snatch the crown from the bed. Shoving it on my head with little care for how it was positioned, or the state of my wild, curling hair, I grimaced and stomped back to the door. "I'm ready."

The sailor looked like he wanted to protest, but seemed to think better of it. "Very good, miss."

I followed him out onto the deck of the ship, feeling like I was walking the gangway to my death. We reached the opposite end of the ship, but instead of climbing the stairs to the navigation deck as before, the sailor gestured me toward a large wooden door. I sighed, bracing myself, and knocked.

24

AMBROSE

ABOARD THE FORESIGHT

"Enter," I called through the door, then waited with bated breath as Lonnie stepped inside.

Her face was screwed up in a scowl, and she gave a disdainful glance around the room as she entered, her eyes finally landing on me. "Am I up to your standards now, my lord?"

I raised my eyebrows. It had been quite some time since anyone called me that. "Sir" or "Commander" was much more common throughout the rebel army, but the phrase sent my mind back to a time long before. It felt like an entirely different person's life, and I supposed, in some ways it was.

"You look lovely," I said honestly. "Would you like to sit?"

Her scowl deepened, and she gave another cursory glance to the room before moving stiffly to take the seat across from me. I wasn't sure what she'd been expecting, but I assumed this wasn't it.

The cabin looked hardly different from the one she'd occupied for the last several days. It was another office type room, with wood paneled walls and bookshelves on both ends. The only difference was this room was slightly larger, and instead of a bed, an intricately carved dining table stood in the center of the room.

The table was adorned with a crimson tablecloth, draped carefully over its smooth surface. Glimmering silver utensils were neatly arranged beside plates of delicate porcelain, each one bearing an intricate floral pattern. A golden candelabra stood in the center, its flickering flames casting a warm glow over the scene.

I reached for a bottle of wine standing near the center of the table. "Would you like some wine?"

"No." She shook her head and the crown placed haphazardly over her wild curls tilted dangerously to one side. "I know better than to drink fairy wine."

I furrowed my brow. "I don't think that will be a problem for you."

She returned my confused look with one of her own. "It always has been before."

That was…interesting.

I'd assumed, given her magic and her family, that she'd have no trouble with the kinds of enchantments that often felled average humans. Was it only the wine that affected her, or other spells as well? Music, perhaps? Could she break an oath? I silently added this to the mental list of questions I'd planned to ask her.

I poured a glass of wine for her anyway, and passed it across the table. She took it, but didn't drink, and a stony silence once again fell over the room.

"How are you enjoying the ship?" I asked.

Her scowl turned instantly to a glare of contempt. "I'm not here to make pleasant conversation."

It was a challenge not to roll my eyes. Of course, I was well aware she was only here to eat—if I hadn't insisted, she likely never would have ventured outside my cabin. Still, wasn't it exhausting for her to maintain such animosity?

Then, I supposed not. I'd seen enough of her long, painfully slow courtship with my brother and cousin to know that Lonnie would hold on to her grudges with her last dying breath. I would have to try to make sure she had no good reasons to hate me then…at least, no more than she already did.

I hadn't meant for our relationship to begin as poorly as it had, but I realized now that I was more dependent on my magic than even I'd realized. I'd never met anyone before without already having some knowledge of how to avoid offending them, of how they would behave, and whether we'd get along or not. I'd already made far too many mistakes with her out of sheer arrogance, assuming she would immediately fall in line with whatever I wanted. I wouldn't make that mistake again. It would be an exciting challenge, I supposed, to win her affection with my personality alone.

The door swung open and one of the kitchen staff entered, carrying a large tray laden with the first course. The woman walked slowly across the room, swaying slightly with both the weight of the tray and the motion of the ship.

I snuck another glance at Lonnie, who now had her hands clenched on the edge of the table. I nodded for the servant to place a dish in front of her, and without missing a beat, Lonnie fell upon it, shoving several lumps of cheese and half a smoked sausage into her mouth at once.

"Hungry?" I asked.

She didn't reply, but took another large bite of sausage. I took that to be a "Yes."

I waited several minutes before speaking again, to allow her time to eat. In the meantime, I watched her carefully.

It had been my own selfish desires that demanded she dress up for dinner, and I'd never been more pleased to give in to something I wanted. This girl, with the wild hair and the crown, was the one I'd watched all these years, and longed to finally see in person. This was how she'd looked when she invaded my dreams, as if we were sharing the same visions, and how I imagined her every time I'd closed my eyes for the last several years.

I'd seen all the other sides of her, and they were also lovely, but this version—the queen—was the one I'd grown enamored with.

For Bael, she was the delicate servant girl, who made him feel useful with how much she needed him.

For Scion, she was the fighter, the equal, who challenged him in a way that no one else could.

And for me, one day she'd be the ruler. The queen, who was both my greatest strength and only weakness.

She just didn't know it yet.

"Do you recall the terms of our bargain?" I asked.

She looked up, seeming annoyed at being pulled away from her meal. "Yes."

"Are you sure? Because you've not yet asked or answered a single relevant question."

She gritted her teeth, and I could practically hear the insults she was biting back. "Fine, then." She attempted a smile that came out more of a grimace. "Would you like to ask the first question?"

I thought I knew what question she would ask first, and I was eager to learn if I was correct. I grinned, unable to help it. How novel to wonder about anything, much less something so mundane. "Ladies first."

Swallowing thickly, she sucked in a deep breath. "Is my mother truly alive?"

My smile widened. I'd been right, which only confirmed how well I already knew her. She couldn't know yet how satisfying that was, but she'd soon find out.

I leaned forward across the table, meeting her gaze. "As far as I know, yes."

Her breath caught, and the most fleeting look of hurt crossed her face before she schooled her expression back to neutral. "Is she in Aftermath?"

"No."

I heard Lonnie's heartbeat speed up, and an image of the last time I'd seen Rhiannon flashed through my mind. That had indeed been in Aftermath, and not so very long ago, but she'd left the province soon after.

Lonnie leaned forward eagerly, slamming both hands down on the table. "Tell me—"

I cut her off. "Stop. It's my turn to ask a question."

"No, but—"

"That was what we agreed, love. A question for a question, and you've already had two."

She savagely stabbed her fork into the sliced meat on the plate in front of her, and scowled up at me. "Fine," she said, shoving a bite into her mouth so her words came out garbled. "Ask your damn question."

I paused, prolonging the moment, if only to annoy her. Was it cruel? Perhaps, but she seemed determined to defy me at every turn, she deserved some small torment in exchange.

I very slowly reached for my glass of wine, taking a long sip while she practically bounced up and down in her seat with impatience.

"What…" I said slowly, as if thinking. "Is your favorite color?"

She gaped at me. "You must be fucking joking."

I clenched my teeth to avoid laughing. I *was* joking, in fact, but her reaction was so intense I now needed to see it through, if only to goad her. "Is that too difficult of a question?"

She bared her teeth. "No, it's too simple. What are you playing at?"

"That's my business," I told her, as I had no good answer to give. "Answer the question or leave the table, it's your choice."

"Purple," she blurted out, then immediately gasped, coughing like pain was searing over her throat. Seeming to not think about what she was doing, she reached for the wine she'd so far avoided, and took a large sip.

I had to forcibly close my mouth to avoid gaping at her. That pointless question had just revealed far more than I'd ever expected. She truly could not lie. I'd noticed her struggling before, when she woke up in my cabin, but I hadn't been entirely sure of what I was seeing. Now, there was no doubt.

"Why lie?" I asked.

"I didn't," she spluttered, and again choked as I knew a second round of pain was now joining the first. "I mean," she coughed. "I didn't think I had."

I winced, knowing the feeling of a falsehood well. "Interesting. I suppose that was more of an answer than I even expected. You may go."

She massaged her neck bitterly, before blurting out: "What's going on?"

I cocked my head. "Be more specific."

She paused, as if realizing she'd wasted a question she could've used to find out more about her mother. I watched the calculation take place behind her eyes, before she snapped her gaze back to me. "Why can't I lie?"

"You could before, I take it?"

Of course, I already knew that Lonnie lied often and well, but waited for her nod of confirmation to be sure. All humans lied, but she was more adept at it than most. I had to assume she'd been taught to lie intentionally, since she spewed the same nonsense that Rhiannon spoke with every other breath without ever flinching.

Conversely, Fae children were taught from an early age *not* to lie, and how to avoid doing so by mistake. It was a half-truth to say we could never do so. We technically could lie, but the resultant pain was so immense it was hardly worth trying. Even now, two hundred years later, I recalled well the pain of misspeaking by mistake back in my youth.

I ran a hand through my hair, thinking. For once, I didn't know the right answer, and could only guess. "I do not claim to know every secret of the source," I said finally. "But I suspect you can't lie now when before you could because you have begun consciously using magic."

"Why would that matter?"

"I don't know." I shrugged. "Perhaps it has always been so. I only know that all creatures who are sustained by the Source struggle to speak falsely…. or," I added, as a second idea occurred to me. "It may have nothing to do with you individually, but because you have recently ingested a large amount of magical blood."

She looked taken aback. "You know about that?"

I snorted a laugh. "There is little you have done that I don't know about, love."

She flushed, but recovered quickly. "If you're expecting me to be embarrassed, I won't."

I grinned. "Only humans would expect you to be embarrassed by sex. You must know that, having lived at the court."

She nodded tersely. "I meant about the blood. Isn't that taboo among you?"

I raised an eyebrow. The Fae viewed blood sharing with the same repressed eyes as the humans viewed pleasure, which was to say, it was not polite dinner conversation. It was taboo, but only for those who were not mated. "Do you wish to waste another question on my opinions of your mating, or would you rather hear about your mother?"

This time, she flushed scarlet and looked back down at her plate. "Fine, where is she?" she asked, in a slightly humbled tone.

I bit my lip. How frustrating it was to have no idea what might have caused her strange reaction. It was really my turn to ask, but she looked so uncomfortable I let it go. "The last I saw her she was on her way to Underneath. Now, I believe she is in the king's dungeon."

She gasped. "Why?"

"She went to Underneath because I asked her to. As for the dungeon, that's a longer explanation."

"Tell me," she demanded.

Alright, that was far more than enough. "You really do not seem to understand how this works. You've now had several questions in a row, but answered none of mine."

She let out an angry growl, and made to stand. "Because your questions are pointless. You already know everything, right?"

"Not everything," I murmured.

There were many things I couldn't know through watching her by way of another's future. And, after the intriguing results of my first question, I was not at all inclined to give up a chance to know more about her.

"What's your favorite pastime?" I asked.

She looked mutinous. "I don't have one. My only goal has ever been survival. I've hardly had time to develop leisurely interests."

I waited a beat, but she didn't react as if she'd lied. Interesting. She at least believed herself, then, though all evidence I'd seen led me to disagree. From what I'd seen, she had carved out a great deal of free time for herself over the years, and seemed to fill it with rule breaking and casual sex. Of everything about her, that was one of her most Fae-like qualities.

"If you did have time for leisure," I asked, "what would you choose to do?"

She grinned widely. "That's a second question."

I smiled, having learned something new from her answer alone. She was a shameless hypocrite. "Fine, answer it and we'll call ourselves even."

"I...I don't know—" She coughed, and changed course midsentence. "I suppose, I like winning."

"Winning..." I said, thoughtfully. She and I had that in common, then. "I suppose we'll have to find a game for you to play."

"Why would you care if I'm enjoying myself?"

"Perhaps I want you to be happy."

She let out a harsh laugh. "Perhaps, but I doubt it."

I took another sip of wine. "Doubt whatever you like. It's your turn."

"Why is my mother in the dungeon?"

"That's a complex question, but the short answer is she went to Underneath looking for someone whom she has not seen in many years. Landing herself in the dungeon…well, I suppose I don't know for certain, but given what I know of that court, I am almost positive she is now a prisoner."

"Who was she looking for?" she demanded.

"My superior," I replied. "The original Dullahan."

She sat up straighter, a spark of genuine excitement flickering through her gaze. "Who is that?"

I scoffed. "Nice try, love. It's my turn."

"Don't call me that."

I raised my eyebrow. "What, you don't like pet-names?"

"Is that your question?"

"No." My smile broadened. "I'd rather find that out for myself, love. Now, let me think…" I paused, mulling over what seemingly "pointless" question would give the best insights.

"Go on," she rushed me.

"Who is your closest friend?"

To my surprise, the smile immediately slipped off her face. "I'm not answering that. Ask something else."

I leaned forward, confusion washing over me. "No, that's my question. Who is your closest friend?"

"Ask something else, or I'm leaving."

"No."

She stood abruptly, the legs of her chair screeching across the floor. Her face had gone white, and her mouth twisted in an angry snarl. "This is pointless. I only came here to eat, anyway. Keep your information, I can find out anything I want to know without your help and without being taunted like this."

She turned on her heel and stormed from the room, and all I could do was stare after her.

What the fuck had just happened?

25
LONNIE

ABOARD THE FORESIGHT

I stormed back across the ship, and threw open the cabin door, still fuming.

Tearing off the stupid, too-tight dress, I threw myself onto the small bed in nothing but my underthings, and buried my head in the pillow.

Fucking Ambrose Dullahan…fucking questions. Fucking Fae.

The bastard had caught me unaware, with the sort of question that shouldn't have stung, but somehow opened up a gaping wound inside me that I was only just managing to not think about on a daily basis.

My sister had been my closest, and only, friend, and it was because of Ambrose Dullahan that she was no longer here with me. It was because of him that she'd charged into battle with the rebels and stood there as King Penvalle murdered her right in front of me…and I didn't even know why.

Of all the questions I had for the rebel leader, what happened to my sister was the most important, and the most terrifying to ask.

Learning about my mother had been painful enough.

For nearly ten years, I'd believed my mother to be dead, and it was only in the last weeks that I'd had any hope to the contrary. If she was alive, then why would she stay away so long? Why would she not return to find my sister and I?

I couldn't face the possibility that I might know just as little about my sister as my mother. That maybe the friendship I'd thought we shared was a lie, just like everything else.

Without warning, the door banged open again. "What the fuck was that?"

I kept my face buried in the pillow, even as I knew Ambrose Dullahan was standing in the doorway, watching me. His heavy boots stomped across the floor, stopped beside the bed, and I felt the radiating warmth of his skin and magnetic presence looming over me.

"Leave me alone," I murmured, my voice muffled. "I'm done talking to you. I'd rather starve."

"I'm sure you would."

He chuckled under his breath, and sat down on the edge of the bed. The mattress dipped with his weight, and I snatched my feet up to my chest, curling into a smaller ball to avoid inadvertently touching him. "I said go away."

"No," he replied calmly. "Not until you tell me what's upset you."

"Used to knowing everything about everyone, I take it. You don't like being in the dark?"

"Precisely," he said flatly. "I know more than any one person ever should, but you, love, are a mystery."

I clenched my teeth together, my anger rising higher at the sound of that nickname.

"Fine." I sat up, hardly even aware of my lack of clothing until his black eyes darted automatically to my body, before flicking back up to meet my eyes. I shivered, but refused to stand to find something to cover myself with. "You want to know what's upsetting me?"

"Desperately."

"You," I hissed. "You're the problem. It's because of you that I do not have a closest friend. She's dead, and you killed her."

He stared at me for several long seconds, and I could practically see the calculation taking place behind his eyes. Perhaps he was running through all the women he'd killed, wondering which might have been a friend of mine. Finally, understanding dawned on his face. "Your sister."

"Rosey," I snapped. "At least say her name when you speak of murdering her."

He cocked his head to the side. "I didn't kill Rosey. You know that, but still you can say so without suffering the pain of lying. How is that possible?"

I shook my head. How was I supposed to know how magic worked? I only knew that I believed, with every fiber of my being, that if it were not for the male in front of me that my sister would still be alive. He might not have wielded the sword, but he killed her. It was as simple as that.

"Tell me what happened to her," I demanded. "How did she know you? What was she doing in the rebel army in the first place? Why did she have to die?"

My voice cracked on the last word, and I looked down, hiding the tears that had sprung, unbidden, to my eyes.

"I'll tell you," he said tonelessly. "But I do not think it will bring you any comfort. You may hurt less not knowing."

I scoffed. It was impossible for this to hurt more than it already did. "Tell me."

"Fine." He sighed. "Some three years ago, now, your sister approached one of my men in the capital."

"She wouldn't do that without some reason," I insisted. "She wasn't the type to break rules, let alone try to overthrow a kingdom."

"She *had* a reason," he said patiently. "You must know she dreamed of the future."

I sneered. "An ability you gave her, I assume."

He let out a bark of laughter. "Not at all. it's impossible to share powers like that."

My brow furrowed. "No it isn't, I've seen it."

I'd certainly seen Bael use my magic before, and even once, I was fairly sure I'd used his. Hell, if I'd had any idea how, and hadn't been drugged, I might be able to use Scion's powers right now. Ambrose was a Fae prince, he had to know more about magic than I did. Except, he was staring at me right now like he had no idea what I was talking about.

His brow wrinkled. "Well, if it is possible, that's certainly not what happened to your sister. Rosey was probably a marginally-gifted seer because it's the most common trait to be mixed into human blood. It could have passed from either one of your parents, and had little to do with your own magic. A lot of my rebels have some vague prophetic ability, but nothing like mine."

But nothing like mine. How arrogant. I snorted a laugh. "So, you're special then?"

"Yes," he replied without a hint of remorse or embarrassment. "Your sister was not particularly gifted, but she did have one very specific ability that made her useful."

"Which was?"

"She could see herself. I don't know why, I've never met another seer who could have visions of their own future, but she did. She was good enough to see some of the most significant paths that the future might take, and to want to stop them, especially when it came to those she was close to."

"Like what?"

"Like you joining the rebellion."

There was a long, charged pause, in which I waited for him to continue, or perhaps jerk in pain as the heat of his lie burned his throat, but he didn't. Finally, I shook my head and leaned forward. "You mean she saw herself joining the rebellion?"

"No, I mean she saw *you*."

"I wouldn't," I hissed. "I would never."

He laughed. "Perhaps not now, but what about two years ago? I've watched you for years, and I know what you were like before all this."

"What was I like?" I snapped, angrily. "Tell me, since clearly you think I don't know myself."

"Angry, rebellious, full of hatred toward all Fae, and the royal family especially. Do you not think it's possible that you would have found your way to me, if my cousin and my brother had never found you in the forest? Or, perhaps, even later, if you'd found me when you spent nights sneaking out of the palace to search?"

I glanced down, horror washing over me and rising the skin on my neck. That did sound like me. Perhaps he was right, then, but if so was it somehow my fault that my sister got involved? Could I blame myself for something I'd never even done, but only could have?

"Fine." I said quietly. "I suppose it's possible I could've joined your rebellion."

"It's more than possible," he replied. "It was likely. Such a strong possibility, in fact, that your sister saw it time and time again. For the year before she sought me out she saw dozens of visions of you in the rebellion, until finally, she saw one that prompted her to go out and stop you."

"Which was what?"

He took a deep breath. "She watched herself die, and thought it was you."

My mouth fell open. Suddenly, as if it were happening all over again, all I could see was the cold madness in King Penvalle's eyes as he raised his sword and sliced once, twice, three times through my sister's body.

All I could hear was the rushing in my ears, the screaming filling the clearing, when, as if in slow motion, Rosey's body fell, her head tumbling onto the ground beside her.

Somehow, I could feel it, as the white-hot, all-consuming fire overtook my entire body, and all I could think of was murdering the male in front of me. Of raising the crown high, and bringing it down again into his smirking, too arrogant face.

"Are you with me, love?"

I heard the voice from too far away, and still couldn't seem to see the room in front of me as I replied. "I don't understand."

"What don't you understand?"

I shook my head to clear it of the screaming. "Why was she there in the first place? Perhaps I believe that Rosey would seek you out looking for me, but once she realized I was not there, why would she stay?"

"For the same reason you would have. She wanted to see your mother again, and I could do that for her."

I gasped, and my heart somehow beat impossibly faster, like I was running for my life rather than sitting on the bed. "Are you telling me that my sister saw my mother before she died?"

He shook his head. "No, Rhiannon was in Aftermath until quite recently, but I knew where to find her and if Rosey had lived I would have made good on my promise to reintroduce them. The problem was, that by the time your sister arrived on my doorstep she was already sick."

I sucked in slow, even breaths, only half listening as I tried to keep myself from breaking open and letting the pain leak out across the floor. "Sick in what way?"

"She'd been fighting a cough for some time."

"I thought she was faking the cough. Those trees that she was claiming to make tea from are poisonous."

"They are," he agreed. "Never hide in a moondust tree at noon."

I glanced up, frowning at the sound of the familiar expression. "My mother used to use that phrase a lot."

"I know. Where do you think I heard it? It's some idiom from the court of Nightshade she must have picked up as a child."

I shook my head. "So what?"

"That expression only makes sense because moondust leaves bloom at dusk and fall to dust by the morning. It was your mother who gave me the idea to use the moondust trees to pass messages throughout my army. The leaves are the perfect place to write a message you want to be sure will be destroyed within a few hours of writing it."

"And Rosey knew that?"

"Yes," he nodded. "After your sister had been with the rebellion for a few months, I asked her to share information with us about the palace. She saw a lot as one of the servants who was permitted on the upper floors, and always knew what courts were visiting, and how often my grandmother ventured out of her room. She would write her reports on the moondust leaves every night for one of us to collect."

"So she wasn't making tea?"

He shook his head. "She was truly ill, that much was true, but I assume she told you she was making tea to cover her frequent trips outside."

I could only stare at him. He'd been right—I would have been happier never to know this. I felt not a shred of closure, only as if I'd been torn open again to bleed anew.

Part of me wished to tell him to stop, that we would pick up this conversation again another time, but I knew deep down that if he didn't finish telling me now, I'd never broach the subject again.

"So she was ill," I reiterated, "and spied for you, but how did that turn into her charging into an unwinnable fight? Why would she try to kill the king for you?"

"A few weeks before the raid on the hunts, Rosey realized she was dying."

I gasped. "No."

"Yes. The cough was not improving, and she was, after all, only human. She didn't have much time left, anyway, and requested to take on the task of going after my uncle. She knew she was unlikely to succeed, but by then I think she'd realized what her original prophecy was—that she'd seen not you, but herself—and wanted to ensure that the correct sister died that day."

"Didn't you try to stop her?" I demanded.

He glanced to the side, as if not wanting to look at me when he answered. "No. Perhaps I would have if she'd had a long, happy life ahead of her, but she didn't. This way, her death served a purpose."

"What was that?" I spat. "She didn't kill Penvalle."

"No," he said slowly, eyes widening at me as if I were missing something very obvious. "You did. Your sister died because she had to for you to become queen."

26
LONNIE
ABOARD THE FORESIGHT

That night, I curled up in a ball on the floor and refused to speak to Ambrose Dullahan.

And so went the next day.

And the next.

Later, I would not be able to recall much of the aftermath of my conversation with the rebel leader. My mind was a jumbled mess of sound and color, not a single coherent thought breaking through the ever present screaming that seemed to echo in the silent room.

It felt as it had in those first days in the dungeon, when all I could think of was my sister. How I'd never speak to her again. Never see her, and how if the dungeon didn't kill me, then the pain in my chest might.

One day blurred into another, and I was hardly aware of the ship moving or how long we'd sailed. Bargains and arbitrary rules ceased to hold meaning. I no longer cared to ask questions, or indeed to speak to anyone, and therefore refused to enter the dining room.

Finally, perhaps fearing I'd actually starve before speaking to him, Ambrose relented on his demand that I only eat while with him. "You need to eat something, love."

I glanced at him with only my eyes, refusing to move my head at all. I was not even sure when he'd entered the room, and only now noticed he was standing before me, holding a heaping plate of stew.

"I thought you planned to starve me," I murmured, my voice scratchy with disuse.

He placed the plate on the desk near the bed, just out of my reach, and cast me a pained look. "No, *you* seem determined to starve *yourself*. Come to the dining room or don't, but please eat something."

He didn't linger to see if I would touch the plate, and when he left the room again, I slowly raised my head to sniff the air. Roast stew, fresh bread, and strong, savory spices.

My stomach growled, and I looked down, almost surprised. I *was* hungry, I realized. Now thinking back, I'd really only had two meals in the last week, and the effects of that were beginning to show on my body and in the dull humming in the back of my mind.

Was Ambrose right, and I was trying to starve myself? I didn't think so. It was more as if I couldn't find the energy to do the things I needed. Eating, drinking, bathing—it all felt too hard. Too strenuous. I wished I didn't have a body that felt things like pain and hunger and thirst. I wished not to feel anything at all.

Ambrose continued to bring food and water, and once some wine. Eventually I found the energy to eat.

My bones aching, I dragged myself off the floor, crawled over to the desk and reached for the plate. Stiffly, as if someone else were controlling my arms, I sat cross legged on the floor and spooned stew into my mouth, tasting nothing as I stared blankly out the window. To my dismay, my too-loud thoughts returned to Rosey.

I could hardly reconcile with myself that my sister had not only known she was going to die, but had planned to for my sake. She'd tried repeatedly to save my life, without ever mentioning it to me, and her final act had been to help me become the queen.

And so far, I'd all but squandered her sacrifice.

I didn't rule anyone or anything. I'd let fear keep me from properly defending myself, or trying to learn to use my magic. I'd gone from being so overtly independent that I would allow no one to help me, to the other extreme of relying too much on others to protect me.

I looked down at the stew, realizing that my spoon was now scraping against an empty dish, and took a deep breath.

What would my sister think of that? What would she say if she could see me now, lying on the floor for days on end?

Certainly, she'd be horrified. She'd say I needed to stand up, dress, rejoin the world of the living.

I thought back to how in the palace, when I was laughed at and rejected by the other servants, she would quietly protect me. How when I could not seem to blend in as others did, I would pretend to be my quiet, capable sister, who always seemed to know the right thing to say. Even then, Rosey had always been the best of us. Always happier than me. Always more the optimist.

Perhaps now, I could pretend to be her once more.

. . .

THE SUN WAS SHINING BRIGHTLY WHEN I LEFT THE CABIN, AND found my way to the captain's deck. Ambrose stood at the wheel, once again flanked by his tattooed male companion and the small, black haired woman. None of them looked at me as I approached, as if I were a startled deer and any movement might send me sprinting for cover.

"Morning," I ground out when I stood mere feet away.

Ambrose glanced over at me tentatively, but didn't mention anything about the last several days. "Hello, love."

I watched him carefully, trying to think what to say.

It was not his fault that Rosey died. If anything, it was mine, and now I would have to find a way to live with that. The realization painted the rebel leader in a slightly brighter light, and now I was not sure how to speak to him.

"I need something to do," I said stiffly.

"Something to do?" Ambrose let go of the wheel, and gestured for his companion to take his place as he turned to face me. "What do you mean?"

I looked to the side, nervously. "You asked about pastimes, remember? Even a job would be fine, I just…"

I needed to get off the floor and out of the damned cabin, is what I meant to say, but couldn't bring myself to actually utter those words. I needed, not just a distraction, but a purpose. Something to focus on beyond the unhappiness that threatened to consume me.

"You need something to do," Ambrose repeated, smiling. "Good. I'll think of something."

"Alright."

"In the meantime," he said, almost nervously. "Will you be joining me for dinner tonight?"

I bit my lip, then sucked in a deep breath, and imagined what my sister would say. "Yes."

WE ATE IN NEAR SILENCE THAT NIGHT, AMBROSE WATCHING ME LIKE an overgrown hawk. Nothing went wrong, however, and after several hours and two courses, I left the table to return to the cabin.

When I pushed the door open, I froze, wondering for a second if I'd entered the correct room.

There, instead of the tiny single bed and the nest of clothing I'd made for myself in the corner, was a wide, comfortable looking mattress. It was more than big enough for two, and looked softer and more comfortable than anything I'd slept in since the four-poster in the obsidian tower.

Had he done this for me?

But why? Why do anything kind at all? Why bring me food, and answer all my questions? Why would he take me as a prisoner, but then treat me as a guest?

Perhaps, I had misunderstood Ambrose Dullahan.

27
SCION

THE WILDES, NEAR THE BORDER OF UNDERNEATH

"Have you ever tried to cross the Hedge?" Bael asked.

I looked sideways at my cousin. "Why the fuck would I have done that?"

"Just making conversation," he replied, his tone singsong. "Have you?"

I rolled my eyes. "Of course not, but I have been here once before."

After we'd both recovered from the incident in Inbetwixt, it had taken only a few days to cross the Waywoods and arrive in the Wilde land outside underneath. As this was a trip I'd made before, it wasn't difficult to picture locations to travel to, and shadow walking was as simple as it was within the capital.

The Hedge was the name of the short stone wall that ran from coast to coast along the border of Elsewhere and Underneath. It had been erected by one of our ancestors long ago, and despite its mundane appearance, did an extremely good job of keeping both the Unseelie out, and the citizens of Elsewhere in. It was heavily enchanted, so that it was impossible to shadow walk past, climb, or tunnel under. The only entrance in and out was a small, heavily guarded pass. It looked like little more than a crumbling break in a stone wall, however, it was rumored that once one stepped over the wall into Underneath, the glamor would lift, revealing what truly lay beyond. Since no one had entered in some time, and even fewer returned to tell tales of the Unseelie realm, I didn't know for certain if that were true, nor what we'd find if it were.

"What were you doing here?" Bael asked.

"Performing an execution on a guard who'd been enchanted by the Unseelie." I cast Bael a sideways glance. "Sorry, I—"

"It's fine," he replied. "I know better than most what monsters they are."

I nodded, still feeling a bit foolish for having brought up the Unseelie at all.

Bael's mood had drastically improved over the last few days, as if he were almost excited to enter Underneath. I couldn't imagine that was the case, but neither could I understand why he'd be putting on such an obvious affect.

I supposed I should simply be grateful.

For weeks things had felt strained between us—perhaps more on my side than his—but now that our goals were aligned once more, things had easily fallen back into the easy companionship we'd shared before I ever laid eyes on Lonnie Skyeborne.

IT WAS MIDDAY WHEN WE FINALLY MADE OUR WAY OUT OF THE Wildes, and appeared on the edge of a town, where the Hedge was visible in the distance. The air was hot and oppressive, and the ground under our feet cracked and dry. The closer one got to the Hedge, the hotter it was…like the land itself was warning us to turn back.

"Do you want to stop in the town?" Bael asked.

"No."

He grinned. "Me either."

I glanced over at the rundown buildings and shook my head. It might have been smarter of us to stop and eat, perhaps catch a few hours of sleep, but now that we were so close I didn't want to waste time. It had been days since the snake told us where to find Lonnie, and I feared she might have landed in the port of Underneath already. Our best chance to reach her would be when the boat came into harbor. Once Ambrose took her wherever he was going, things would get dramatically more complicated.

"The break in the wall is just over that hill." I pointed, and Bael followed my gaze toward the outline of a reddish-brown slope in the distance, that was really more of a small mountain than a hill.

"Shall we go then?" he asked, moving as if to walk through the shadows once more.

I put out a hand to stop him. "No, we'll have to walk. The magic from the Hedge will stop you from shadow walking, and I'm not sure what would happen if you were halfway into the shadows."

He grimaced, perhaps also imagining the potential horror of being stuck between two places indefinitely. "Right. I suppose we'd better start walking, then."

The entrance to the Hedge was just as I recalled it. The wall was only about three feet high, and the break within it looked more like a failure of time and weather than a gate to another realm.

Standing beside the wall—or rather, leaning against it—were two obsidian armored guards.

Bael and I had agreed that I would do the talking when it came to the guards. It would have been easier to simply kill them, but as magic didn't work well so close to the Hedge I was not sure if it was worth getting into a physical fight with our own, well trained, soldiers.

As we approached, it became clear that I needn't have worried.

The two guards looked neither well trained, nor capable of winning any kind of fight. The closer of the two, a tall thin human, appeared to be asleep. The other, a middle-aged Fae male, stared off in the opposite direction from which we approached. He, at least, should have heard our footsteps long ago. I sighed. Fucking idiots, giving a bad name to the army as a whole.

I plastered a false smile onto my face, trying my best to seem as unthreatening and empty headed as the guards. "Hello," I called, loudly enough to alert anyone in a mile radius.

As expected, the Fae guard jumped, startled, and the one who'd been sleeping stirred.

I'd often had the occasion to notice that outside the capital, Fae rarely recognized me without Quill on my shoulder to provide them a clue of my identity. Still, I tensed slightly as the guards turned to look at us. They barely reacted, not a hint of recognition in either male's gaze.

I relaxed. "We're here to relieve you," I said when we stood only a few feet away.

"Ah, excellent." The human guard grinned, blinking the sleep from his eyes, and leapt to his feet. "Cheers, mates."

He took a few steps forward, as if to walk past us, but the Fae guard threw out his hand to block his partner. "Hang on." He gave us a skeptical once over. "Never seen you before. Where'd you come from?"

Part of me was almost relieved. I was glad he didn't recognize us, but if both the soldiers had left without question at the word of two strangers, it would have shattered my faith in our army as a whole.

"Inbetwixt," I said vaguely. "Just arrived today."

The Fae male cocked his head, his skeptical expression melting. He laughed. "Too bad. I was hoping you were from the capital."

I furrowed my brow. "Why?"

The soldier sneered. "The rumor around the village is that the royal family had their asses handed to them by the rebel army. We sent word to the capital and all the nearby outposts hoping to get some confirmation, but haven't heard anything."

"Why does that matter to you?" Bael asked, seeming unable to keep his mouth shut any longer.

The guard laughed again, giving Bael a once over. "You must be new. If you'd done as many years of service to those bastards as I have, you wouldn't be asking why it matters. The moment I know for sure they're all dead, I'm leaving and never looking back."

"Then I'm sorry to tell you they're not all dead," I said through gritted teeth.

The male frowned. "That's a shame. Any idea who survived?"

Bael and I glanced at each other. Of course, we were all well aware of how the people of Elsewhere despised us, but it was fucking surreal to hear oneself talked about like this. At least he hadn't said anything about Lonnie.

"Does it matter who survived?" Bael asked.

"Course," the guard said easily. "You know they used to send their precious raven prince down here to hunt down deserters? I want to get out of here, sure, but I'd slit my own throat before willingly meeting him. I'd reckon he's more monstrous than anything over the wall."

I smiled tightly. "Yes, I'm sure he is."

I stepped forward to brush past the guard, aiming to end this conversation quickly. We'd pretend we were taking their place guarding the wall until they were out of sight, then cross the border without any further trouble. Easy, except…

"I don't know what you're so worried about, Cyrus," the human guard said. "The royal family isn't even in charge anymore."

I jerked, having nearly forgotten he was here until he'd spoken. In response, the Fae guard—Cyrus—grinned at Bael and I, as if we were sharing a joke at the expense of the human. "Ignore him. I've tried to explain the hunts to him a dozen times, but he doesn't understand."

"I do fucking understand," the human snapped. "We threw a party in the pub in the village when that human girl took the crown. I'm telling you, Cyrus, you don't have to worry about the bird king or whatever the fuck he's called."

"And I've told you," Cyrus sighed, exasperated. "They killed her. Must've done, right? Since nothing really changed after she won."

"You don't know that," the human grumbled.

Cyrus grinned at us again. "I swear, he never shuts up about the Slúagh queen. All the humans act like she's the incarnation of Aisling herself, but I'm sure that either that girl is long dead, or they're keeping her as a pet and by now she's been fucked so hard she'd wish she was they killed her."

My pulse pounded loudly in my ears, like the ominous ticking of a clock. Then, before I could think what I was doing, my fist connected with the soldier's jaw, sending him crashing to the ground with a resounding thud. "That's my fucking wife you're insulting."

With a maniacal chuckle, Bael swiftly took down the other guard, his lion-like strength evident as he effortlessly subdued the man. The air crackled with tension, and within seconds, we were standing in a puddle of fresh blood, two obsidian armored corpses at our feet.

I breathed heavily, and looked over at Bael, almost anxious. I wasn't really sure what had come over me, but certainly that had been an overreaction and I didn't want to hear him point it out.

To my great relief, he only shrugged. "No great loss, I'd say. They wanted to be free of their post anyway…now they are."

I let out a long breath. "We need to move," I said sharply, my mind "Before someone else comes looking for them."

Bael grinned, seeming invigorated by the violence. "Lead the way."

Nodding, I turned to face the Hedge once more. With a deep breath, I took a resolute step over the wall, and blinked as the glamor immediately faded and it suddenly became very clear why this was the only point at which one could cross into Underneath.

Before us stood a massive and seemingly endless chasm. Jagged rocks jutted out from the fiery lava below, and the foul-smelling steam rising from the depths only added to the ominous aura of the place. The sound of crackling lava and hissing steam echoed, and the air was thick with the pungent smell of sulfur and ash, reminding me uncontrollably of the scent of Wilde magic that hung over Aftermath and followed wherever the afflicted went.

Directly beneath our feet, a narrow bridge stretched precariously over the gaping chasm, its length disappearing beyond my range of vision.

I looked back at Bael, and was slightly unnerved to find him beaming with excitement. A sense of unease washed over me, but I shoved it to the back of my mind. Somewhere beyond this chasm, my brother was holding Lonnie hostage and I would find her…even if it killed me.

28

LONNIE

ABOARD THE FORESIGHT

"Why did you leave the royal family?"

"To join the army," Ambrose replied without inflection. "Did you love any of your human lovers?"

"No." I took a bite of toast. "I thought you started the army...?"

He shook his head. "No, I took it over. What about the man who brought you food in the dungeon?"

"What about him?" I countered.

"Did he love you?"

I laughed. "Not at all."

"Then why bring the food?"

I grinned. "It's my turn. Save your question."

We were sitting at the breakfast table in the same cabin where our dinner had been interrupted several days before. Only I was eating, while Ambrose simply sat, his feet up on the table, watching me.

Somehow, my pretending to be Rosey was becoming easier with each meal and against my better judgment, Ambrose and I had fallen into something of a rhythm.

We didn't interact outside of meals, not even when he came to the cabin to sleep at night. I'd thought perhaps he would stop watching me so carefully, after the gift of the new bed, but he did not. Still, he never so much as brushed against my side at night, giving me all the space possible. With time, I was beginning to think he was not quite so abhorrent as I'd originally thought.

Ambrose hardly ever asked anything serious, and steered noticeably clear of mentioning any of his family, especially Bael and Scion, or discussing my magic. He seemed to want to know only mundane things—my favorite food (I didn't have one), did I prefer the morning or the evening (morning), and if I missed living in Aftermath (yes). This morning, he'd fixated on my love life prior to winning the crown, and wanted to know all about every guard who'd ever looked twice at me.

It could've been far worse.

For his part, he held true to his word and answered everything I asked him. The only problem was, he refused to give more than the most direct answer, forcing me to yank every detail out of him like pulling teeth.

If I didn't know better, I would've said he was doing it on purpose. Perhaps trying to keep me at the table longer.

I put my fork down with a definitive clang.

Ambrose sat up slightly straighter at the sound, leaning forward to fix me with one of his bottomless stares. "It's your turn."

"I've finished eating," I replied, scooting my chair back from the table. "Isn't that how this works?"

He scowled, looking slightly aggravated, but raised a hand to wave me off. "Fine, go."

My eyebrows pulled together. We'd been sitting here for several hours already, to the point that soon one meal would bleed into another and lunch would begin. Yet, for some reason, he seemed bothered that I was leaving. Perhaps if he'd ever asked anything serious, I would've understood, but how interesting could it be to make me recount my various likes and dislikes in excruciating detail?

I didn't understand this male at all. Could he be all bad? What would have happened if I'd met him without all the preconceived opinions I'd formed, ever since losing my sister?

Except, there had to be more to it. He was still a killer, still the head of an army. Moreover, Scion hated him…there had to be some reason for that. I supposed, I would simply have to work up the courage to ask…perhaps during lunch.

I stood, and turned toward the door, ready to return to my cabin. However, I hadn't taken more than a step when he called me back.

"Wait!"

I glanced over my shoulder, my hand on the door. "Yes?"

He was biting the inside of his lip, in one of the most distinctly human expressions I'd ever seen on his face. Having sat across from each other for several meals now, I'd come to notice that Ambrose often moved like a human. He fiddled with his utensils, blinked often, and slouched in his chairs. It was at complete odds with Bael and Scion, who'd never once looked human to me in the time I'd known them. Their posture was too good, their movements too fast. I had to assume that spending twenty or more years surrounded by mortals had forced the rebel king to pick up some habits.

With a start, I wondered if I would pick up Fae mannerisms in as many years? Had I already?

After an inordinately long pause, in which I began to wonder if I'd imagined him calling me back, Ambrose opened his mouth to reply, but did not get a chance.

Without warning, a tremor rocked the ship. Plates and glasses slid from the table onto the floor, shattering at our feet. Outside, I heard the distant sounds of other things crashing against the deck, then the beginnings of screaming.

"What was that?" I demanded, stumbling back.

Across from me, Ambrose's black eyes widened, as if he were shocked by the words coming out of his own mouth. "I have no fucking idea."

Ambrose stared off into the space over my head, as if he could see something more than the dark, wooden wall behind me. His eyebrows came together. "Fuck."

"How can you possibly not know what's causing this?" I asked, frustration evident in my tone.

"I don't know everything, nor do I have time to discuss it with you." He turned on his heel and sprinted toward the door, leaving it wide open behind him.

Grasping the edge of the table to steady myself as the boat rocked once more, I stared after him, my mind moving sluggishly, seeming unable to make a decision. I supposed, if we were about to sink at the mercy of a thunderstorm, I'd be worse off inside than out.

Tripping over my dress, I stumbled after him, and emerged outside to find the entire crew in chaos. People were scurrying in all directions, slipping on the wet surface of the deck and screaming as the ship tilted back and forth. I looked up in bewilderment at the serene sky above. There was no sign of a storm or even a slight breeze to disturb my hair, yet the ground beneath me swayed as if caught in the midst of a hurricane. What the hell was going on?

As the thought entered my mind, it was immediately answered by a rush of sea water that sprayed into the air. An all too familiar reddish-brown tentacle burst from the ocean and flopped hard against the deck, writhing like the body of a gigantic snake.

I shrieked and jumped back. Was it the same monster I'd encountered while in the row boat, or another of the same type? I didn't know, nor did I care to wait and find out.

Before I could even react, however, a second tentacle snaked out of the water and landed beside the first. Both were covered in suckers the size of dinner plates, and were thicker even than the snake I'd met in Inbetwixt.

My eyes widened as the two slimy tentacles writhed and reached out, searching for something to cling onto. I could feel my heart racing in fear as I took a step back, trying to avoid their grasp.

The one closest to me wound its way around the thick central mast, and the wood creaked dangerously. My eyes bulged, and my mouth opened in a shrill scream, joining the cacophony of panicked voices that reverberated throughout the ship.

For a long moment, I couldn't bring myself to move. Fear rooted me to the spot, and I stood frozen, until out of the corner of my eye I saw Ambrose dashing in the opposite direction from the rest of the crew. They were fleeing from the monstrous creature, while he charged toward it, drawing his sword from its sheath at his waist.

I watched him for a split second before snapping myself back to reality. What was I thinking? I couldn't be of any assistance in this situation, I needed to get out of the way as quickly as possible.

I sprinted along with the panicked crowd, desperate to reach the cabin where I had been sleeping. My heart raced in my chest, and my feet struggled to maintain traction on the slippery dock, making it a challenge to keep my balance. Sea water sprayed over my head, and I choked when it burned my eyes and throat, soaking me entirely.

I was only a few steps away from the door to my cabin, when a giant shadow loomed over me. A third long tentacle ascended from the dark water and struck the ground with a loud thud, blocking my path to the door. My mouth fell open with another scream.

The slimy arm slithered toward me, as if reaching for a lifeline. It twisted and turned, searching for something to grip onto. My heart raced as it inched closer and closer, its searching motions sending shivers down my spine.

Without thinking, I threw my hands up in front of me and closed my eyes. I hadn't been using magic long enough to be sure why, but it seemed as if I performed better when my life was truly in danger. I was certain that when I looked, the serpentine thing would be engulfed in foot-high flames, charred to a crisp.

But nothing happened.

I looked down at my hands, then it hit me like a ton of bricks and I screamed, this time with anger. I was incapable of performing magic. If we lived through this, I would kill Ambrose myself for giving me that power deadening potion.

I backed away from the cursed tentacle, real fear washing over me. It was driving me back toward its other wandering arm, and in a matter of seconds one of them was bound to snatch me up. or, perhaps worse, swat me like a fly until I smashed against the boat.

My heart raced and my breathing was rapid. The tentacle inched closer to me, and I squeezed my eyes shut.

The telltale swish of a sword cut through the air, followed by a dull thud. My breath caught in my throat and I forced my eyes open to look up into the face of my savior, already knowing who I'd see there. "Fuck you."

Ambrose's lips curled up into a grin as he pulled his sword out of the tentacle he had just expertly severed. The limp appendage flopped against the deck, and he quickly wiped away the purple-ish blood with the leg of his trousers. "That's not a nice way to thank someone who saved your life, love."

"Yeah?" I shouted. "How about the bastard who put me on this ship in the first place and took away any ability to defend myself?"

"I'm not sure if I should be offended, or glad your fire has returned enough to hate me." He mused, already backing away to return to the fight, he pulled another long blade from his belt and tossed it at me. "Here, Defend yourself with that."

I jumped backwards out of the way of the flying blade, letting it crash against the deck. "Are you insane? You're going to cut my hand off."

He looked genuinely perplexed. "Not if you caught the handle."

I gaped at him in complete disgust. Not only was that blade far too heavy for me to ever lift on my own, the fact that he would expect me to catch it and hadn't seen the monster coming had me questioning everything I'd ever known about Ambrose Dullahan. "What kind of a seer are you?"

"The kind who wasn't paying attention for the last hour," he yelled over the wind and creaking of the ship. "If you want to blame someone for this, blame yourself. I couldn't possibly be expected to look away from you in that dress."

I felt my cheeks redden. It wasn't really my fault, of course, but he had seemed…engrossed in our conversation.

"What is that thing?" I demanded before he could run away again.

"It's a Charybdis," he said as if it were obvious. "Every time one of the tentacles is severed it will grow two more in its place."

I gaped at him in horror. "Then how do you kill it?"

"Cut all of them off at once before any others can grow," he replied.

"Oh, is that all?"

Without any warning, Ambrose barreled forward and collided into me. My breath was knocked out of my lungs, and we tumbled onto the hard surface of the deck. I let out a gasp and saw stars explode in my vision from the impact. And then I felt his weight come crashing down on top of me.

I lay flat on my back, disoriented, while Ambrose leaned over me. Our chests rose and fell in unison as we caught our breath, and I gazed into his intense, black eyes. In an instant, my entire world was consumed by his magnetic presence. I couldn't tear my eyes away from him, his sheer attractiveness captivating me and igniting an unexpected surge of desire within me.

I must have hit my head too hard.

"Get off me," I demanded, pushing at his chest.

He shifted back and, disgusted with myself, I looked past his head instead, and noticed two more tentacles above us. They were smaller than the first one, but still just as menacing, and they were moving in the exact spot we had been standing moments ago.

"Again, love, that's a terrible way to say 'thank you.'" Ambrose grinned, almost as if he were enjoying himself, and jumped to his feet. "Go back to the cabin. If I don't join you within the hour, you can assume I've been eaten."

I blanched, staring after him, as he darted away. To my surprise, I felt...nervous. Worried for his safety, and whether he might return or not...and I didn't like that. Not one bit.

29

LONNIE

ABOARD THE FORESIGHT

As it turned out, I needn't have worried. Ambrose returned to the cabin within mere minutes of my closing the door.

I sat on the bed we'd silently shared for the last few nights, and blinked at him across the room. Suddenly, the room felt too small, and I felt heat rise inexplicably in my face.

"Did you kill that thing?" I asked briskly. The boat was no longer rocking, but still, I felt the need to be sure the monster was well and truly gone.

"Yes," he said, as he closed the door behind him, locking out the whistling of the sea breeze.

I let out a sigh of relief, even as the rebel king leaned against the door, looking as close to exhaustion as I'd ever seen one of the Fae. His face and clothing were smattered with blood, and the side of his hair that was not shaved up to the scalp had fallen loose from its braid. His eyes flicked up to meet mine, and I immediately turned away.

"That was quicker than I'd expected."

"Did you expect me to return at all?" he asked, pushing off the door. "Or were you hoping the Charybdis would take care of all your problems for you."

I scowled. That was a little too close to what I'd been thinking for my comfort, and I still didn't have a good answer for him. "Let us say, I'm glad I don't need to sail this ship on my own. I don't even know where we're going."

He laughed quietly under his breath, and stalked across the room to the trunk at the foot of the bed. Throwing it open, he pulled out a clean shirt, and again raised his eyes to meet mine from beneath his lashes. "Is that your way of asking where I'm taking you?"

I bit my lip. "I don't suppose you'd answer, anyway. We're not eating."

He smirked, then straightened back to standing. "I'll tell you, but only if you answer a question for me."

I blinked. The way his questions had gone so far—my favorite color, my favorite pastime, and other such nonsense—I'd be a fool not to agree. "Fine."

His grin took on a wicked gleam. "We're on our way to Underneath."

"Why?" I demanded.

He shook his head, still grinning. "I said I would tell you where, not why."

I bit back a growl of frustration, and looked down. With my eyes on the bed, I almost didn't see him reaching behind him for the neck of his blood stained shirt, he pulled it off with one swift motion. I blinked in surprise.

"Are you ready for my question?" he asked.

I shook my head to clear it. "Fine."

I needed to get a grip on myself. I shouldn't have noticed or cared what his body looked like, but it was hard not to stare at all the hard muscles, covered almost completely in black, swirling tattoos. They started at his neck, and extended all the way down, disappearing past his belt.

"What are you thinking about?" he asked. "At this very moment."

I flushed scarlet, and quickly looked away. I was an idiot, and that was a cruel question, but only because I should not be wondering how much lower those tattoos ran. I should not be thinking of anything, except why we were bound for Underneath.

I refused to answer honestly. There had to be some technical truth I could give him, that would not burn my throat and also wouldn't reveal how absurd my thoughts had turned.

"I was thinking about how very stupid I am," I said.

To my surprise, he grinned. "An answer worthy of a Fae queen."

I flushed deeper, and turned away.

"Wait, he said, finally pulling his shirt over his head. "I wanted to tell you something earlier, but did not get the chance."

For some unknown reason, my heartbeat sped up, and I was nervous as I replied: "What was that?"

"I've thought of something for you to do."

"For me to do?" I raised an eyebrow in confusion.

He sat up straighter, focusing on me again, as if coming to a more concrete decision. "You said you have no pastimes."

Oh. A beat too late, I recalled the request I'd made of him. I needed something to occupy my time. "Right. What is it? It's not as if I'm about to take up painting while in captivity."

He stood, seemingly not listening to me, and walked around the side of the table until we were only a few feet away from one another. "You like winning, as do I, and you complain you have no way of defending yourself, which I can also understand."

I wrinkled my nose. "I don't know what you're angling for, but I cannot imagine that you have ever understood being unable to defend yourself."

"I don't have any offensive magic," he said, as if it were obvious.

"Perhaps, but you seem perfectly well acquainted with those swords."

Ambrose grinned at me. "Exactly. I'm going to teach you to use them."

THERE WAS NOT A SINGLE PROTEST I COULD'VE MADE THAT SEEMED to make any difference to Ambrose. Therefore, I found myself out on the deck that afternoon, preparing for my first lesson.

In truth, I should be jumping for joy at this offer. Ambrose had been right in his assessment of me: I'd complained bitterly and often about being outmatched, and unable to do much more than flee in a fight. Except, I remembered all too well Bael's early attempts at teaching me to use a blade, and how poorly they'd gone. I was simply uncoordinated, and that was all there was to it.

The afternoon sun was shining brightly, bringing some much-needed warmth after days of chilly weather. As I stood on the upper deck of the ship, I could still feel a slight chill in the air but it was nothing compared to the freezing temperatures of previous days. Ambrose and I stood facing each other, a sense of tension between us as I waited for him to speak. The crew had given us a wide berth, but I saw them casting curious looks at us as Ambrose presented me with a sword.

I eyed the blade skeptically before taking it, testing its weight in my palm. It wasn't small exactly, but neither was it as heavy or bulky as the enormous two-handed blades he favored. "Where did you get this?"

"It's Lin's," he replied easily. "So make sure not to lose it or she'll have my head."

I tilted my head questioningly, trying to think of who he could possibly be talking about. I'd never seen him interact with anyone besides the imposing guard, Riven. Who would have such a close connection to the rebel leader that they could borrow his possessions or even dare to intimidate him? "Who is Lin?"

In answer, he jerked his head toward the bow of the ship, where the short, dark haired woman from the other day was standing at the wheel. "My first mate, I suppose one would call it. Although, as she does far more in the way of navigating than I do, she's really the captain in all but name." He grinned. "Now, stop changing the subject, you're here to learn."

I grimaced. "I should warn you, I'm awful at combat."

His brow wrinkled. "I don't believe that."

I laughed. "Then you haven't been watching me very carefully."

He gave me an odd look, and ran his tongue over his bottom lip. "On the contrary, love. There's hardly been a moment since you were eighteen that I've been able to look away."

A sudden warmth spread across my cheeks. "Why? How would you have even known of me for that long?"

He grinned. "A question for another time, love. Let me see you wield the sword."

My cheeks still warm, and feeling incredibly foolish, I whipped the blade through the air a few times. He grimaced, and I stopped, growing defensive. "I told you, this is entirely pointless."

"It's not," he said quickly. "For starters, try not to flop your wrist so much, you'll break it the moment anyone combats you with any measure of force, and keep your sword as close to the center of your body as possible," he held out his hand to demonstrate.

With a hesitant grip, I grasped the weight of the sword in my hand, following his instructions to swing it through the air. The blade whistled, flowing in a wide arc. I turned my gaze toward Ambrose, eagerly awaiting his praise for my efforts. However, his face remained unreadable.

"You're too stiff," he said.

"Well, I did sleep on the floor for the better part of a week," I snapped, growing seriously annoyed.

Without commenting, he walked around to stand behind me and gently took hold of my sword arm. "Bend your elbow," he directed. "Don't stab, like you're using a fire poker. Slash, like this…"

His rough, calloused grip shifted my arm, and guided my movements in fluid motions.

"Fine," I breathed, and repeated the motion.

"That's better." he nodded and stepped closer. He placed his hands on my hips, his fingers pressing firmly into my skin as he shifted my stance. "You need to loosen up. Allow your body to move, like you're dancing."

A spark of desire shot through me, beginning where his hands burned into my sides, and flooding my entire body. I shivered involuntarily, feeling his words on the back of my neck. *Oh gods.*

I took a large step forward, breaking our contact. "I've got it."

A tense and drawn-out silence hung in the air before he finally emerged from behind me and retreated to his previous position, keeping a safe distance between us. Pressing his lips together in a flat line, he gestured for me to try again. And again. *And again.*

The sun had moved from overhead to low in the west before he declared that I was even holding the sword correctly.

I ran my sleeve across my forehead, wiping away the sweat dripping down my face. My body ached and I let out an exhausted sigh, shifting my weight to ease the tension in my stiff muscles. "I can't keep doing this."

Ambrose, who looked just the same as he had this morning having not exerted himself at all, raised his eyebrow at me. "But we haven't even gotten to spar yet."

I shook my head, and my skull pounded. "And we never will if you force me to continue because I'll drop dead right here and now."

He cocked an eyebrow. "Do you really mean that, or has your ability to lie returned at last?"

I fixed him with a withering stare, and turned to stomp back toward the cabin. "What do you think?"

30
SCION

UNDERNEATH

The last golden fingers of the sun clawed at the horizon as we reached the city of Underneath.

Smoke rose in the distance, and the air was thick with the smell of roasting meats and unwashed bodies—a stark contrast to the sterile desert that lay beyond the Hedge.

"This place is a fucking cesspool," I muttered.

"I love it," Bael said without a hint of sarcasm in his tone.

I caught the gleam in his unnerving yellow eyes, and I shook my head. "That?" I gestured pointedly to a group of ramshackle buildings, crumbling under the weight of their red-stone roofs. "You love *that*?"

"There's a strong energy here, don't you think?"

"If by 'energy' you mean 'chaos,' then yes. It's quite strong."

My cousin was far too happy to be here, and it was setting my teeth on edge. As far as I was concerned, we would find Lonnie and get the fuck out of here. Bael, however, seemed a bit too at home.

"You do remember why the fuck were here, right?" I muttered as we passed a ramshackle tavern.

"Yes, of course," Bael replied, the humor falling from his tone. "You do not need to keep reminding me that it has been nearly a week since we saw our mate. I feel it as much as you do."

I ground my teeth. I didn't like it when he said "our mate" as if it were fact, but for once I let it go. As long as he was focused on the point of our visit, and not distracted by the revolting spectacle of the unseelie city, that was all that mattered.

*

As we walked further along the road, a group of red-robed men tumbled out of the tavern we'd just passed. I stopped, and looked back at them, unease crawling up my spine.

I knew fucking soldiers when I saw them, armor or not.

"Wait," I motioned for Bael to stop. "Look."

He turned and followed my gaze. The red-robed soldiers were lounging outside the tavern, drinking from tankards that caught the dying light, making the liquid inside look like molten gold.

"King's lap dogs seem to be enjoying themselves," I observed, my lips curling in distaste.

Bael raised a skeptical brow. "You think those are guards?"

"Definitely."

"Hmmm," Bael hummed, his voice tinged with a dark amusement. "And to think, I thought your uniform was the ugliest one imaginable."

"Shut the fuck up, I'm being serious."

"As am I," my cousin replied. "If that's what the guards here wear, then don't you think we might stand out at the harbor?

Your armor screams 'Fae nobility' louder than a banshee at a funeral."

I glanced sideways at him. Bael might not have been destined for the throne, but he was every bit as dangerous as any royal I'd ever known. He also wasn't stupid, as much as he liked to pretend otherwise. "Maybe you're right."

"Trust me," Bael said with a flash of his sharp teeth in a semblance of a smile. "When have I ever led us astray?"

"More times than I care to count," I shot back.

"Then what's one more time to add to the list?"

I sighed, and looked down at my own shiny stone armor, before reluctantly nodding.

He was right, but trading the armor I'd worn religiously for years outside the palace was not something I looked forward to. I'd already had to send Quill away, telling him to circle the area outside the Hedge and wait for us. It seemed that this mission was determined to strip everything from me.

THE ALLEY BEHIND THE TAVERN WAS A NARROW GASH BETWEEN TWO hulking buildings. The uneven cobblestones were slick with garbage, the remnants of ale, and other less savory liquids. I pressed my back against the cold stone wall, my eyes scanning the back door.

"How long do you think it would take to sail from Inbetwixt around to Underneath?"

"By boat?" Bael mused, his yellow eyes reflecting the last light of the sun as it bled away into dusk. "Days. Perhaps a week?"

I nodded sullenly. That was what I'd thought.

It had been nearly a week already, and my greatest fear was that Lonnie would arrive in the harbor before we did. If she disappeared into the lands of Underneath before we could find her, I couldn't imagine any way to track down where she'd gone. "If she's already here—"

"I know," Bael cut me off. "Then we're fucked."

"But what if she is?" I pressed. "Where would Ambrose take her? To the king?"

"By Aisling, I fucking hope not," Bael muttered. "Even Ambrose can't be stupid enough to visit the king."

"Shut your mouth," a gruff voice hissed from the darkness nearby, and I jerked to a tension.

We both spun around to look as a ragged figure emerged—an unseelie beggar. Horns protruded from his temples, and his completely black, bug-like eyes wild with fear or madness. Possibly both.

"What did you say?" I hissed angrily.

"I said to shut your mouth, Idiots," he hissed. "After dark, the king hears everything. Even the walls have ears."

"Then you'd best be on your way," I snapped. "Or the walls will hear me cracking your skull against the pavement."

Nervously, the man retreated back into the shadowy embrace of the alley, muttering curses or prayers—I couldn't tell which. As he disappeared, I shared a look with Bael.

"Is that true?" I asked him.

Bael shrugged. "I don't know."

I ground my teeth in frustration, not liking to bring up my cousin's clear connection with the King of Underneath any more than absolutely necessary. "Can you…"

He shook his head, already knowing what I was going to say. "I can only see, not hear."

I couldn't ask anything else, as then, heavy footsteps sounded inside, and two red-robed guards stumbled out, drunk on ale and their own inflated egos.

"Ready?" Bael whispered.

I nodded, even as bile rose in my throat. There was no honor in this, only necessity.

As the first guard fumbled with his belt, I stepped forward.

The man was a bulky bastard, all muscle and no finesse. He barely had time to register our presence before I struck. I reached behind him, and twisted his neck with a sickening crunch. The guard crumpled to the ground.

Meanwhile, behind me, Bael had made quick work of the second guard. "Do you think you should take the time to behead them?"

I glanced down at the crumpled soldier. High Fae might be able to heal a broken neck, but I wasn't sure about the Unseelie.

"No," I said, reaching down to pluck the sword from the guard's belt. "It will take too long. Even if they eventually wake, it will be to find their robes and weapons gone."

Bael shrugged. "Fair enough."

I dragged the body of the first guard behind a barrel, and bent to pull off his robes. Then, out of the corner of my eye, I spotted a flash of crimson. A third guard was creeping out of the shadows behind my cousin, a long, Source-forged knife clutched in his shaking grip.

"Bael!" I called out, "Behind you."

Later, I'd realize it was that yell that sealed our fate. That the walls really did seem to hear all, and that mentioning Bael's name after dark was perhaps the most foolish thing I'd ever done in my immortal life.

Like he'd been summoned by my yell, a silence descended, profound and chilling. Then, out of the shadows, a hulking figure emerged, flanked by more guards than could be counted in a single gasp. They swarmed like locusts, their red robes a sea of blood against the city's cobblestones.

"Seize them," the king commanded, his voice devoid of emotion. "My son and I are long overdue for a talk."

31
AMBROSE

ABOARD THE FORESIGHT

"You seem to be getting along better." Riven said by way of greeting as he stepped up behind me.

I nodded slowly, and crossed my arms, leaning against the side of the ship. "Only because she's adaptive."

"What does that mean?"

Out of the corner of my eye, I watched Lonnie dancing across the deck of the ship, practicing the swordplay I'd spent every moment of the last several days teaching her.

After a difficult first session, in which I expected she would never pick up a sword again, she'd steadily impressed me with her improvements. With each new move she mastered, my apprehension lessened. At least now, she would be able to defend herself when we arrived in Underneath.

"If I didn't know her magic was suppressed, I'd say she has some enhanced ability to survive, no matter the circumstances," I told Riven. "Maybe it's just a learned personality trait, what with all the times Rhiannon moved her family around."

Riven didn't say anything to that, but he didn't have to. Voicing the thought aloud made me all but certain it was true. Rhiannon had been, and still was, a terrible mother, but she'd certainly raised capable daughters—if only by accident.

I smiled widely, as I watched Lonnie take a large slash in the air, and spin around, as if fighting two invisible opponents.

Riven looked sideways at me, his expression assessing.

"What?" I asked.

"Have you told her where we're going, yet?"

I nodded slowly. "Yes."

"Did you warn her about Rhiannon?"

"Not yet." I frowned. "Let me worry about that. I'll tell her when the time is right."

"And when is that?" Riven asked.

"When I think she'll believe me, and not go running straight to her mother and into a trap."

"There's hardly any time left. We'll be arriving tomorrow evening."

I pushed off the edge of the ship, and strode in the direction Lonnie had gone. "Then I'd better make tonight count, hadn't I?"

LATER THAT NIGHT, I EASED THE CABIN DOOR OPEN TO FIND THE lamps already extinguished, and Lonnie lying in bed, her back to me. I sighed. Despite what I'd told Riven, I was not willing to wake her just to continue my efforts to make her like me.

It sounded absurd. I was over two hundred years old, and I was spending my time trying to slowly coax a woman into wanting me, like some inexperienced nineteen year old. It was possibly the most ridiculous thing I'd ever bothered doing, and by far the most difficult.

Lonnie was emotionally broken, confused, and incredibly stubborn.

In the days after we'd talked about her sister, I'd been afraid I'd made a terrible mistake bringing her here, but somehow, she'd seemed to pull herself back from the brink of devastation.

I thought her cold shell was finally thawing, ever since I'd saved her from the Charybdis. Of course, there was still an absurdly long way to go, and a disheartening number of obstacles in our way.

For one thing, despite her appearance to the contrary, she was clearly still grieving.

For another, she had some absurdly human views about monogamy that made her unwilling to even acknowledge half of what I said or did near her. That hadn't come up per se, but I'd watched her excruciating back and forth with my brother for long enough to know it was the case. Even without prophecy, I knew that one day I'd become as frustrated as Bael, trying to convince Lonnie that it was perfectly possible to have more than one mate. In fact, for her, it would be almost impossible not to... at least, once she finally started using her powers correctly.

Of course, that was one of the problems in and of itself. Until Lonnie accepted her own magic, and stopped acting like the human she'd been raised to be, instead of the future queen that she was, we'd never get anywhere.

I walked as silently as possible across the room, trying not to wake her. At least she was sleeping in the bed now, rather than on the floor.

That had been another miscalculation on my part. I'd thought she would eventually relent, and sleep in the bed with me, but clearly I'd underestimated both her inflexibility and her resilience. Of course she would refuse to give in, unless the alternative would actually kill her as with the dinners I'd forced on her. I took it as a good sign, therefore, that she'd accepted the peace offering of the larger bed.

If I were a gentleman, I would have left her to sleep on her own.

But I wasn't.

I felt in my gut that once Lonnie truly came into herself, she'd be a force to be reckoned with—strong and erotic and entirely in control of herself. She wasn't there yet, though, and I knew that pushing her would only prolong the moment when I finally got to taste my queen.

Until then, every night we spent next to each other was a pleasant sort of torture.

Tonight was no different, and I bit back a curse as I slipped off my boots and shirt and climbed into the bed beside her. She didn't move an inch as I moved into a more comfortable position, so I was startled when she spoke into the darkness. "Thank you for helping me today."

I jumped, both at the shock that she was awake, and at the strange feeling of being surprised in the first place. It had been an entire week since I first found her in the barn, and I still wasn't used to how if we were alone together, I was entirely blind to our future.

I raised an eyebrow. I would've bet she was allergic to the word thank you, as I didn't think I'd ever once heard it escape her lips.

"You're welcome, love," I replied.

"Why do you keep calling me that?" she asked.

I stared up at the ceiling, unseeing, unsure what answer I could give her. I wasn't sure if she would want to know, or how she would take the knowledge that what had begun as a way to test myself, had long since turned into a personal obsession. How would she react if I confessed everything? How lovely I thought she was, how fascinated I was with everything about her, and how even though she held me at arm's length, this past week had been the best I'd experienced in two hundred years.

"You must be accustomed to nicknames by now," I said, flatly.

She stiffened. "I suppose."

I looked over at her, curiously. She reacted strangely every time I made the briefest mention of either Bael or Scion, and until now I'd ignored it, assuming she was preoccupied with her grief and anger. Now, though, I felt compelled to question it. "What are you thinking?"

"I'm wondering why your brother hates you?"

"Sorry?" I asked, startled. That wasn't what I'd thought she would say at all.

She shifted very slightly into a more comfortable position, but still didn't roll over to look at me. "Why does your brother hate you?"

That was what I'd thought she'd asked, but hearing it again didn't make the question make any more sense. We hadn't discussed Scion at all in the last week, except when I'd mentioned how she'd been healed after Riven shot her. I'd planned to heal her myself, thus making our week together easier from the onset, but I couldn't say I was sorry that things worked out the way they had.

I wanted her to be happy, even if it wasn't with me.

"Does Scion hate me?" I asked, stalling for time.

She snorted. "You must know he does. What happened between you?"

"Why do you want to know?"

"I'm wondering if I misjudged you."

My heartbeat sped up. That was good—perhaps I would be able to make this evening count after all. "Scion might be angry that I left," I began. "But more likely it's because I killed our father."

She stiffened, and finally rolled over to look at me. "Why?"

I appreciated that she assumed there was a reason, rather than immediately condemning me as a murderer. "It's difficult to explain."

"Try."

I sighed. I rarely explained myself to anyone, and even when I'd tried, few people understood.

I raised a hand in the darkness, tracing patterns through the air like the branches of a tree. "This is how the future looks to me. Like thousands of paths—of branches—all stemming off from a single decision, then each of those branches starts another set, and so on. There are endless possibilities, and every single moment could start the world off on a new path."

"I didn't ask for a lecture on prophecy."

"It would be easier to justify myself if you could see every decision made in the last one hundred years, as I can. If you knew every decision that could've been made instead. Let's say that my father wasn't a good male, and letting him get anywhere near the crown would've spelled disaster for more people than you can probably conceptualize."

"Why not just tell him that?"

I sometimes felt like the only player in an enormous game of chess, carefully planning out every decision to marshal my knights across the board toward the queen. My plans had been decades in the making, and now I was so close, I felt as if someone would knock my game board to the floor at the last possible second.

If anyone were capable of that, it would be the woman beside me.

"Because Scion, like me, believes in enacting the greater good for the largest number of people at the cost of anything else. If he knew everything I know, and was able to weigh that on the whole, Penvalle was a better choice than Belvedere, he would probably agree with my decision."

She gave me a skeptical sideways glance. "But…that would be good, right? If he agrees with you."

I pinched the bridge of my nose. It was a good question, and one I'd certainly wrestled with. "No, it wouldn't. Him forgiving me would have far reaching consequences that might derail everything I've spent thirty years lining up."

"Lining up to break your curse," she said.

It wasn't a question, more of a loose statement, but I answered anyway. "Yes."

"Because you've spent those thirty years searching for a worthy wearer of the crown," she said. "You'll be the villain who burns cities to the ground until you can pull a single worthy hero from the ashes."

I blinked at her. *What?*

It was such an odd statement, and so out of character for her, that it took me a moment to realize she was quoting *me*. Repeating what I'd said to her the day we destroyed the obsidian palace.

In retrospect, I might have said something a bit less dramatic… too late.

I shook my head, realizing I hadn't yet answered her. "Yes."

She looked me in the eye, and though it was dark, I could see every line of her face perfectly. "So…everything you're doing is to break the curse?"

I nodded again. "Yes."

"I want to help. I don't know why I landed where I am, if it was fated or if I was maneuvered into place just like you've done with everyone else, but I'm done pretending it doesn't matter."

I furrowed my brow. Despite having an army at my disposal, I'd never had anyone help me who truly knew the purpose behind everything we did.

Would she turn away as soon as she realized that my every decision was morally gray, at best? What would happen when she was forced to decide between her own life, my family's lives, and the lives of thousands of strangers?

I'd spent years searching, only to finally realize that there wasn't any one person alive able to break our curse, so eventually I'd realized I would have to create one. Originally, I'd intended Scion to be the worthy one—the last Everlast king.

Now, I was more convinced than ever that it was Lonnie who ended our long suffering—one way, or another.

"It's not a simple mission," I told her. "You could easily die."

"I would rather die a mortal death in battle than spend a thousand years in hiding."

I let out a long breath. Fuck, she was amazing.

Without thinking about it, or planning why I did it, I put out a slow, tentative hand. To my relief, Lonnie did not pull away and I gently ran my fingers through her long curls.

I tilted my head, slowly closing the distance between us until our lips were almost touching. Her eyes darted down to my mouth and her lips parted. She didn't flinch away, and I inched even closer, my breath mingling with hers.

As my mind went blank, a bright flash of colors and images flooded my vision, blocking out everything else. The walls of the room blurred, and my surroundings disappeared as I was pulled into someone else's mind.

Huddled in the dim, musty dungeon beneath the castle, I could feel the cold stones closing in on me, draining any glimmer of hope for escape. The only source of light was a small grate high above, casting eerie shadows that seemed to dance across the floor. The clanking of chains echoed throughout the cramped space, and I shifted uncomfortably on the rough floor. My back burned, as if I'd been whipped, and every movement was agony.

I blinked rapidly, and Lonnie came back into focus. Her face was a breath away, but she stared at me, bewildered and unsure. "What's wrong?"

I released my hold on her. There were more pressing matters that demanded my attention, now. As much as it pained me, she would have to wait.

"I've just had a vision. There's more than one person we need to save from the dungeons of Underneath."

"Who?" She demanded.

"Your mates."

PART THREE
Legacy and Ruin

32
LONNIE
ABOARD THE FORESIGHT

"How old are you?" I demanded.

The fairy looked down at me. His eyebrows pulled low over eyes so dark they appeared black. "Go away, infant."

I stayed exactly where I was. Fae were terrifying, generally, but mother had told me to trust this male. If mother said something, it had to be true.

Anyway, he looked like a prince from a storybook. Anyone this lovely couldn't be all evil.

"I've only seen gray hair on old people before, but I thought fae didn't age." I continued as if he hadn't spoken. "Unless you are very very old?"

He sighed. "Stop. It is humiliating enough to be sent outside like a servant. I won't debase myself further by talking to a human."

I blinked at him, somewhat confused. He'd used several words I'd never heard before, but I understood generally that he was insulting me. "Is it not defacing yourself to bother insulting a human child?"

"Debase," he corrected.

"Child, not infant," I replied. "Surely you know the difference, unless you are so old you have forgotten."

The corner of his mouth tipped up ever so slightly. "I have always had this hair color. Now, go away."

A pang of offense shot through me. "What's your name?"

He sighed, looking up at the sky. "What's yours?"

I paused for half a second. Earlier, when he'd asked my name I'd refused to answer. But, if mother trusted him…

"Elowyn," I replied, using my full name to sound more grown up.

The Fae glanced sideways at me, black eyes assessing. "That was an incredibly stupid mistake, Elowyn," he said, sounding almost bored. "I assume you have some sort of nickname. You should only ever use that."

My brow furrowed. "Why?"

"Do you know what a powerful fairy can do with your real name?"

I sucked in a breath. I wanted to say yes, but in truth I didn't know. My mother had warned Rosey and I never to give out our names, but she never said why. Like everything else, she never explained her reasons, only saying that she'd tell us when we were older.

"For the rest of your life, you'll never be able to deny a direct order. You'll always have to come when I call you. You'll never truly be free."

My stomach sank. "I don't believe you."

"Fae can't lie," he said, sounding bored. "But I'd be happy to demonstrate for you. You have a sister, do you not?"

"Yes."

"What if I told you to go murder your sister?"

Angry heat licked up my spine, dancing over my arms and making my fingers tingle. "Then I would kill you first so you could never make me do that."

The fairy laughed, a cruel, musical sound that made the hair on the back of my neck stand up. "Interesting. Well, let me tell you a secret, infant human. I can tell you exactly how unlikely that is."

He glanced off to the side, as if looking at something far in the distance.

In what was only a couple of seconds, but felt much longer, the fairy blinked and looked back at me.

His brows knitted again, seeming distressed. "What are you?"

"I assume you know at least something about Underneath?" Ambrose asked.

I nodded. "Yes."

"Good, then you know that it's far more dangerous than every city in Elsewhere combined."

We were standing once again on the upper deck of the ship, but for once there was nothing going on that might require the use of a sword. The sails billowed as the ship cut a silent path through the placid waters, drawing ever closer to the harbor of Underneath. I leaned over the railing of the captain's deck, peering into the heavy mist that hovered on the horizon, trying to catch the first glimpse of the shoreline.

I wondered how many people had sailed this close to the forbidden city before?

How many humans?

Had my mother made the same trip, or had she crossed the Hedge?

There were so many questions swirling through my brain, I didn't know where to begin.

"Why is it so dangerous?" I asked.

"Unlike Elsewhere, Underneath is an absolute monarchy."

I raised an eyebrow. "So is Elsewhere, or have you not been living in the same country I have all this time?"

He shook his head. "No. Elsewhere is a kingdom in a traditional sense, meaning the actual day-to-day governing has very little to do with the royal family. I would know, having been part of the court for more years than you've been alive."

I frowned. I sometimes forgot how old he was, because the silver-haired prince looked roughly twenty-five by human standards, and because the other fairies I knew—namely Bael and Scion—were not actually that old in the grand scheme of things. Bael was only about ten years older than me, in his thirties, and to my knowledge Scion was somewhere between fifty and seventy, give or take. Ambrose, however, was over two hundred, and had only been exiled from the royal family for the last several decades. He'd had an entire life at court before I was born, and while it felt unimaginable to me, there were many alive today who recalled when The Dullahan was called "Prince Ambrose."

How surreal it was to realize that the castle which he'd destroyed, had been his home once. How strange to think he'd likely been friends with Gwydion at one point, had verbally sparred over breakfasts with Raewyn, and terrified servants, just like me. The man in front of me didn't seem to fit that role at all.

I shook my head to clear it, realizing that Ambrose had still been talking the entire time I'd been thinking, and I hadn't heard a word of it. "Sorry, could you repeat that?"

Ambrose gave me an exasperated look, but obliged. "Elsewhere is made up of multiple independent territories, each of which is governed by its own High Lord and Lady. At one time, every province was its own independent kingdom—"

"Until Queen Aisling mated with all the High Lords and united the country—yes, I know the story."

He raised an eyebrow. "It's not a story, it's a historical account. At the time of Aisling, Underneath did not exist as it does now, nor did the capital city. Everything below the Waywoods was Wilde land, overtaken by creatures either too monstrous, or too uncivilized to assimilate with the Fae—or the Seelie, as we were called in the old tongue."

"Which is why Underneath is now full of Unseelie."

"Yes. Back then, the Unseelie were not organized as the Seelie, but they did have a king who was their absolute ruler."

I nodded. I knew this part of the story as well.

The unseelie king had been furious at not being included in Aisling's circle of mates, and had therefore attacked her kingdom. He killed her mates, and all but one of her children, before stealing the crown of Elsewhere, raping the queen and taking her as a hostage back to his court. As punishment, Aisling asked the source to curse the Unseelie king, and all his descendants with never-ending misery until such time as the crown was returned to its rightful wearer.

It was a story I understood well, because the Everlast family were the many generations removed descendants of Aisling and the Unseelie king. For thousands of years, they'd been unable to find the worthy wearer of the crown, and therefore remained cursed with unhappiness.

"You do not have to explain your curse to me," I said. "I'm all too aware already."

He looked at me gravely, and nodded. "Fine, then I won't bore you with details you already know. What I mean to make you understand is that there is only one power that matters in Underneath, and that is the king. There are no lesser lords, no governors or dukes, and no real court to speak of. The position of Unseelie king is not inherited, but won, by way of killing the previous monarch."

I snorted a humorless laugh. "That sounds familiar."

He shared my smile. "Yes, quite. Only Underneath has never put as many rules or arbitrary events in place as we have. There, one simply challenges the current king, and the victor gets the crown."

"That sounds messy," I mused. "And violent."

"For many years, it was. They used to cycle through kings as often as seasons."

"All kings?" I asked. "Were there no queens?"

"The term "king" is not gendered there, as many of the Unseelie are fluid shapeshifters, or don't ascribe to a humanoid gender. Anyone can be the ruler, but for many years now the position has been held by only one male. King Gancanagh."

As if summoned by the king's name alone, the shoreline emerged out of the mist on the horizon. It was still too far out to make out any distinct details, but mountains seemed to rise in the distance, like the back of a dragon, or the sharp points of the obsidian crown.

"I've heard of him," I said vaguely.

"From Bael?"

I nodded. "And because of the dust. You trade your drugs with the kingdom, do you not?" I asked, tearing my eyes from the first glimpse of land I'd seen in a week.

"Yes," Ambrose said. "And I won't pretend that's merely a ruse to cross the border. Gancanagh's dust has been instrumental in the success of the rebellion thus far. In fact, we'll be entering the kingdom because I have a meeting planned with the king, but it should also provide a good opportunity to search for Bael and Scion, as well as your mother."

"Right," I said nervously. "But do you not think anyone will question my presence there? Who am I meant to be?"

"Yourself," he replied, as if it were obvious. "Believe me, King Gancanagh will not question why I'd have a hostage with me, especially one who matters to the royal family. He, himself, has two consorts."

"I thought you just said that the king was the only one with power?"

"He is. The consorts don't control anything. I don't even know their names."

I raised an eyebrow. "How is that possible when you've met them?"

"You'll see when we arrive."

The shore was well and truly visible now, and I stared out over the landscape of red-rock cliffs, and jagged mountains. It looked similar to the landscape of Aftermath, if perhaps, dryer. Where the valleys in the north were green and full of life, it didn't look to me as if a single green thing had ever been seen growing in the sandy soil of Underneath.

"It's beautiful," I remarked, my gaze lingering on the city's skyline, where the dying light cast sinister shadows that danced like specters against the rock face.

"Yes," Ambrose replied with a bitter laugh. "Beautiful like a siren song. Alluring, yet deadly."

As dusk fell, we sailed into the bustling harbor of Underneath.

The harbor was set into an alcove in the rock face, mostly hidden until we were right upon it. The water itself glistened with a reddish sheen, no doubt caused by the red and orange sand that cascaded down the sides of the crimson mountains. It gave the harbor an almost blood-like appearance.

I hoped it was not an omen.

I leaned over the edge of the ship as we arrived, fascinated by the activity of the harbor.

Though it was evening, the docks bustled with life, like the market vendors had only just begun work for the day. Ships of every conceivable design jostled for space along the crowded docks—galleons with sails like the wings of giant moths, sleek vessels that shimmered with a pearlescent sheen, and rough-hewn barges that looked as if they'd been carved from the very bones of the earth. Still, our ship glided to a gentle stop, and was tethered securely by the deft hands of the crew. They moved as if they'd done this many times before–which, I supposed, they had.

Ambrose stepped up behind me and put a large hand on my lower back. "Ready?"

I turned my head to look up at him, and jerked back in surprise. He was wearing a long, black cloak with a hood pulled up to cover all of his gleaming silver hair, but that was not what startled me. "Why the mask?

"Because this will draw far less attention than my face would, I promise you."

I cocked my head to the side, unable to imagine how that was possible. He was wearing the same stag-skull mask I'd first met him in, and it added a dark, powerful quality to him that was impossible to ignore.

"Everything will be fine," he promised. "Underneath is only two thirds as frightening as everyone says."

I stared at him, and it took me a long moment to realize he was joking. "Two thirds? So there are no dragons at every gate, or horrible Unseelie monsters lurking at every turn."

"Oh, there are," he replied, "But I won't let anyone touch you."

A slight shiver traveled up my spine, and it had nothing to do with my nerves.

33
LONNIE

UNDERNEATH

My legs wobbled as we made our way down the gangway to the dock, the crew trailing behind us. I swayed slightly, and Ambrose threw out a hand to steady me. "You'll get used to dry land again within a few hours. Until then, perhaps hold on to my arm."

I sighed, but took his arm anyway. As we stood, watching the crew unload all manner of crates and barrels, a tall, thin man approached us down the long dock. He wore a robe of deep crimson, the same shade as the distant mountains, and an expression that was neither pleased, nor particularly hostile.

"Say nothing," Ambrose muttered under his breath.

"Why?"

He shook his head, indicating that I would have to wait for explanations, and turned to face the oncoming man. "Good evening."

The man stopped in front of us, and I pressed my lips together to keep from gasping out loud. From afar, I'd assumed he was human, but up close I could see that his eyes were a green far too bright to be normal, and slitted, almost like a snake. I silently wondered what else might be hiding beneath his long billowing robes. Scales perhaps? Did he have a tail?

"Lord Dullahan," the snake man said stiffly, reminding me a bit of Mordant—the Everlast's unpleasant household advisor. "Welcome to the dark court. The king was expecting you several days ago."

Ambrose stiffened at my side. "Odd then, that you're waiting here to collect us."

"Not at all," the servant said without inflection. "We see all that goes on beyond the Hedge."

Ambrose barked a bitter laugh. "As if I could forget."

The servant glanced at me. I caught a glimmer of recognition in his eyes—swiftly masked—but not before sending a shiver down my spine. He looked back to Ambrose. "Will it be you alone joining us in the palace, or…?"

"Me, and my companion," Ambrose said shortly. "The crew will find their usual accommodations."

"Very good, my Lord. If you'll follow me, the King is eager for you to join the court for supper."

THE DOCKS OF UNDERNEATH, AND THE MARKET PLACE BEYOND, were far more lively than I would have expected. There were hundreds, if not thousands of shoppers, chatting, laughing, and stopping to admire the various stalls. It might have looked like any other market square in Elsewhere, except that I'd never seen so many Unseelie as long as I'd lived.

Unseelie were rare within the city of Inbetwixt, and nearly nonexistent within the capital, but here it was we who stood out among all the horns and teeth and bright, scaly skin. Ambrose had been right—his mask did blend in far better than his too-perfect Fae features.

"Might I speak now?" I hissed.

Ambrose gave a tight shake of his head, causing his mask to wobble. "Later."

Furrowing my brow with annoyance, I entertained myself watching the crowd as we passed by vendors selling foods and glittering gems I'd never seen before. There was even a group of small, green skinned unseelie children crouched on the ground, playing some game that looked like a mixture of checkers and tic-tac-toe.

We trailed behind the servant as we exited the marketplace and emerged onto a bustling main street. Here, the houses that lined the street were constructed from stone and clay instead of brick or wood, and the road itself was paved with large, orange-red stones that resembled thousands of raw-cut rubies. In the center of the empty road stood a massive black carriage, pulled by two enormous black Fae horses, with eyes that glowed as if they were fueled by an inner fire.

The snake-like servant held the carriage door open for us. Ambrose strode in first, his long black cloak brushing against the servant's red one. I hopped in after him, and the servant followed me.

As if anticipating the questions I was burning to ask, Ambrose shot me a warning glare. I slumped down into my seat, tapping my foot impatiently as the coach took off.

After what felt like hours, the coach finally came to a stop and I eagerly leaned out the window. I gasped.

There was a huge, ornate castle, seemingly built into the side of a mountain. Its black towers looked like shards of glass, and the last rays of the setting sun bounced off the polished glass-like surface, creating a dazzling spectacle of red and gold. Running alongside the castle, almost like a moat, a huge volcanic chasm, stretched as far as the eye could see.

Finally, I could not keep my mouth shut a moment longer. "How are we meant to cross that?"

"Bridges," Ambrose said roughly, his brow wrinkling with annoyance. "Nearly everything is accessible by bridge the further you go into the mainland. That chasm stretches almost the length of the entire wall, so without being able to cross, they would lose access to half their land."

"Why not build within it?" I asked. "It is, after all, called 'Underneath.'"

Ambrose chuckled. "They have. The bottom of the rift is home to many creatures that I doubt you would want to meet."

When we finally made it to the other side, we stepped out of the coach with relief.

"Will you be wanting your usual room?" the servant asked.

"Yes," Ambrose replied.

The servant glanced at me, addressing me for the first time. "And for you?"

"She'll stay with me," Ambrose said, before I could answer.

I looked down, avoiding his gaze. I didn't feel like debating over where we would sleep tonight. We had been sharing a room for the past week. Plus, this city was notorious for its danger - possibly the most dangerous on the entire continent - and I didn't want to be left alone to face the wrath of the Unseelie.

The servant beckoned us inside the massive castle, and my eyes traced the intricate carvings on the stone walls as we walked through dimly lit corridors. On the third floor, he stopped in front of a large, round-topped door. "The king has requested your presence in one hour."

I frowned. One hour was hardly enough time to, not only rest, but discuss our next plans. Apparently, the king was eager to discuss business with The Dullahan, and my presence here didn't change that.

The servant scurried off, and Ambrose opened the door to our room, ushering me inside. Velvet drapes kissed the floor with a regal elegance, and golden chandeliers overhead dripped with crystal, like frozen rain touched by Midas himself. It was as if the room breathed in wealth and exhaled extravagance.

And I didn't care for any of it.

Ambrose closed the door behind us with a heavy snap, and I immediately rounded on him. My voice dripped with derision. "Am I allowed to speak now, your highness?"

He pulled off his mask, and rolled his eyes. "Would it matter if I said 'no?'"

"Not at all," I snapped. "What the fuck is going on?"

Shaking his head, he pressed his finger to his lips, then grabbed my hand and half dragged me behind him across the room. Out of habit more than fear, I resisted, digging my heels into the carpet. "What are you doing?"

"Shhh!"

Ambrose threw open a door to the attached bathing room, and pulled me inside. Like the bedroom, the bathing room was a luxurious space with polished marble floors and golden fixtures. The large shower stood in one corner, while a freestanding tub sat in the center of the room, beckoning me to soak in its depths.

Ambrose turned on both faucets, filling the room with the soothing sound of running water. "I forgot to tell you," he hissed, looking furious with himself. "Within the lands of Underneath, King Gancanagh can hear anything you say after dark, and if he chooses, he can see you as well."

I raised an eyebrow. "How is that possible?"

Ambrose shook his head. "I don't truly know how he does it, but it's quite disturbing to watch. His eyes roll into his head, and he can look upon anywhere within his kingdom."

"Ah," I said quickly. "Like Bael."

"Shhh!" Ambrose hissed, glancing at the running faucets with apprehension. "Do not say his name. I doubt this is doing us much good as far as muffling our voices."

Dread sank in my gut, at the realization that if the king could hear, and worse, see us, we would not be able to immediately go searching for the dungeon as I'd planned. "Then how are we going to discuss…" I searched my mind for words that wouldn't give away exactly what I meant. "What we came here for?"

"The king's power is strong, but it is limited only to the hours of darkness. Simply try to remember not to mention anything you would rather not overheard unless it is daylight."

I nodded stiffly. "Fine."

Ambrose relaxed slightly, a mirthless smile flickering at the edge of his lips. "There is one other thing. The very stones of this castle are mixed with Gancanagh's dust. The dust is used here to neutralize magic within the castle's walls. Except for the king, all magical abilities are rendered useless."

My mind raced, piecing together the implications. The absence of our magic meant no premonitions to guide us. It also landed some much-needed clarity on how Bael and Scion could ever have been captured.

"Great," I muttered, feeling as if a stone dropped into my chest. "So we're as helpless as lambs in a lion's den. Perfect."

"It's not only that. There's a high likelihood that you'll find your inhibitions lessened."

I cocked an eyebrow at that, already feeling heat creep up my neck. "Meaning?"

Ambrose stepped closer, his silver hair a stark contrast against the shadows that played hide and seek across his features. "Meaning, I would be careful to think twice over any decisions you would not normally make. The king is the basest form of our kind, as such, he enjoys a spectacle as much as a cruel trick."

"Understood," I replied, though my stomach coiled tight with anxiety. Without magic, every step was a gamble, but for Bael, for Scion, and for my mother, I was willing to play the odds.

34
LONNIE

UNDERNEATH

After only a brief hour's rest, a knock sounded on our door.

A different red-robed servant, this one with blue-tinted, leathery skin and long spindly fingers, arrived to lead us down to dinner.

Ambrose and I were already ready and waiting to go—having bathed and dressed quickly, in case we were dragged from our room sooner than expected. I'd stuffed myself into the same burgundy gown from the ship, and had brief cause to wonder if Ambrose had always intended me to wear it here, rather than on the boat.

We hadn't spoken much since he'd warned me we were unable to use magic, except so long as it took him to insist I wear the obsidian crown to dinner.

I got the impression that Ambrose was on edge, feeling crippled by his inability to see prophecies. I was only just starting to realize how many visions the rebel king must see at any one time. I remembered what Bael had told me about Queen Celia going effectively blind toward the end of her life, and wondered if that would be Ambrose's future as well.

For my part, I was a torrent of mixed emotions. I was desperate to look for Bael, Scion, and my mother, and simultaneously terrified to leave this room. If we were caught searching for them, and ended up in the dungeon ourselves, then…well, I didn't see it likely that I would be rescued from a dungeon by a prince two times in the same lifetime.

I practically shook as we walked down to dinner—somehow terrified that I'd blurt our plans by mistake.

The obsidian crown felt too heavy on my head, and despite my insistence that I could handle this, that I wanted to help, I didn't feel particularly adept or royal when surrounded by the all too foreign walls of Underneath.

I couldn't help but let my gaze sweep over the opulence that surrounded us—vaulted ceilings reaching into shadows, tapestries that told of ancient victories and tragedies, and statues of fairies caught mid-flight, their faces twisted in expressions of rapture or agony. The only sounds were our footsteps, and the notes of some ethereal melody that seemed to bleed from the very walls.

We reached the ground floor, and stopped in front of a set of black obsidian double doors, almost identical to those of the Everlast palace. I cast Ambrose a sideways glance, wishing I could speak out loud to ask why there were so many similarities between here and the capital.

Was it simply because the obsidian palace was originally built by the Unseelie king, perhaps in the image of his own home? Or was there another reason behind the similarities?

The dining room doors swung open with an almost ceremonial gravitas, revealing a hall so grand it would've put the obsidian palace to shame. The ceilings towered so high it was hard to tell if they opened to the sky, or if they were simply painted to resemble distant stars. In the corner, sat a golden—robed string quartet, but they were not playing. In the center of the room, was a long table, so laden with food it could have fed an army—or at least a small battalion of gluttonous nobles.

The golden silverware gleamed, and crystal goblets stood poised to catch the light, fracturing into a thousand dancing reflections. Platters overflowed with fruits that shone like jewels, meats roasted to a succulent sheen, and pastries that were airy puffs of temptation. There were dishes I couldn't even name, exotic concoctions that promised flavors as complex as the politics of this cursed court.

We walked in and sat down at the table. No one moved to touch any of the food, and I followed their lead. My stomach growled loudly, and I pressed my fingers to my abdomen, willing it to be quiet.

Servers appeared, carrying huge ceramic pitchers. One stopped behind my chair. "Wine, my lady?"

I swallowed a lump in my throat, remembering how I too had once carried a pitcher like that. How I'd spilled it across Scion's boots, in what felt like another lifetime. "No, thank you."

Beside me, Ambrose accepted his own wine with a whispered "thank you," through his mask.

Finally I could not keep silent any longer. "How are you going to eat with that thing on?"

He turned to me, and though I could not see his face, I knew he was scowling. "I'll take it off when the king arrives. He knows what I look like."

"Where is the king?" I asked pointedly.

"He likes to make an entrance."

I bit back a snort. Of course he did. What fairy did not?

A hush descended upon the room, thickening the air with expectation, or perhaps dread. My heart danced a nervous rhythm.

That's when he entered.

The doors flew open once more, and a tall, painfully beautiful man stepped into the room.

I stifled a gasp, and schooled my face into benign interest, but inside I was reeling. I supposed I'd expected the king of Underneath to be monstrous, or at least as unusual as some of the servants and market-goers. But he was not.

The King looked like Bael.

Or rather, Bael looked like his father.

Even if I hadn't known already that Bael's father was Gancanagh of Underneath, it would have been evident from a single glance. They had the same dark, dangerous beauty, the same square jaw and high cheekbones, and—most obvious of all—the same cat-like, yellow eyes. More disturbing still, immortality gave the impression that both were about the same age, so that they could have more easily passed as brothers than as father and son. The only obvious differences between the two, as far as I could see at a glance, were that Gancanagh's pin-straight hair was a dark, chestnut brown, and he was somewhat taller than Bael, so that the king towered to nearly seven feet.

The king crossed the room, flanked by a small group of nobles. Several, I assumed to simply be his inner circle—advisors, and court flies alike. Two, however, caught my attention.

They were small—shorter than the rest by several inches, and appeared slight of bone. "Appeared" as I couldn't see anything of them, aside from the long, red-silk robes they wore. Both were veiled from head to their toes, making me wonder how they could possibly see where they were going.

The two veiled companions hurried to the king's side, as he stood behind his chair at the head of the table. He smiled at everyone, flashing razor sharp teeth. When he glanced at me, his eyes flicked up to my crown, before he immediately looked away.

As I watched the king, transfixed, I almost didn't notice the servant who scurried forward with a golden pitcher, pouring wine into his goblet with hands that trembled like leaves in a tempest.

"Welcome," the king said finally, raising his goblet high.

As he sipped, I noticed that where hands should be, he had monstrous, cat-like claws. I shivered.

Everyone around me, Ambrose included, raised their own goblets and sipped, and I suddenly realized I should have accepted the wine. I sat awkwardly, unmoving, as I waited for everyone to drink.

Then, without warning, the king smashed his glass upon the ground with a loud crash. The others followed suit, the sound of shattering crystal echoing through the room, and as if it were a signal, music suddenly erupted from the players in the corner, and talking commenced.

"Welcome, Lord Dullahan," the king leaned toward Ambrose, smiling as if they were sharing a private joke. "I trust the journey was not too strenuous?"

To my surprise, Ambrose pulled off his mask with a flourish and grinned back, like King Gancanagh was an old friend. "Only two run-ins with Charybdis, and not a single dragon. Hardly anything worth mentioning."

The king's face fell comically, like that of a child. "How disappointing."

I choked on air, thinking of the monsters we'd encountered while at sea. I certainly would not have called that "disappointing" as if to see more would've been all the more enjoyable.

The sound of my cough turned the king's attention to me, and his vibrant yellow eyes bore into me, flickering with interest. "Did you not enjoy the journey?"

My chest seized, meeting his too-familiar eyes. Looking at him it was hard to imagine that it was under his orders that Bael himself was currently trapped beneath the castle. "It was… eventful."

"I don't believe we've met," the king said to me, leaning all the way forward. "What's your name?"

Before I could reply, Ambrose cut me off. "You must remember Rhiannon."

Gancanagh cocked his head, clearly curious. "I do, but this is not Rhiannon."

"One of her daughters," Ambrose said smoothly. "The one who was a seer, Rosey, joined my cause several years ago."

"Hmmm," the king replied, looking away from me as if his interest had died. "It's a shame you couldn't get the other one."

I sat frozen, a buzzing starting up in the back of my mind. Ambrose had done quite well, in hiding my name without lying. He'd spoken only technical truths, leading to the conclusion that I must be my sister. Except, in doing so he'd revealed new questions. How did the king know my mother? And more importantly, why would he find it "a shame" if I were Rosey, rather than myself?

"So, daughter of Rhiannon," the king said, addressing me directly once more. "How did you come to wear that crown?"

"I gave it to her," Ambrose said, again cutting me off before I was forced to reply. "I took it during the battle over the castle, and it looks lovely on her, don't you think? Besides, I thought it might be enjoyable to have three queens with us, rather than two."

Gancanagh grinned. "Ah, thank you for reminding me. Allow me to introduce my wives." He gestured to the two veiled figures beside him.

An awkward silence followed, as neither woman spoke, and the king did not offer their names to us.

"Hello," I said finally to the nearest veiled woman.

She didn't so much as twitch, and didn't reply. A strange, uneasiness fell over me in the following silence.

Thankfully, at that moment, the servants returned and began doling out food onto our golden plates. Conversation stopped for a few minutes, as everyone ate, and when it started up again the king seemed to have moved on from questioning my presence.

Ambrose and Gancanagh spoke animatedly as we ate. They discussed only business; the success of their trade routes, and politics that flew directly over my head. My mother was not mentioned again, and as the meal progressed, I began to tune out the conversation.

Perhaps I should have listened, tried to learn their secrets, but my thoughts kept wavering to other parts of the castle. Were my mother and my mates starving, while we sat at this feast? Would I know if they were seriously harmed, as they seemed to with me? Or could they be dead already, and I was too human to notice. When would we be freed from this pointless charade so that I could go search for them?

"You will have to join us for the hunt tomorrow," Gancanagh was saying to Ambrose, their business evidently having concluded. "Or, are you planning to return right home? If I'd recently acquired a palace, I cannot say I'd have left so soon for a simple business meeting."

Ambrose stiffened beside me, and I was not sure why. "The palace is currently not fit for visitors. It's being rebuilt after the unfortunate damage it sustained in battle."

"You will have to invite me to visit when the repairs are complete."

Again, Ambrose went stiff, but his voice was even when he replied: "Of course."

A spark of anger flitted through me. They were discussing travel, as if the king was not holding his own son beneath the castle. Perhaps torturing him, or worse.

With a smile so brittle it could shatter, I pushed back my chair, the sound jarring against the marble floor, and rose to my feet. I couldn't sit through another moment of this or I would scream. "I believe," I blurted out, my voice cutting through the drone of pleasantries like a blade, "a breath of fresh air would do wonders for me."

Ambrose's gaze flickered to mine from across the table, dark and sharp as obsidian. His gaze bore into me with a silent warning, but I turned away.

"Of course," came the king's honeyed reply. "My dear," he intoned, addressing his veiled queen with a nod so subtle it was almost imperceptible. "Would you be so kind as to escort our guest to the terrace?"

Fuck.

Ambrose's silent reprimand still lingered in the air, but at the king's command one of the veiled queen's rose, and beckoned silently for me to follow.

I ground my teeth. Now, there was no chance of me searching for anyone, but I couldn't very well pretend to have changed my mind. I would simply have to get some air with the queen, and return.

The queen led me silently out of the hall and down another opulent hallway.

"Your home is quite lovely, Queen…" I trialed off, hoping she would interject her name.

She did not respond, her veiled gaze fixed on the path ahead. I shivered again. Her silence was a tangible thing, wrapping around me with unease. My eyes flitted from one dark corner to another, seeking any hidden threats.

Then, the queen opened a door onto a large terrace, and I stepped outside, my mouth falling open.

The sky stretched on forever, the stars twinkling over the tops of red mountains. Strangely, I felt my throat tighten at the sight. It looked like the mountains of Aftermath, and after the casual mentions of my mother and sister, my emotions lingered too close to the surface.

"It's beautiful," I said honestly, glancing over at the queen.

As I turned, a flicker of motion caught my eye, and I whipped around sharply, only to see nothing but the dance of candlelight against stone. I bit back a curse, chastising myself for nerves that felt like rampant lightning beneath my skin. This castle, these people—they had a way of burrowing under the skin, of making you doubt your own senses.

And then, without warning, the shadows burst into life.

A robed figure stepped out of the darkness of the terrace, a long blade raised to strike.

"Look out!" I cried, throwing myself toward the queen.

Time seemed to stutter, like a heartbeat suspended in the mid-air.

The assailant's blade sliced toward us, its whistle a discordant note against the hushed silence of the balcony.

"Behind me!" I snapped at the queen, shoving her roughly out of the way.

Before leaving, I had carefully concealed a small blade in my boot, hidden from view by the flowing layers of my dress. Now, my hand instinctively went for it as the assassin bore down on us.

I didn't have time to wonder why this was happening, or who the man was. My hand found the familiar grip of my hidden dagger, and I lurched forward.

The assassin slashed the air in front of me with his long sword, and I met his strike with my own blade. Everything Ambrose had taught me flew from my mind, yet somehow, the memory of the movements had not left my muscles.

We danced across the balcony, his long sword clashing against my short dagger, each strike echoing through the night. My breaths came in quick gasps as we danced and dodged, both determined to win this fight. As I parried his blows, my heart thumped wildly in my chest, adrenaline coursing through my veins.

With each clash, I wove my way closer, reading the attacker's rhythm. Their strength was formidable, but it was brute force, lacking the subtle artistry of true skill.

Seizing an opening, I feigned right, and the assailant took the bait, lunging with a thrust meant to end me. But I was no longer there; In the space of a faltering heartbeat, I struck back.

My dagger found home, plunging into the throat of the mysterious attacker, and he finally let out a single, long shriek.

I dragged my blade downward, and the man crumbled onto the ground. Quickly, I crouched atop his chest, my own breath heaving as he sputtered and died, blood pouring out across the terrace.

"Are you harmed?" I asked the queen without looking back.

She was ominously silent, and I glanced back to look at her, forgetting for a moment that I would learn nothing from her covered face. She appeared to be uninjured, and the red splatters of blood on the ground and my dress did not seem to have any effect on her equally crimson robe.

My chest heaved, and a cold realization washed over me as my adrenaline slipped away. I looked down at the assassin beneath me.

This close, the darkness was no longer able to hide his identity, and with a gasp I recognized his too-green, snake-like eyes.

The servant from earlier.

Unfortunately, his identity provided more questions than it answered. Why? What did the servant have against me? Or, perhaps I was not the target, but the queen was.

Moreover, Ambrose had just told me that the king could see everything that went on in his castle. Why then, had he allowed not only me, but his own wife to be attacked?

It seemed entirely too obvious.

This was intentional.

A test.

And I wasn't sure if I'd passed or failed.

35
LONNIE
UNDERNEATH

I threw open the doors to the banquet hall, and a dozen eyes turned to me.

I let them stare, feeding off their shock as I crossed the threshold with purpose etched into every stride.

On the balcony, I'd remembered the conversation that Bael and Scion and I had back in the inn. My dagger was not made from Source-forged metal, which could mean that the assassin would heal his wounds and eventually wake. However, as Scion had told me, there were very few creatures who could live without their heads.

I strode toward the table, my head high, and for once I didn't mind the weight of the obsidian crown. Blood from my blade, and the gift I'd brought the king dripped onto the floor, leaving a long crimson trail behind me.

King Gancanagh rose, his regal composure marred by a frown that seemed out of place in his court of mirth and splendor. "What is the meaning of this?" he demanded, his voice the crack of an unyielding whip.

"Lonnie!" Ambrose exclaimed, seeming to forget he'd aimed to hide my identity.

He jumped to his feet and rushed forward, but I brushed him off, my gaze fixed firmly on the king.

Approaching the table, each step was a deliberate punctuation in the silence that had befallen the room. The nobles recoiled as if I were a tempest unleashed. And perhaps, at that moment, I was.

I stopped before the king, and with a flourish, I dropped the head in the center of the table. It rolled across the polished wood, and came to rest before the king, its sightless, snake-like eyes accusing. "Your hospitality is unmatched, King Gancanagh."

"What the fuck happened?" Ambrose paced angrily across our room, the rage practically radiating from him.

As soon as I'd dropped the head, Ambrose had whisked me from the room before the king could react. It was probably for the best. If he'd meant to kill me with his assassin he no doubt would have found a way to deny it. If perhaps he wanted to try again…well, then we would lose the opportunity to search for Bael and Scion.

"I thought we couldn't speak," I murmured under my breath.

"Fuck that, I don't care," he yelled loud enough to shake the crystal chandeliers. "Who hurt you?"

I shook my head vigorously. He might not care, but I did. I wasn't about to destroy my chance to find both my mates and my mother, simply because he was worried about me.

Annoyed, Ambrose dragged me into the bathing room and turned on the shower. "Talk to me."

I quickly recounted the attack, and as I spoke a small smile curved his lips. "What?"

"Nothing. I'm just pleasantly surprised at how well you have mastered your lessons. It seems you can hold a sword correctly, after all."

"I don't know about 'correctly' but I can certainly point it in the right direction." I muttered. "But I would have preferred not to have to. If the king can see everything, how could he miss an assassin in his own home?"

"I don't know," Ambrose said, looking even more frustrated by that statement alone.

"True," I agreed begrudgingly. "Why don't the wives speak? Even when we were attacked, the queen just stood there, completely silent."

"Again, I don't know. They never have in all the times I've visited this place." He let out a loud, frustrated growl. "I fucking hate it here. Not being able to see is infuriating."

"Now you know how the rest of us feel."

He glared at me. "That is not amusing. If I could see, we would know who tried to hurt you, since I doubt any servant of Gancanagh would act without orders."

"Do they take orders from anyone but him?"

"I don't believe so, but it seems strange he would have sent them on purpose when his own wife was put in danger."

I paced the bathroom, thinking. "How do you know the king?"

"I told you, we do business together—"

"No," I said sharply. "How did you meet? Why would he know my mother?"

Ambrose sighed, running a hand through his long silver hair. "Gancanagh has always been interested in power. It's his primary driving trait, he wants to rule and believes he was born to do so."

"Well, he does rule," I snapped. "He has my fucking congratulations."

"Yes, but he has been the king of Underneath for about thirty years, which must seem long to you, but to me is hardly anything. Before then, he spent ten years or so making a bid for the crown of Elsewhere. We met because it was he who marshaled the prisoners and afflicted in Aftermath. He is the original Dullahan."

I gasped, leaning back, as if I could evade the very implications that came with that statement. "Then how did he become king? How did you take over the army?"

He sat on the edge of the large bathtub, leaning his elbows on his knees. "After some time in Aftermath, Gancanagh made his way to the capital. He met Raewyn, and learned from her that he was unlikely to ever capture the obsidian crown."

"Due to the curse?"

"Right. He was hardly worthy on his own, and did not have the patience to wait for Grandmother to die so another hunting season would begin. Gancanagh is not a foolish male, and decided to leave his pursuit of Elsewhere and return to Underneath to fight for that crown instead."

I furrowed my brow "But isn't Raewyn his mate? Why leave her?"

Ambrose shrugged. "In my opinion, he lacks the emotional range necessary to complete a mating bond. Or, perhaps it was that he was unwilling to risk his life to be with her. He's selfish above all else, and it only took a few short years after he left for him to kill the king and assume their role. Since then, not much has changed within this court."

"And you became the Dullahan?"

He nodded. "It really wasn't all that difficult to imply I always had been. The mask makes it so that even some of my most loyal soldiers don't know what I look like, and I still felt that the rebellion was necessary for the long-term benefit of the country."

My mind reeled, and I took a deep breath. "How did you both know my mother?"

He shrugged. "She was part of our army. Not a particularly relevant member in some ways, but she'd grown up in the court of Nightshade and had an almost fanatical hatred of the High Fae."

"Oh."

I couldn't think of anything else to say. It made sense, yet for some reason, hearing the truth for the first time did not make me feel any better. The reality was almost anticlimactic.

"Wait," I demanded. "Is that how you knew my true name—because you knew my mother? Have *we* met before?"

He grinned, as if remembering something amusing. "Once."

I reeled back, shocked. "I don't remember."

"You were very young and, I might add, *very* annoying. I all but forgot you existed entirely until you were perhaps seventeen."

"Why then?"

"By that point, I was working on expanding my magic. I needed something to measure my progress by."

My brow furrowed. "What? I don't—"

He waved his hand, and cut me off. "This is all ancient history, and has little to do with the original matter at hand, which is that

I can't think of any reason Gancanagh would bother to kill you."

"Kill Rosey, you mean. You implied I was her."

"Only because I believe he knows your true name from many years ago, and I do not want to test if he would be powerful enough to use it on you. Ambrose moved closer, until I had to tip my head up to meet his gaze. "I won't let anyone harm you, especially not the king. You will not go anywhere without me from now on."

My breath caught, and as I looked up at him I suddenly forgot the rest of the questions I'd meant to ask. "I'll have to, if I'm going to find—"

He pressed a finger to my lips, quieting me. "Perhaps, we can discuss it more in the morning."

When it's light out, and our conversation will not be overheard, I finished silently. I nodded.

Ambrose glanced at the still running shower, and stepped back, reaching down to pull off his shirt. "If that's all, I may as well use this, as long as it's running. Proper baths are the thing I miss most while on the ship."

"Oh…" I muttered, and began to back out of the room. "Alright then."

"You're welcome to stay and assist," he called, his voice taking on a flirtatious edge. "You too need to wash that blood off."

"Er, no," I stammered, still backing up. "I'll wait until you're finished."

"Suit yourself."

I darted across the bedroom, and only then realized I'd forgotten to close the door behind me. I hastily averted my eyes, heat flooding my cheeks. *Oh gods.*

As the sound of water cascading echoed through the chamber, I closed my eyes and tried to steady my racing heart. *How had he managed to so quickly turn my thoughts from miserable questions, to...other, far less upsetting things.*

This was neither the time nor the place for such thoughts.

Darting to the bed, I flopped down on top of the crimson blanket, and closed my eyes. However, the sound of the shower would not let me forget what was going on only feet away.

The sound of the shower continued, so loud I could almost imagine I were standing beneath it as well.

I closed my eyes and, feeling slightly guilty, let my hand travel down my side. My fingertips skimmed the edge of my trousers, then quickly, as if I couldn't stop myself, I slid my fingers lower.

My clit throbbed with anticipation, and goosebumps rose all over my body.

I dragged one delicate finger between my folds, then rubbed faster, tracing little circles.

My skin got hotter, and I opened my eyes to peer through the open bathing room door. I let out a breathy moan. "Oh."

Ambrose faced the wall, not looking at me, but still I could see all too much. My traitorous gaze lingered a moment too long on the planes of his sculpted chest, his body, the water pouring over him...

I whimpered and arched off the bed, sinking two fingers into my core."

36
AMBROSE

UNDERNEATH

I stood beneath the steady stream of water, reveling in the feeling of warmth flowing over my head.

I hated this castle and everything in it. I hated the feeling of stumbling in the dark, completely blind to everything around me, and I hated having to play nice with my former commander, Gancanagh.

But, if there was one thing I didn't mind about underneath, it was their hot water.

Rebel camps and sea travel didn't often provide opportunities to be truly clean, and I had to admit that I took advantage of the showers every time I visited Underneath.

Reluctantly, I switched off the faucet and stepped out. Droplets of water flew across the bathing room as I stepped out of the shower and shook out my wet hair. I grabbed a large towel from the pile on a nearby shelf, and wrapped it loosely around my waist.

I'd been in the bathing room for the better part of twenty minutes, so when I strode back into the bedroom I was unsurprised to find Lonnie sprawled on the bed, her fiery mane, rebellious and untamed, fanned around her head like a halo. She'd changed out of her gown, and had taken the liberty of wearing one of my shirts like a nightgown.

For a heartbeat, or perhaps an eternity, I stood rooted to the spot, ensnared by the sight. *Fuck.*

Her eyes were closed, and so for a moment I let my gaze linger over the curve of her neck, the freckles that dusted her shoulders like a constellation charting my downfall. The scent of honey and something wilder, unmistakably Lonnie, permeated the cool air, stirring a hunger within me.

The image of Lonnie standing in the grand hall flashed before my eyes—her arm outstretched, her hand unflinching as she dropped the bloody head onto the polished surface of the king's table.

It was brutal, violent, and the sexiest thing I'd ever seen.

Shaking from my revery, I strode across the room and sat on the edge of the bed, the mattress dipping beneath my weight.

Lonnie didn't move, but here, the air was even thicker with a fragrance that sent my senses into disarray.

My nostrils flared. Oh. *Oh, fuck.*

The scent of Lonnie's arousal wrapped around me, and the sudden realization of what she'd been doing while I stood feet away hit me like a bolt of lightning. I closed my eyes, drawing in a deep breath. How the fuck could I be expected to resist that?

"Did you come yet, love?"

She let out a soft gasp and stiffened, betraying what I suspected the moment I scented the air. She was not asleep. No, she was far, far from it. The entire time I'd been just one room over, she'd been in here, petting her pretty cunt to make herself come.

She opened one eye to look at me, and I leaned toward her as if pulled by invisible strings. A pretty flush crossed her cheeks, and it was like a flag waving me toward her. A beacon coming alight, telling me to take her. Taste her. Give in to what I'd wanted for years, long before I'd ever met her in person.

"No," she whispered.

For a moment, I faltered. No? Fuck, I thought she wanted this too.

Then, I remembered the question I'd asked her, and a smile curved my lips. I looked directly into her honey-brown gaze, asking again just to be sure. "You haven't come yet?"

"No," she breathed, softer this time. "Not yet."

"That's a shame," I found myself replying, my words running away from me, tumbling out of my mouth before I could stop them. "You should."

Her breath hitched, a sharp intake that cut through the thick silence of the chamber. "Excuse me?"

"Continue," I found myself saying, the command resonant in my tone. "Make yourself come, love. I want to see you touch your pretty little cunt for me."

Her eyes went wide and her blush deepened, but from the way she looked at me, and ran her tongue over her lips I was sure it was curiosity, not fear, I saw in her expression. Arousal. Want.

There was no mistaking the challenge in her face, like she was daring me to stop her, to change my mind, as she slowly lifted her hand and sucked her fingers into her mouth.

Fuck me.

I watched her swirl her tongue around her middle and pointer finger, wetting them, and showing me exactly what she'd do if ever I had her for real.

Then, she pulled her finger from her mouth, and let her hand travel lower. Her fingers dipped beneath the hem of the shirt she wore—my shirt, and I watched her trail her hand up the inside of her thigh.

"Show me," I commanded. "Pull your shirt up."

She obliged, obediently reaching down with her other hand to pull the hem of the shirt up to rest against her stomach. "Like this?"

My eyes widened, my pupils dilating, and I ran my tongue over my lips. "Higher."

Her smile turned teasing, and she inched the shirt slowly over her body, tormenting me with how slow she could move.

"I will rip that fucking thing off you right now," I said roughly.

She laughed, and tugged it over her head, baring her entire body to me.

I sucked in a breath, and had to close my eyes for a moment to bring myself back under control. Her body was perfect, soft in all the right places, but it was more so her confidence that held me captivated. It was the way she watched me, like she could see right through me, and although she was naked, I was the one who was vulnerable.

"Begin again," I told her roughly. "Lick your fingers."

She obliged, smiling as she did so, and then popped her hand back out of her mouth. "Now what?"

I froze. By the gods, if she let me direct her, tell her what to do…

"Run your hand over your inner thigh."

She settled back against the mountain of red pillows covering the bed, and again obeyed, trailing her fingers slowly against her too-soft skin until I felt it was me she was teasing, rather than herself.

"Use your other hand to play with your nipples."

Her nipples, already peaked, turned impossibly harder as she circled them with one long finger. "Don't you want to help?"

I shook my head, as I couldn't tell her "no" without lying. Fuck, I did want to "help" as she put it, but more, I wanted to see how far I could push her. How long would it take before she balked, or would she meet my every challenge with one of her own.

"I'll join in when you've earned it," I told her. "Spread your legs wider. Good. Now, run your fingers through your cunt."

I watched her falter slightly, and for a moment I thought she would tell me to fuck off. That this was over. She certainly didn't need any more males directing her, or treating her as if she couldn't care for herself.

But then, as if she were pushing away any embarrassment, she obeyed.

I smiled. Perhaps she liked giving in to others' direction, in the same way I craved the control of commanding everything around me. Perhaps in the way that my greatest desire was total omniscience, Lonnie preferred the freedom of being taken care of, and not having to worry about everyone around her.

I stared down at her, wet and ready for me, and licked my lips. In a moment, she'd forget that hesitation entirely—I'd make sure of it.

At my direction, she trailed her fingers up and down, growing wetter with every pass. Her mouth opened, and I watched her entire body relax, the tension draining from her, as she let out a long sigh.

"I want you to massage just around your clit, now," I told her. "Not too hard."

She closed her eyes, and did as I asked, brushing soft circles over her most sensitive parts until her legs began to shake slightly.

"Are you wet for me, love?"

"Yes," she breathed.

"Good, now you can touch your clit. Use one finger, and do it gently. Imagine I'm touching you."

She looked at me then, and I relished her whimper, and the raw desire in her eyes. The tension coiled between us, a serpent waiting to strike, potent and primordial.

"Are you going to come for me, love?"

"Mmmhmm," she moaned.

"Ask my permission. You should always ask to get what you want."

She kept rubbing, and I watched her hungrily, as she leaned her head back, and closed her eyes. "May I come?"

"Yes, love."

She opened her mouth in a silent scream, her face scrunching up almost as if she were in pain. Then, the moment stretched taut—a bowstring pulled to its limit, then her back arched, and the air itself vibrated with the force of her climax. The sight was a revelation, a tapestry of ecstasy woven from the threads of restraint and longing.

When finally she came down, she looked up at me with some combination of apprehension and expectation painted across her face.

"Well done," I praised her.

I grabbed her hand, and pulled it toward me. Her eyes widened, when I sucked her fingers into my mouth. Gods, she tasted like magic and damnation.

She pulled her hand back, breathing heavily.

"Don't you want…" she trailed off, her question hanging in the air.

Ignoring my own aching cock, I reached for her, wrapping her in my arms. "Not tonight, love. Tonight, I just want you to sleep."

She laughed softly into the darkness. "If I didn't know better, I'd call you a liar."

"But you do know better," I pointed out.

I moved us both to the center of the bed, and held her there, petting her hair, until her breathing evened out.

"Ask me what I'm thinking," Lonnie said.

I froze. "What are you thinking?"

"I'm thinking I'm a terrible person."

I raised an eyebrow. She was far from that, but what would make her think so? "Why?"

"Because I think I must be fated to destroy your family. I already left your brother and cousin to make sure that my presence wouldn't kill them, and now you're being…like this," she waved her hand aimlessly in the air. "And I'm wondering if I'll end up killing you all, anyway."

My eyes went wide. Somewhere in there, between all the guilt and self-loathing, I was fairly sure she was admitting to wanting me.

I wished I could reassure her, except, I was fairly certain she was right.

If history was anything to go by, then she probably would end up killing me—all of us—in the end.

I only hoped the sacrifice would be worth it.

37
LONNIE
UNDERNEATH

The following morning, the predawn sky was a brooding tapestry of purples and grays as Ambrose and I made our way down to join the king's hunting party.

After last night, my thoughts were a jumbled mess, but externally I wouldn't let any of it show. We had important things to do today—perhaps the most important thing I would ever do, and I needed to remain focused.

The path leading from the castle to the encampment unfurled like a serpent, winding through the forest and toward the rocky and volcanic landscape that promised danger at every step. The earth beneath our boots grew increasingly treacherous, and it seemed as if we were walking straight into the jaws of a great beast.

"What are we hunting?" I asked Ambrose. "This doesn't seem like the sort of land that would draw deer or foxes."

"Dragons," Ambrose replied, his gaze sweeping over the gnarled trees that gave way to barren stone. "At least, if Gancanagh is to be believed."

I raised an eyebrow. "Why wouldn't he be?"

"I've never been entirely sure if the Unseelie can lie. Sometimes it seems like it, so keep that in mind when they speak to you."

I nodded in wary acknowledgement. It seemed like there were a great many important things he'd forgotten to tell me, but now it was far too late.

A MIST CLUNG TO THE EARTH, SHROUDING THE VOLCANIC LANDSCAPE in mystery as we advanced, joining the small circle of Unseelie warriors, lingering at the edge of the great chasm that ran alongside the castle. They were each dressed in leather and reddish silk, and moved with a lethal grace that made my fingers twitch at my sides—the memory of last night's attack still fresh in my mind.

As we grew nearer, I couldn't help but notice that where one would expect to see horses, or at least weapons, the king's men had neither.

I would have thought dragon hunting would require swords, at least, but what did I know?

I didn't have a chance to ask about it, because just then the crowd parted, and King Gancanagh stepped forward to greet Ambrose.

Again, I was startled by his alarming resemblance to Bael. It was as if the latter had inherited nothing from his mother except her golden hair, and was instead a nearly identical copy of the male before me.

"Good morning to you," Gancanagh called, his voice echoing off the walls of the chasm. "I trust you had a peaceful night?"

"Of course," Ambrose answered for both of us. "Your castle is always far more comfortable than I even remember."

The king smiled, as if flattered and waved us over to join them.

I bit the inside of my lip to keep from commenting. If I didn't know that the king was dangerous, deadly, and currently had nearly everyone I loved locked in his dungeon, I would have likely found him rather pleasant. He didn't give off the aura of a killer, and everything he said seemed carefully polite and cheerful.

Still, there was something off about him that made the hair on the back of my neck stand up, and despite Ambrose's disagreement, I was still all but certain he'd aimed to kill me last night.

"Where are the queens?" I asked loudly. "I hope they weren't too scared by the attack last night."

Gancanagh glanced at me, as if only just then realizing I was there. "No. Thanks to your…efforts, both my wives are safe and accounted for."

I smiled sweetly. "I was glad to help. Did you discover why your servant might have wanted to attack us?"

He shook his head, and for the briefest moment I saw a spark of rage fly across his too-handsome face. It twisted his features, turning them ugly and monstrous for the briefest moment, before he smiled again. "Unfortunately not, but don't fear. I will find out soon enough. Nothing in this land goes on without my knowing."

I flinched back, disconcerted by his abrupt change, and could only nod in reply. "Thank you."

The king turned back to Ambrose. "I should warn you, this hunt may be too difficult for her. Would your…woman…not be better off staying here?"

"Hmmm," Ambrose mused. "Perhaps you are right."

"Excuse me?" I scoffed, feigning anger. "I'll be fine."

"No," Ambrose said flatly. "I forbid it."

I looked down to hide my face in case any of our true plans showed in my expression. We'd discussed this already, just as the sun was rising. The hunt was the perfect—and perhaps the only—opportunity for me to search for the dungeons without the king being aware of it.

The plan was for the king to believe it was his own idea that I stay behind, so I would have the opportunity to search for the entrance to the dungeons. Ambrose was nearly positive that the king couldn't use his powers of searching during the day, and so even if I were spotted by a servant, it would take hours for him to be warned.

The only problem was, once I found Bael, Scion, and my mother, I had no idea how to get them out of the castle or get back to Ambrose. That was a problem for a later time, however. I'd figure it out as I went along.

"Fine," I sighed dramatically. "I'll just stay here, then. Enjoy your fucking hunts."

A smirk teased the edges of Ambrose's lips, as he stepped closer to me, as if to say goodbye.

For the sake of our audience, I supposed, he leaned in, his lips brushing mine in a quick, chased kiss.

A jolt ran through my entire body.

It was an act, I reminded myself, a performance for the benefit of those who watched. Yet the warmth of his mouth against mine felt anything but feigned.

Without thinking, I reached up and pulled him back. My arms wound around his neck, my fingers finding the end of his long, silver braid. With my heartbeat thrumming fierce as a war drum in my chest, I tilted my head to deepen the kiss.

Following my lead, he opened his mouth, then he pressed his tongue against the seam of my lips, seeking entrance. I moaned, allowing him to explore the inside of my mouth with his tongue, igniting a fire within me. My teeth brushed against his bottom lip, and I bit down, hard. The taste of him was like honey, intoxicating and addicting.

"We must go!" King Gancanagh's angry voice broke through the haze in my mind. "Leave your pet or bring her with us, but don't waste our time."

We broke apart, and Ambrose blinked at me, seeming a bit dazed before he reached up and brushed blood off his lip with the pad of his thumb.

"Ambrose!" the king screamed. "Let's fucking go."

Ambrose craned his neck to call over his shoulder. "I'm coming. Go on without me, if you must."

The king yelled back something unintelligible, and I just stood there, my head spinning.

"I need to go," Ambrose said under his breath. "If anything goes wrong, or if you…need to leave before we get back, I'll meet you at the ship."

I nodded sharply. "Alright."

"Stay safe, love," he said loudly for the audience we had amassed. Then, softly so only I could hear, he added, "I couldn't bear it if anything were to happen to you."

With a final look that seared into my memory like a brand, Ambrose turned and strode toward the waiting hunters. I watched him go, and it was only because I did that I saw the moment that the majority of the group shifted into…something else.

Where before, there had been some two-dozen men, I was now looking at a motley collection of creatures. Wolves, bears, monsters too unusual to name...

Then, a tremendous roar rattled through the canyon, and my eyes landed on a tremendous mountain lion. The gigantic cat turned to look at me, and its familiar yellow eyes flashed with rage.

38
LONNIE

UNDERNEATH

I rushed back up to the castle, my heart beating so hard I thought it might burst from my chest.

I was supposed to have several hours on my own in which to search for the dungeon, but something about the look in the king's eyes when he left made me feel as if I needed to hurry.

Bursting back into the castle, I immediately went to look for a staircase that might take me down to the lower levels. I doubted the dungeon would be on the higher floors, so there were only so many places to search. This would be easy...or so I thought.

After an hour of roaming the halls, I was forced to concede that it was not, in fact, easy.

My determination had long since turned to frustration, and I began to suspect that the enchantment on the obsidian palace—which made it so those who were not meant to be there might find themselves lost—had also been cast upon this castle.

Still, I could not give up. Bael needed me. Scion, and my mother needed me. I wouldn't stop.

I combed through each room, every hallway, and corridor.

The longer I searched, the dim light played tricks on my vision. The opulent rooms stretched out before me endlessly, a dizzying display of luxury that overwhelmed my senses. I began to feel as if I were being watched, but every time I turned, nothing looked back at me but shadows.

Finally, I descended a long stone staircase into yet another gleaming corridor. All the while, the sense of something watching grew stronger, a palpable pressure against the nape of my neck.

At the base of the stairs, I reeled back and gasped.

Like a silent wraith, one of the veiled queens stood in the center of the hallway in front of me. Before I could speak, the queen raised one gloved hand and gave a small wave.

My eyes widened in surprise. She could see me then, but could she speak?

I stared directly into where her eyes would be beneath the veil, and felt a bit foolish as I said: "Hello...are you alright after last night?"

I had to assume this was the same queen who'd been with me on the balcony, and my theory was confirmed when she nodded.

A sudden spark of excitement shot through me. The queen would likely know where the dungeon was, would she not? But, could I trust her enough to ask?

On second thought, it didn't matter whether I could trust her or not. I was getting nowhere on my own, and the possibility that she might be able to help was too important to ignore. Anyway, if I found them then we'd be long gone, back to the ship, before the queen ever had the chance to tell her husband.

"Are you able to speak to me?" I asked.

She nodded this time. Perhaps she was simply afraid to speak, or maybe the king was holding her captive?

"Listen, I'm looking for something…" I frantically cast my mind around for some excuse I could give her, and came up with nothing. Finally, I gave in to the necessity of asking directly. I only hoped I would not regret it. "Can you show me where the dungeons are?"

She nodded again, and beckoned more urgently for me to follow before turning to walk down the hall. Excitement quickening my heart, I darted after her.

We moved in silence.

The queen's crimson robes whispered against the floor, and the only sound was that of my heavy boots and labored breathing as she led me deeper into the bowels of the castle. With each echoing floor we descended, my anticipation swelled, pressing against the walls until it felt as if the very stones held their breath.

Finally, the queen stopped and turned to me. Behind her, a smooth, stone door was set into the wall. She gestured toward it, nodding.

I tensed. Perhaps this had been painfully stupid. But then, I had the dagger in my boot and, if nothing else, the crown on my head had killed a far more powerful fairy than whatever could be under that veil.

Still, I hung back from the door. "You first."

To my surprise, the queen immediately turned and reached for the handle. She swung the door wide, and all at once a familiar scent whooshed out to greet me.

The stench of the dungeon filled my nostrils, bringing back memories of the long year I spent trapped beneath the obsidian palace. The musty, damp odor was suffocating, like a heavy blanket pressing down on me. Decay, despair…It was a scent that would forever be etched into my memory, haunting me even now as I stood outside the fortress walls.

For a moment, I swayed on my feet, giving in to the horrible memories that came along with the scent. Then, I blinked, my mind snapping back to reality.

"The dungeon?" I asked the queen, pointing at the dark hallway beyond.

She nodded, and stepped through the door. Filled with anticipation, I leaned in and followed.

Like the obsidian castle dungeon, each side of a long, winding hallway was filled with iron-barred cells, their rusted bars casting menacing shadows on the stone floor below. Dust motes danced in the still air, and the silence was only broken by the occasional moan or whimper from within.

I ignored all of it.

I dashed inside, quickly overtaking the queen. My boots pounded the damp floor, as I glanced right and left, scanning each cell for a familiar face.

As I hurried down the long corridor, my heart raced with worry. Each door I passed looked the same. The flickering torches cast dancing shadows across my face, making it difficult to see, and I began to fear I would never find them. Panic set in as the hallway seemed to stretch on forever.

Then, a sudden noise to my left made me stop.

Peering carefully into the dark cell beyond, my heart swelled with both excitement and relief. "Bael."

39
LONNIE

UNDERNEATH

Bael looked up at me from where he sat on the floor of the filthy cell. Mud caked his clothes, and a deep gash ran across his chin.

Still, the moment he saw me, his yellow eyes lit up and a wide grin stretched across his face. The prince sprang to his feet and rushed toward me. "What are you doing here?"

Without waiting for my reply, he extended one muscular arm through the bars and dragged me forward.

Our lips met with urgency, our bodies pressed against the cold metal bars separating us. I shook with a mixture of fear and desire as I poured out all my emotions into that one desperate kiss. Every inch of my being longed for this moment, and as we finally connected, it was like a floodgate had been opened, releasing all the pent-up feelings of terror, longing, and relief that had been building inside me.

This was more than just a kiss. It was a release, a connection, a promise of everything to come.

"How are you here?" he asked again, pulling back to look me dead in the eyes.

"I'll always find you," I replied with a smile.

He grinned back. "How did you get into the castle, though? Are yo—"

I pressed my fingers to his lips to quiet him. "I'm fine, and the rest doesn't matter right now. Where's Scion?"

His smile slipped from his face faster than a flame winking out. He pointed vaguely to the right, down the darkened hallway behind me. "I don't know, little monster."

"What do you mean, you don't know?"

He looked pained. "He stopped responding to me."

My heartbeat jumped again, my excitement at finding Bael immediately clouding with fear. I pulled out of his grip, and ran down the rest of the hallway in the direction he'd pointed. "Scion?" I yelled. "Where are you?"

Several cells down, I found him.

But, it was not the same happy reunion I'd just had with Bael.

Scion's cell seemed darker, as if the prince were shrouded in his own illusions. He looked in worse shape than Bael had been, either because the king's guard had used more force, or because he'd fought harder to escape—I couldn't tell which. As I approached, he looked up at me, but his silver gaze held no recognition.

"Scion?" I demanded, rattling the bars of his cell. "My lord!"

His silver eyes met mine, the magnetic pull of them tainted by the pain etched around their edges. "Go away," he muttered. "You're not real."

"Like hell I'm not." My voice cracked as I desperately clung to the prison bars, my knuckles turning white from gripping them so tightly.

What the fuck was going on here? What could've possibly happened to change him—confuse him—make him not know me? "Please," I pleaded, tears pricking at the backs of my eyes. "It's me."

He turned away from me, showing me a back that had clearly been whipped with Source-forged steel. "Get the fuck out of my head."

"Don't do this to me." I choked, real tears pouring down my face. "I fucking hate you for this."

His back stiffened, and he slowly turned back around. "Say that again."

For a moment, I couldn't fathom what he was getting at, but then I understood. "I hate you," I insisted, ignoring the pain that burned my throat. "I hate you, I hate you, I hate you."

His gaze finally lifted and met mine again, and I saw recognition spark in his silver eyes. "Rebel?"

"Yes."

He murmured something too fast for me to hear, his lips moving rapidly as he jumped to his feet and rushed toward me. I reached through the bars, and held on to him, never wanting to let go again.

He pressed his forehead to mine through the bars, and finally I was able to make out what he was saying: "I love you. I love you, I love you."

Tears still streaming down my face, I finally laughed. "I'm going to get you out. Both of you."

I scanned the room, searching for any object that could break open the cell doors. A key on a hook, a lever, even a rock would do.

My hands shook as they skimmed over damp walls, tracing the lines of mortar between stones, hoping for some hidden mechanism, some secret lever to reveal itself beneath my desperate touch.

"Stay calm," I muttered to myself, the words a mantra against the rising tide of panic. "There has to be a way."

My fingers traced the cold, unyielding iron of the cell doors, the chill seeping into my bones as I let out a frustrated sigh. The keys, if they even existed, were nowhere to be found, and the locks were unlike any I'd seen before—imbued with a magic that repelled every attempt at picking them.

"There's no point," came a voice, ancient and gravelly like stones tumbling down a mountain. "You'll never find a way out."

I whirled around and my gaze snapped toward a neighboring cell where another prisoner sat in the dark. He looked like nothing but eyes glinting out of a pile of hair and rags, and I wondered how long he'd been down here.

"Shut up," I snapped. "There has to be a key somewhere."

"No key," he chuckled dryly. "It's only the king who can open the doors."

"Well how does he do that?" I demanded.

"Blood," he replied bitterly. "*Royal* blood."

The words resonated within me, setting off a flicker of hope in the darkness of my despair. Without hesitation, I reached for the dagger in my boot and sliced my palm, smearing my blood across the lock of Scion's cell.

Nothing happened. The door remained firmly shut, mocking my efforts.

"Fuck," I growled, bitterness coating my tongue.

I was no true royalty; my blood was as powerless here as I was.

"Let me try," Bael spoke up, his voice cutting through my defeat.

"Why?" I asked. "I'm wearing the damn crown and it didn't work. It has to be Gancanagh's blood."

Bael looked at me, his eyes widening. "I know."

Oh. *Oh.*

I rushed over to him, my excitement rising once again. I passed him my dagger and he cut his own hand, and smeared it over the lock as I'd done.

I held my breath, watching the blood trace a path over the intricate carvings of the lock. There was a moment of silence, so profound that even the whispers of the castle seemed to pause in anticipation.

Then, the door began to groan, a sound that seemed wrenched from the very bowels of the castle itself. As the door yielded, inch by grudging inch, I could almost sense the reluctance in its movement. Bael's hand remained pressed against the cold metal, and with a final, resentful creak, the cell door swung open.

"Yes!" I screamed, practically giddy from success. I rushed into the cell and threw my arms around Bael. He held me tight for a long moment, and once again I felt tears pricking the backs of my eyes.

Quickly, Bael moved to Scion's door, repeating the blood ritual. Again, the castle relinquished its hold, and the door opened.

I didn't hesitate. My arms flung wide, I rushed forward, embracing them both in a tangle of limbs and emotions. We stood there for a long moment, before Scion pulled away.

His dazed gaze had mostly cleared, but he still looked a bit wild, untethered. "Let's not celebrate yet," he growled. "We've still got to get out of this damned place."

His statement was like a rock falling into the pit of my stomach.

A wave of guilt washed over me, realizing that I'd been so focused on getting my mates back, I'd completely forgotten about the other person I loved.

"Wait, we can't go yet," I insisted. "Have either of you seen my mother?"

Bael cocked his head to the side, bewilderment in his eyes. "Your mother?"

I nodded, already pulling away from them to peer into the other cells. My heart sank with realization as I checked those at the end of the row.

She wasn't here.

I'd already gone past every cell in this place, and Bael and Scion were practically at the end. The only other person held deeper than them was the old man who'd known how to open the door.

My gaze landed back on the old man. "Are there more cells somewhere? Another room perhaps?"

The man rose to his feet, more gracefully than I would have expected possible. He chuckled darkly. "You have a lot of questions, girl."

"Yes," I said desperately. "Can you help?"

He moved toward the bars. "Let me out, and I'll help you with whatever you like."

My eyes widened as we came face to face, and I realized that he wasn't old at all.

A strikingly young, handsome face emerged from a tangle of waist-length hair and an unkempt beard. His hair was so matted and filthy that it could have been any color, but his violet eyes shone with clarity even in the darkness.

I hesitated. "Why are you in here?"

"Let me out, and I'll tell you."

"Tell me now," I demanded.

He laughed again. "I would, but it's a long story. I've been here for nearly seven-thousand years."

That...couldn't be right. He was mad, or confused, or...something. Wasn't he? A shiver traveled up my spine and I shrank back. "No..."

"Wait!" the man said desperately calling me back. "I could help you."

"Do you know where my mother is?"

"No," he admitted, as his eyes flicked to the crown on my head. "But I could still help you. Wouldn't you like to know where that crown came from? Would you like to know how it's supposed to be worn?"

"I—"

Before I could answer, the sound of sudden footsteps pounded behind me, and the mysterious prisoner yelled in alarm. "Behind you!"

I whirled around, my eyes frantically scanning the room for the king, or perhaps the guards, but instead they landed on the figure of the veiled queen sprinting toward us.

For a moment, I'd completely forgotten she was there. Apparently, that had been a deadly mistake.

40
LONNIE

UNDERNEATH

The queen rushed toward us, her long, red robe swirling around her. While her veil concealed her face, I could feel the intensity of her gaze as she sprinted toward us, the sharp edge of a sword gleaming in her hand.

I didn't understand anything that was happening. Why would she attack us? Why now, when she'd been standing behind me for the last several minutes.

I didn't have long to wonder.

My muscles tensed as I gripped my dagger, ready to strike. But before I could make a move, Bael pushed me roughly aside, and charged toward the queen. Fear gripped me, and every second felt like an eternity as the two of them met in the middle of the hallway.

I watched in abject horror as the queen's sword pierced Bael's skin. My scream of fury and fear echoed through the room, and I started forward to help. Except, then Scion's furious voice rose behind me. Suddenly, I felt a sharp tug as his muscular arms wound around my waist, yanking me backwards into his cell.

"Let me go!" I shouted. "He's hurt."

"He's fine!" Scion held me tighter.

I kicked at him, but he ignored it, reaching forward to pull the door of the cell closed behind us with a heavy metal snap.

"What the fuck are you doing?" I demanded. "We'll be trapped in here."

"Better that than torn to bloody shreds."

I had no clue what he was referring to, until a guttural growl echoed through the dungeon.

I gasped, and even the veiled queen seemed to falter as Bael's body contorted and stretched, his skin bulging and shifting into the form of a massive lion. His powerful muscles rippled beneath his tawny fur as he let out a fierce roar.

For a fraction of a second, I wondered how Bael was able to wield magic within the castle walls. Then, I realized that the only individual allowed to use magic in this fortress was King Gancanagh. It seemed Bael had inherited more than an ability to open doors.

"I need to help him," I hissed at Scion.

"If that bitch doesn't kill you, Bael will," Scion yelled back. "He'll kill all of us. It's not…him when he's like that."

As if to illustrate the point, Bael let out a fierce roar and charged after the queen with lightning speed, his powerful paws pounding against the ground as he closed in on his target.

Furious, I kicked harder against Scion. "He won't hurt me. Let me fucking go."

Scion ignored me completely, and as I thrashed and screamed, the fight in the dungeon hallway only grew more intense. The queen dodged and weaved, seeming desperate to get to us—to me.

Bael's powerful claws sliced through the air, narrowly missing the queen's head. Despite his strength, the narrow pathway of the dungeon was a hindrance, making it hard for him to stand to his full towering height, or land a fatal blow.

With each swipe, the queen deftly blocked or evaded, her sword glinting in the dim light. Panic began to rise in my throat, and I hardly noticed when the bars of our cell seemed to crumble, Bael's magic tearing through the prison and causing total destruction.

Then finally, with a swift motion, Bael slashed his claws across the queen's abdomen.

There was a beat, where she seemed to realize she was hurt and looked down. Then, for the first time she made a sound. A piercing shriek of pure agony escaped her lips.

My ears pricked up.

I knew that scream. I'd heard it over and over again in the back of my mind for half my life. Ever since…

no…it couldn't be.

"Wait!" I screamed. "Stop! Bael!"

Bael turned his enormous feline head to look at me, and in that moment the queen struck.

One of her hands was clutching her stomach, as if she were holding her inners inside her body with her fingers alone. The front of her red robe looked slick with blood, and I could hear her breath, gasping and ragged, as she stumbled forward. She raised her shaking sword, and with what seemed to be her final burst of energy, she sunk her blade into Bael's shoulder.

He whirled back around, hissing, and swatted her with an enormous paw. It was like she was nothing more than a fly, her blade merely an annoyance, as she went flying backwards against the stone wall.

As she slumped to the ground, her veil slipped.

Red hair tumbled out from beneath the crimson silk, and my eyes bulged with horror. The confirmation of what I'd already known when I heard her voice struck me like lightning, sending electric pain through every inch of my body.

It was my mother, and she'd just tried to kill me.

41
LONNIE

UNDERNEATH

"We need to get the fuck out of here," Scion yelled.

I felt a surge of energy pulsating in the air, followed by a deafening roar. The ground beneath us began to shake violently as cracks formed in the walls and ceiling. Bael's immense powers were ripping through the dungeon and castle, leaving behind nothing but destruction.

But I couldn't see any of that.

All I could see was my mother, bleeding and unconscious on the floor, dust and debris from the crumbling ceiling falling on top of her. If she was not already dead, she would be in a matter of seconds.

I needed to get to her.

"Let me go," I demanded of Scion once more.

This time, he dropped me, seeming to think I was aiming to escape the crumbling building. Instead, I dashed out of the now-open cell, and fell to the ground beside my mother.

Nothing made sense.

How was she here? What had happened? And, most importantly of all, why would she want to kill me?

I would never get the answers if we let her die here.

"Help me!" I demanded, whipping my head around.

Bael did not seem to understand the words I was saying, and Scion didn't so much as look at my mother as he reached for me, picking me up and dragging me toward the door.

"Let's fucking go."

"We need to save her!"

I screamed with frustration, as Scion threw me over his shoulder, holding my legs against his chest. "Not if the castle is about to fall on top of us, I don't give a fuck about anyone but you."

"I'll hate you for this!" I yelled, and for once as I spoke there was no pain in my throat.

"Fine, hate me," he growled. "I love you enough for both of us."

Tears streamed down my face, and I watched in desperation as the dungeon moved further and further away. Bael ran behind Scion, his eyes on me, and I pleaded silently with him to understand what I was saying. To care. To save my mother.

But, he didn't. Even if he'd been himself at the moment, I knew deep down that he would have agreed with Scion. Neither one of them would risk my life to save the woman who'd just tried to kill me.

Even if she was the one who'd given me life to begin with.

Despair nearly drowned me, but then, my eyes caught a glimpse of the man with striking violet eyes. I lifted my head up, my heart beating faster once more.

Bael's dark magic had torn through his cell, setting him free, after all. His grin was one of victory as he chased after us, with a strength I would not have thought possible after so many years underground.

"Wait!" I yelled out to him, panic rising in my voice. I frantically gestured toward my mother's lifeless form behind Scion's back. "Please, save her!" My voice cracked. "You owe me."

In truth, it was Bael who he owed his freedom to, but without me, Bael would never have been freed in the first place. The man faltered, and looked directly at me for a long second. He bent and scooped my mother into his arms.

A wave of relief washed over me. She may die anyway, but at least now there was a chance.

We sprinted out of the dungeon and fled from the collapsing castle. Scion, in the lead with me over his shoulder, Bael the lion loping behind us, and the violet eyed stranger carrying my mother taking up the rear.

This time, we quickly located the stairs that would take us to the upper levels. I wondered vaguely if it was because of Bael, or perhaps the magic of the castle was collapsing along with the walls. Still, in no time at all we burst through the heavy wooden doors and into the blinding sunlight outside the ancient palace.

"We need to get back to the ship," I insisted.

Scion dropped me back to my feet so I could meet his scowling gaze. "The ship? No. The bridge is right fucking there, rebel." He pointed wildly at one of the several long rickety bridges that crossed the chasm.

"No, but—"

I broke off. In the confusion, I'd forgotten to consider that Scion hated his brother. Both Bael and Scion viewed Ambrose as nothing more than a villain, and they wouldn't be likely to trust him.

In that same moment, I realized that I *did* trust him.

Ambrose had promised that he would meet me at the ship, and that was where we needed to go. We couldn't leave him behind, any more than I could've left my traitorous mother.

I set my jaw, and glared determinedly up at Scion's silver eyes. I pointed toward the city lights shimmering in the distance. "I'm going this way. You can come with me, or part ways right here."

As I'd known would happen, Scion's conviction crumbled. We'd already nearly died countless times to find each other, the means of our escape would not be the thing that divided us.

We sprinted down the rocky path of the mountain, our feet pounding against the dry, rocky ground as we sprinted through the unforgiving desert landscape. My lungs burned with each breath and my muscles ached from the steep incline, then finally, we burst onto the busy streets of Underneath.

As I rounded the bend of the narrow cobblestone street, the salty scent of the ocean hit my nose, and I could see the vibrant blood-red waters of the harbor in the distance. My heart filled with joy as I quickened my pace toward the docks.

Except, just as joy flooded me, the ground behind us began to shake. People screamed, and the wind whipped faster as if a sudden storm had fallen upon us.

I looked over my shoulder and my blood ran cold.

In the distance, I could hear the thunderous gallop of hooves and the growls and roars of wild animals. My heart pounded as I saw the king's hunting party charging toward us.

Leading the pack, Gancanagh was immediately visible. His massive lion form towered over every other creature, radiating a fierce power that sent shivers down my spine. Even from here, the sharp gleam of his teeth and his piercing yellow eyes gutted me.

With one mighty roar, he commanded all attention to him. It was like a hunting horn, telling his army to charge.

I glanced at Bael, and all I could think was how he'd warned me time and time again never to run from monsters.

Except, when the monsters were hunting us, what other choice was there?

42
LONNIE

UNDERNEATH

As the king drew nearer, Bael erupted into motion.

He charged toward the enormous lion—a golden streak against the darkening sky. His own lion form was lithe and powerful, and seemed to drag tendrils of smoke in his wake, like he was made from magic itself.

Screams erupted from the marketplace and over the harbor, and I realized distantly that one of those screams was me.

My voice had gone hoarse from all the yelling. My mind was a twisted jumble of questions and fear, overstimulated and on the verge of collapse. Still, I yelled for Bael, and refused to tear my gaze away as the prince and king collided.

A thunderous roar echoed over the harbor. The two beasts met, and it was hard to make out who was whom in the frenzy of fur and blood. Even in this form, Bael and his father were nearly identical and I struggled to know who was winning. With every sharp blow, I gasped, unsure if I should cheer or scream.

"Rebel, we have to go!" Scion's hand gripped my arm, pulling me back to the harsh reality of our situation.

I turned to meet his gaze, and my vision swam, barely seeing him. He dragged me toward the water, apparently no longer bothered by the ship if it meant keeping me away from the battle in front of us.

"Stop!" I demanded. "We can't go."

"We can't help, either," he said, sounding as frustrated as he was desperate.

Dust and debris flew up as the lions swiped and clawed at each other, their fierce battle shaking the ground beneath our feet.

Scion turned and watched the battle for a moment, and I could see the conflict in his gaze. Without magic, Scion wouldn't stand a chance against Gancanagh, but he seemed to still be considering going to help. I loved him all the more for it.

"No," he tore his gaze away. "You're what matters. We need to go."

"I don't care about me," I insisted.

"Lonnie, go!"

My brow furrowed with confusion. I heard the yell, and my brain could not process it. I was looking at Scion and he hadn't opened his mouth, yet I heard his demand.

For a moment, I thought I was losing my mind.

Then a silver-haired figure broke free of the oncoming army and sprinted toward us.

Ambrose skidded to a halt beside me, his black eyes were twin obsidian stones, hard and reflecting a resolve that brooked no argument.

For a long second, he and Scion stared at each other and the tension rose. I couldn't have guessed what they were thinking if my life depended on it.

"We need to get her to the ship," Ambrose snapped.

"Right," Scion agreed, and picked me up once more.

Air whooshed from my lungs, and I struggled to breathe as we sprinted to the ship. Still, I managed to voice my protests, screaming curses at the pair of them as we ran.

The ship was anchored exactly where we'd left it, and on the deck I could already see Lin and Riven marshaling the crew into action. The sails were being hoisted, and crew members ran back and forth up and down the gangway, loading cargo back onto the boat.

We drew nearer, the male's boots pounding against the wooden dock and my entire body bouncing with every step they took. I squinted toward the ship, and a small sense of relief washed over me.

The mysterious prisoner was easily identified, his long hair and beard standing out even at a distance. He was leaning over the side of the ship, watching us approach. If he was aboard, so too must be my mother.

"Go!" Ambrose pushed Scion forward ahead of him, and the two of us traveled quickly up the gangway onto the ship.

Scion dropped me, but didn't fully let go, his arms still wrapped around my waist and holding me in place.

"Set sail!" Ambrose barked at the crew, and Lin echoed his yell, urging everyone to move faster.

"No!" Tears stung my eyes, the salt of them mingling with the brine of the sea. My chest heaved as if I'd run for miles rather than stood frozen to the spot. "We can't just leave him!"

"He can use magic here, Rebel. We can't."

"So?" I demanded, new tears choking me.

"He can shadow walk to reach us," he replied. "Once you're safe I'm sure he'll follow, if…"

He broke off, a spark of pain appearing behind his eyes.

"If he's still alive," I shrieked, my hysterical yell drawing the crew's attention away from the battle on land. "That's what you mean, isn't it?"

Scion's gaze was haunted, but he nodded. Then, seeming to want to distract me, he gestured to something behind me. "Go see to your mother."

I glared at him. For a moment, I really did hate him.

RIVEN TOOK CHARGE OF BRINGING MY MOTHER AND THE ESCAPED prisoner below deck. My mother was still alive, but barely, and it was worry over her and Bael that drove the prisoner from my mind. I forgot to warn anyone where we'd found him or that he might be dangerous.

I forgot everything else entirely.

My gaze clung to the shore, trying desperately to keep Bael in sight. The sails unfurled, catching the wind and the ship lurched forward, like a beast awakening from slumber.

Dread sunk into my chest. We were truly leaving him behind.

In two strides, I lunged for the ship's side, my hands grappling for purchase on the slick wood.

But Ambrose was quicker.

His warrior reflexes honed by years of conflict, this time it was the elder brother whose arms encircled my waist, pulling me back with an iron resolve.

"Let me go!" I raged against him, my voice rising like the howl of the wind. "He needs me!"

"Love," Ambrose's voice was a whispered plea, his breath warm against my ear. "If you interfere, you'll die."

I heard him, but I didn't care. It wasn't myself I was concerned about.

It was the golden-eyed prince that I loved, the one whose very presence had always been both unsettling and intoxicating. He needed me now, more than ever.

Just as I prepared to unleash another volley of protests, a guttural roar tore through the air, silencing all other sounds. Time and motion seemed to crystallize, the world narrowing down to a single point.

There, amid the chaos of the harbor, the two lions clashed with primal rage. Blood covered the sand, and both beasts seemed to be gravely injured.

From this angle, high above on the ship, it was easier to tell who was whom. Gancanagh was larger, but Bael was far faster and more brutal. As I watched, he danced around his father's bulk with deadly grace, then struck, sinking his teeth into the king's jugular.

"Look!" I pointed.

Distracted by the fight, Ambrose's grip loosened around me. My heart hammered, my breath caught in my throat as Bael tore again and again into Gancanagh's throat.

The king's roar turned into a strangled gasp, the sound of tyranny ending with a whimper, and he collapsed onto the sand. With one enormous paw, Bael dragged his claws down the other lions chest, splitting him open to reach his heart.

"Fuck," Ambrose's amazed voice cut through the pandemonium, to rise above the crash of the waves and the screams of fleeing townsfolk. "This makes him king!"

I barely heard him. I didn't care.

With a wrench of my body, I tore myself from Ambrose's grasp.

I didn't hear his protestations, nor did I see the shock on the faces around me as I dove headfirst over the railing.

The wind whistled past me, the long fall stealing my breath and making my stomach climb into my throat. I plunged into the icy embrace of the harbor, and the cold rocked me. My legs flailed as I spun beneath the surface. Then, with a splash I resurfaced, gasping for air.

My entire body screamed in pain as I swam frantically toward the shore. Saltwater stung my eyes, blurred my vision, yet I propelled forward, like I were drawn by an invisible string.

As I stumbled onto the rocky beach, coughing the sea from my lungs, I saw him.

Even in his exhaustion, Bael's cat eyes found mine amidst the chaos. He was still a beast, but I could tell just from the way he looked at me that it was him. I stumbled forward out of the water, and ran to meet him.

In the distance, I thought I could hear Scion's frantic yell, and the gasps of onlookers as I launched myself at the bloody lion, wrapping my arms around his neck.

Beneath my fingers, his form shimmered and shifted before my eyes. The lion's mane receded, the tawny fur melted away, until there stood not a beast, but the man. *Bewitching. Beguiling. Beloved.*

"Don't cry, little monster," he croaked.

I only cried harder.

43
LONNIE

ABOARD THE FORESIGHT

The evening was surprisingly warm, the weather pleasant, as we sailed back out of the red waters of Underneath. Out on the dock, Lin shouted orders at the crew, and Riven steered the ship toward home.

Inside, however, we couldn't hear any of it.

It had been several hours since the fight on the shore, and after proving many times over that I was unharmed, I now found myself back in Ambrose's cabin. The room had always felt small, but now, it seemed impossibly overcrowded. Between Ambrose, Bael and Scion, there was hardly any space left for me. For once, I didn't mind.

I couldn't wrap my head around the fact that we were all still alive, and the overwhelming feeling of joy drowned out any other emotions.

At least, it did for me. The same could not be said for all of us.

Ambrose and Scion stood on opposite sides of the room, refusing to look at one another. Whatever brief truce they'd shared to reach the ship had evaporated, and the air between them was thick with unspoken animosity. Fortunately, it didn't matter, as Bael and I seemed to have made a silent agreement to broker the tension.

In any case, we had far more important things to focus on than the feud between the two brothers.

When we'd boarded the ship, Riven had taken charge of my mother, immediately bringing her below deck. She was still alive–for now–but unconscious. If and when she woke up, we were due for a long conversation. However, thinking about it caused me so much anxiety that I'd all but pushed it from my mind for the time being.

In the meantime, it had taken over an hour for me to relay everything we'd done while in Underneath to Bael and Scion, and in turn, for them to recount where they'd been this last week. I was pleased to hear that they'd managed to void my bargain with the quarry serpent, but shocked by what they'd learned from it before it died.

It was almost too much to process that Scion was now the King of Elsewhere, and more importantly, my husband. The only person unsurprised by that revelation was Ambrose, who insisted he'd known all along. Personally, I didn't know how to feel about it. For me, it didn't change much. I was already certain we were mates.

What interested me more, was the fact none of my princes were princes any longer.

They were kings.

A knock sounded on the door, which pulled all of us from our respective musings. I stood to answer it, but three Fae males moved to shove me back. I sighed. I had a strange feeling that I was about to have even less freedom than I'd had before.

Bael–who was closest to the door–went to open it. On the threshold, stood the prisoner we'd rescued from the dungeon. We all tensed as one.

I realized in that moment that it was not only my mother I'd pushed from my mind. I'd all but forgotten the prisoner was here. I certainly hadn't thought to warn anyone where we'd found him, or that he might be dangerous.

For the first time, I realized that beneath all his hair and the rags that had once been clothes, he was not as thin nor as injured as I might have expected. In fact, he was quite as muscular as Bael and nearly as tall as Ambrose. For some reason, that made the hair on the back of my neck stand on end. Not that size was always an indicator of strength, but what kind of magic must this male have to survive in a dungeon for seven-thousand years?

With me still unable to use magic, and both Bael and Scion recovering from the dungeons, only Ambrose's sword stood between us and potentially deadly power.

The prisoner stepped inside, seeming to either ignore, or be unaware of the tension in the room. He glanced around, his violet eyes flashing with interest. "I apologize for interrupting."

"You didn't," Scion spat. "What do you want?"

"I was hoping to speak to you."

Bael narrowed his gaze on the male. "All of us?"

"No." The prisoner smiled slightly beneath his matted beard. His eyes fell on Ambrose. "Only the seer."

I felt a tension fall over the room, and was sure that we were all thinking the same thing: what did this male want to know, and why couldn't he ask in front of all of us?

"I don't think–" I began, just as Ambrose shoved past Scion and toward the door.

"It will be fine, love."

Scion stiffened at the sound of Ambrose's endearment toward me, while Bael simply looked curious. Neither commented however, their attention still focused on the prisoner.

"Are you certain?" I asked, my voice wavering slightly with nerves.

Ambrose tapped his head and grinned at me, before stepping out onto the deck. "Very certain. I'll see you soon."

The door closed behind them with a defining snap, and an ominous silence rang through the room.

"What do you think he wants?" I asked to break the silence.

"Hopefully to commit a quick murder," Scion mumbled. "If we were not in the middle of the ocean, I'd–"

"Well, it's a good thing we are, then," I interrupted, having no wish to hear all the ways he wanted to kill his brother.

"You don't understand."

"I do," I said. "Perhaps better than you do, for once."

Scion glared at me, practically vibrating with an anger that seemed a bit disproportionate to the issue at hand.

I glanced at Bael, and found that he too was scowling. With a start, I realized that the last time we'd been together like this, all three of us, had been the night in the inn. The night of the bathing tub…and the night I left.

"If you're both angry at me, just say so," I said, my own frustration rising.

"This isn't about you," Scion snapped.

"Isn't it?"

I held my breath as the air seemed to thicken, my eyes darting between the two males.

"Fine," Scion burst out. He rose from his chair and strode over to me, intense fire burning in his silver eyes. "You fucking left."

"I know," I swallowed thickly. "But if I hadn't—"

"It doesn't matter," he raged, moving so close I had to back against the wall to keep him in view. "You could've fucking died."

"And you would've died if I stayed," I snapped, fire rising within me.

He shook his head. "I don't care."

He might not care, but I did.

No matter how painful this last week had been for all of us, I wasn't sorry for what I'd done. If I could go back and live that night over again, I would still leave. Leave to keep them safe, and because ultimately it had led to so many other things. To meeting Ambrose, to finding my mother…to this moment, right now.

I suddenly entirely understood what Ambrose had been trying to tell me about prophecy. About how a single decision would have far reaching consequences.

The thought of losing them, of being responsible for their deaths, felt like an anvil hanging over my head. I couldn't bear the weight of that guilt, the knowledge that I could have saved them. They may not care, but I did. They were everything to me, and I couldn't bear the thought of losing them because of my own mistakes.

I looked to Bael over Scion's shoulder. "Don't you have anything to say about this?"

His face held a serious look, unlike the usual playful expression I was accustomed to seeing. When our eyes met, there was a strong intensity in his gaze that I had never noticed before.

Silently, he rose from his seat on the bed and moved across the room. My heartbeat began to pound with some strange combination of fear and anticipation.

He pushed Scion aside, making his way to me. Surprisingly, Scion didn't object and simply moved over. The two of them stood next to each other, gazing down at me.

Bael's hand closed around a fistful of my hair, tugging me toward him. My head tilted back, and I found myself staring into his too-intense eyes. A shiver ran down my spine as he whispered, "Look at me. Never do that again. Do you hear me?"

I sucked in a sharp breath. "I can't—"

He let out a frustrated growl and forcefully tugged me toward him. Bending his head down, he captured my lower lip between his sharp teeth. "Promise me."

"No," I whispered against his mouth. "I won't help you die."

With a guttural sound, he flipped our positions, holding me firm against his chest. "I daresay you've solved it, little monster. I will never be fucking happy knowing you have one foot out the door."

My chest panged. He was wrong, and I was likely lying to myself. I didn't think I'd ever be able to leave him again—any of them—but if believing I would kept them breathing...

"Good," I breathed. "I hope I make you miserable."

Bael bent his head to my neck and ran his tongue over my skin up to the shell of my ear. I gasped.

Feeling a pair of eyes on us, I glanced up to see Scion staring at us with a hungry expression. With only a look, I beckoned him to approach, and he did so without hesitation.

As Scion pressed in toward me, his hot breath tickling my lips, I could feel Bael's soft kisses trailing down the side of my neck from behind. My heart raced with anticipation as their combined touches sent warmth skating over my skin.

I opened my mouth wide to Scion, and playfully flicked my tongue against his lips in a slow, leisurely kiss.

I was still fully clothed, but my skin felt like it was on fire.

I bit down on his lip, but he pulled back before I could break the skin. "None of that, rebel."

My eyes were glassy and dazed as I looked at him. "But—"

Did that mean he was finally admitting we were mates, as well as husband and wife? My heart pounded a rapid staccato against my ribs, as Scion's intense gaze gave me all the confirmation I needed.

Bael chuckled against my neck. "Just because we're not likely to fall off the tower doesn't mean we should jump. No biting, little monster, but don't worry. You'll hardly notice when we're done with you."

Bael held both my arms behind my back, trapping me as Scion lowered himself to the floor in front of me. Scion's knees hit the ground with a loud thud, and his eyes burned with hunger as he reached for my boots. His fingers clumsily fumbled with the laces, eager to take them off. I felt a surge of heat spread through my body.

"What are you doing?" I demanded, though I already knew the answer.

He tugged off one boot, then the other, and tossed them unceremoniously across the room. Then, I held my breath as he ran both hands up and down the outside of my thighs. I moaned, unable to help myself.

Bael clapped a hand over my mouth. "You don't want to have the whole ship running in here, do you?"

Scion reached up slowly, never breaking eye contact with me, as he undid my belt and slid my trousers down my legs. The cold air hit my bare skin and I gasped against Bael's hand covering my mouth.

Scion smiled, wickedly. "I'm going to fucking destroy you."

Oh gods. I could swear I'd had a dream like this once, but the real thing was so much better.

Releasing my arms just long enough to tug my shirt over my head, Bael continued to hold my hands behind my back with one large hand. He removed his free hand from my mouth, as he whispered in my ear. "Not too loud, little monster. Do you think you can do that?"

No, I absolutely did not think I could do that, but I wanted his hands all over me. I wanted him to touch me.

As if reading my mind, he massaged my breast, pinching my nipples just hard enough to hurt.

My body responded to his touch, and my back arched, as Scion leaned forward and pressed his forehead against my lower belly. His hair tickled my skin, his warm breath sending sparks of anticipation flying through me.

Behind me, I could feel Bael growing hard and I pressed my hips back, grinding my ass against him. He hissed.

"Patience, little monster. I want you already wet and trembling when I fuck you."

I moaned. I didn't think there was any doubt he'd get his wish.

Scion pressed a kiss right above my core, and ran his hands along the sides of my thighs. Then, he lifted one of my legs, throwing it over his shoulder, and dug his fingers firmly into my ass.

The first brush of his tongue sent tingles all over my body, and I closed my eyes tilting my head back.

Scion gripped my legs tight, not letting me squirm away as he dragged his tongue over and over me, in torturous, long strokes. I spread my legs wider, and Scion traced his mouth lightly over my throbbing clit. "Please…"

He lifted my other leg, until I was suspended between them, sitting on Scion's shoulders while Bael supported my weight from behind. He thrust his tongue deep inside me, curling his tongue to lick my innermost walls.

I felt my entire body begin to tighten, and warmth and pressure grew deep in my core.

Bael reached over my shoulder, and grazed his fingers over my clit, rubbing small, intense circles. Bael's hand brushed against Scion's head, but they didn't seem to notice or care, both entirely focused on me.

The building pressure inside me became too much, and I threw my head back against Bael's shoulder as everything turned white hot. My legs shook, and I clamped them around Scion's head. He didn't stop licking inside me, and my face turned hot. I whimpered, my entire body feeling fluid and wrung out.

Scion stood, and Bael picked me up, whisking my trembling body across the room to the bed. He lay me flat on the soft mattress, my head facing the foot of the bed. I was completely naked while they were both still fully clothed, but it wouldn't stay that way for long.

Bael undid his belt with a torturous slowness that had me quaking from anticipation once more. Then, with my legs hanging off the bed, he positioned himself over me. His hard cock pressed against my throbbing core in all the right ways.

I arched my back and pressed my hips against his. A low groan escaped from both of us as he slid into me, filling every inch. He set a steady rhythm, driving in and out with precision. Each thrust sent shivers through my body as I gripped the sheets and moaned in pleasure.

Scion approached and gracefully lowered himself onto the bed beside me. He must have undressed at some point, as I couldn't help but stare at his too-perfect body. My mouth watered as my eyes roamed over him.

He knelt beside my head, and I turned my face to take his hard cock into my mouth. Reaching up with my left hand, I gripped the base, covering what I couldn't with my lips. He groaned, and leaned forward, catching himself against the bed.

Bael tilted my hips to get a better angle as he furiously thrust into me.

I was overwhelmed, feeling more aroused than I had ever been before. My mind was a jumble, unable to articulate the intense sensations that were pulsing through me.

Bael pushed my legs even wider, holding my knees open against the mattress. He moved slowly, going impossibly deep within me, and I let out a long groan.

Scion's fingers found my clit, rubbing teasing circles, and once again tension started to rise within me.

I wondered suddenly what it would feel like to have both of them inside me at once…perhaps one day I'd get to find out.

Scion's fingers moved faster against my clit as his movements began to stutter within my mouth. With his free hand, he gripped the back of my head, urging me to go faster.

"Oh fuck," Bael murmured, watching us.

I smiled slightly around Scion's cock, liking the attention of Bael's eyes on me.

Suddenly, a tension spread down my spine again and I couldn't help but whimper as my body writhed in pleasure. Another intense orgasm rippled through me, leaving me shuddering and breathless.

My stomach clenched, and I rose slightly off the bed as I came, driving Scion's cock deeper down my throat. He made a strangled noise and followed me into orgasm, Bael not far behind.

44
LONNIE

ABOARD THE FORESIGHT

Several hours later, I woke in the quiet darkness of the cabin. I was wrapped in a comfortable tangle of blankets and bodies. For the first time in a long time, I felt truly content.

Or, at least, *almost*.

Some strange thought nagged at the back of my mind. Like, a misremembered dream, or as if I were looking for something, and I could not recall what.

Quietly, so as not to wake them, I rose from the bed.

Quick as a whip, Scion's large hand shot out and circled my wrist. I stopped, startled, and turned back.

His silver eyes shone in the darkness, and his expression was almost resigned as he looked up at me. "Where are you going, rebel?"

I could hear the panic raw in his voice, and something inside me broke. "I'm just going outside." I smiled. "It's a ship, remember? I'll be back."

He relaxed, and let go of me. "You better."

My chest felt slightly lighter as I made my way across the room. Slowly, I turned the brass knob and gently pushed the heavy wooden door open.

The salty scent of seawater filled my nostrils as I stepped onto the creaky deck of the ship. It was late at night, and the only sounds were the gentle lapping of waves against the hull and the occasional flap of sails in the wind. The stars above shone brightly, their reflection dancing on the water below.

I let the door close behind me, and strode purposefully out onto the deck.

Out of nowhere, a massive bird swooped down and perched itself on my shoulder. Its weight caused me to stumble, and I felt a sharp pain on my shoulder as talons dug into my skin. I let out a yelp of surprise as I struggled to regain my balance.

Then, I turned my head and grinned. "Quill!"

The bird tittered at me, almost like a greeting. I smiled wider.

I had no idea where he'd come from, or what he was doing here, but I couldn't deny that I'd missed the strange raven—nearly as much as the prince he belonged to.

Quill and I continued my walk across the deck, and I stopped when I spotted another figure outside in the clear night.

Part of me had suspected that I'd find him here.

Ambrose's attention was fixed on the horizon as he guided the ship, so he didn't notice me until I walked toward him. At the sound of my footsteps, he turned to face me. He smiled as our gazes connected, but all too fast, his face fell.

Ambrose took a startled step backwards, his eyes widening with horror. "Where the fuck did that come from?"

I looked around, confused. "What?"

He reached down and began to draw his sword from his belt. "Move very slowly toward me, love. I do not wish to anger it."

I glanced from him, brandishing his sword as if his life depended on it, to the enormous bird on my shoulder. "Do you mean, Quill?"

"What?" he spat, distracted. "No, I mean that *monster*." He pointed with his non-dominant hand at Quill, keeping his right hand gripped firmly on the hilt of his sword.

"Yes." I raised my eyebrows, wondering if we could possibly be seeing the same thing. "This is Quill. He's Scion's bird and he's harmless."

"*Harmless?*" Ambrose let out a bark of harsh laughter. "That thing is vicious. I swore blood-price to end its miserable existence if ever we crossed paths again."

I scoffed. "Well, you can try, but you'll have to go through me first, and I've recently had some excellent fighting lessons."

Quill made a cooing sound, and nipped affectionately at my hand. Part of me could swear the bird was laughing.

I stepped closer, coming to stand next to Ambrose looking out over the silent water. "How was your chat with the prisoner?"

Ambrose cast another wary glance at Quill, before he answered: "Informative."

I raised an eyebrow. "Aren't you going to tell me?"

He reached for the wheel of the ship again, and rotated it slowly the right, seeming to buy himself time. "Eventually," he mused. "Soon, even."

"Why not now?"

"Because I'd rather you talk to Rhiannon first. I think it will make any conversation we have about our new passenger far simpler."

"Did you see that? Are you sure, or…"

"No," he shook his head and smiled at me. "I can't ever see you, love. I just think you deserve answers directly from the source, for once."

We stood in silence for several long minutes. It wasn't awkward or charged, simply comfortable. I listened to the sound of the ocean and the ice rocking against the ship, and felt oddly calm. I couldn't remember the last time I'd felt calm–if perhaps, I ever had.

"Where are we going?" I asked.

"Home."

I chewed on my lip. "Where is that?"

There were many places he might consider home–the rebel camps, the capital, this ship…

"I assumed the capital. We can figure out the rest from there."

I looked out over the water, then off in the direction of the cabin I'd just left. I couldn't imagine that he and Scion would be able to both exist in the capital at once without the castle burning down all over again. "What about…"

"We'll figure it out. There are no secrets too horrible to be forgiven, or grudges that can't be undone, love."

"I don't know about that." I murmured.

"I do." He chuckled softly, and tapped his temple. "Everything will work out, you'll see."

I grinned, and leaned against his side. I hoped he was right, not just about him, Bael and Scion, but about me too. Me and my mother, and all the pain that came along with it.

I hoped, and more so, I believed.

I didn't know exactly how it must feel to be Ambrose–to know nearly everything long before it happened, but if I were to make a prophecy I would say everything would work out in the end– for all of us:

The Rebel King, the King of Elsewhere, the King of Underneath, and me: the queen who ruled them all.

ALSO BY KATE KING

WILDE FAE

Lords of the Hunt

Lady of the Nightmares

The Last Heir of Elsewhere

Kingdom of the Monsters ~ Summer 2024

WILDE THIEVES

The House of Doublecross ~ Coming Soon

THE GENTLEMEN

Red Handed

Thieves Honor

Damned Souls

THE BLISSFUL OMEGAVERSE

Pack Origin

Pack Bound

Pack Bliss

STANDALONES:

By Any Other Name: A Deliciously Dark Romeo and Juliet Retelling

COMING SOON!

THE STORY CONCLUDES IN:

Wilde Fae Book Four:
A KINGDOM OF MONSTERS

Coming October 2024

THE WORLD OF Wilde Fae

THE WORLD OF WILDE FAE

YOUR GUIDE TO EVERYTHING YOU NEED TO REMEMBER FROM BOOK ONE!

1. Book Two Recap
2. The Extended Everlast Family Tree
3. The Calendar
4. Pronunciation
5. Map of Elsewhere
6. Glossary of Characters
7. Glossary of Places
8. Glossary of Terms, Items and Creatures

BOOK TWO RECAP:

In a flashback, we learn that Ambrose Dullahan believes he is working for the greater good of Elsewhere by rebelling against his family (The Everlasts). He is a powerful psychic and has spent 30+ years attempting to force events to occur, thus creating the future he thinks is best.

Knowing that he needs to speak to his brother, Scion, at some point in the future, Ambrose intentionally gets caught by the royal guards and thrown in the palace dungeon. Ambrose thinks about how he will be "blind" for the next several weeks until Scion comes to see him, as he cannot make predictions about himself, only those around him. Then, he realizes that Lonnie is in the cell next to him. He calls her his weakness, and the source of everything.

In the present, it is hunting day in Inbetwixt. Lonnie is making her way up the quarry and attempting to win the second hunt. She is distracted from the hunt by thoughts of Bael's revelation that they might be mates, but she is unharmed because Prince Scion has threatened to kill anyone who touches her. She encounters a monstrous snake, and considers using magic to escape. Lonnie remembers how her mother told her never to use her magic or something horrible would happen, and thinks about how she doesn't know how to use it because she has never tried. Ultimately, she escapes after bargaining with the snake; telling it her true name, Elowyn, and swearing to return at a future date with a gift of royal blood.

Meanwhile, back in the capital, Scion believes that Ambrose Dullahan will use the second hunt as an opportunity to attack the castle, and demands that his family stay behind to fend off the rebel army. Scion is in a foul mood, due to the bargain he struck with his brother, Ambrose, early that morning. Ambrose told Scion he would marry Lonnie, and now he has been freed from the dungeon.

Bael agrees to stay behind initially, but is distracted and irritable. He tells Scion that he believes Lonnie is his mate, and Scion is horrified. Scion realizes that Ambrose's marriage prophecy now makes sense, as the Everlasts have a long history of marrying fated mates to close family members, since they cannot claim them due to their curse.

Bael learns that Lonnie has encountered the snake, and leaves immediately for Inbetwixt to help. He rushes to her aid, and they argue about their feelings for each other and have a sexual encounter.

Lonnie wins the hunt, and she and Bael return to the camp where the court has gathered to watch the hunters. Lonnie's servant, Enid, is in her tent and reveals that she brought all of Rosey's journals with them to the hunting grounds. Bael and Lonnie read part of Rosey's journal, which turns out to be mostly accounts of her dreams from the previous year. Bael theorizes that Rosey may have been a seer, like his grandmother and Ambrose, which could be why Ambrose was interested in her. Lonnie questions Bael about the powers of himself and the other Everlasts, but refuses to admit to her own possible magic. Bael's powers are explained–he has limited power over time, which manifests in the ability to destroy objects or enemies. He can also see echoes of times past, in the form of spirits.

The following day, the court procession rides back to the capital. Bael teases Lonnie, showing her he still has the ability to conjure fire. This is a power that he has only gained through their blood sharing, and is rightfully hers. She is terrified, due to her mother's warnings that her magic would cause something horrible to happen. Before she can voice this concern to Bael, they are attacked by a hoard of afflicted. Bael exhausts himself, using nearly all his magic to escape the afflicted and protect Lonnie. Because they are connected, he accidentally drains Lonnie's life-force as well to save them. Lonnie and Bael make it back to the obsidian castle, where Lonnie collapses into Scion.

Scion spends several days calling multiple healers to revive Lonnie, who has not woken up since the incident. Bael, meanwhile, is also unresponsive but stable. Scion realizes that Bael used too much magic to escape the afflicted, and has drained Lonnie. Knowing that it will temporarily bind her to him, Scion feeds Lonnie his blood and resolves never to tell her or Bael about it.

While passed out, Lonnie dreams about an unknown masked fairy. She wakes up to find Scion with her, and they fight. Scion reveals that Bael has been trapped in his cage since the incident with the afflicted, and will eventually recover on his own. Lonnie demands to see him and is denied.

Scion and the other Everlasts explain that they believe the afflicted were sent by Ambrose Dullahan to destroy the capital. Lonnie fears they are wrong, and that she is the cause of the afflicted, but doesn't tell anyone.

Scion wants to go search for Ambrose in Inbetwixt, and needs Lonnie to go with him. Lonnie will not agree, and demands to see Bael. Scion abducts her and forces her to accompany him against her will.

Lonnie is furious with Scion the moment they arrive in Inbetwixt and attempts to escape when he binds her to him with a shadow rope. They ultimately agree to stay in Inbetwixt for three days, and if they cannot find Ambrose Dullahan, then Scion must take Lonnie back to Bael in the capital.

Lonnie and Scion go to speak to the Lord of Inbetwixt to ask for the soldiers to help search for Ambrose. The Lord denies the request, due to thieves stealing ships from the harbor. Lonnie suggests that they address the problem with the thieves, so that the soldiers will be available, and everyone begrudgingly agrees.

It turns out that Scion knows the thieves, and he and Lonnie immediately set off for the guild headquarters. The guild leader, Cross, turns out to be a former member of Scion's army unit, and a close friend. Cross agrees to help them find Ambrose. Later that night, a shapeshifting incubus attempts to sexually assault Lonnie by pretending to be Scion (whom he assumed was her mate). Scion dismembers the incubus and nails him to the wall of the thieves den.

Over the next few days, Lonnie and Scion live with the thieves and plan a heist to locate Ambrose. Lonnie continues to dream about the mysterious masked fairy. While on a shopping trip to the local market, Lonnie and Scion discuss their different understandings of how to rule a country and the greater good. Having been raised to rule since birth, and then spending years in the military, Scion believes in using any means necessary to protect the largest number of people. He acknowledges that he is not sorry for imprisoning Lonnie, because if she were a threat to the kingdom it would have been worth it to him.

To locate Ambrose and his rebels, the thieves determine that they will need to break into the local brothel and steal the madam's client book. Lonnie and Scion agree to provide a distraction, although Scion is dubious about putting Lonnie in danger. In the brothel, they are mistakenly poisoned by "Gancanagh's dust," an illegal fae drug which causes insatiable lust. They nearly have sex, but after biting Lonnie's neck Scion comes out of the trance and takes her back to the thieves den.

The following morning, Lonnie is horrified by what they did while under the influence of Gancanagh's dust, and the fact that the mark on her neck seems to be permanent. Scion tells Lonnie not to be embarrassed because he would still want her anytime, all she has to do is ask.

Lonnie and Scion speak to Cross, and learn that while they were under the influence of Gancanagh's dust, he and his thieves were able to steal the client book. They discover that the Lord of Inbetwixt's son is a rebel, and go to confront him. The son tells them that the rebellion has been shipping Gancanagh's dust in and out of Underneath, and tells them he hopes they burn up with their castle.

That night, the thieves have a party, and Lonnie and Scion dance. Back in their room, Lonnie tells Scion she wants him. They have a sexual encounter. Scion panics, thinking that he may have real feelings for Lonnie, and Lonnie realizes she can no longer lie.

Overnight, Lonnie dreams that the obsidian castle is burning and Bael is trapped. In the morning, Lonnie's ability to lie has returned, and she and Scion return home to the capital. There, they find the castle under attack by the rebels.

Scion is concerned with retrieving the obsidian crown because without it their curse cannot be broken. Lonnie wants to find Bael, who may be stuck in his cage inside the burning castle.

Scion admits he cares about Lonnie, and traps her in the stables to prevent her from getting hurt.

Lonnie manages to use magic to escape the stables, and appears in the castle. She helps her friend Iola escape, then goes looking for Bael. Lonnie finds Bael, and discovers that his "monster" form is an enormous beast-like lion. He saves her life, and they reunite.

Bael goes to help Scion and the rest of his family. Scion is able to use Lonnie's fire magic, and doesn't understand why. Bael tells him he believes that Scion is also one of Lonnie's mates, but Scion disagrees. He feels guilty for getting between Bael and Lonnie, and tries to apologize for his feelings.

Meanwhile, Lonnie runs into Ambrose Dullahan on the grounds. Ambrose has taken the crown, and wants Lonnie to leave with him. He promises her information if she will go with him, and implies her mother is still alive. Ambrose mentions to Lonnie that it is possible for two fated mates to be together, because Bael's parents were mates. His real father is an Unseelie named Gancanagh.

The castle collapses, and Lonnie assumes that both Bael and Scion have died. She lets out a burst of magic, and accidentally summons the afflicted to her. Bael, who was not harmed, is able to calm her down.

Lonnie, Bael, Scion and the rest of the Everlasts who survived the battle (Gwydion, Aine, Thalia and Elfwyn) all escape. They flee to a nearby coastal town, and commandeer an inn.

Bael and Lonnie finally have sex, but cannot complete their mating bond because of the Everlast curse. The following morning, Scion kisses Lonnie before telling her to stay away from him from now on.

Lonnie announces to the group that she will not be participating in the third hunt. She intends to travel to Aftermath and search for her mother so she can finally learn about her magic and who she is.

The Everlast Family Tree

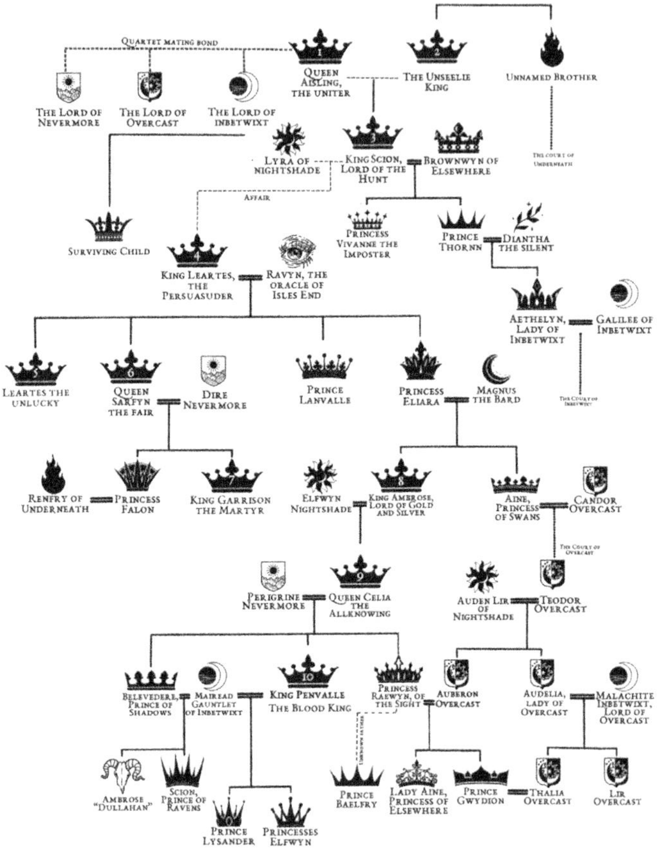

CALENDAR

- January — Danú (Da-new)
- February — Imbolc (Im-blk)
- March — Ostara (Ow-staa-ruh)
- April — Walpurgis (Wal-pur-gus)
- May — Beltane (Bel-tayn)
- June — Litha (Lee-tha)
- July — Annwn (A-noon)
- August — Lammas (la-muz)
- September — Mabon (Mah-bon)
- October — Samhain (Sow-wen)
- November — Bálor (Baw-lor)
- December — Yule (Yule)

PRONUNCIATION

- "Acacia" —Uh-kay-sha
- "Aine" — An-ya
- "Aisling" — Ash-lin
- "Ambrose" — Am-broz
- "Auberon" — O-ba-ron
- "Baelfry" or "Bael" — Bale-free or Bale
- "Beira" — Bay-ruh
- "Belvedere" — Bell-ve-dear
- "Caliban" — Cala-ban
- "Celia" — See-lee-uh
- "Ciara" — Keer-ah
- "Dullahan" — Doo-luh-han
- "Elfwyn" — Elf-win
- "Elowyn" — El-lo-win

- "Gancanagh" — Gan-can-ah
- "Gwydion" — Gwid-ee-in
- "Iola" — Eye-oh-luh
- "Kaius" — Kai-us
- "Lysander" — Lie-san-der
- "Mairead" — Muh-raid
- "Mordant" — Mor-dnt
- "Penvalle" — Pen-vail
- "Raewyn" — Ray-win
- "Rhiannon" — Ree-ann-in
- "Roisin" — Row-sheen
- "Scion" — Sigh-on
- "Siobhan" — Sh-von
- "Slúagh" — Slew-uh
- "Thalia" — Ta-lee-uh

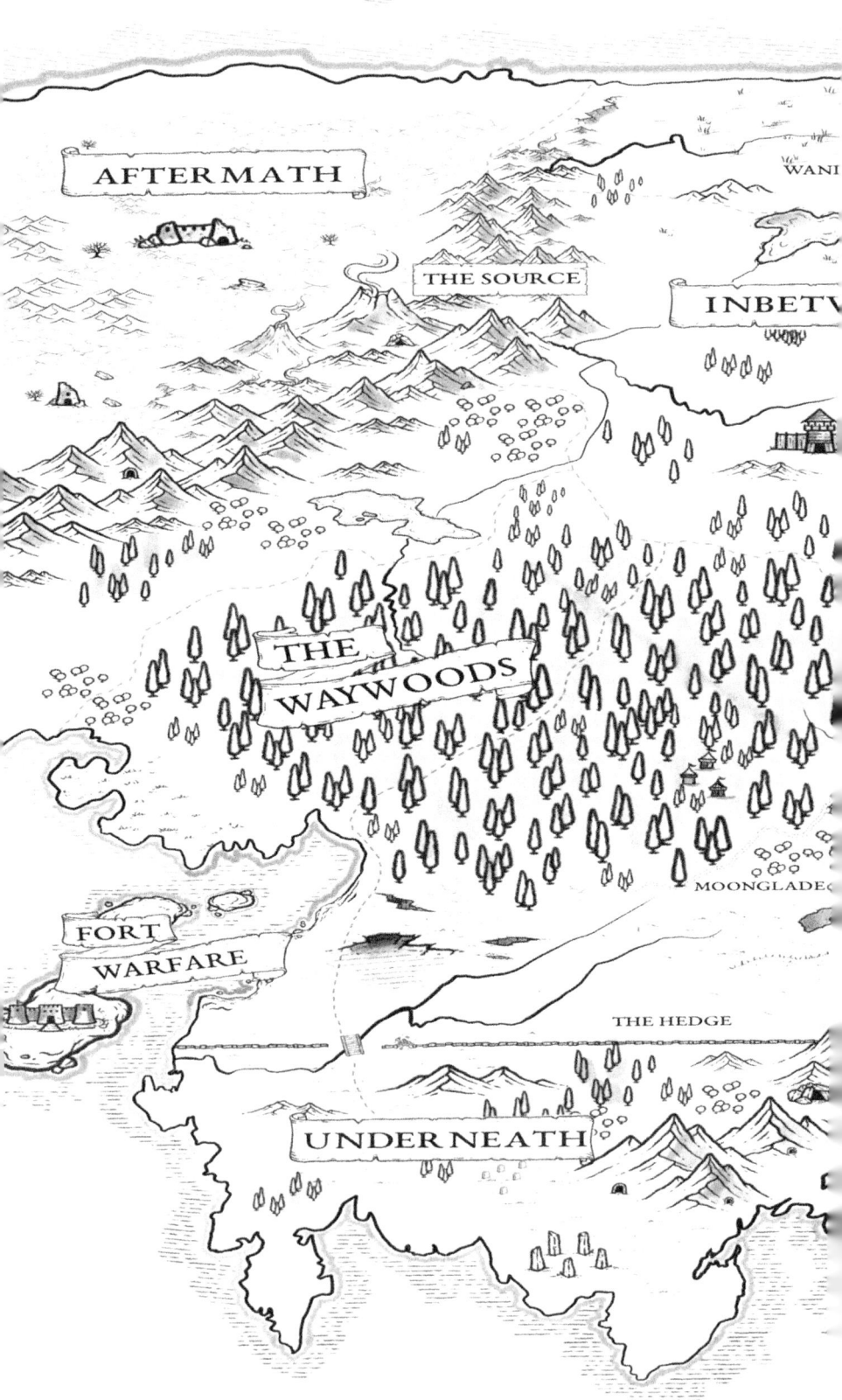

GLOSSARY OF CHARACTERS

If you need an instant character index, here it is! This information is as of the end of *Lords of the Hunt*, so there are many spoilers in here for that book, but none for *Lady of the Nightmares*. I hope this is helpful!

PRIMARY CHARACTERS AS OF *LORDS OF THE HUNT*:

LONNIE SKYEBORNE:

At the start of *Lords of the Hunt*, Lonnie is a twenty-year-old kitchen maid, but by the end of book one, she is twenty-one and the first human queen of Elsewhere. She has no known powers and is not a particularly adept fighter, however, she is unusually good at surviving deadly circumstances and alludes several times to having powers that have not yet been revealed. Due to drinking Prince Bael's blood in *Lords of the Hunt*, she was temporarily able to use his powers.

Lonnie has curly red hair, brown eyes, and a scar on her ear where the tip appears to have been torn off. She is extremely mistrustful and fearful of Fae, who killed her mother and sister. Her mother taught her to avoid Fae at all costs, but the Fae have always been extremely interested in her. During *Lords of the Hunt*, this is not fully understood but seems to be attributed to giving off a magical scent or aura. Bael and Scion note that she "tastes like magic." She seems to have some immunity to the Everlast's powers but insists that the immunity doesn't extend to all Fae.

Lonnie may be the fated mate of Prince Bael, but that has yet to be confirmed. He believes that she is. Lonnie has also expressed sexual attraction to Prince Scion, although she does not like him.

By the end of *Lords of the Hunt*, Lonnie has been revealed as an unreliable narrator as she lies often to protect herself from the Fae. As Bael says, Lonnie lies so often that she herself isn't sure what the truth is anymore.

SCION, THE PRINCE OF RAVENS (SIGH-ON):

"The Prince of Ravens" is the kindest name given to Prince Scion, the heir apparent of the Everlast family. He is also sometimes called the Prince of Nightmares, the Queen's Executioner, or the God of Pain.

A former soldier in the queen's army, Scion spent his adolescence and adulthood fighting rebels in Aftermath. Scion's magical ability is illusion, which he primarily uses to inflict crippling pain on opponents in combat. He also creates shadowlike visual illusions. Like a bomb, the prince can clear entire battlefields on his own, so often his presence is enough of a threat to end a conflict. Scion hates the northern rebels due to his experiences fighting them and reacts harshly to any mention of them.

Scion is described as handsome and dangerous, with black hair and magnetic silver eyes. He is second in line to the throne after

Penvalle. His father was Celia's first son, Belvedere, who is dead. His mother is Mairead, who is now married to Penvalle. He often expresses that he dislikes everyone, including his family, but this is shown to be mostly untrue in practice. He views lifting the curse on his family as his responsibility and believes he is destined to be the last Everlast king. He has two half siblings through Mairead and Penvalle (Elfwyn, 9, and Lysander, 15) and one significantly older brother through Mairead and Belvedere (Ambrose).

PRINCE BAEL (PRONOUNCED "BALE" NOT "BAY-EL"):

Bael is the youngest of the adult children in the Everlast family. He is described as angelic-looking but slightly unnerving. He has blond hair, yellow catlike eyes, and unusually sharp teeth. During *Lords of the Hunt*, he tells Lonnie he was twelve during the fall of Nightshade, making him about thirty-three years old.

Bael is as powerful or possibly more powerful than Scion but is not in the running to be king because his powers are chaotic and potentially dangerous. While it is not clear by the end of book one exactly what the full extent of Bael's magical abilities are, he is seen to have some powers relating to conjuring smoke as well as making objects turn to ash. It is mentioned that he has "bad nights," and he has a cage in his bedroom.

Publicly, Bael's parents are Princess Raewyn and Lord Auberon, but it is an open secret that he has a different father than his two older siblings (Aine and Gwydion).

Bael wants Lonnie to win the Wilde Hunts and give him the crown but says that he does not personally want to be king. His best friend is Scion, and he believes Lonnie to be his mate.

LADY AINE (AN-YA):

Raewyn's daughter, Bael and Gwydion's sister. Aine is thin and willowy, very tan, with curly honey-colored hair. She is a cynic with unclear motives. She is good friends with Scion and her brother Bael. Her mother wants her to marry her cousin, Scion. She is a princess like her brothers but is never called Princess Aine. She mentions to Lonnie once that she hates her title. Her magical talent is unknown.

PRINCE AMBROSE EVERLAST/AMBROSE DULLAHAN:

"Dullahan" is a major player in the rebellion against the Everlast family and the person responsible for Rosey attempting to kill King Penvalle. It was revealed at the end of *Lords of the Hunt* that Dullahan is actually Ambrose Everlast, Scion's brother. His parents are Belvedere and Mairead, and he is a seer like his grandmother Queen Celia. Since the death of Queen Celia, Ambrose is now the strongest seer alive. Ambrose had a letter sent to Lonnie asking her to meet him during the second hunt and then was released from prison by his brother, Scion, later that same night. He is the visual opposite of his brother, possessing black eyes and silver hair.

CALIBAN:

Lonnie's former lover, Caliban, is a guard at the palace. While Caliban and Lonnie did not have any great affection for each other, he did help her stay alive in the dungeon. He is often used by Scion to do errands he does not want to take credit for (like bringing Lonnie food). The last time we saw Caliban, Scion had him stationed in the dungeon, guarding Ambrose.

PRINCESS ELFWYN (ELF-WIN):

Penvalle and Mairead's daughter. She's nine with black hair and silver eyes and has similar powers to her half brother Scion, whom she idolizes. Elfwyn tried to kill Lonnie in *Lords of the Hunt* because she thought Scion would be proud of her. She has no personal ill will toward Lonnie.

ENID:

Lonnie's former nemesis turned sometimes ally. Enid is a maid in the kitchens who is only out for herself and her own survival. She doesn't dislike Lonnie but wouldn't lay down her life for her either.

PRINCE GWYDION (GWID-EE-IN, RHYMES WITH GIDEON):

Bael's older brother, Gwydion, is a healer with an excellent court reputation. He is large and muscular, very tan, with curly dark blond hair. He is everyone's friend, and even the servants say he's not that bad. He is betrothed to Thalia. During *Lords of the Hunt*, Gwydion showed his cunning side by forcing Lonnie into an alliance in exchange for healing her friend Iola, who had been poisoned.

IOLA:

Lonnie's former maid and friend Iola was poisoned at a ball but is recovering due to Lonnie's bargain with Gwydion.

PRINCE LYSANDER (LY-SAN-DER):

Penvalle and Mairead's son. He's fifteen, and his powers have not yet emerged. Lysander hates Lonnie for killing his father.

MAIREAD GAUNTLET (MUH-RAID):

Scion, Lysander, and Elfwyn's mother, Penvalle's wife. She has the power of illusion but doesn't use it. She has not spoken much in years. She is originally from Inbetwixt (for more on this, see the glossary entry on Inbetwixt). Mairead has technically held the position of princess (through marriage) and queen consort, but she is not treated as such.

MORDANT:

The Everlasts' stuffy and prejudicial head of staff.

KING PENVALLE (PEN-VAIL):

Celia's only living son at the time of her death, Penvalle is murdered by Lonnie early on in *Lords of the Hunt*. Prior to his death, Penvalle was cruel and barely sane and considered to be dangerous even by other Fae. His magical ability was mind control.

He was married (not mated) to his brother's former wife, Mairead, and father to Lysander and Elfwyn. Prior to his death in *Lords of the Hunt*, it was mentioned that Penvalle and Scion looked very similar.

PRINCESS RAEWYN (RAY-WIN):

Queen Celia's daughter. Raewyn married the lesser lord Auberon Overcast and has three children: Gwydion, Aine, and Bael. Raewyn's greatest ambition is for one of her children to take the throne so she can rule by proxy. She is a seer like her mother but far less powerful. She is very accurate, but her visions are random and infrequent.

ROSEY SKYEBORNE:

Lonnie's mild-mannered identical twin sister. Although Lonnie and Rosey look the same, Rosey does not attract attention from the Fae in the same way as her sister. She is much less rebellious and cynical as a result. She writes daily in journals and seems to have no secrets until she suddenly is seen to be part of the rebellion against the Everlasts. In the month or so prior to her death, Rosey was very sick and drinking tea from a tree that only bloomed at night.

THALIA OVERCAST (TA-LEE-UH):

Gwydion's fiancée. She was originally brought to the royal court as a bride for Scion (they are both illusionists) but is now betrothed to Prince Gwydion. This situation has not been explained as of the end of book one. Thalia is described as pale and unusually beautiful, even for a fairy, but always looks like she was recently crying.

Thalia is technically a cousin of the Everlasts several times over. She is a first cousin of Gwydion (her mother is his father's sister). She is also a second cousin through Queen Celia, who was her great-aunt.

MENTIONED OFF PAGE OR DEAD AS OF *LORDS OF THE HUNT*:

QUEEN AISLING THE UNITER:

The long-dead historical queen of the Fae who first united all the provinces into the country of Elsewhere. She had three mates, but her story ended tragically when her family was murdered and she was violated by the Unseelie king. She cursed the king, leading to the curse on the Everlast family.

PRINCE BELVEDERE:

Scion's father, Mairead's former partner, Penvalle's brother. He was the heir to the throne before he was killed in the war with the rebels.

QUEEN CELIA THE GREAT:

The longest-reigning Everlast queen, who has just died as of the beginning of *Lords of the Hunt*. She was a very powerful seer who left letters for some members of her family with instructions after her death. Only Scion's letter has been revealed so far.

RHIANNON SKYEBORNE:

Lonnie and Rosey's mother. Seen only in flashbacks in *Lords of the Hunt*, Rhiannon was a changeling child stolen from the human realm and brought to Elsewhere to serve the Fae. She was stolen as a child (not an infant) and lived in the North of Elsewhere (Nightshade). Eventually, she became the mother to Lonnie and Rosey. She spent her entire life training her daughters to hate the Fae, likely due to her own upbringing and early memories of being stolen.

She was taken away by Fae soldiers for punishment due to some unknown transgression and never seen again. Prince Scion was part of the group that captured Rhiannon.

A/N: When Rhiannon is speaking a language that Scion does not understand in LOTH, it is English. Being a changeling, Rhiannon speaks English, while her daughters do not.

THE KING OF UNDERNEATH/UNSEELIE KING:

The monarch of the separate realm below the border.

THE KING CONSORT:

Queen Celia's late husband and father/grandfather to all the Everlasts, who died before the events of book one. Though it is not relevant to the events of *Lords of the Hunt,* his name was Peregrine, and he was from the province of Nevermore. For more on this, see the glossary entry on Nevermore.

GLOSSARY OF PLACES

ELSEWHERE:

The country where the story takes place. It is located "beyond the veil," somewhere in the North Atlantic Ocean.

EVERLAST CITY (INTERCHANGEABLY "THE CITY OF EVERLAST" OR "THE CAPITAL"):

Not to be confused with the Everlast family, this is the capital city of Elsewhere. It is named after the royal family. It is mostly populated by wealthy Fae (some noble, some not) and free humans. There is a large class divide between even the poorest Fae and the wealthiest human.

The capital city is extremely small compared to other cities in Elsewhere in terms of both size and population. In technical terms, it is more of a vassal township than a city, being only a tenth the size of Inbetwixt. It is bordered by the Waywoods on one side and farmland on the other.

The most important (and only) landmark is the obsidian palace. The palace is over seven thousand years old and built by the former Unseelie King of Underneath. The palace is the southernmost structure in Everlast, and there is nothing but untamed wilderness between the palace and the Hedge.

NEVERMORE:

The richest and most insular of the four provinces, Nevermore sits on an island slightly separated from the rest of Elsewhere. They speak in a different dialect than the mainland (Referred to by the characters as "the old tongue") and are governed by a council rather than a single governor. Nevermore might govern themselves if not for their friendly relations with the Everlast family and prosperous trade with Inbetwixt. Queen Celia's late husband, the king consort Peregrine Nevermore, was integral in making sure that Nevermore did not succeed from the rest of the kingdom. The royal-appointed governor now acts as an ambassador. Their climate is temperate to cold, and most of the island is covered in mountains. The Fae of Nevermore live peacefully alongside some species of non-combative Unseelie, such as dwarves and sirens. Since the fall of Nightshade, Nevermore now has the highest population of druids and witches (human magic users). Fae with particular magical talents in Nevermore tend to possess mental abilities like mind-control and clairvoyance.

INBETWIXT:

Inbetwixt is a trading port that grew into a city of travelers with a violent reputation for being unwelcome toward outsiders.

They have the largest and most diverse population of non-noble Fae, Unseelie, free humans, and hybrid monsters. Their climate is warm and often rainy. They are bordered on all sides by the Source Mountains, the Waywoods, the Wanderlust, and the

Undertow, making it easy for Inbetwixt to control access to the city. Every road in and out is guarded, and tolls are high.

The governing noble family of Inbetwixt has been loosely at odds with the Everlast family for the last century. Lady Mairead Everlast was born Mairead Gauntlet in Inbetwixt. She was not a noble but the daughter of a wealthy merchant who met Crown Prince Belvedere while he was traveling with the queen's army. Mairead was a talented illusionist and came with a large dowry, and therefore, her non-noble blood was completely ignored by Queen Celia and King Consort Peregrine, who favored Prince Belvedere above their other children. This incident enraged the Lord of Inbetwixt and his family, and they are still bitter about it.

OVERCAST:

Overcast is a small but relatively prosperous northern seaside province known primarily for its political neutrality and lack of army. Their governing noble family is heavily enmeshed with the Everlasts, as they are all not-so-distant cousins. Their governor is Thalia's mother (Lord Auberon's sister), but it will likely soon pass to Thalia's brother.

Overcast sits in the shadow of the Source Mountains, directly downwind of Aftermath. In the years since the disaster that destroyed Nevermore, they have had increasingly erratic weather and are now struggling to deal with the toxic clouds rolling in from their neighbors to the northwest. There are only two ways into Overcast: through the Wanderlust or across the Undertow. It is far easier to cross the Undertow, especially in the twenty years since the fall of Nightshade. Thalia marrying into the Everlast family is intended to ensure that Overcast is not overlooked and cut off from the rest of the country, as they need their own expanded water access unhindered by Inbetwixt. The population of Overcast is almost entirely Fae, and there are no free humans in their city.

AFTERMATH:

Previously called Nightshade, the mountain province of Aftermath sits at the northernmost part of Everlast. A third of the population died in the initial volcanic eruption, with another third dying in the following weeks from injury, starvation, and effects of the Wilde magic. Survivors quickly fled to the valleys on the opposite side of the mountain, closer to the Waywoods, and most eventually left entirely. Aftermath is considered mostly uninhabitable, with a climate similar to Underneath.

After the disaster, Queen Celia began sending prisoners and slaves to Aftermath to assist in rehabilitating the area. This punishment was viewed by many as cruel and unusual and led to the beginning of the organized rebellion.

NIGHTSHADE (ALSO SEE AFTERMATH):

Nightshade was the fourth province in Elsewhere until the disaster roughly two decades ago that destroyed the land and population. Their city was very large and beautiful, having been built by Queen Aisling as the original capital of Elsewhere, and they were an area of high magic concentration. Despite this, they did not pose much political threat to the Everlasts as most of the population were highly religious academics. The noble court of Nightshade trained spiritual leaders and magical practitioners and sent them out to proselytize to other courts about the way of the Source.

UNDERNEATH:

The home to all hostile Unseelie and monsters, The Underneath is part of the continent of Elsewhere but separated from the kingdom by the Hedge. It is ruled by the Unseelie King. The Hedge is patrolled on the Everlast side at all times to prevent any monsters or Unseelie from crossing over into the capital.

WANDERLUST:

A large marsh between Inbetwixt and Overcast, populated by thousands of Underfae. It is extremely easy to get lost in the marsh and wander forever in the fog or sink into the waters. Crossing it is difficult without an undersea guide.

THE UNDERTOW:

A small sea filled with pirates and traders.

THE WAYWOODS:

A seemingly endless forest that stretches through the middle of the country. No one person has ever explored every part of the Waywoods, and it is said that there are things in there that predate the Everlast family themselves.

FORT WARFARE:

An enchanted prison on an island in no-man's-land on the west side of the continent. It is used most often by the Everlast family, but they do not exclusively control it.

THE HEDGE:

The wall separating Underneath from the capital of Everlast.

MOONGLADE LAKE:

A lake in the capital that is rumored to be enchanted. Queen Celia walked into this lake when she decided to return to the Source.

THE SOURCE:

The volcano that is believed to be the source of all magic. Gods are said to live in the mountains surrounding the Source.

GLOSSARY OF TERMS, ITEMS, AND CREATURES

FAE:

The dominant species, Fae have become the ruling class by numbers alone. They are also called Seelie, to differentiate them from the Unseelie, but this is typically not a necessary conversational distinction to make. All Fae possess some inherent magic and are immortal (though not impervious to death), but only some possess unusual magical abilities. Fewer and fewer Fae are born with special abilities with each generation.

HIGH FAE:

Fae of the noble class. Sometimes interchangeably used to mean Fae with magic, but typically referring to social standing.

"FAIRIES":

Catch-all term for anything non-human, including High Fae, monsters, hybrids, Underfae, etc.

UNSEELIE:

Sentient non-human, non-Fae creatures. The Unseelie are not always malevolent (though they often are). In Nevermore, some of the non-hostile Unseelie, like dwarves and sirens, live alongside the Fae. On the continent, almost all Unseelie are confined to Underneath, although there are some exceptions (like Beira, the palace cook). Some examples are succubi, spriggans, púca, incubi banshees, and shape shifters. The Unseelie are different than monsters, which are abundant everywhere, although some are just as dangerous.

UNDERFAE:

Magical creatures that cannot speak or be reasoned with but are sentient (like pets). Will-o-whisps and all the plant guardians fall into this category.

SLÚAGH:

A rude name for humans. This roughly means "the crowd" or "the army," but the intention is to mean "peasant" or "sword-fodder."

THE WILDE HUNTS:

The competition where the ruler proves their worthiness to keep their crown. There are five hunts, the first taking place on May 1 and the last one taking place on June 21. Every hunt is in a different province in this order: the capital, Inbetwixt, Nevermore, Overcast, Aftermath. Anyone who wishes to challenge the monarch for their crown must kill them on hunting night and take it. If the monarch dies, the hunts end until the following year.

MOONDUST TREES:

Trees that only sprout leaves at night. Their leaves are white and turn to dust in the morning.

THE COMMON TONGUE:

The language spoken most commonly on the continent. It is used by both Fae and humans.

THE OLD TONGUE:

The language spoken most commonly below the Hedge (Underneath) and in Nevermore. This is where the word "Slúagh" originates.

The Everlasts speak old tongue because their grandfather, Peregrine, was from Nevermore. Now, they complain that others don't speak it, when in reality, if they had not been forced to learn, it is likely they would not have bothered.

ALSO BY KATE KING

WILDE FAE

Lords of the Hunt

Lady of the Nightmares

The Last Heir of Elsewhere

A Kingdom of Monsters ~ October, 2024

WILDE THIEVES

The House of Doublecross ~ Coming Soon

THE GENTLEMEN

Red Handed

Thieves Honor

Damned Souls

THE BLISSFUL OMEGAVERSE

Pack Origin

Pack Bound

Pack Bliss

STANDALONES:

By Any Other Name: A Deliciously Dark Romeo and Juliet Retelling

ABOUT THE AUTHOR

USA Today and International bestselling author Kate King loves sassy heroines, crazy magic, and alpha-hole heroes.

An avid reader and writer from a young age, she has been telling stories her whole life. Ever a fan of the dramatic, she lives in an 18th century church with her husband and two cats, and often writes in cemeteries.

STALK ME!

Visit my website at Katekingauthor.com

Follow me on Instagram and Tiktok @katekingauthor

Join my Facebook reader group "The Kingdom: A reader group for Kate King"

Printed in Dunstable, United Kingdom

78188001R00238